BOOKS BY SHYAM SELVADURAI

Funny Boy (1994)
Cinnamon Gardens (1998)

Cinnamon Gardens

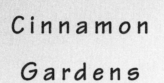

Cinnamon
Gardens

Shyam Selvadurai

M&S

Canadian Cataloguing in Publication Data

Selvadurai, Shyam, 1965-
Cinnamon gardens

ISBN 0-7710-7955-9

I. Title.

PS8587.E445C56 1998   c813'.54   C98-931435-9
PR9199.3.S45C56 1998

We acknowledge the financial support of the Government of Canada through the Book Publishing Industry Development Program for our publishing activities. We further acknowledge the support of the Canada Council for the Arts and the Ontario Arts Council for our publishing program.

Typeset in Centaur by M&S, Toronto
Printed and bound in Canada

The quotes from the *Tirukkural* are taken from *The Kural* by Tiruvalluvar. Translated from the Tamil by P. S. Sundaram and published by Penguin India. Reprinted by permission.

The author would like to thank the Canada Council and the Ontario Arts Council for their financial support during the writing of this book.

McClelland & Stewart Inc.
The Canadian Publishers
481 University Avenue
Toronto, Ontario
M5G 2E9

2 3 4 5   02 01 00 99 98

To my aunt, Bunny (Charlobelle) De Silva,
for all the books bought, all the stories read.

To Andrew, with all my love.

". . . for the growing good of the world is partly dependent on unhistoric acts; and that things are not so ill with you and me as they might have been, is half owing to the number who lived faithfully a hidden life, and rest in unvisited tombs."

— George Eliot, *Middlemarch*

Book One

1

However great the hardship,
Pursue with firmness the happy end.
— The Tirukkural, *verse 669*

Annalukshmi Kandiah often felt that the verse from that great work of Tamil philosophy, the *Tirukkural* — "I see the sea of love, but not the raft on which to cross it" — could be applied to her own life, if "desire" was substituted for "love." For she saw clearly the sea of her desires, but the raft fate had given her was so burdened with the mores of the world that she felt it would sink even in the shallowest of waters.

Like most visionaries, Annalukshmi somewhat exaggerated her constraints. For a young woman of twenty-two from a good Tamil family, living in the year 1927, her achievements were remarkable — or, depending on your conviction, appalling. She had completed her Senior Cambridge, an accomplishment fairly rare in that time for a girl; she had stood first islandwide in English literature, much to the discomfiture of every boys' school. Then she had gone on to teachers college and qualified as a teacher.

Annalukshmi's qualification as a teacher was held to be her greatest crime by her mother's relatives, the Barnetts. A career as a teacher was reserved for those girls who were too poor or too ugly to ever catch a husband. They saw it as a deliberate thumbing of her nose at the prospect of marriage. She might as well have joined a convent. They blamed her wilful, careless nature on both parents. Her father, Murugasu, had gained notoriety in his village in Jaffna for beheading the Gods in the household shrine during a quarrel with his father, running away to Malaya, and converting to Christianity. Louisa, her mother, had defied family dictates and married Murugasu. The Barnetts were one of the oldest Christian Tamil families of Ceylon. Murugasu was too recent a convert to have, like them, generations of the civilizing influence of Christianity behind him.

Louisa placed the blame for her eldest daughter's nature squarely on her husband's shoulders. In the absence of a son – there were three daughters in the family – he had raised Annalukshmi as if she were a boy. *He* was responsible for her reckless nature, a disposition that would have been admissible, even charming, in a boy, but in a girl was surely a catastrophe. Louisa had tried to warn him of his mistake. She had tried to curtail Annalukshmi's freedom, to inspire in her an understanding of the necessary restrictions that must be placed on a girl to protect her reputation and that of her family's. Yet her attempts were useless, with her husband taking Annalukshmi off to the family rubber estate on inspections, teaching her tennis and swimming.

Louisa would have liked to feel satisfied that the entire blame rested on her husband, but she had to admit that the estrangement between Murugasu and her, which had finally forced her to return to Ceylon from Malaya, had sundered the close bond between father and daughter as well. It had left Annalukshmi with a deep hurt. Louisa had, indeed, agreed to let

Annalukshmi go to teachers college in the hope that the responsibility of teaching would finally settle her down.

If Annalukshmi had been asked the reason for her nature — which she considered not wilful but that of the "new woman" who was not ashamed or afraid to ask for her share of the world — she would have pointed to two people: Miss Amelia Lawton, the missionary headmistress at the school she had attended and where she now taught, and her adopted daughter, Nancy (whose parents, impoverished villagers, had died of cholera when Nancy was thirteen years old). Annalukshmi felt that it was Miss Lawton and Nancy who had provided the cheer and pleasure in her life after her parents' marriage failed and she and her sisters had returned to Colombo with their mother. Their bungalow had become her second home, and she spent most of her spare time with them, going for sea baths and occasionally taking holidays in the hill country. It was through Miss Lawton that she learnt about the struggles for women's rights in England and Miss Lawton's own small part in them during her college days. It was Miss Lawton who had encouraged her reading habit, which, she knew, had led to her standing first in English literature. It was the headmistress who had truly supported her in the decision to be a teacher.

When Miss Blake, the assistant headmistress, presented Annalukshmi with a gift of her bicycle on the day Miss Blake returned to England, Annalukshmi was spurred on to accept because of the smiling faces of Miss Lawton and Nancy, standing on the verandah steps above Miss Blake, nodding their approval.

❧

That afternoon, Louisa was kneeling at one end of the back verandah. The heavy wooden box in which she stored her dry rations and spices was open before her as she measured out the ulundu to be soaked overnight for the morning's thosais. She was disturbed from her task by the exclamations of her two younger daughters, Kumudini and Manohari. She dropped the lid shut and, not even waiting to padlock the box, picked up her bunch of keys and hurried through the drawing room. She came out onto the front verandah to find Annalukshmi standing by the bottom step with a bicycle.

Louisa drew in her breath in astonishment. "What on earth is this?"

"A bicycle," Annalukshmi said, trying to sound as if it were the most normal thing in the world for her to turn up with one.

"I can see it is a bicycle. But what is it doing here?"

"It's Miss Blake's. She gave it to me as a going-away present."

Annalukshmi pushed aside some hairs that had strayed from her plait, which she wore in a knot at the nape of her neck. In her mind, she went over the arguments she had rehearsed with Nancy to combat her family's resistance.

Louisa clicked her tongue against her teeth in annoyance. "Don't talk rubbish, Annalukshmi. You know you can't go around on a bicycle."

"And why not?"

Louisa's face flushed at Annalukshmi's impertinent tone.

Before she could proceed further, her middle daughter, Kumudini, laid a warning hand on Louisa's arm. Arguments between her mother and older sister were often overheated, and Kumudini frequently had to step in as peacemaker. "Akka, be reasonable," she said to Annalukshmi. "You can't. People will say all sorts of things."

Though Kumudini was twenty-one, and a year younger than Annalukshmi, she was regarded by everyone as the eldest because she was such a model of propriety.

"And look at the state of your sari," Kumudini continued. "It's ruined." She shook her head. Though only a five-rupee Japanese Georgette sari, it was lovely, with a clover-leaf design on an off-white background. Now there was a grease stain along the bottom of it. Kumudini had, with great care, stitched this sari onto a length of belting because, at that time, a sari was sewn onto belting that hooked around the waist very much like a skirt, the only dressing required being the pleats and the fall draped once about the body and over the shoulder. Her efforts had been in vain. The sari was probably ruined. Further, the white sari blouse had two very unladylike sweat stains under the arms.

"We should put a chain around her neck and take her from door to door," Manohari, the youngest, put in sarcastically. "She looks just like a monkey on a bicycle, and I'm sure people will pay us a lot of money to see her do tricks."

Manohari, who was sixteen, actually thought the whole thing a bit of a lark. The situation merely presented her with an opportunity to exercise the wit she was famous for and lord it over her eldest sister.

"Excuse me for pointing out the obvious," Louisa said, "but decent, respectable girls don't ride bicycles."

"They do," Annalukshmi replied. "Lots of Burgher ladies and European ladies ride bicycles. Look at Miss Lawton."

"Miss Lawton!" Manohari cried. "Miss Lawton says no rickshaws, Miss Lawton says ride a bicycle. If Miss Lawton told you to go and jump in the well, will you do that next?"

"So Miss Lawton is encouraging you in this nonsense." Louisa fiddled with the keys on her triangular silver key ring so that her daughters would not see the hurt she felt when Annalukshmi valued the opinions and advice of another woman above her own mother's.

"Akka, be sensible," Kumudini said. "It's one thing for European ladies to ride bicycles. We can't."

"And we never will, unless someone makes a start," Annalukshmi replied. "How will the women of this country ever progress? European women can ride bicycles and do all sorts of other things because a few brave women made a start."

"I don't care what Miss Lawton says," Louisa said as she hooked her key ring onto the waistline of her sari. "You cannot ride that bicycle, Annalukshmi. It's simply out of the question."

Annalukshmi started to protest, but her mother waved her hand to say that she would not entertain any further pleas. She went back into the house to continue her duties.

"I shall ride it anyway," Annalukshmi called out after her mother.

Louisa chose to ignore the taunt.

Annalukshmi now glared at Kumudini and Manohari. "Thank you very much for your sisterly support," she said.

She stalked off, wheeling the bicycle in front of her.

After Annalukshmi had leant the bicycle against the side of the house, she stood brooding over her possession. She thought of the sheer pleasure she got from riding the bicycle, of the exhilaration that rose in her as she felt the bicycle gather speed under her, the panting sense of accomplishment as she reached the top of a slope and the rush of wind in her hair and under her sari as she went down the other side. Then there was the freedom to come and go as she pleased. Already she and Nancy had made numerous expeditions on Miss Lawton's and Miss Blake's bicycles whenever Annalukshmi had stayed over at the headmistress's bungalow. She recalled one in particular now: a Saturday morning she and Nancy had got up while it was still dark and ridden to the Galle Face Promenade to watch the sun rise over the sea. They had sat on a bench by the sea wall in contented silence, wrapped in their shawls, the air misty around them, the taste of salt on their lips. It had been a spectacular sight, the first slivers of light on the rolling waves like silver-coloured sea creatures that surfaced and dipped, surfaced and dipped. Then the splinters of light had turned gold and, as more and more of them appeared, the sea seemed alive with golden fish.

Annalukshmi was not going to let herself be stopped by the ridiculous conventions of society. She convinced herself that it was only fear of societal censure that made her mother forbid her and no personal repugnance on Louisa's part. After all, when they were girls in Malaya, her mother had not protested when her father had taught her to ride her cousin's bicycle. Annalukshmi glanced contemplatively at the bicycle. It really was a very jolly bicycle, the frame a shiny red. There were red, white, and blue streamers at the ends of the handlebar, with corresponding colours on the seat. The wicker basket attached to the handlebar proudly displayed a Union Jack. A plan began to form in her mind. Tapping her chin thoughtfully, she went inside to wash before tiffin.

❧

Colombo, with its fine port, its midway position between East and West, was one of the great junctions of the shipping world in the 1920s. It was thus of immense importance to the commerce of the British Empire. Yet, the city had none of the chaos of masonry, the hustle and bustle that one associated with the other great cities of the East, be they Singapore or Shanghai or Bombay. Instead, the principal impression of Colombo was that of trees and water. The city was flanked on one side by the ocean, and its inhabitants were never very far from the salty smell of the sea air and its cooling breezes. In the middle of the city was the extensive Beira Lake, from which tributaries snaked their way through the city, forming smaller lakes at various junctures. The waters of the lakes were bordered by foliage of unrivalled beauty, palms of every variety, masses of scarlet flamboyant blossoms, the waving leaves of plantain trees. The streets of Colombo were tarred and kept in good condition. They were wide and lined on both sides by huge trees that cast their shade over the roads. The most common of these was the suriya tree, whose profuse blossoms often formed a carpet of primrose yellow on the pavements. Even the Fort, the commercial district of Colombo, had broad streets with grand, whitewashed buildings. The merchant offices and stores were capacious and often had colonnaded verandahs running the length of them to provide shade for pedestrians.

The only part of Colombo that possessed the chaos and scramble of other large cities was the Pettah, where the colourful bazaars were always raucous with the cries of vendors, the fierce bargaining of women shopping. Here the streets were narrow, the buildings huddled together, the shops and domestic dwellings often open to the streets, the activity of selling and living going on on the streets themselves. The air was pungent with the odour of fruits, spices, dried fish, meat, the blood from butcher shops running into the open drains. The roads were crowded with people, cows, goats, pigs, and the constant flutter of scavenging crows.

The Kandiah family lived in Cinnamon Gardens, a suburb of Colombo. A century ago, the entire area had been a protected cinnamon estate cultivated by the colonial masters for gain, the cinnamon peelers almost bonded slaves, the price of cutting down a tree, death.

Cinnamon Gardens was laid out around Victoria Park, a pleasure ground with meandering walkways, shaded by fig trees and palms, with benches under clumps of graceful bamboo and araliya trees. Along the numerous archways that provided entrance into the park crept the purple bell-shaped flowers of the thunbergia and within the park were passionflowers, orchids, bright-leaved caladiums, and a multitude of other tropical plants.

To the north of the park was the Town Hall. To the south, Green Path led all the way up through the suburb of Colpetty to Colombo's main thoroughfare, the Galle Road. To the east of the park was Albert Crescent, from which branched off the main residential streets of Cinnamon Gardens: Ward Place, Rosmead Place, Barnes Place, and Horton Place, most of them named after former British governors of the Crown colony of Ceylon.

These streets contained within them many grand mansions, situated well away from the road, some barely visible for the greenery that surrounded them. They were the homes of the best of Ceylonese society, whose members had thrived under the British Empire and colonial economy. This gentry had attained an affluence they never could have foreseen, through trade in rubber, coconut, plumbago, and – this a well-covered fact – the distilling of arrack. The drawing rooms of these homes were appointed with the very best that Europe had to offer, the finest chandeliers, Waterford crystal, curtains from Paris, damask tablecloths, Steinway pianos. Everything that made the occupants faithful servants of the British Empire or, if not the Empire – as this was the age of agitation for self-rule – at least loyal to the principles of the colonial economy that had placed them where they were. The fine residences bore names such as Ascot, Elscourt, The Priory, The Grange, Chateau Jubilee, Rosebank, Fincastle, The Firs; and the names of the occupants – Reginald, Felix, Solomon, Florence, Henrietta, Aloysius, Venetia, Tudor, Edwin.

Perhaps one of the grandest houses of Cinnamon Gardens was that of the Mudaliyar Navaratnam. He was kin to Annalukshmi and her sisters, their paternal grandfather and the Mudaliyar being first cousins. His property on Horton Place was named "Brighton" after the Brighton Pavilion, which the Mudaliyar had visited as a young man. A large, three-storeyed, Georgian-style house sat at the end of a long driveway that curved both ways around an oval garden and met under the front porch. The roof of the front porch was flat and served as a balcony, a balustrade running around it. French doors led into the second floor. The façade of this floor consisted of a series of arched windows, in comparison to which the windows of the third floor were but slits. Along the edge of the roof there was another balustrade, which hid the low-pitched, red-tiled roof. An arched, colonnaded verandah ran around the house. The verandah had elaborate flowered-tile flooring and large reclining chairs of teak and caning.

Brighton's oval front garden was extensive, with stone benches at each end for viewing the vista. A carefully tended lawn was broken by flowerbeds of cannas and roses. Royal palms had been planted at regular intervals around the edges of the driveway, their feathery, soaring leaves giving a sense of lightness and whimsy to the entire garden. To the left of the garden, beyond the driveway, was a thick clump of trees. This vegetation separated the grounds of Brighton from the property belonging to Annalukshmi and her family.

The Kandiah bungalow — Lotus Cottage — was a simple two-bedroom bungalow with whitewashed walls and a red-tiled roof. It might have been spartan but for carved verandah pillars whose design of lotus flowers and vines was picked up on the fretwork mal lallis above the doors and windows and on the carved valance boards that ran along the bottom edges of the roof. The house was small and would have been unbearably cramped for a family of four if not for the deep front and back verandahs. Like most inhabitants of Ceylon, or indeed any tropical country, the Kandiahs conducted a large part of their living — the entertaining of guests, tea, sewing, reading, some cooking — on these verandahs.

A set of front doors opened directly onto the drawing room, to the right of which were the entrances to the two bedrooms. One was occupied by Louisa, the other by the three girls. They were neat, cheerful rooms. Though the furniture was inexpensive and the three beds a bit of a squeeze, the brightly coloured floral coverlets and curtains adequately compensated for these shortcomings. Beyond the drawing room, and separated only by an archway, was the dining room, with a carved ebony table and matching chairs. From the dining room, a pair of doors led onto a U-shaped back verandah. Along the left arm of the verandah was the bathroom and store rooms; along the right, the kitchen and the servants' quarters. The back garden was extensive and contained a variety of fruit trees — jak, banana, papaw, breadfruit, mango; beds of vegetables – brinjal, murunga, okra, pumpkin; and herbs – curry leaves, rampe, lemon grass. At a fair distance from the verandah was the toilet. Lotus Cottage still used the bucket system, a latrine coolie coming by every morning to collect the night soil in his cart.

The front garden of Lotus Cottage was carefully landscaped by Louisa, who was an avid gardener. A tamarind tree, two king coconut trees, and a flamboyant tree spread their shade across the lawn. Carefully tended beds of red crotons, pink and yellow ixoras, balsam and ferns surrounded each tree. The hedge that ran the length of the property was bright with red hibiscus and, on this November day, under the cooling breeze brought by the northeast monsoon, the flowers nodded in a friendly fashion to any visitors coming up the small lane that led from Horton Place to the wicket gate of Lotus Cottage.

That afternoon, a visitor would have found the Kandiah family at tiffin on the front verandah, their white wicker chairs pulled around the matching table, Louisa presiding with the teapot. A lively conversation was in progress between Louisa and Kumudini about the pattern for a tablecloth Kumudini was completing for her sewing class at the Van Der Hoot School for Ladies she attended. Louisa had been a great beauty in her time. None of her daughters had inherited her charm, though they were by no means unattractive. Kumudini had that much-valued fair complexion. Her front teeth stuck out slightly, but she had a way of drawing her upper lip over them that gave her a prim and timid look that a young man would find charming. Manohari was almost as tall as a man and gangly. Her classmates had nick-named her Giraffe, which was, unfortunately, an apt description. Yet she had a pert nose and nicely shaped lips. Annalukshmi was dark-skinned. She had a long face with a high brow, large ears, and no chin to speak of. Her body was thin and angular. These disadvantages were offset, to some extent, by her eyes, which were large and fringed with long lashes. They sparkled with intelligence and vivacity. Her hair was thick and had an attractive kink to it. She usually wove it into a plait, which she then knotted at the back of her neck. When released from the knot, it spread out like a veil down to her waist, giving her a sudden and startling beauty. At present, Annalukshmi sat with her teacup in her hand, trying to be attentive to the conversation about the tablecloth. Yet her mind was far away, contemplating the plan she had come up with that would allow her to ride her bicycle to school the following day.

❧

The next morning, as Annalukshmi got dressed, she tried to appear serene, to act as if nothing out of the ordinary was about to happen. Yet her mouth felt dry and she had to concentrate while she draped her sari, nervousness making her fingers stiff.

At breakfast, Louisa noticed her oldest daughter did not bicker and quarrel with her sisters like she usually did but, instead, asked them to pass the thosai and sambar with a politeness that made her eyes narrow in suspicion.

"Merlay," she said, leaning forward, "are you all right?"

"Of course," Annalukshmi replied. "Why shouldn't I be?"

Before Louisa could question her further, the rickshaw men banged on the gate.

"Ah, the coolies are here," Louisa said, still not satisfied that all was well with her daughter. She stood up and tied her kimono around her ankle-length nightdress.

The girls rose from the table and washed their hands at the sink. Their bags were on the settee in the drawing room, Annalukshmi's and Manohari's small hard suitcases, one in brown, the other in navy blue, Kumudini's a straw sewing basket with a lid. They picked up their bags and went onto the verandah.

The rickshaw men, bare-bodied with turbans and knee-length sarongs, were out on the lane, crouched between the shafts of their rickshaws, chewing beetal. They stood up when the girls and Louisa came through the gate. Louisa watched as each daughter stepped in between the shafts and climbed into their respective rickshaws.

Louisa gave the signal and the rickshaw men began to move forward. When they were almost at the bottom of the lane, Louisa cried out, as she always did, "Girls, girls, open your umbrellas, for heaven's sake. You don't want to turn black, do you?"

They waved in reply.

Each girl had been given a gift by their father of a flower-patterned, paper Chinese umbrella from Malaya. Once they were on Horton Place, Manohari and Kumudini dutifully opened their umbrellas. Annalukshmi, however, pulled out an old, battered cloth hat from her bag, put it on her head, and slipped the elastic under her chin.

"Stop!" Annalukshmi called to her rickshaw man. He halted and she got down quickly.

"Akka?" Kumudini signalled to her man to stop.

Ignoring her, Annalukshmi hurried towards the hedge that formed the border of Brighton. She stepped through a gap and, after a moment, returned with the bicycle. The edges of her sari were wet with dew and a twig had caught in her hat.

"Brilliant plan, don't you think?" she said with attempted cheerfulness to ward off the aghast looks on her sisters' faces and the growing heaviness in her stomach at what she was about to do.

Kumudini snapped her umbrella shut and stepped down from her rickshaw. "Are you mad or something, akka? You are sure to be spotted and Amma is going to hear about it."

"By then it will be too late," Annalukshmi said, yet her voice caught.

"You think you are wondrously adventurous, akka," Manohari said, "but the truth is you look an absolute fright on that bicycle."

Annalukshmi put her bag in the wicker basket attached to the handlebar. "Goodbye," she said, afraid her resolve might give way if she listened to her sisters any longer. She began to ride away.

"Akka, wait, stop!" Kumudini cried out after her, but Annalukshmi pretended she had not heard.

Once Annalukshmi had gone past Horton Place and was on Green Path, heading towards Colpetty, she began to be filled with elation. She looked up at the canopy of leaves created by the huge trees on either side of Green Path and she smiled. Her plan had succeeded. Here she was riding her bicycle to school. The deliciously cool wind flapped against her sari and crept underneath it. She pulled off her hat, threw it into the wicker basket, and rose in her seat. She began to pedal faster, blissfully unaware of the looks she was getting from pedestrians and motorists.

❧

Galle Road ran parallel to the coast, about two hundred yards inland. The residents of Colombo thus identified buildings and other landmarks on Galle Road as being either on the "sea side" or the "land side" of Galle Road.

The Colpetty Mission School, where Annalukshmi taught, was on the "sea side" of Galle Road, in the suburb of Colpetty. A wrought-iron front gate opened onto a courtyard, from which two paths forked off in opposite directions, one leading to the Colpetty Mission Church, the other to the buildings of the school. The church, heavy and sombre, was made out of stone and looked like it belonged in Scotland rather than Ceylon. The inside of the church was bare and functional, its only redeeming feature the stained-glass window of Christ as the Good Shepherd above the pulpit. In contrast, the school buildings had a cheerful, light feeling to them. They were made of brick and had been whitewashed. The proximity of the school to the sea meant that the sunlight against the buildings had a muted, golden quality. Flowering creepers – bougainvillaea, morning glories – grew up the walls, providing splashes of colour.

A netball court and a drill ground formed a quadrangle around which the school buildings were situated. To the "sea side" of the quadrangle, bordering the railway line and the beach, was the senior classroom block. To the "land side" was the headmistress's office and the staff room. The other two sides had the boarding and the junior classroom block, respectively.

Any girl who had been through the Colpetty Mission School knew that the students divided their teachers into two groups – the confirmed hags and the potential hags. The confirmed hags were women who were well past the marriageable age and to whom life offered only a bleak spinsterhood on a meagre teacher's salary. The potential hags were former students whom

Miss Lawton invited back to teach in the junior classes until such time as they found husbands. The more of a confirmed hag a teacher became, the more ridiculed and despised she was. The distinction between the two groups was, thus, strictly and rancorously maintained.

Margery De Soysa, the leader of the potential hags, was standing at the window of the staff room when Annalukshmi came sailing in through the gate on her bicycle into the midst of the students who were gathered in the courtyard.

"My heavens!" she said, raising her eyebrows in astonishment.

The other teachers were chatting with each other around the long staff table in the centre of the room. They looked up at her.

"You absolutely must come and see this," she said.

They all came to the window.

Annalukshmi had now got off her bicycle and was surrounded by the students, most of whom were expressing their admiration, a few pleading to be allowed to do a turn on the bicycle.

"What utter lunacy," Ursula Gooneratne, the leader of the confirmed hags, said. "That Kandiah girl, sometimes I think her brains must be in her backside."

The confirmed hags nodded in agreement.

"But where did she get that bicycle, is what I want to know." Margery De Soysa said.

"Miss Blake gave it to her. A farewell gift."

Miss Lawton's adopted daughter, Nancy, stood in the doorway, trying to conceal her amusement at their disapproval. Unlike the other teachers, who wore saris, Nancy had on a daringly high knee-length dress and her hair was bobbed. Though she was extremely pretty and had a shapely figure, there was none of the jauntiness to her one might have associated with such a fashionably turned-out young woman. Rather, her manner was sedate, and, when she spoke, there was a flowing elongation to her vowels that showed that, while her English was perfect, she had learnt the language later in life.

"Slavishly imitating," Ursula Gooneratne said. "I suppose she thinks she looks like a European now. More like a peon to me."

Margery De Soysa had, until this moment, been as critical about the whole thing as Ursula Gooneratne. Yet, hearing her arch-rival's disapproval, she decided to take the opposite track just to provoke her. "Nonsense," she said, tossing her head, her earrings clinking as she did so. "I think it's absolutely delightful. I have a good mind to go out and get one myself."

"Why don't you?" Ursula Gooneratne retorted. "That way your car will no longer have to bring you the hundred yards from your house to school."

This comment about Margery De Soysa's notorious indolence was not received well. A flutter of anticipation went through the staff room at the possibility of an argument.

"At least I have a car," Margery De Soysa declared.

Before the argument between them could go any further, Annalukshmi walked in.

"Shhhh-shhhh," somebody cried and the staff room became silent.

Annalukshmi paused for a moment, bag in one hand, hat in the other, realizing that they had been discussing her and the bicycle. She was grateful to see Nancy standing by the cubicles at the back of the room, her eyebrows raised in sympathy.

"Annalukshmi," Margery De Soysa cried, stepping towards her, "how tremendous you looked on that bicycle. I was telling everybody that I have a mind to go out and get one myself."

"That's good," Annalukshmi answered. She moved past her and walked over to where Nancy was standing.

Annalukshmi always felt awkward around girls like Margery De Soysa, with their delicate French-chiffon saris and high, tinkly laughs. She dressed for school in simple Japanese Georgettes and, next to the likes of Margery, she knew she was plain.

Nancy touched Annalukshmi's arm. "Congratulations," she whispered. "I thought you looked splendid as you sailed in through the gate."

"How is our European miss today?" Ursula Gooneratne said to Annalukshmi.

The other teachers snickered.

"Next thing you know, our European miss will be talking with an English accent."

Annalukshmi was about to retort, but Nancy, who still had her hand on her friend's arm, tightened her grip, advising her to ignore Miss Gooneratne's taunt.

Though emancipated and modern, Nancy, who was twenty-five, asserted her will and bore any criticism with quiet equanimity. She was often a check on her younger friend's excesses.

The headmistress's door opened and Miss Lawton came out. She looked around. "Hasn't the bell rung yet? Nancy dear, could you please go and tell that groundskeeper to ring it now."

Nancy nodded and left.

"Ah, Anna, there you are," Miss Lawton said to Annalukshmi. "Come in, I want to talk with you."

She followed Miss Lawton into her office.

Though Miss Lawton ran the school with clockwork efficiency, her office was always a mess. Her desk was covered with papers and books through which Miss Lawton seemed to somehow know her way. The rest of the office was similarly cluttered. Against one wall, a dusty, glass-fronted cupboard was crammed with old cups and shields that the school had won over the years, the excess trophies on top of the cupboard, on the floor, and on the windowsills. A sofa seemed to have caught the spillover from Miss Lawton's desk and was in danger of being submerged by papers too. One corner of the room, however, was neat, the surface of the desk bare. This had been Miss Blake's area, and she had maintained it in her orderly fashion.

"Anna dear," Miss Lawton said as she bustled around to her side of the desk and indicated for Annalukshmi to sit down, "I have a favour to ask you. I am in the midst of finding a replacement for Miss Blake and it might take more than a few days. Would you be able to assist me with Miss Blake's work?"

"Me, Miss Lawton?" Annalukshmi said, surprised and pleased. "But I don't know anything about the assistant headmistress's job."

"Well, of course I wouldn't expect you to do all of it," Miss Lawton said, rolling her eyes. "That would be beyond you. What I need help with is the office work, filing, answering some of the correspondence."

"I . . . I'd be delighted, Miss Lawton," Annalukshmi replied, proud that Miss Lawton considered her for the task.

"I'll be eternally indebted to you."

At that moment, the telephone rang and Miss Lawton went to get it. Annalukshmi looked at her beloved headmistress – her hair parted down the middle and wound around her head in a braid, glasses perched on the edge of her nose, her long-sleeved plain dress that hung unfashionably loose to a little below her knees – and she felt an enormous affection for this woman. Miss

Lawton had picked her from amongst all the teachers, some of them much senior to her, for this task. She resolved to do her very best so that Miss Lawton would see that her confidence in her had been well placed.

2

A wise son gives joy not only to his father
But to all the world.
— The Tirukkural, *verse 68*

The Mudaliyar Navaratnam's birthday was one of the grand-est, most looked forward to social occasions of Cinnamon Gardens. For the family, however, it was a day tinged with sorrow. Twenty-eight years ago, on the Mudaliyar's birthday, his older son, Arulanandan, had stabbed his father in the arm because of the Mudaliyar's resistance to his affair with a low-caste woman who worked as a servant at Brighton. This incident had forced the Mudaliyar to banish his son and the woman to India. His birthday had thus always brought with it the discord of that time and sadness for the loss of a son.

The memory of his brother was very much with the Mudaliyar's younger son, Balendran, as his car turned into the gates of Brighton on the morning of the Mudaliyar's birthday. Balendran had received a summons. The Mudaliyar had tele-phoned him last night and requested his presence early this morning about a matter of importance. He felt sure this meeting had to do with the recent misappropriation of the brass lamps in their temple in Pettah. The chief priest had gone over Balendran's head and appealed directly to the Mudaliyar. Balendran felt a twinge of nervousness, wondering whether his father disapproved of his actions with regard to the lamps.

In the days before European domination, a mudaliyar, in the domain in which he held sway, had served as a representative of the king. The British had continued the mudaliyarships, but now it was an appointment by the governor based on loyalty to the Empire. The mudaliyars served as interpreters to the British government agents in the different provinces of Ceylon, and they helped the agents execute colonial policy. They were also Legislative Council members.

As usual, the long front verandah at Brighton was crowded with petitioners seeking favours from the Mudaliyar Navaratnam – posts in government, letters of recommendation, help in settling land disputes. The more important, or those who considered themselves so, were seated in the large reclining chairs. The poor simply sat on the outer edge of the verandah or loitered in the shade of the araliya trees.

Balendran had grown up in this house and knew it intimately, yet he felt himself a stranger as he got out of the car and walked up the steps. In fact, he hesitated briefly, too timid to actually ring the bell and have himself admitted to the vestibule. When he did visit Brighton at this time of day, he would usually have the driver take him to the back, where he was sure to find his mother in the kitchen, her palu wound tightly around her waist as she worked alongside the servants. This morning, however, he did not wish to disturb her, as she would have her hands full with the birthday dinner.

"Sin-Aiyah!"

He turned to see his father's old retainer, Pillai, in his white coat and cloth, his long grey hair in a knot at the back of his head. He was hurrying down the verandah towards him.

"What is Sin-Aiyah doing here?" Pillai asked in Tamil as he came up to him.

"The Peri-Aiyah sent for me," Balendran replied in Tamil.

"But nobody told me. You could have stood here for half an hour and we would not have known." His eyes widened with horror at the thought that the son of the Mudaliyar Navaratnam might have waited on the front verandah of his ancestral home like a lowly petitioner.

He took a large ring of keys that hung from a chain around his waist and selected one.

The heavy front doors of Brighton were panelled and made of teak. Above them was an elaborate, floral-patterned fanlight of stained glass. Pillai unlocked the doors and pushed one of them open for Balendran. "Does at least Peri-Amma know you are here?"

"No," Balendran replied, beginning to feel annoyed at the big to-do Pillai was making over something inconsequential.

Pillai shook his head at this state of affairs. He shut the front door after him and hurried away, no doubt to inform the Peri-Amma and Peri-Aiyah of their son's arrival.

Balendran stood in the vestibule, gazing around him. It had been a long while since he had been in the house at this time of the day. Wide wooden stairs, with a red carpet in the centre, rose from the vestibule to a landing. From there, a set of doors led into the ballroom and the banquet hall. Sunlight streamed down on the landing through a stained-glass skylight. Balendran looked up at the landing and was reminded of his childhood –

of those years before he started school when he would lie on the landing and imagine the brightly-coloured patterns of light on the floor to be deer or monkeys, then wriggle around to catch the patterns on his body.

Balendran had a sudden wish to see the designs of light again and he walked quickly up the stairs. As he stood looking down at the configurations, however, another memory from his childhood came back to him. The school holidays when he and his brother would play cards on this landing. A familiar gloom descended on him at the thought of his brother. He turned abruptly and walked down the stairs.

When he reached the bottom step, he stopped in surprise. His father's secretary, Miss Adamson, was standing by the study door, watching him.

"Good morning," he said.

She bowed humbly in reply.

Balendran found, as he often did in the presence of this American woman, a desire to laugh at her incongruence in a white sari, her long fair hair pulled into a tight knot at the back of her head.

"The master will see you now," she said softly.

She turned and led the way into the study. He followed, thinking how her accent, the way she dragged out the vowels of "master," made the word sound almost like a caress.

The Mudaliyar Navaratnam's study was an unfortunate example of what happens when the furnishings of Europe are adapted, without modification, to a tropical climate. The curtains and the upholstery of the *chaise-longue* and chairs were all of a thick red velvet. The upholstery had very quickly worn off in places, and the curtains, despite repeated cleaning, were always full of dust. The effect was gloomy and musty, and, as Balendran walked in, he could feel a tickling in his nostrils.

The Mudaliyar pushed his chair out from his desk and leant back in it as he watched Balendran, escorted by Miss Adamson, come towards him. Very little brought him such pleasure as this, the sight of his son, and one of the Mudaliyar's favourite verses from the *Tirukkural* came back to him. "The service a son can render his father is to make men ask 'How came this blessing?'"

For a moment, because his face was in shadow, the Mudaliyar let his normally stern expression soften.

Birthdays are often a time for recollection and nostalgia, and the Mudaliyar felt he was looking at a younger version of his own late father. Balendran had inherited his grandfather's small but well-proportioned frame and fine features, his long eyelashes and aquiline nose, his mouth with its thin upper lip and full lower one. At forty, Balendran's hair was greying slightly at the temples, but this only enhanced the dark glow of his skin. His being clean-shaven, at a time when moustaches were the fashion, gave him a youthful look. He wore neatly pressed, white drill trousers and a coat for, despite the heat, most Ceylonese gentlemen conformed to the standard of European attire and dressed in a suit. The Mudaliyar's pride in him was well warranted.

The Mudaliyar, at seventy, was still healthy and robust. He was tall and strongly built and had stately features — a long nose that flared out at the nostrils, a high forehead, slightly hooded eyes, and a neatly curled moustache. He was an imposing and handsome figure in his cream cotton sherwani and matching turban, with the holy ash and the sandalwood potu on his brow.

Balendran had reached the desk now and he shook hands with his father, wishing him a happy birthday.

"Pillai says you came through the front entrance."

"Yes, Appa."

"Next time use the back. We were not ready and you could have been standing there for an hour. It would not do for people to say that the Mudaliyar Navaratnam keeps his own son waiting like a common petitioner."

"Yes, Appa."

The Mudaliyar indicated for Balendran to sit. Miss Adamson had seated herself cross-legged on a cushion. She was looking at some correspondence on the low table in front of her.

"I asked you to come today because something important has taken place."

"Appa, if it is about the lamps, I can explain . . ."

The Mudaliyar waved his hand, dismissing this triviality about which he wished to know nothing.

"After meeting with members of the Ceylon Tamil Association yesterday, I have decided to throw in my lot with them."

Balendran frowned in astonishment. His father belonged to the Queen's House set. They were statesmen whose only loyalty was to the British governor and Empire and they had no interest in local associations and their demands and needs.

The Mudaliyar shrugged, reading his son's mind. "I hold my post because I am nominated by the governor and I intend to stay in the Legislative Council only so long as I am nominated. However, the arrival of this Donoughmore Constitutional Commission in two weeks makes it necessary that we Tamils unite together. It is rumoured the commission will be granting greater self-government in the new constitution. This must be stopped. The governor must retain all the powers he possesses.

Otherwise, we will replace a British Raj with a Sinhala Raj and then we Tamils will be doomed."

Balendran tried to keep his expression attentive so his father would not be able to perceive how much he disagreed with his political views; how much he hoped for, prayed for, the possibility of self-government. He was a respectful son and hence had never expressed his views to his father. Further, Balendran felt sympathy towards him. His father belonged to the old breed of statesman who had come of age at a time when even the mention of self-government would bring the mighty fist of the British Empire down on them. They had learnt to negotiate themselves within this tyranny. His father was like a prisoner who had spent so much of his life in a penitentiary that he was unable to accommodate himself to a life outside of it.

"Besides, self-government would be fatal to this country economically," the Mudaliyar continued. "We are a mere dot in the ocean. Without the might of the British Empire behind us, we would be reduced to penury. Let us first put our house in order, show that we are worthy of self-government, before it is granted to us."

The Mudaliyar leant forward in his chair, silent for a moment. "Fortunately, the commission is to be headed by Lord Donoughmore, a man of noble standing. The pale horse in the whole thing is, of course, that Labourite, Dr. Drummond Shiels, who has very fixed ideas on what is good for Ceylon. European ideas that are at odds with our great cultural tradition." The Mudaliyar paused. "I am speaking specifically about universal franchise."

Again Balendran had to struggle to keep the disagreement from his face. The one thing that Balendran hoped for, even above self-rule, was the possibility of universal franchise and the vast and beneficial change it would bring to Ceylonese society, with its feudal subservience and loyalties.

Balendran looked up from his thoughts to see that his father was examining him carefully. Then, strangely, he lowered his eyes and looked away, as if embarrassed to be caught staring at his son. Balendran sensed immediately a change in the air and glanced around, half expecting to see something different in the room. After a moment, the Mudaliyar continued, still not looking at Balendran. "I received a very important and interesting phone call yesterday from someone in the colonial secretary's department. It seems Dr. Drummond Shiels may not be the problem we anticipate him to be. He has an adviser, a gentleman who evidently exerts great influence over him, a gentleman to whose opinions Dr. Shiels is known to listen."

He paused again and toyed with the cap of his inkwell.

A strange suspicion began to form in Balendran's mind. He felt the air close in around him.

"A gentleman you knew very well during your London days."

A coldness rushed up the back of Balendran's neck.

"I am talking of Mr. Richard Howland."

Balendran felt light-headed, felt the need to put his head between his legs, to have the blood enter his head again. But, at the same time, he had an equally strong need to maintain his dignity, his calm, in order not to betray in his father's presence the impact that name still had on him after all these years, the combination of regret and dismay that arose in him.

Balendran felt hands on his shoulders. He had been unaware that his father had come around the desk and was now standing behind him. His father squeezed his shoulders and their pressure was the steadfastness Balendran needed. He felt himself coming into his own again.

"Miss Adamson, you can call in the next petitioner," the Mudaliyar said.

Balendran watched Miss Adamson walk towards the door that led out onto the front verandah. Her simple action gave him a further grip on himself.

The Mudaliyar sensed Balendran's return to normality. He let go of his son's shoulders and went back around the desk, where he picked up his papers and straightened them. "It might be a good idea to open communications again."

"With Richard . . . Mr. Howland?"

"Mr. Howland struck me as a fine man, a sensible man. A man who would be sensitive to the differences between the Orient and Europe and not confuse one with the other. I have found out he is to arrive with the commission and stay at the Galle Face Hotel. You will speak with him?"

Miss Adamson entered with the next petitioner, and Balendran stood up.

"Yes, Appa," he replied distractedly. One thought and one thought alone was in his mind. Richard Howland, his Richard, was going to be in Ceylon in two weeks! Staying at the Galle Face Hotel. Balendran knew he had to be alone, to try and work his mind around this stupendous notion. He began to walk towards the door that led to the vestibule.

The moment Balendran left his father's study, his mother — a diminutive, plump woman — rose from the chair where she had been sitting in the hallway and held out her arms to him. Nalamma came to her son and he bent down towards her. She took his face between her hands and kissed him on both cheeks.

"You came to the front door, thambi-boy. What were you thinking?" she asked in Tamil, for she spoke no English.

She put her hand on Balendran's. "Come with me. I want to talk to you about something."

"I can't, Amma," Balendran said quickly. "I . . . I have things to do. I must go to the temple."

"The temple business is more important than your own mother?" Her grip tightened on his arm. "I'll only take a few minutes of your precious time."

Balendran saw that he had no choice but to obey. He did not have the faculties at the moment to extricate himself.

From the landing at the top of the stairs, two sets of steps curved off in each direction only to meet again at the next floor. Here there was a wide foyer, with entrances to the bedrooms on either side of it. At the far end, a set of French doors opened onto the balcony above the front porch, with a fine view of the oval garden. Nalamma used this foyer as her drawing room and, unlike the Mudaliyar's study, it was light and airy, a settee, carpets, and cushions being the only furniture in it.

When they were seated, Nalamma turned to Balendran and said, "I can't stop thinking of your brother and all that happened."

Balendran nodded. For the past twenty-eight years, this had been his mother's refrain on the Mudaliyar's birthday.

"Have you heard anything from him, thambi-boy?"

He looked at her, surprised. "Of course not, Amma."

After his son had left, the Mudaliyar had made them swear in front of the Gods in the household shrine not to have anything to do with Arul.

She glanced down at her hands. "It was silly of me to ask. But I was hoping."

"Why?" he said, trying to keep his mind on her need.

"Last night I dreamt we were at Keerimalai on the beach. It was one of our Jaffna holidays. He was still a child. I took his hand and went with him towards the sea. Then I lifted him in my arms and walked into the water."

Inebriated, Balendran suddenly thought. This was what he felt. As if he were back in his college days, intoxicated far quicker than his companions and too proud to admit it. His college days, however, were inextricably bound with the memory of Richard. He hastily tried to recover what his mother had said and make an appropriate reply. "But that's a pleasant dream, isn't it? We loved those Jaffna holidays."

She shook her head. "But you are forgetting, Keerimalai is the place where we scatter the ashes after the funeral. You walk into the water and release them to the sea."

The seriousness with which she had spoken should have made him feel solicitous towards her, instead a silly college drinking song went through his mind. He drew himself together. He had to end this conversation quickly. He patted her knee and stood up. "It's nothing, Amma. You wait and see."

"I wish we had some news of him," she said, rising too.

"He no longer exists for Appa," he reminded her gently. "We have no choice but to obey."

"And the boy . . . his son, Seelan. He must be almost twenty-seven now."

"'Laugh at misfortune — nothing so able to triumph over it,'" he quoted from the *Tirukkural.*

Nalamma sighed and said, "Men don't understand. The cord may be cut at birth, but the attachment remains."

Before Balendran left, his mother gave him some money to put in the offerings box at St. Anthony's Church in Kochchikade.

Though a staunch and fervent Hindu, Nalamma, like many Ceylonese, deemed divine favour to exist in all faiths. Thus, she had no compunction about appealing to a Catholic saint or making an offering at a Buddhist shrine, along with her daily pooja to Ganesh.

※

Balendran's car was a black 1910 Model T Ford. It had originally belonged to his father, who, when the "Tin Lizzie" became a common automobile, got tired of it and moved on to a more sleek and expensive car, something he would do every few years. He always offered his son his old cars before selling them off, but Balendran, despite the fact that the Ford had to be hand-started, had always stuck with his "Tin Lizzie." There was a jauntiness to it that reminded him of nothing so much as an intelligent, alert terrier. He liked its shape, its angles, the brass radiator shell, the broad running boards, the large wheels with fenders raised well above them, which gave the car a buoyant look. The top folded back easily and this allowed Balendran, when he chose, to travel with the wind blowing through his hair. When Balendran was in his car again, he leant back against the seat.

"To the temple, Sin-Aiyah?" his driver, Joseph, asked.

"Yes . . . no . . ." Balendran tried to decide what he wanted. He needed a place where he could walk and think. "The Galle Face Green," he finally said. "Take me there."

Joseph was looking at him, puzzled. Not wanting his scrutiny, Balendran waved his hand impatiently for him to drive on.

Once the car started to move, Balendran shut his eyes. He had to think, he had to order his thoughts. Yet his mind had developed a capricious determination of its own and, instead of thinking about Richard's arrival in two weeks, he found himself fixated on that ridiculous drinking song and, with it, the remembrance of that pub in St. Martin's Lane, the Salisbury, which he and Richard used to frequent. As the song filled his mind, it brought back the image of Richard standing by the piano, his face flushed with drink and the effort of singing, a lock of his blond hair fallen over his forehead, his hand around Balendran's waist. As the evening progressed and their inhibitions fell away, Richard's hand would invariably slip under Balendran's shirt. He would gently run his fingers up and down Balendran's spine until Balendran had to lean against the back of the piano so that the other patrons would not notice his arousal. At the thought of Richard's caress, Balendran felt his blood thud against his temples.

The Galle Face Green was an open lawn about one mile in length and three hundred yards wide. It was flanked on one side by the sea and the other by Beira Lake. It was a public recreation ground and, of an evening, was always busy with cricketers, football players, kite flyers, horse riders, and strollers. Three roads passed through it: the Esplanade, a perfectly smooth carriage drive and promenade by the sea wall; a similar drive by the lake; and a central road for commercial traffic.

When the car reached the Galle Face Green, Balendran got out hurriedly, feeling as if he were escaping from some stifling room. He instructed Joseph to park on the side of the central road, then he set out across the nearly deserted green towards the sea wall. He breathed in deeply, the sting of the salty air in his nostrils, the breeze cooling his face. His thoughts felt like the jumble of different-coloured threads in his wife's sewing box, and he knew he had to unravel them one from the other. The Galle Face Hotel at the other end of the green, however, made him stop. The hotel was a long, rectangular block, three storeys high. End bays and a centre entrance bay had been brought forward to break up the monotony of the façade, an effect further accentuated by the bays being one storey higher and having individual pitched corner roofs. The front porch, at the base of the entrance bay, was a hive of activity as cars and carriages pulled up, deposited guests, and drove away. The very concreteness of the hotel gave a sudden solidity to the notion that Richard would be here in two weeks. There had been no communication between them in more than twenty years. Balendran felt an apprehensiveness rise in him, but he tried to reassure himself it was natural. After all, they had been in love. Like any two people who had been intimately connected in the past, there was bound to be awkwardness at first. After that, the meeting would go smoothly. They already had something to discuss. The Donoughmore Commission would regulate any gaps or bumps in their encounter.

He stared at the hotel again, imagining their meeting. Richard would step out of the lift and see him sitting on one of those lovely antique ebony sofas in the lounge. They would both raise their hands in greeting. He, Balendran, would stand and straighten his coat, waiting for his friend to come up. They would extend their arms to each other, their hands meeting in a firm clasp. "Bala," Richard would say, "what a pleasure after so long." "The pleasure is all mine, old chap," Balendran would reply.

The sight of a kite whirling its way drunkenly into the sky momentarily distracted Balendran from his thoughts. Then his mind, the great swindler, summoned up a recollection of Richard. His friend's freely flowing, instantaneous anger. The way Richard would storm around their flat, slamming doors, banging plates, once even throwing a vase against the wall. Public places were not inviolate either, and Richard would think nothing about yelling the word "bastard" at him on Tottenham Court Road or in Russell Square. Now an alternate scenario of their first meeting presented itself: Richard storming out of the lift and, even before he got to him, letting fly a string of invectives, accusing him of desertion, of cowardliness, of not loving him. Balendran clicked his tongue against his teeth, dismissing his vivid fancy. He turned away from the hotel and began to walk towards the sea wall. "We are both twenty years older," he told himself. "Much has happened since then." In fact, Balendran assured himself, such meetings were often painful precisely because both parties found themselves irritated they had actually felt such an intensity of feelings for each other. Bad habits, annoyances would be recollected with a wonder that one had been foolish enough to tolerate them for love.

Love. He rolled the word around in his mind. He knew that his love for Richard was long dead. The passing of twenty years, a wife whom he loved in his own way, and a son, whom the very thought of filled him with happiness, ensured that. As for the type of love Richard and he had had, he accepted that it was part of his nature. His disposition, like a harsh word spoken, a cruel act done, was regrettably irreversible. Just something he had learnt to live with, a daily impediment, like a pair of spectacles or a badly set fracture.

"'As one by one we give up, we get freer and freer of pain,'" he said, citing to himself that verse from the *Tirukkural* on renunciation. How often he had repeated it during that first year of his marriage, to comfort himself for the anguish he had felt, the suffocation, lying next to his wife, Sonia, at night, unable to sleep. His suffering had been intensified by knowing that she despaired along with him, felt his alienation, almost hatred towards her, without knowing its cause. Yet no life is without its compensations. In the first year of their marriage, two things had happened to counteract their unhappiness with each other. The first, and most important, was the arrival of their son, Lukshman. How quickly that had altered their relations with each other, how easily they had learnt to love through their son. The second had been that his father, after the birth of his son, had finally grown cordial towards him. After a prolonged period of thirst, he had felt the assuaging waters of his father's love, his restoration as the much beloved son.

For a moment, Balendran allowed himself to think of that terrible time when the Mudaliyar had come to his flat in London, somehow knowing of his relationship with Richard. Balendran immediately shuddered and turned away, not wishing to dwell on that memory. Instead, he made himself recall his father's forgiveness. His father, as a gesture of his pardon, had bestowed on him the running of the family rubber estate and the temple, which he now managed and from which he drew his income. The granting of control and responsibility was the way the Mudaliyar expressed his affection.

Balendran stopped walking, a sudden significant idea before him that he had not thought of before. His father was *asking* him to renew contact with Richard! This request was not simply about the Donoughmore Commission. It went much deeper than that. His father was saying that he completely trusted him, that anything there was to forgive was forgiven. He recalled the pressure of his father's hands on his shoulders. They were the clasps on the mantle of societal approbation that Balendran now drew around him. He saw himself as he was. Much adored father of a handsome, intelligent son, their open, equal relationship the envy of all his son's friends; gallant spouse to a wife who was constantly told by her friends how lucky she was to have such a gentle, humane husband; dutiful, ministering son who eased his parents' burden in their old age. While other men might have taken these positions for granted, passed them off lightly, for Balendran they had an inestimable value. They were hard won, they had been laboured for, they were the sustenance from which he drew the strength for his daily life. Now the reminder of his charges gave him a mastery over his mind and emotions. Like someone emerging from a fever, he felt exhausted but also a clear-headed relief at being lucid again.

Balendran had reached the sea wall. He turned around and began to walk back towards the car. The meeting with Richard, which had seemed so earth-shattering a prospect a short while ago, now promised to be curiously banal. Apart from an initial moment of awkwardness, their meeting would be no different from the visit of any of his old London friends passing through Colombo.

3

A house divided like a vial and its lid
Seems one but comes apart.
— The Tirukkural, *verse* 887

The morning Annalukshmi rode her bicycle to school, Louisa was in the garden, supervising Ramu, her odd-job man and gardener. She wore a large straw hat with netting over it, making her look like she was bee-keeping. The hat was to guard her complexion, the netting to protect her from the mosquitoes. She was disturbed from her task by the postman, who stopped outside their gate and rang his bell in that maddeningly prolonged way he had. Louisa shaded her eyes against the sunlight and sent Ramu to fetch the letter the postman was waving at them. When Ramu passed it to her, she saw that the handwriting on the envelope was her husband's, the address barely legible because of his impatient scrawl. She told Ramu to carry on with his work, then, pushing the netting over her hat, she went up the verandah steps and sat down in one of the wicker chairs.

"Wife," the letter began, causing Louisa to frown at its peremptory tone. "Prepare Annalukshmi to get married. The young man in question is Muttiah, my nephew, Parvathy Akka's son." Louisa leant forward and went over this sentence again, unable to believe what she had just read.

"Muttiah has just secured a job," the letter continued. "He is at the Land Office in Kuala Lumpur on a steady salary and is able to support a wife and family. I have known him these last few years and find him serious and dependable. He fits all my expectations and I am sure will make Annalukshmi very happy. I will notify you of Parvathy Akka and Muttiah's forthcoming visit to settle the matter."

Louisa gasped. She reread the letter, shaking her head, unable to believe its contents. Ramu had stopped work and was watching her. She got up and, with as much calm as she could muster, went inside.

Once in her bedroom, Louisa removed her hat, sat on the edge of her bed, and stared at the letter again. A myriad of thoughts went through her mind at the same time, but, out of them, one took precedence. Her husband's nephew was a Hindu.

It was Murugasu's reversion to Hinduism that was the final blow to their already crumbling marriage. Louisa, a preacher's daughter, had been biased against Hinduism anyway. The fact that her husband had forsaken Christianity and returned to Hinduism marked the demise of her own happiness. Now, by Murugasu's command that Annalukshmi marry Muttiah, a Hindu, her husband was conveying to the world that their marriage held no meaning for him, that he was her husband in name only. "The mockery," she said to herself. "This is a slap in my face. He might as well take me out into the street by my hair and spit on me, such is the insult."

She now thought of Annalukshmi and a dread took hold of her. Louisa could not imagine her daughter, or indeed herself, in that house. Parvathy, her sister-in-law, kept a strict Hindu household, and Annalukshmi would be forced to conform to the ideals of a Hindu wife, cloistered like a nun, her movements restricted, her thoughts and opinions suppressed in favour of her husband. Then there was the groom himself. His physical attributes were not wholly unpleasant, but whatever charm there was in them was completely negated by his clumsy, oafish manner. In fact, when she had first met him, Louisa had wondered if he was a simpleton. She resolved that, come what may, she would not allow her daughter to go through with this.

Louisa recalled the terrible quarrel between father and daughter that had led her to leave Malaya, fearing for Annalukshmi's safety. Even now, she could hear Annalukshmi's scream of pain when Murugasu pulled her by her hair and slapped her. All ostensibly because Annalukshmi had not swept the drawing room. Yet Louisa later found out that the real cause of violence was the severing of the bond between father and daughter ever since Annalukshmi had seen Murugasu coming out of a Hindu temple and known that her parents' marriage was falling apart. Louisa looked at the letter on the bed and shook her head at the possible havoc this proposal brought with it. She decided to spare her daughter this news. She would handle it herself.

As well as sealing her daughter's fate, by this proposal Louisa also saw that her husband was binding her hands, forcing her to support him. If she protested, it would only expose to the world the state of their marriage and bring shame and disgrace to her daughters. Instead, she would have no choice but to support him, to say to her amazed family that she did not see why her daughter should not marry a Hindu. Such marriages, though rare, had happened in the past, some of them very good marriages, all this religious intolerance was ultimately very un-Christian. Louisa lowered her legs over the side of the bed.

Somehow this train of events had to be stopped before it led to catastrophe. But who could she appeal to in her predicament?

❧

Colombo being such a small place, Annalukshmi had, of course, been seen on her bicycle. By no worthier a figure than Louisa's cousin, Mrs. Philomena Barnett, who was taking her morning constitutional — which in Mrs. Barnett's case meant collaring some poor rickshaw man to trundle her around Victoria Park. She had seen Annalukshmi riding up Green Path and gasped in astonishment, raising her handkerchief to her mouth. What was Cousin Louisa thinking? Had she completely lost her mind? She signalled to her exhausted rickshaw man to take her home. Philomena had to go to Brighton later this morning to supervise the preparations for the Mudaliyar's birthday dinner. She vowed to have a talk with Cousin Louisa on the way there.

Philomena Barnett (whom Annalukshmi referred to as the Devil Incarnate) believed in the notion that a person's character was in their physiognomy. She herself was respectably stout and plain, the only note of frivolity seen in her garishly patterned saris of flowers, birds, and animals. In her opinion, Louisa's curvaceous figure could have led to nothing but trouble. Elopement. Even now the word stuck in the back of her throat. How selfish and thoughtless Louisa had been to do that. It had nearly destroyed the impending marriage of Philomena's sister. The groom's family, thinking that all the Barnett girls were flighty, had withdrawn their proposal and only the inducement of a larger dowry had mollified them. Philomena thought of her last unmarried daughter, Dolly, and her recent attempts to find a husband for her. Annalukshmi riding the bicycle had to be arrested immediately. She, a widow with scant resources, did not want any scandal spoiling her Dolly's chances.

So it was that, later in the morning, Cousin Philomena descended from her rickshaw at Lotus Cottage with a great heaving and panting, climbed laboriously up the verandah steps, and found Louisa sitting on the verandah, gazing dejectedly out into the garden.

"Cousin," she cried, "this time you have gone too far."

Louisa had been lost in her thoughts and she stood up quickly, confused.

"Don't give me that look. I have seen her today on the bicycle."

"Annalukshmi? But how did she? I saw her off in the rickshaw."

Philomena shook her head. She wiped her brow with her handkerchief and sat down in a chair. "So you didn't know," she said. "This is serious, very serious. We all warned you about giving that girl notions that were above her. I have no objection to a girl dabbling in a little teaching, but to go and get a professional certificate! What do you expect after that?"

"Well, I'll give her a good scolding and confiscate the bicycle," Louisa said, not wanting to hear a litany of her errors in the way she had brought up her daughters.

Philomena was not satisfied. It was clear to her that Cousin Louisa did not view this infraction with the seriousness it deserved. The time had come for her to take charge. And she knew just the solution for that Annalukshmi, the remedy that never failed.

"Listen, cousin," Philomena said, sitting forward in her chair. "I'll tell you what we will do. Let's marry off Annalukshmi. Best thing. Nothing settles a girl like marriage. There are some nice Tamil boys in our congregation and I could easily arrange a match."

Louisa was, at first, surprised by the suggestion. Then a sense of relief took hold of her.

"Do you actually have any one in mind?"

"Well, there's that Worthington boy who's just got a good position in the Postal Services. The Lights are looking for someone for their son and so are the Macintoshes."

Louisa clasped her hands together. "How wonderful!"

Philomena frowned, disconcerted by her enthusiasm.

Louisa grasped Philomena's hand tightly. "Now remember your promise, cousin. I wish to see these young men as soon as possible. I shall be very disappointed if I don't."

"I . . . I shall see what I can do about it." Philomena stood up. She bid her cousin goodbye and went down the verandah steps to her waiting rickshaw, a little suspicious. Her plan had been too eagerly seized upon.

Once Philomena had left, Louisa felt tired. She sensed a terrible headache coming on and retired to her room to lie in bed with the blinds rolled down, a handkerchief soaked in eau de cologne on her forehead. Though she had every intention of reprimanding Annalukshmi, Louisa could not bring herself to be truly upset about her daughter riding that bicycle. Hadn't she herself rebelled once, thought she was above societal regulations. Hadn't she eloped and married Murugasu? Still, she knew that she had to protect her daughter's reputation. Louisa, all the same, could not help smiling when she thought of the look of horror that must have crossed her cousin's face when she saw Annalukshmi flying by on her bicycle.

Louisa's mind dwelt for a moment on Miss Lawton. Though she disapproved of the headmistress's progressive ideas filling her daughter's head, she could not help but be flattered and honoured that such an influential, almost legendary, figure like Miss Lawton had bestowed friendship on her daughter, had taken such a personal interest in her. Though Miss Lawton was in her fifties and hence only about ten years older than her, Louisa had to admit she was a little in awe of her. She had been a student at the Colpetty Mission School when Miss Lawton first arrived as assistant headmistress. Even then she had commanded respect from teachers and students alike.

Murugasu's photograph was on the bedside table. Louisa picked it up and looked at it. It was one that he had given her while they were courting. There he stood, leaning on a pedestal, one arm on his hip, his left foot crossed over his right. He was wearing a light-coloured suit, a sola topi in hand, his moustache stylishly curled at both ends. He radiated vigour and satisfaction, but also impatience, as if he had been walking along and the photographer had begged him to pose for a moment. His half-smile said he was merely humouring the photographer and he would be off about his business in a moment.

Louisa thought of the first time she had met him. It had been at the Kuala Lumpur Mission Church, where her late father, Reverend Barnett, had been sent to administer to the needs of the numerous Jaffna Tamil Christians who were employed in the Malaya Civil Service and railways by the British. Jaffna, because of its arid, infertile environment and its proliferation of missionary schools, had provided the necessary recruits to Malaya. Louisa had gone to keep house for her father, as her mother had long been dead.

Murugasu's reputation had preceded him, and even before she met him, she knew of him as the man who had beheaded the Gods in his family shrine before coming out to Malaya a

Christian convert. While she served tea and biscuits to the parishioners, she had been aware of him staring at her. When she felt he was not looking, she had glanced in his direction too, feeling admiration for the passion with which he had acted. Even then he had been rotund, his stomach pushing out his coat. She could tell he was very uncomfortable in his white cotton suit, that it restricted him, made him sweat constantly. Yet his very lack of comfort, the way he wriggled his shoulders, the damp stains in the armpits of his coat, had caused a pleasant sensation to spread through the back of her neck.

Of course, her relatives, the Barnetts, had objected and continued to object long after they were married. Their list of complaints was long. He peppered his English with too much Tamil; refused to take a Christian surname like other converts (since Hindus had only one appellation, it was customary for them to take a Christian surname. Murugasu had chosen instead his grandfather's name, Kandiah). He had refused to give his daughters Christian names; chewed beetal leaves; belched after a meal; did not know how to use cutlery properly; smelt of stale sweat because he didn't use talcum powder. He was just too newly Christian. The things they disdained – his sweating, his red skin, his smell – Louisa associated with his ardour. For when she had looked at the pinched faces of her cousins, especially the female ones, she had known they had not experienced true passion.

Louisa recalled Murugasu's first visit to her house. Her father had left them unchaperoned for a moment. The instant he had gone in, Murugasu rose from his chair and, with absolute confidence, as if he were going to get a biscuit from the table, crossed over, took her startled face in his large hands, and kissed her expertly. If any other man had done that, she would have protested, if only for the sake of conformity. Yet, with him, it seemed squeamish to do so and would have earned his scornful puzzlement.

Louisa rubbed the side of her arm at the thought of the love and passion they had shared. She looked at the empty space of bed beside her, not even a pillow on it, the bare clothes-horse on his side of the room. She wanted to weep at how desolate her marriage had become. His sister, Parvathy, she blamed her. Yet, even as Louisa said this to herself, she knew it was not really Parvathy's fault. She had simply been the bearer of bad news.

Parvathy's husband had got a job on the Malayan railways and they had come to Kuala Lumpur. After fourteen years, Murugasu met his sister again. Louisa marked that meeting as the beginning of the demise of her marriage. When Murugasu saw his older sister standing there in the doorway of their house, he silently fell to his knees and touched his hand to her feet in a gesture of respect. Parvathy raised him up. She ran her hand over his head and said, "Appa is no longer of this world." Then Murugasu began to weep. Louisa had run to him, had tried to hold him from behind, but he had twisted out of her grasp and fallen at his sister's feet again, burying his head in her lap.

Later, through various conversations with Parvathy, Louisa, in an attempt to understand her changed husband, had come to know of the troubled relationship between Murugasu and his father, which had culminated in his walking into the family shrine room with a wooden stick and mutilating the clay idols. It was a relationship between two people who loved each other deeply but were too similar in temperament to ever exist in peace side by side.

When the girls returned home for lunch, they found the drawing room deserted. They went to see if their mother was in the kitchen. Their servant, Letchumi, was alone in the kitchen grinding some spices, the oblong rolling stone rumbling as she pushed it back and forth over the flat slab on which the spices lay. Then she scraped the spices off the rolling stone, only to repeat the laborious process many times.

Letchumi informed them that Louisa was lying down.

"Is something wrong?" Kumudini asked.

"Barnett Amma came to visit," Letchumi said in a tone which implied that was explanation enough.

The sisters looked at each other nervously.

"I wonder what the Devil Incarnate wanted," Annalukshmi said.

The girls went to Louisa's door. Kumudini opened it quietly and put her head inside. Louisa seemed asleep. She was about to shut the door again when Louisa said, "Come in, girls. I'm awake."

Silently they filed in and stood at the foot of the bed. Kumudini took Louisa's handkerchief off her forehead and checked to make sure that she was not running a temperature.

"It's nothing. Just a headache."

She waited until Kumudini put the handkerchief back. Then she looked at Annalukshmi. "Aunt Philomena came to visit. She saw you on Green Path."

Annalukshmi's eyes widened in dismay.

"You deliberately lied to me," Louisa said, raising her voice. "You went behind my back and did what I forbade."

Annalukshmi swallowed, not knowing what to say. She saw that she had exposed her mother to the scornful gossip of her family, betrayed her to their common enemy. From the time they were very small and pestered their father to repeat over and over again the story of how their parents fell in love, the Barnetts had always been the dragons that guarded the princess. "Ah come on, Amma," she said after a moment, her voice cracking slightly. "It was just for fun."

Louisa thought she was trying to be dismissive of her reprimand. "Fun!" she cried, sitting up in bed, the handkerchief sliding off her forehead. "How dare you . . ." But then she lay back in bed, her headache coming on again. She waved her hand, dismissing her daughters. "Go and have your lunch." When they had reached the door, however, Louisa said, "Kumudini, tell the gardener to take that bicycle and lock it in the shed."

She glared challengingly at her daughter, and this time Annalukshmi did not protest.

4

Of the folly which takes the unreal for real
Comes the wretchedness of birth.
— The Tirukkural, *verse 351*

During their youth in London, the Mudaliyar Navaratnam and his younger brother had been quite the darlings of the Mayfair set. Their handsome appearance, their willingness to expound on Hinduism, Eastern thought, and, perhaps more important, their introduction of the *Kama Sutra* to many a Mayfair matron had meant that they never lacked for dinner invitations.

The Mudaliyar's brother had married an Englishwoman named Julia Boxton. Their only daughter, Sonia, was Balendran's wife. Sonia, whose parents had died of smallpox soon after her birth, had been brought up in England by her aunt, Lady Ethel Boxton. It was in London that she and Balendran had met. In high-caste Tamil society, the marrying of cousins who were the children of sisters and brothers was held in esteem. Besides keeping wealth within a family, it also served to ensure that the bride's husband and in-laws would not be strangers to her. However, the marriage of the children of two brothers or two sisters was considered almost incestuous, and such cousins even referred to each other as "brother" and "sister." Balendran and Sonia's alliance had thus raised a murmur of disapproval. Sonia being of half foreign blood and a stranger to Ceylon had, however, somewhat mitigated the objections.

❧

Balendran's house was a short drive from Lotus Cottage and Brighton. Unlike the rich neighbours his father had in Cinnamon Gardens, Balendran's neighbours were middle-class people. He and Sonia had chosen to live in this unfashionable area because they loved being close to the sea, and because of the rustic environment around them. Their road, named Seaside Place, was not even tarred and there were only three houses on it, his being the last before the railway line and the sea beyond. His property, which he had named Sevena, from the Sinhalese word for shade or shelter, was vast and included all the land between his house and the sea. Except for a small, cultivated garden, the rest of the land had been kept in its natural state, with coconut trees and cacti of various types.

At lunch, Balendran said to Sonia, "I had an interesting talk with Appa this morning."

"Ah, yes. I was wondering what all that was about."

"It seems that a friend of mine, a certain Richard Howland, might be travelling with the commission to Ceylon. As Dr. Shiels' right-hand man."

Sonia stopped eating. "Appa wants you to get Mr. Howland to influence Dr. Shiels," she said indignantly. "You're not going to, obviously."

Balendran did not reply. For the first time, the reality of what his father was asking was before him — that he set aside his own opinions on the commission and persuade Richard to see things his father's way. He had been too arrested by the thought of Richard's arrival to really comprehend this.

"Bala! Tell me you're not going to."

Balendran glanced down at his plate, disconcerted. "I . . . I don't know. Appa has asked me to –"

"For God's sake, Bala, be serious. Are you going to tell this Mr. Howland that you believe universal franchise is the worst thing for Ceylon? Especially female franchise, for women are needed for – what is it – ah, yes, 'the quiet discharge of important duties at home.'"

Balendran was taken aback by the extent of her anger.

"And what about self-government?" Sonia continued. "Will you tell him you believe none of the powers of the governor should be altered? That he should continue to be a despot? It's a betrayal of all we believe in. After all we've discussed and hoped for, how can you turn around and do this?"

Sonia began to eat again, angrily clinking her cutlery against her plate.

Balendran had to admit that his wife was right. It was indeed a betrayal of everything that not just he, but Sonia also, believed in. Still, he had already promised his father that he would speak to Richard. Balendran sighed.

Sonia heard his sigh, but she read it as impatience with her charges. She shook her head. The greatest dispute between her husband and herself was over his blind obedience to his father and her constant irritation and annoyance at it. It made little sense to Sonia, like a man of science believing in goblins. Balendran, she knew, was not an ineffectual man. After he had taken over running the family estate and temple, they had flourished in a way they had never done under his father. Intellectually, he was his father's superior and was thoroughly knowledgeable on all aspects of Tamil culture and religion. In fact, she had often told him he should put his knowledge down in a book. He always demurred, and she could not help but feel that it was in deference to that atrocious book the Mudaliyar had written, entitled *The Splendours of the Glorious Tamil Tradition*. She thought of how the Mudaliyar had been invited to America because of the book and passed himself off as a great Hindu sage; how those gullible Americans had flocked to his classes to learn meditation from a man who had not gone much further in meditation than any woman who did her daily pooja at the family shrine. Renunciation was the first step to true meditation, something her uncle knew nothing about. He had become even more indulged since he returned with that foolish Miss Adamson and her master-this and master-that.

The Mudaliyar was a son, a first son at that. Sonia knew, from various conversations she had heard, that he had been hopelessly indulged. From the time he was a child, he had been taught to feel his superiority, his right never to be thwarted. He was free to interrupt his mother's conversation with his childish pipings, sure that he would be greeted with a fond "Ah, Sinna-Rajah is speaking." When he wished, for his amusement, to horrify his elders, he would attempt a household chore. Then he would be sure to be greeted with appalled cries of "Sinna-Rajah is touching a broom!" "Sinna-Rajah is lifting a pot!" "Sinna-Rajah is cleaning his shoes!"

Such a child, once he became a man, was like a blunt knife, unsharpened on the hard stone of adversity. In the twenty years of her marriage, Sonia had once or twice been forced to battle the Mudaliyar, and she had found that her uncle, when faced with the assertion of another's will over his own, often reacted excessively out of a fear at his authority being questioned, a sense of the world falling away from him.

Balendran and Sonia had finished eating and the houseboy began to remove their plates. Sonia glanced at her husband. A letter from their son in England had arrived this morning, but she did not wish to tell Balendran the news when such conflict hung between them. It would stain his joy in receiving the letter.

"Who is Richard Howland?" she asked as a gesture of reconciliation. "Haven't heard you mention him before."

"An old school friend," Balendran said, glad of the change of subject and her conciliatory tone. "We used to share a flat in London for a short while."

Sonia nodded and waited for him to continue, but Balendran, as always, did not elaborate on his London days and she dropped the subject.

"By the way," she said as they began to eat dessert. "We got a letter from Lukshman this morning."

"A letter!" Balendran cried in delight, putting down his spoon. "How is he? No, don't tell me. I want to read for myself."

She smiled at his happiness and felt, as they did in anything to do with their son, a sudden closeness between them.

Once they had retired to the drawing room for coffee, Sonia gave him the letter and then sat down across from Balendran. He opened it and began to read. When he smiled and laughed out loud, she cried, "What? Which part are you reading?"

"The part where your Aunt Ethel descended on his digs, declared them unfit, and had him removed to her house."

Sonia laughed. "Poor Lukshman," she said.

"Poor Aunt Ethel."

When Balendran finished reading the letter, he put it down

on his lap and stared ahead of him. Sonia could tell he was filled with the same melancholy she had felt after reading it.

Balendran sighed and shook his head. "We shouldn't have let him go."

"We had to, Bala. He needed to further his education. We parents are simply the bows. Our children the arrows we shoot into the future," she said, citing the thought from the philosopher Khalil Gibran that she had often used to comfort them.

He nodded and opened his hands, palms upward, to show that he submitted to the necessity that his son, in the interest of his education, should be halfway around the world from him.

❧

Sonia volunteered a lot of her time and effort to the Girls' Friendly Society on Green Path. It had been set up for single working girls — secretaries, teachers, shop assistants — who had come to Colombo for employment. The society ran a boarding for some of them, but, more important, it provided a meeting place in the evenings and this kept many of the girls from the vices and dangers of the city. Sonia had been one of those instrumental in setting it up. She helped in the administration and taught the girls English and other skills.

Soon after lunch, Sonia left for the Girls' Friendly Society and Balendran went into his study to attend to the temple accounts. He found it in disarray. Sonia and the houseboy had taken down all the books from their shelves, so that the bookcases could be cleaned. The books were in high piles on the floor, and, as he walked around them to get to his desk, Balendran noticed a copy of Edward Carpenter's *From Adam's Peak to Elephanta:*

Sketches in Ceylon and India sitting on top of one pile. He picked it up. It had been a gift from Richard. He opened the book and read the dedication Carpenter had written to him, recalling the trip Richard and he had made to see Carpenter after reading his *Intermediate Sex*. Seldom had a book had such a profound effect on him. There, for the first time, he learnt that inversion had already been studied by scientific men who did not view it as pathological, indeed men who questioned the whole notion that regeneration was the sole object of sex.

Richard had sought out other books by Carpenter and discovered *From Adam's Peak to Elephanta*, which he bought for Balendran. He had been surprised to find that Carpenter had visited Ceylon and was good friends with the famous Arunachalam, first president of the Ceylon National Congress. Richard, meanwhile, made inquiries about Carpenter and found out that he lived at Millthorpe, in the countryside near Sheffield, with his companion. He had pressed Balendran to write to Arunachalam, who was a family friend, and ask for a letter of introduction. Balendran had refused, for fear that he might arouse suspicion about himself, even though Richard pointed out that Arunachalam must approve of Carpenter's way of life if they were such good friends. Finally, Balendran had agreed to write to Carpenter himself, as a family friend of Arunachalam, and ask if they might visit.

Balendran recalled now the long walk from Sheffield to Millthorpe. What a glorious summer day it had been, warm but not enough to make walking uncomfortable, rolling fields on either side that sloped down to the road, the light green of the grass contrasting sharply with the dark colours of the trees that bordered the fields and clustered here and there in small copses.

Then there had been Carpenter's house, nestled amongst foliage, a charming brook running at the foot of his property.

When Richard and he had met Carpenter and his companion, George Merrill, Balendran had been amazed and then intrigued by the way they lived, the comradely manner in which they existed, the way they had carved a life out for themselves, despite such strong societal censure.

Balendran shut the book. The visit had given Richard and him such faith in the future of their own love. But a month later, that hope had been destroyed by the arrival of his father and, with him, reality. Youth is terrible, Balendran thought as he put the book back on the pile. Alive, beautiful, but ultimately painful. He was glad to be free of the searing ache of it. Youth was like that proverbial konri seed – red to view but with a black tip – its vitality and radiance deceptive. The passage out of youth was an acceptance of this deceptiveness, the stripping back of life to what it really was. That was the way he thought of his time with Richard. How foolish to have imagined that the world would change over for them. Balendran knew, now that he was a father himself, that his father had done the right thing. The Mudaliyar's terrible anger at the time had been the roar of a bear protecting its cub. It had been out of love for him.

At forty, Balendran felt that, despite the difficult years of his marriage, despite the necessary compromises he had to make, his father had acted wisely and correctly. He looked around his study. It was vastly different from the Mudaliyar's, light and airy, with lace curtains that constantly moved in the sea breeze. There was a callamander antique desk and chair in the centre of the room, one wall was taken up with bookshelves, a brass bowl filled with araliya flowers sat on an ebony stand. Balendran compared his present comfort to the meagre life he might have had in London. He would have never amounted to anything but a junior partner in some barrister's firm and he would have remained so to this age. The only flat he could have afforded would have been similar to the one he had as a student with its unbearably cold hall and toilet. As for Richard, surely their love would have withered under Balendran's increasing frustration and envy as he watched his friend soar to the heights of the legal profession. There had been a shabbily dressed Indian gentleman who had lived in the same crescent as them. He had seemed ancient then, but he was probably close to Balendran's present age. He had a constantly apologetic manner about him, an excessive deference, the way he would unnecessarily step off the pavement to let others pass. This was the image Balendran held for himself when he thought of what might have happened if he had stayed in London with Richard. He had his father to thank for saving him from such a fate.

The thought of his father made Balendran recollect the promise he had made to him about Richard. He sighed. He had undertaken to do this for his father and so must follow it through. Otherwise, he would have to explain his own political views to his father and this he did not wish to do. Yet could he really present his father's opinions as his own? He tried to imagine doing that and saw the growing dismay in Richard's eyes that his friend, champion of socialism and other liberal causes in his student days, had ended up so conservative. Balendran shook his head. He could not do that. He frowned, considering his predicament. Then he had an idea. Rather than giving his father's opinion as his own, he would talk to Richard about the various views by Ceylonese on what the commission should do.

In the process, he would present his father's point of view. Balendran, satisfied that he had found the solution, began the temple accounts.

❧

The different stages of a man's life are often reflected in the guests he invites to his annual dinner. Nowhere was this more so than at the Mudaliyar Navaratnam's birthday. For amongst those invited were comrades from his Mayfair days, their conversation, after all these years, consisting of nothing more than horses, motor cars, and cricket. Miss Lawton was also a regular guest. She had known the Mudaliyar from the time she had arrived as a young assistant headmistress in Ceylon. Though it would be hard to believe now, the Mudaliyar had been a strong advocate of education for young women in those days. Then there were his colleagues from the forty-five years he had served in the Legislative Council. While some of them had remained faithful members of the Queen's House set, others had gone on to join the Ceylon National Congress and agitate for self-rule, thus setting their political path in direct contradiction to the Mudaliyar's. Still, the Cinnamon Gardens circle was tight and to have not invited them would have caused an unpleasant social reverberation for host and guests alike. At this year's dinner, there were a few new invitees. Members of the Ceylon Tamil Association, with whom the Mudaliyar had recently thrown in his lot. It promised to be a controversial evening.

Sonia and Balendran arrived early. The Mudaliyar liked to have Sonia receive the guests with him as his wife did not speak English and was usually too busy with the preparations in the kitchen.

Torches on high poles had been placed at regular intervals along the driveway, giving Brighton a festive air. When Balendran's car stopped under the porch, Pillai came down the steps to open the door. In keeping with the occasion, he was wearing his gold-buttoned white coat. The proudly displayed gold watch-chain denoted his position as head servant. Later, before he supervised the serving of dinner, he would put on his white gloves.

Pillai smiled in pride and admiration at how fine the Sinn-Aiyah and Sin-Amma looked, the former in his black dinner jacket and white bow tie, the latter in a dull-gold French-lamé sari with a chilli-red border. The colour of Sonia's sari brought out her milk-tea complexion and dark, glossy hair. Her black-lace sari blouse was of the latest fashion, with a mere frill for a sleeve. She had on gold jewellery.

"Peri-Aiyah is still dressing," Pillai said, "but the rest of the family is in the ballroom."

Balendran and Sonia went up the stairs to join them, accompanied by Pillai.

Brighton's ballroom was one of the loveliest rooms in the house. Along the back wall was a series of glass doors that opened out onto a balcony with a black-and-white checkered floor. A stuccoed pattern of grape vines ran along the top edges of the wall, and the design was picked up in a circular grouping at three points on the ceiling. From the centres of these circles, two-bladed wooden electric fans hung down. Tonight practically the entire ballroom was spanned by the dining table. It sat sixty people. A single white damask tablecloth ran the length of the table and, at regular intervals, there were flower arrangements. Menu and place cards in sterling-silver holders were in front of each place setting.

Balendran and Sonia entered to find the family gathered there, dressed in their very best.

The short, form-fitting Indian choli that exposed a good deal of midriff had not yet come into fashion. It was considered peasant attire. Sari blouses resembled their modest English counterpart. They were fairly loose and waist-length, the sleeves to the elbows or wrists. Rather than matching the hue of the sari, they came in standard colours of white, cream, grey, black, or brown. Some of them had ruffles along the neckline and on the sleeves, some were embroidered or had lacework on them. For formal occasions, a sari was always worn with a "set" — matching earrings, necklace, bracelet, and a broach to hold the sari in place on the shoulder.

Louisa, wearing a black charmeuse sari with tiny pale-pink rosebuds scattered over it and a Matara diamond set, was checking the place settings to make sure nothing had been forgotten. Philomena Barnett was fussing around her, picking up the various place cards and commenting on the genealogy of the guest and any gossip she could think of about them. For the grand occasion, she was wearing one of her flashiest saris, which featured Japanese maidens in kimonos daintily crossing butterfly bridges. She had on a set of brightly coloured Ceylon stones. Her unmarried daughter, Dolly, a jittery girl who had spent her whole life being cowed by her mother, sat on one of the chairs along the wall, nodding and blinking rapidly any time Philomena addressed a comment to her. Manohari sat by her. She was too young to be invited and, when the guests started to arrive, she would make herself scarce. Nalamma, wearing a bottle-green Benares sari with an intricate silver border and a silver set, was in conversation with one of the houseboys, giving him last-minute instructions. Kumudini, in a printed floral French chiffon, was at a side table making some final adjustments to the table plan. Her jewellery set was one very popular at the time for young women, pearls arranged in a design of grape clusters. It had been a gift from Balendran and Sonia on her twenty-first birthday.

Balendran noticed that his favourite niece, Annalukshmi, was not present. (He thought of the girls at Lotus Cottage as his nieces, even though their paternal grandfather and the Mudaliyar were only cousins.)

At that moment, there was an exclamation from Philomena. She had come upon the place card with Nancy's name on it.

"That girl has been invited too."

Philomena always referred to Nancy as "that girl," because of Nancy's low, village origins. She thoroughly disapproved of her friendship with Annalukshmi and this extending of the invitation was the limit.

"My husband and I felt it would be a slight to Miss Lawton not to include the girl," Nalamma replied. "Besides, I feel sorry for her. Twenty-five years old and hardly any chance of getting married."

"These Europeans and their big ideas," Philomena said. "Miss Lawton might have thought she was doing a charitable thing adopting her, but, at the end of the day, look where it's brought that girl. Neither fish nor fowl. She has all the upbringing of one of our girls, but no decent boy would touch her for all the gold in Christendom. Better to have left her in the village."

Manohari, who loved nothing better than to add fuel to Philomena's fire, said, "Nancy has gone and bobbed her hair."

Philomena stood still, her hand on the side of her cheek, to convey just how appalled she was.

Sonia walked over, picked up a menu card, and read it aloud, "Hors-d'oeuvres: prawn cocktail; soup: dhall consomme" – she lifted her eyebrows slightly at the pretentiousness of the appellation – "fish: grilled seer in a white sauce; entrée: chicken voul à vent; main course: roast duck; dessert: charlotte russe followed by petit fours." She looked at Philomena admiringly, "You have really outdone yourself this time, akka."

Philomena pursed her lips modestly, very pleased.

Nalamma was not proficient when it came to European cooking. The task of planning and supervising the dinner thus always fell on Philomena, who had turned up this morning with her culinary bible, *Mrs. Beeton's Cookery Book*, tucked under her arm.

At that moment, the ballroom door opened and Annalukshmi entered. Balendran called to her and she went towards him with a smile.

"You look very nice," he said, glancing at her turquoise Kanjivaram silk with its purple border and her white laceworked blouse. Her jewellery was in a pattern of delicate turquoise and gold flowers. Also a gift from her aunt and uncle on her twenty-first birthday.

She nodded her thanks.

Nalamma had by now crossed the room to her son.

She took his arm. "My dream was prophetic," she said in a low tone. "Your brother is in trouble."

Balendran stared at her in surprise and dismay.

"We heard through the bank manager, Mr. Govind, who gives him that monthly allowance your Appa sends. He was climbing the stairs at work, became breathless, and fainted."

"But is he all right now?"

She nodded.

Balendran sighed with relief. "It's probably nothing, Amma. Just tiredness."

"Nothing? How can you say nothing? He should go and get an examination. But I know how your brother is. So stubborn. As a mother, I feel helpless. If he were here, I would have forced him to see a doctor."

Balendran could tell that she was suggesting again that he renew contact, but he chose to ignore the hint.

Nalamma sighed, "And his son, Seelan." She waved her hand to encompass the ballroom, "I can't help thinking of what he has been denied."

The Mudaliyar, resplendent in a black dinner jacket and white bow tie, entered at this moment, putting an end to Nalamma and Balendran's conversation. They went forward to greet him.

Annalukshmi, even though she knew it was rude, had listened keenly to their conversation. The girls at Lotus Cottage were of course familiar with the story of their uncle's expulsion from Brighton and his marriage to a woman who had worked in Brighton's kitchen.

Annalukshmi had quickly become intrigued by the romance of the story. An avid reader at that time of Gothic and romance novels, she had seen that her uncle's story was a strange instance of real life imitating the world of fiction. Later, as a girl of fifteen, her romantic feelings about the story had come to fix themselves on her cousin, Seelan. The fact that he was a mysterious, doomed young man, in exile from his family heritage, raised him to the level of a hero of Gothic fiction or medieval romance. Annalukshmi smiled now to think that she had actually read those books and had thought of her cousin in that way. Like most revealed secrets, the novelty of it had worn off over the years.

The first cars could be heard coming up the driveway, and everyone began to leave the ballroom. Annalukshmi, as she came down the stairs, saw that among the first guests were Nancy and Miss Lawton. With a smile of pleasure, she went to greet them. Before she could reach them, however, Miss Lawton was cornered by one of the other guests, an old pupil who was now married to a member of the Legislative Council. The woman, a well-known doyenne of Cinnamon Gardens society, shyly introduced herself to Miss Lawton. When the headmistress immediately remembered her, she blushed with pleasure.

Nancy and Annalukshmi exchanged looks and smiled. This would likely be the pattern for the rest of Miss Lawton's evening.

The Wijewardena family were regular guests at the Mudaliyar's birthday dinner. The son, F. C. Wijewardena, was Balendran's best friend. Their friendship went all the way back to when they had studied at the Colombo Academy. They had left together for England, as well.

It was a ritual at the Mudaliyar's annual dinner for F. C., his wife, Sriyani, Balendran, and Sonia to gather for a chat on the side verandah, outside the drawing room where the party was in progress. Since most of the guests were of the Mudaliyar's generation, they had very little in common with them.

F. C. was a prominent member of the Ceylon National Congress, and they had no sooner sat down in the verandah chairs when he brought up the subject of the Donoughmore Commission and the new constitution.

"Well, the gold rush will be on in two weeks."

"Gold rush?" Sonia asked.

"Yes," F. C. replied. "All this hullabaloo reminds me of a gold rush. Everyone running to stake their claim, to carve out their piece of the land."

He brought out a tortoiseshell cigarette case from the pocket of his coat. "Divisions are appearing where I didn't even know there were any." He lit himself a cigarette. "Up-country Sinhalese versus low-country Sinhalese, Karava caste versus Goyigama caste, Moors, Malays, Christian Tamils, Hindu Tamils, Buddhists, and so on and so on. And not a bloody bugger is thinking nationally, except us in the Congress."

"Perhaps the Congress needs to redefine what 'national' is," Balendran said.

Sriyani and Sonia exchanged glances. These discussions between their husbands were always lively.

"What do you mean?" Sriyani asked Balendran.

"I'm not the first one to refer to it. Two of your former Congress presidents, C. E. Corea and Arunachalam, talked about it. Before foreign rule, we had a constitution and a system of government that was suited to our needs."

F. C. groaned. "Not that damn village and district council theory again."

"Why not?" Balendran said. "Village councils that send elected members to a district council, which in turn sends members to a council of the ministers of state. That way all the various groups get to feel that they have a hand in governing this country. In other words, more or less a federal state. One of your own men, S. W. R. D. Bandaranaike himself, suggested it, but now that he is Congress secretary he has conveniently forgotten."

"It would be an administrative nightmare," F. C. said. "No, no. The only system is the parliamentary one, modelled on Whitehall. These bloody people have to learn to look past their feudal loyalties and to think of themselves as Ceylonese first."

"Two hundred years of foreign rule hasn't changed those loyalties."

F. C. drew on his cigarette and exhaled. "So, you are becoming a Ceylon Tamil Association man," he said teasingly, with a nod in the direction of the drawing room, where he had noticed the presence of the new guests. "Slowly, slowly moving in that direction. Between you lot and the damn Kandyans wanting their separate state, you will split this country into a thousand pieces."

"It already is in a thousand pieces," Balendran said. "You Congress chaps just refuse to see it. Like an Arabian mosaic. Take one tile out and you might ruin the entire design."

"We forgot to tell you a piece of delightful news," Sonia began. When she saw the expression on Balendran's face, she stopped.

"What news?" Sriyani asked.

They looked at her expectantly.

"It seems," Sonia said reluctantly, "that a good friend of Bala might be coming with the commission."

F. C. and Sriyani turned to stare at him.

"Who is this?" F. C. asked. "Someone I know?"

"Oh, I'm not sure if you remember him," Balendran said. "One Richard Howland."

"What are you talking about, Bala?" F. C. said. "Of course I know him. You shared a flat together."

Before anyone could comment further, they heard the sound of raised voices from the drawing room. Balendran stood up quickly.

A hush had fallen over the party. Two men were arguing. One of them was a member of the Ceylon National Congress, the other of the Ceylon Tamil Association.

"Why should we support your Congress on self-rule when you are going to ask the commission to abolish communal representation?" the man from the Ceylon Tamil Association cried.

"Communal representation simply forces people to think in terms of their race and not as a nation," the Congress man replied. "We are proud to take a stance for territorial representation."

"And that is why we will never support your claim for self-government."

"You may be content to live in a servile fashion under the British, howling and bowing like coolies, but some of us are more manly than that."

"Give us a British Raj any day to a Sinhala Raj."

He had gone too far. As long as the discussion had been about the Congress versus the Tamil Association, the obvious undertones of Sinhalese against Tamil had not surfaced. It was necessary for someone to step in, and the Mudaliyar did so with great suavity.

"Gentlemen, whatever our differences, we are agreed on one thing. Universal franchise would be the ruin of our nation."

A collective murmur went through the party and someone said, "Hear, hear."

"People like Dr. Shiels do not understand what it would mean to an Oriental society like ours. It would put the vote in the hands of the servants in our kitchen, labourers, the beggar on the street. Illiterate beings to whom the sophistication of politics is as incomprehensible as advanced mathematics to a child. It would lead to mob rule."

"It would lead to A. E. Goonesinha and his Labour Union thugs running this country," a guest said.

This was greeted with another murmur of agreement.

Goonesinha was the *bête noire* of the Cinnamon Gardens élite and the British administration. A few years ago, he had led a general strike that had crippled the country. His was one of the few groups asking for universal franchise.

"In the good old days, people like him would have had to go around to the back entrance," a guest said, alluding to Goonesinha's low caste. "Now we have to shake their hands and treat them like equals."

At that moment, dinner was announced. The guests began to pair off and leave the drawing room, mounting the stairs to the ballroom. Balendran offered Sriyani his arm, and F. C. did the same to Sonia.

"I don't know what gets into people sometimes," Sriyani said to Balendran as they went in. "After all, we are one country, one people. Why can't we just exist amicably."

Balendran did not reply. He felt that Sriyani's sentiment dismissed the obvious fears and concerns of the Tamils.

When limited franchise was granted in 1921, six years ago, the Tamils, who until that time had been treated by the British as a majority community, alongside the Sinhalese, found themselves a minority because of the numerical superiority of the latter. The behaviour of the Sinhalese members of the Ceylon National Congress had done nothing to assuage the fears of people like his father about a Sinhala Raj. When the Tamils, after the 1921 elections, had requested a special reserved seat in the Western Province, the Sinhalese had refused. Balendran felt that the Sinhalese politicians had been obtuse in the matter. By granting this minor request, they could have easily won over the Tamils to the Congress. Now he felt that it was too late for sentiments that suggested they should all simply exist amicably.

Sriyani tugged at his arm, distracting him from his thoughts.

"I want to talk to you about your wife," she said softly. She waited until Sonia was far enough ahead of them, then she turned to Balendran. "You men never notice things, but I am worried about her. What on earth does she do all day now that Lukshman is gone?"

Balendran was confounded by the question. "I . . . I don't know," he said. "She has the Girls' Friendly Society."

Sriyani waved her hand in dismissal to say that such work was hardly enough to occupy a person's time.

"And then there are her tasks around the house. You know she relishes gardening."

"But it's unhealthy, Bala. A woman, of course, must attend to her household duties, but to spend so much time at it? What on earth are servants for? The other day I visited and found her up a ladder breaking cobwebs and the houseboy standing there looking very put out that he had been denied his work." She shook her head. "You should be encouraging her to go out more. I try and try to get her to attend at-homes with me, but it's like enforced labour. If you're not careful, she'll become a real hermit."

"I'll have a serious talk with her," Balendran said playfully. "I shall order her to attend a minimum of two at-homes a week from now on."

Sriyani sighed. "I see you are no help. Well, I have just the plan for your wife. Something that will get her out of that house and into society a little more."

They had reached the stairs now and they began to go up to the ballroom.

Balendran glanced ahead of him at Sonia. He was, of course, aware of Sonia's deep attachment to their home and to domesticity. He had only understood it many years into their marriage when the Mudaliyar had tried to send Lukshman off to boarding school in England. It was one of the few times his wife had openly clashed with his father. She had firmly refused to acquiesce, even in the face of the Mudaliyar's wrath. Sonia, so she told Balendran then, had always felt the lack of a real home, real parents, despite Lady Boxton's kindness. Further, she had spent her youth in boarding schools, only returning to her aunt's for holidays. This was simply the way things were done in that set, but Sonia had been miserable. That was why she had determined her son would not suffer in the same way. Balendran, at the time he had found this out, had felt a new, protective tenderness towards his wife. Before, she had always struck him as extremely self-sufficient, but, after that conversation, he had come to understand how very much her home, her husband and child meant to her. They were her world.

As for refusing to attend at-homes, Balendran knew that his wife, who had been sent to finishing school, who had been trained to be the perfect society lady, abhorred and rebelled against that schooling.

The meal, efficiently served by a host of houseboys under Pillai's supervision, was impeccable. After dinner, as was customary, the men remained in the ballroom to have port. The women began to retire to the drawing room, where the men would presently join them for coffee.

Sonia was descending the stairs with Annalukshmi when Sriyani caught up with them. "I've been meaning to talk to you, but you know how it is with men. A woman can't get a word in edgewise."

Sriyani took Sonia's arm. "Some women from the Congress are getting together to form a Women's Franchise Union. To press the Donoughmore Commission for female franchise. What do you think about women fighting for the vote? Are you interested in joining?"

"It's not just Congress women," Sriyani added hastily, in case that would put Sonia off. "Lady Daisy Bandaranaike has agreed to be the president." She listed the other women involved, most of whom were well-known society ladies. "Please say you will join."

Sonia frowned contemplatively. "And will they ask for limited or universal female franchise?"

"It's thought best to ask for limited," Sriyani said, somewhat apologetically.

"But the poorer women need it most," Sonia said, thinking of her students at the Girls' Friendly Society and their difficulties.

"I know, I know," Sriyani said placatingly. "However, we do think it might be wiser in the first instance to limit the franchise to the better-educated and better-qualified women. Later we can broaden it out to include others."

Sonia sighed. "Let me think about it," she said. "If one joins an association, one must comply with its rules and I am not sure I will be able to do that."

As Sonia spoke, however, she happened to glance at Annalukshmi and saw that she had been following the conversation with much eagerness. "Are you interested, Annalukshmi?" she asked.

"Oh yes, Sonia Maamee."

"Then you'd like to attend?"

Annalukshmi nodded enthusiastically.

Sonia smiled and lifted her eyebrows. "Well," she said to Sriyani, "looks like we might come after all."

She offered her arm to her niece. Annalukshmi took it and squeezed her hand to express her thanks. They had reached the bottom of the stairs and walked on into the drawing room.

A lively discussion was in progress, with Miss Lawton at the centre of it.

A former pupil of hers, Lady Dias-Rajapakse, a wealthy heiress, had decided to build a school for girls in the district of Ratnapura, where her ancestral home was located. She wanted to name the school after Miss Lawton.

"Absolutely not, my dear," Miss Lawton was saying when Annalukshmi came in. "I do my work for the Lord. If you wish to please me, you must name it the Ratnapura Mission School."

"But, Miss Lawton, you have done so much for female education in Ceylon," Lady Dias-Rajapakse said. "You deserve to be honoured in this way."

A number of the assembled women nodded in agreement. Since the Colpetty Mission School was one of the best girls' schools in the country, many Cinnamon Gardens women had attended it.

"I would never have gone on to be a doctor if you hadn't come personally and cajoled my father into letting me go to medical college in England," one of the women said.

"Never mind being a doctor," another added. "My grandmother was trying to pull me out of school when I was fifteen and marry me to some cousin of mine. If Miss Lawton had not spoken to my father, I would be an ignorant, unhappy woman now."

"Look at the difference between us and our mothers," Lady Dias-Rajapakse said. "Because we have education, we have been able to be helpmates to our husbands rather than millstones around their neck. And our children have benefited too. All because of the tireless effort of people like you."

"I don't see why you won't let her do this," another former pupil added. "Other headmistresses have had streets and schools named after them in Ceylon."

"Exactly," Lady Dias-Rajapakse said.

Miss Lawton began to demur again, but her protests were drowned out by the voices of the other women telling her that she should allow such an honour to be bestowed on her.

Annalukshmi, who was standing against the wall near the door, felt an intense glow of pride that so many of these well-known women esteemed Miss Lawton in this way. She thought of a dream of hers, the possibility that, one day, she, as head-mistress, would find herself surrounded by grateful pupils who had gone on to lead fulfilled lives as a result of her efforts.

Balendran felt it important to impress on Sonia the need to keep his acquaintance with Richard secret. The reason he gave himself was that it would damage his father's reputation if people thought he was using his personal contacts to affect the decisions of the commission.

When they got home, he said to her, "You were a little indiscreet this evening, Sonia."

She felt annoyed by his righteous tone. "Why shouldn't I mention that a friend of yours is part of the commission?"

"You obviously don't understand. It was a private conversation. Between myself and my father. Appa will not like F. C. knowing about my connection with Richard. He is, after all, a Congress man."

"Don't be silly, Bala," Sonia said. "You sound as if you are involved in some important espionage."

Her dismissive tone irritated him. "You have to be careful what you say around these politicians."

"But he's your friend," Sonia said.

"Nevertheless."

"Don't you feel any shame pressing your father's views on your friend?"

Balendran turned away and began to walk towards the study door.

"Ah, I see. You do feel some qualms. That's interesting."

Balendran slammed the door.

Sonia clenched her fists, feeling the frustration she always felt when they argued, the way Balendran would shut off her needs, her emotions, her convictions. She turned and walked away.

In her bedroom, Sonia sat down in front of the mirror and took off her jewellery. Then she removed her sari and underclothes and put on her nightdress. She had just finished when she heard her husband's study door open and the sound of his footsteps going towards the front door. He was off on one of those late-night walks he took when he had eaten too much or was too agitated to sleep. The thought of his leaving her alone in the house filled Sonia with a sudden, irrational dread. Before she quite knew what she was doing, she was at the bedroom door.

"Bala," she called out.

She was too late. He had already left and she could hear his footsteps going down the front drive.

Sonia felt foolish now at her impulse, her childish fear at being left alone when there were so many servants in the house. She turned and went back into her bedroom.

As she sat down at her toilette table to wipe off her make-up, the mirror reflected her bedroom. It looked cavernous and forbidding. Her grand four-poster bed, made of ebony, was covered on all sides with mosquito netting. Elevated high above the floor, it suddenly reminded her of a funeral bier. She shivered. The side panel of her toilette-table mirror was positioned in such a way that she could see through the connecting door into her son's room. After he had left, she had kept the door open. Sonia closed her eyes tightly and tried to conjure up his image in the other room, to will him to be there if only in her mind. It did not help. She opened her eyes and stared at the reflection of his empty room. Then a swift sadness rose in her and, before she knew it, she had put her head down on her arms and was sobbing. "I miss him," she murmured to herself. "Oh God, how I miss him." After a moment, she looked around agitatedly for her handkerchief and blew her nose. She got up hastily and went towards her son's bedroom, taking his letter with her.

Lukshman's room was small and Sonia felt secure in its tightness. She sat down on the bed, reassuringly narrow and hard, unlike her own, whose softness made her feel, of late, as if she were drowning in it. She looked around the room at the cheery prints of childhood scenes, children fishing, picnicking, an Impressionist reproduction of a woman walking in a field of poppies hand in hand with her child. Unlike her room, where the electric light did not reach the shadowy corners, this room was completely illuminated.

Sonia made herself comfortable in the bed and began to reread the letter. As she did so, she imagined Lukshman in her Aunt Ethel's house, occupying the bedroom that had been hers as a girl. The thought of that room, with its chintz curtains and view of the park, made Sonia homesick. It was odd that she had never missed England until now, never thought of it with nostalgia. These days, she thought about her life there all the time and with those memories always came the thing that had brought her here to Ceylon. Her love for Balendran.

She had heard about her cousin Balendran in letters her Aunt Ethel wrote to her while she was at finishing school in France. Even after she came back, she did not meet him for a while, as he had come down with pneumonia after his father's arrival in London. Their first meeting had been at her aunt's autumn ball. A young man who was interested in her had accompanied her outside to the garden. They had just come in again and she was removing her cape when she had seen Balendran at the front door with his father. The Mudaliyar had signalled to her to come over and meet his son. Balendran, who was handing his coat to the footman, had turned to her and she had almost stepped back at the sight of his face. She had expected him to look sickly, but the haggard look in his eyes made her feel that she was looking at a dying man, not one who was in recovery. He had shaken her hand, his lips pressed together diffidently, and she had seen, despite the illness, that he was handsome. Sonia always traced the moment she fell in love with him to that first meeting, the feel of his hand in hers, the beautiful vulnerability of his face with its long eyelashes, fine nose, clearly defined cheekbones.

What a difference there was between her expectations and what her marriage had really turned out to be. She belonged, she knew, to that group of women from Europe who had married non-European men as an escape from the strictures of their world, a refusal to conform. What they did not know, could not have known, was that these men, so outcast in Europe and America, were, in their own land, the very thing women like her were trying to escape. This was what she had not been prepared for. Balendran's unquestioning obedience to familial and social dictates, his formality even in their lovemaking, his insistence that they maintain separate bedrooms.

Still, there was love. Despite the roughness of the early years of their marriage, despite his aloofness, she had always known that she loved him.

The thought of her love for Balendran made Sonia shake herself mentally. "I'm being ridiculous and morbid." She got up and went to stand at the window, which looked out to her garden. In the moonlight, she could see the plants and trees, all so well known, all bearing testimonial to years of care and the pleasure she had derived from tending them.

After a while, she went back to Lukshman's bed and lay down. Thinking of her love for her husband and her son, she drifted off to sleep.

❧

Balendran's house was the last one on the road and then it was only vegetation that opened out to the railway line and the sea beyond it. He could make out the silhouettes of coconut trees against the night sky, swaying in the wind like ghostly apparitions.

When he reached the end of his street, he began to walk along the railway line, away from his property. It was rare that a train came by at this hour. Still, he always made sure to pick the line along which the trains came towards him. In a couple of minutes his eyes adjusted to the dark and he looked out at the sea. It shimmered in the moonlight like black silk. Against the horizon, he could see the lights of a ship and far ahead of him the illumination of the Fort area. He walked about a mile, not meeting anyone. The railway tracks, popular with strollers in the evening, were now deserted. Balendran finally rounded a bend and saw ahead of him the Bambalapitiya railway station. Though long closed for the night, the platform was busy with men, cigarettes butts glowing red in the dark. Balendran faltered, as he always did, the blood rushing to his head. He knew what it took to keep walking, had taught himself how to go on. He closed his eyes and willed himself to take the next few steps. Then he opened his eyes and continued, pulling his hat low over his forehead.

There was a roof over the portion of the tracks in front of the platform. It was supported by a wall on the other side. Balendran avoided the railway platform. Instead, he walked quickly along the deserted outer edge of the wall, his head lowered. He saw ahead of him the one he always went with, Ranjan, a private in the army. The young man was leaning up against the wall. He noticed Balendran approaching and stubbed out his cigarette.

"Good evening," he said in English as Balendran came up to him.

"How are you, Ranjan?" Balendran replied softly in English, for he knew that Ranjan liked to practise his English with him. "How is your mother? Did she finally see a doctor about her problem?"

"Thanking you very much, sir," Ranjan replied.

The last time Balendran was here, he had learnt about Ranjan's mother's illness and given him money to take her to a doctor.

They began to walk away from the others, and Balendran asked him a few more questions about his mother's health. Balendran was fond of Ranjan in a disinterested way. Mostly, he felt gratitude because Ranjan was extremely discreet. The one time he had seen him in public, he had taken the initiative and ignored him. Further, he never haggled over money, took whatever was given to him. Occasionally he would mention something, like his mother's illness. When Balendran gave, he did so generously to ensure Ranjan's tact.

They were a sufficient distance from the wall now and they scrambled down the rocks to the beach, Ranjan taking Balendran's hand and helping him. Amongst the rocks, they found a fairly private place, a smooth flat stone for them to sit on. A silence fell between them. After a while, Ranjan put his hand on Balendran's crotch and began to gently massage it. He undid the buttons on Balendran's trousers, and Balendran lifted himself slightly, so Ranjan could slide his trousers down his thighs. Ranjan bent over him and, at the feel of Ranjan's breath on his arousal, Balendran sighed and lay back on the rock. He closed his eyes for a moment, then opened them and looked up at the night sky.

Balendran liked to take his time with Ranjan, to prolong his bliss as long as possible. For, once it was over, he knew he would be visited by a terrible anguish. Then, walking quickly away from the station, he would curse himself for his imprudence, for putting everything at risk, his marriage, his family name. The precautions he had taken would seem absurd: the fact that he had avoided the station altogether; the fact that, were Ranjan not there, he would have turned around and gone back home. Balendran would look back to see if he was being followed, step off the tracks, and stand in the bushes to ascertain this was not so. He would not be comforted by the fact that Ranjan did not know his name, that Ranjan was discreet. He would find himself attributing to Ranjan the worst characteristics, make him out to be a devious blackmailer who was waiting to seize the right chance. Then Balendran would vow never to visit the station again.

5

Weigh well before you plunge
The inputs, impediments and gain.
— The Tirukkural, *verse 676*

Philomena Barnett acted quickly in the matter of finding Annalukshmi a suitable groom.

A week after the Mudaliyar's birthday, Louisa was gardening one morning when she saw Philomena come in through the gate of Lotus Cottage. She removed her straw hat and anxiously went to meet her cousin. Philomena signalled to her that she was in no fit state to talk until she was seated comfortably on the verandah. Louisa sent Letchumi to bring a glass of thambili, which always worked wonders on Cousin Philomena's humour.

Philomena gulped down the thambili, wiped her mouth with her handkerchief, and said, "Cousin," in a tone that portended no good.

Louisa moved to the edge of her chair.

"I am afraid it is not good news. The Lights and the Worthingtons have both declined."

"But why?" Louisa cried in dismay. "If it's a matter of dowry, there is the rubber estate in Malaya."

Philomena raised her hand mournfully to say it was not. She looked down at her lap before she spoke. "The unfortunate thing is, cousin, Annalukshmi has gone and got herself a reputation."

Louisa's eyes widened. There was no worse predicament for a girl in Ceylon than to have a "reputation."

"They say she is fast."

"Our Annalukshmi *fast*? She has nothing to do with boys."

"I know that. But the Lights have a relative who teaches at the mission school and the report was not good."

"What has she done to deserve a reputation?" Louisa queried, completely bewildered by the whole thing.

"It's not what she has done. It's what she might do after marriage, once —" Philomena coughed. "Once she has been . . . you understand me, cousin. A woman who has a wild temperament may be chaste before marriage but once exposed might seek other fields . . . numerous other fields."

Louisa had heard this argument before but had never thought it would be applied to her daughter.

"There is also the matter of education, the one I warned you about so much." Philomena could not keep the vindicated tone from her voice. "The Worthington boy, for example, barely passed his Senior Cambridge. The only reason he got into the Postal Service is because his uncle is chief clerk. So, of course, they don't want a girl better qualified. After all, Annalukshmi passed with honours and now she has a *teacher's certificate*." Philomena stressed the last two words to remind Louisa that she had been cautioned about this. "Flora Worthington says she wants a girl who will build up her son, not try and cut him down."

Louisa's spirits sank. These premier families should have welcomed Annalukshmi with open arms.

"Don't be disheartened, cousin," Philomena said, satisfied that Louisa was suitably chastened. "All is not lost. The Macintoshes have agreed to look at Annalukshmi."

The Macintoshes were the last ones Louisa had expected to be interested, given their wealth and prestige. She narrowed her eyes. "Why? Is there something wrong with the boy?"

"Cousin?"

"He's not epileptic or simple, is he?"

"Of course not."

Louisa was not satisfied. She was sure that the Macintoshes had said yes, despite Annalukshmi's "reputation." There had to be something wrong with the boy.

"This is a golden opportunity. Let me arrange a preliminary meeting."

After a moment Louisa nodded reluctantly. She had to at least see the boy. Something was better than nothing. Yet she felt frightened that people did talk of Annalukshmi in this way. She had thought that they might say she was headstrong, even a little rash, but she had never expected that Annalukshmi's behaviour had garnered her a "reputation."

The window-seat in the drawing room was Annalukshmi's favourite place to read. She would switch on the lamp by the window, draw the lace curtains to cut off the world, prop a pillow behind her back, and, with her knees drawn up to her chest, the book on her thighs, she would lose herself in the world of her characters.

That afternoon Annalukshmi was seated in the window-seat when Louisa, who was also in the drawing room sewing with Kumudini, got up and approached her. She advanced on her with some trepidation, knowing her daughter's dislike for these matchmaking attempts.

Annalukshmi was completely lost in her book and did not notice her mother until a shadow fell across her page. She looked up to see Louisa on the other side of the lace curtain, an expression on her face that made her immediately draw her knees even closer to her chest.

"Merlay," Louisa pushed aside the curtain. "I had some news this morning. Some very good news." She sat down on the window-seat.

Annalukshmi simply looked at her, holding the open book to her chest as a shield.

"It's a possible meeting with a young man, kunju," Louisa said. "For you. Arranged by Aunt Philomena."

Annalukshmi had an instant image of the boys Philomena had found for her own daughters. Young men without looks or any real brand to them but who would remain in their dull civil-service jobs and retire with a pension. "Pleasant boys" as everyone charitably described them.

"No," Annalukshmi said. "I will not do it. You know how I feel about proposals."

Kumudini, who had been following the conversation with great interest, now came and joined them. "Who is the boy, Amma?" she asked.

"A Mr. Macintosh. You know, *the* Macintoshes on Ward Place."

Kumudini drew in her breath, impressed. "Akka," she said, "this is not one of Aunt Philomena's usual types, not some thuppai government clerk. Don't you remember Grace Macintosh? She was in my class. In fact, she was in your house when you were house captain."

"She was a good sprinter?" Annalukshmi asked, not sure if they were talking about the same girl.

Kumudini nodded. "She was lovely. Fair and pretty. And so vivacious too. A beauty spot in one eye. Like a tea leaf."

The little detail was what Annalukshmi needed and she promptly remembered Grace Macintosh. "Yes, her," she said, interested now, despite herself. She had liked Grace and her witty manner.

"The brother probably looks like Grace," Kumudini said. "My, he must be very handsome. And they're rich, akka. A big house on Ward Place and everything."

Annalukshmi recalled that a Rolls-Royce was sent to pick Grace up from school, liveried chauffeur and all. Yet, unlike a lot of rich girls, Grace was unaffected. She had also been an avid reader like herself.

"What do you think, merlay? Shall I ask Aunt Philomena to arrange a meeting?"

Annalukshmi imagined the eyes of the parents and whatever relatives they brought with them surveying her person. She always hated these meetings; thought of them as cattle markets in which a girl was on display like a prize cow.

"No," she said. "I won't put myself through something like that. It's a completely barbaric way to meet someone."

"But, akka," Kumudini said, "how else do you plan to meet young men?

She let the question hang in the air for a moment. "It's not as if we are lucky enough to have brothers and might be introduced to a friend of theirs and then slowly-slowly fall in love. If we don't agree to these proposals, we can look forward to a life of spinsterhood for sure."

In Annalukshmi's mind, she had always imagined meeting her husband in precisely the way Kumudini had described. When she sat in the window-seat daydreaming, she imagined a young man coming up the steps of their verandah, hat in hand. She would be reading and someone (an always unspecified someone) would make the introduction. His hand would be dry and warm in hers, the hairs delicate on his wrist. He would ask her what she was reading and then they would discuss the book. Love would proceed from there.

Her sister was waiting for a response, and Annalukshmi said lamely, "There are other ways."

"Such as?"

Annalukshmi was silent.

"This is not *Pride and Prejudice*, akka," Kumudini said, making crushing use of her knowledge of literature. "Your Mr. Darcy isn't going to ride up on a horse."

"Why don't you just give it a try, merlay," Louisa said. "It's only a meeting, after all. If you don't like him, I promise that will be that."

"The meeting will be pleasant, akka," Kumudini said. "I am sure Grace will come along, so we can talk about our school days and not have to sit there like deaf and dumb types."

Annalukshmi was silent considering all this. Her mother had promised not to pursue the matter if she was not interested. The presence of Grace would ease the awkwardness of the situation. Indeed their talk about school would show her in a favourable light as both house captain and later head prefect. Then there was the boy himself. He might, after all, be handsome and charming like Grace. She turned to her sister and mother. "Well, I suppose there is no harm in seeing what he's like," she said grudgingly.

The moment her mother and sister had left her alone, however, Annalukshmi sat, thinking. From the time she had been a small child, she had always wanted to be a teacher. When she got older and discovered the world of books, she was single-minded in her desire to inspire a similar love in others for learning; to one day, perhaps, be headmistress in a school of her own. Though she had been made aware by her family all along that a decision to marry would end her teaching, that, unlike certain other professions, women teachers, by regulation, could not continue in their careers once they were married, she had not allowed this to stop her. She had never really contemplated that she would ever have to make this choice.

❧

The headmistress's bungalow was on Mission Road, the lane that ran by the school. Thick foliage and a hedge screened it from the road. A wicket gate opened onto a narrow front path that led up to the house. Most Ceylonese wives would have been appalled by the garden. It lacked the symmetry, the ordered flowerbeds so dearly loved by them. The lawn was well cut, but, other than that, no attempt had been made to tame or order the vegetation. The bungalow, despite all the years Miss Lawton had lived there, still had a feeling of temporariness to it, like a place used by a succession of travelling officials. The sturdy, extremely plain furniture and the lack of bric-à-brac was what created this effect.

Annalukshmi often spent part of her weekend with Miss Lawton and Nancy. That evening, it being a Friday, she went to their house for dinner. Annalukshmi was to spend the night there, as early the next day they were planning to go to Kinross Beach for a swim and a picnic breakfast.

The next day, when Annalukshmi awoke, the sky was a dark grey, the sun not having risen yet. As she lay there under the mosquito net, her thoughts returned to that conversation with her mother and sister last afternoon about Grace Macintosh's brother. From the verandah she could hear the clatter of cups and the low murmur of Miss Lawton's and her servant, Rosa's, voices.

When Annalukshmi came outside, Miss Lawton glanced at her, surprised, and said, "You're up early, Anna."

Annalukshmi nodded and sat down next to her.

"You look worried. Is anything wrong?"

"I was just lying in bed, thinking."

Miss Lawton poured Annalukshmi a cup of coffee and passed it to her.

"What my life would become if I got married."

Miss Lawton looked at her keenly. "And what has prompted these thoughts?"

"Oh, just wondering about it." She smiled. "Early-morning thoughts."

Miss Lawton gestured to her to go on.

"I want more than anything else in the world to continue to teach. I've always wanted this . . . to be like you."

"I'm flattered, Anna, but you must realize my life has its limitations too."

Annalukshmi stirred her coffee. "And what about love? Where does that fit in to all of this?"

"Aaah," Miss Lawton said. "That is a tough one, isn't it?"

"But other people . . . you . . . made a choice."

Miss Lawton stood up. "Yes, I made a choice. But choices are never easy."

At that moment, the morning newspaper was thrown over the gate and fell onto the front path with a thud. Miss Lawton, rather than waiting for Rosa to get it, went down the verandah steps herself. She picked up the paper and came back, tapping it against the palm of her hand. "You know, Anna," she said when she reached the verandah steps, "I never tell anyone what to do with their life. I can only explain how it was for me. Then one must decide what one wants to do." She came up the steps and sat down in her chair again. "I am where I am by choice. And do I regret my decision?" She smiled. "Sometimes. When administrative problems are too bothersome or on the first day of holidays when the school is deserted and forlorn, or at the end of the year when my Senior Cambridge girls, whom I have known as if they were my own, leave, never to return." She shrugged. "But what life is without its regrets?"

Kinross Beach was a favourite bathing spot because the proximity of the reef to the shore created a peaceful bay where a swimmer was safe from the currents of the open sea. By the time Miss Lawton, Nancy, and Annalukshmi got there, it was busy, as the morning was a popular time for a swim, before the sun got too hot. The sea was a greyish blue, the cream-coloured sand cool beneath their feet. They found a spot underneath a coconut tree and laid out their mat and picnic basket. Nancy had a proper one-piece bathing suit with a sailor collar, but Annalukshmi, whose mother would never consent to a bathing suit, wore an old sari blouse and a long underskirt. As they hurried down the beach, she was aware that they were the only women about to swim in the sea. The others sat in the shade of the coconut trees, their umbrellas open over them, watching their husbands and sons and brothers frolic in the water and on the beach.

As Annalukshmi went into the sea, she felt the coolness of the water soak through her blouse and slip, touching her skin underneath like gentle hands. She glanced back up the beach at the other women and it came to her that if she did marry she would end up like them, forced to sit in the shade, only a spectator. Nancy was floating on her back and she called to Annalukshmi to come and join her. With an overwhelming gladness that she was not one of those women, Annalukshmi fell back into the water and gave herself up to the flow of the sea, feeling the waves carry her along towards the shore.

Once she felt the scrape of sand underneath her, she sat down on the beach, the waves washing around her. Nancy had joined Miss Lawton. Annalukshmi surveyed the beach, and her gaze came to rest on a young man who was playing an impromptu game of cricket with his friends. He was wearing a style of bathing suit that had just become fashionable in Ceylon, a black singlet joined up to a pair of close-fitting shorts, all in one piece. The young man was the wicket keeper and was squatting, waiting for the ball to come towards him. The batsman missed the next ball and it landed in the water near Annalukshmi. The young man sprinted towards her, recovered the ball, grinned, said, "Sorry if I disturbed you," then ran back. In that instant, Annalukshmi saw all she needed to. His handsome face and nice teeth when he smiled, the straps of his suit slightly awry over his smooth chest, the shape of his crotch clearly outlined in the bathing suit. She felt the heat release itself from somewhere in her lower back and spread down her legs. She surreptitiously watched the young man. Before he could field another ball, however, a woman called out to him. He ran up the beach, flung himself on the sand next to her, took her hand, kissed it, and then listened attentively to what she was saying, nodding his head. As Annalukshmi looked at the couple, she knew that this was what she would have to give up if she did not marry. Miss Lawton and Nancy were calling to her and she saw that the picnic breakfast was already laid out. She stood up and began to walk towards them, her slip heavy and cumbersome against her legs, her hair bedraggled and messy down her back.

"Oh look, Anna," Miss Lawton called out gaily, "Rosa has made your favourite. Pol roti."

The sight of her beloved headmistress reminded Annalukshmi of their conversation early that morning, the fact that no life was without its regrets, that one had to make a choice. She smiled as she sat down next to Nancy and Miss Lawton. She picked up a pol roti and began to munch on it contentedly. Choices had to be made and she was fairly certain now which one was hers.

Once they had finished their picnic breakfast, Annalukshmi and Nancy went for a walk along the beach to search for unusual seashells. They walked some distance in companionable silence, then Annalukshmi turned to her friend and said, "I have some news. My Aunt Philomena is trying to set me up with a boy."

"I'm all ears," Nancy said with amusement, aware of just how much her friend abhorred these arrangements.

"His surname is Macintosh."

"Grace Macintosh's brother?"

Annalukshmi nodded.

Nancy raised her eyebrows, impressed. "A very good Christian family. Very wealthy as well." She bent down to pick up a shell. "And is your plan to give up teaching and get married if it works out?"

"I don't think I'll ever get married. Instead," Annalukshmi smiled, "I might lead a life of unmitigated spinsterhood."

"Oh?"

"Like Miss Lawton. She never married, yet you can't say she isn't happy. Her life is full of satisfactory things. A school of her own to run, the rewards of girls going on to become doctors and lawyers. Friend, guide, confidante to so many. It seems like a very good life to me."

She bent down to dig up an interesting shell out of the sand. As such she did not see the slightly worried expression with which her friend regarded her.

Once they were walking again, Nancy said, "Yes, Miss Lawton has a good life, but it's not the only life."

"But think of how much one has to give up in marriage," Annalukshmi said. "Stuck at home all the time. No money of your own. Always having to ask your husband. And what if he is the jealous type, forbids you to leave home or thrashes you?"

"Not all marriages are like that, not all men are cruel and thoughtless."

"He could be a charmer and a deceiver and then what? One can't very well get divorced, you know. And don't forget the children," Annalukshmi continued. "God help you if you are fertile. Remember that poor Zharia Ismail who used to be in our class. Married at sixteen and already five children. She looks like a wrung-out rag." Annalukshmi stopped walking. "What about you? You're a modern woman. Would you give up teaching and get married, knowing all the disadvantages?"

Nancy became serious. "Well so far no one has come around asking. But if it did happen and I loved him, I might consider it." She turned to her friend. "All I am saying is that Miss Lawton's way is not the only option."

∾

On Monday morning when Annalukshmi arrived at school, she found the teachers in the staff room in excited conversation. "Miss Lawton is talking to Miss Blake's replacement in her office," one of the teachers informed Annalukshmi. "No one knows who it is."

Annalukshmi glanced at Nancy, who betrayed nothing.

Just then, the headmistress's door opened and Miss Lawton came out. "Ladies, ladies," she said, "I have an announcement to make."

The teachers waited expectantly.

"I would like to introduce you to the newest member of our staff." Miss Lawton turned and signalled to someone in her office. After a moment, a man appeared in the doorway.

A rustle went through the staff room.

"With the departure of our beloved Miss Blake," Miss Lawton continued, "I have decided to fill in her position not with another teacher from England, but with Mr. Jayaweera here, who will take over most of the clerical and accounting aspects of my work, thus leaving me free to do what I love most. To teach."

Annalukshmi studied Mr. Jayaweera. He was tall and well built and she judged him to be about thirty-five years old. His skin was dark, his jawline sharp. It was a face that she found too angular to be called handsome. There was a reserved, dignified air to him, and Annalukshmi noted that his white drill suit, though neatly pressed, was threadbare. She wondered what misfortune had befallen his family and had caused him to have to work as a clerk.

The school bell rang to announce that chapel was about to start. Miss Lawton glanced quickly at her watch. "Oh dear, I didn't realize it was so late." She looked around at the teachers. "Anna," she said, "aren't you free the first period this morning?"

Annalukshmi nodded.

"Good. Could you show Mr. Jayaweera to my bungalow? He will be living with us until such time as he finds suitable accommodation in Colombo."

Having stayed over so often at the headmistress's bungalow, Annalukshmi knew that Miss Lawton reserved a special room for gentlemen visitors, travelling preachers, male missionaries who had come into Colombo from outstation on some business, a few English tea-planter friends. The room was outside the bungalow, at the far end of the back verandah, which meant that the male guest did not actually share the house with Miss Lawton and Nancy, thus ensuring propriety on all levels.

Once Mr. Jayaweera had retrieved his suitcase from Miss Lawton's office, Annalukshmi led him across the school quadrangle, off which there was a doorway that opened directly into Miss Lawton's back garden. At first they walked in silence, but the quiet soon became awkward and, to relieve it, Annalukshmi began to point out the various school buildings and tell him what they were. He nodded politely and asked interested questions. Although his English was, for the most part, correct, he spoke with the accent of a Sinhalese person for whom English was not their first language, mispronouncing his "w" as "v," elongating short vowels, substituting "p" for "f." And, from time to time, he dropped his "the's" and "a's." Annalukshmi, again taking in his shabby suit, felt now that he must be from a poor, rural background and she wondered where he had learnt to speak English. Once she had shown him his room, he bowed slightly and said, "Thank you very much for your kindness."

Annalukshmi inclined her head in reply. She left him and returned to the school, as chapel was ending.

Annalukshmi took the morning roll call in her class, and then returned to the staff room. The door in the back of the room led into Miss Lawton's office. It was open and Annalukshmi could hear the headmistress reprimanding a student for being habitually late.

When the student left, Annalukshmi went to stand in the doorway of the office, curious to ask Miss Lawton more about Mr. Jayaweera.

"All is well, my dear?"

She nodded.

"And what do you think of our Mr. Jayaweera?"

"He seems very pleasant."

"I had some reservations about hiring him, but Mr. Wesley, the headmaster of the boys' mission school in Galle, highly recommended him. He's an old pupil of his."

Annalukshmi now understood why he spoke English fluently.

"Mr. Jayaweera was working on a tea estate as a clerk," Miss Lawton continued. "He was fired through no fault of his own." She grimaced. "Poor man is saddled with a very bad egg, an older brother who is a notorious troublemaker. A member of the

Labour Union. The brother, it seems, was paying secret visits to the estate workers, informing them of their so-called rights, urging them to unionize. The workers finally staged a strike, which the head tea planter and the police soon put a stop to. They caught the brother, put him in jail for a month, then packed him off to India. Mr. Jayaweera lost his job as a result. Mr. Wesley assures me that Mr. Jayaweera is not at all interested in the union. A very decent man, really. Supports his widowed mother and two unmarried sisters at great sacrifice to himself."

Before Miss Lawton could proceed further, Mr. Jayaweera entered the staff room. "Do come into my office," Miss Lawton called out. "Let me show you what needs doing before I begin my rounds of the school."

Annalukshmi moved away from the doorway and went to sit at the table. She had before her a stack of exercise books that needed correcting and she picked one up and opened it. After a few moments, she found herself studying Mr. Jayaweera with curiosity as he stood talking to Miss Lawton. She had often read accounts in the newspapers maligning the Labour Union and its supporters. Yet she had always found herself admiring those who were outspoken about something they believed passion-ately, their willingness to make sacrifices for those less fortunate than themselves. Miss Lawton was clearly disapproving of what his brother had done. But, try as she might, Annalukshmi could not bring herself to believe it was wrong. She thought instead what a fine person he would have to be to make such an effort on behalf of the poor estate workers.

Just then Miss Lawton came into the staff room. "I have given Mr. Jayaweera some work to do, Anna," she said. "Since you have been helping me with the office work these last few weeks, perhaps you can assist him if he needs anything."

Annalukshmi nodded and Miss Lawton left the room.

Mr. Jayaweera was seated at the desk in Miss Lawton's office that had been Miss Blake's. He was reading through the letters that had come in that morning. After a while, he stood up and looked around him uncertainly. Annalukshmi got up and went into the office.

"Do you have everything you need, Mr. Jayaweera?"

He had not heard her enter and he started slightly.

"I have been helping Miss Lawton in her office, so if you need anything please feel free to ask."

He held out the letters to her, "Where would I put these, miss?"

She looked through the correspondence and showed him which ones to file and which ones to put on Miss Lawton's desk. "Thank you very much," he said and smiled.

His smile was open and friendly, inviting conversation.

"Not at all, Mr. Jayaweera."

"Miss is from Jaffna?" he asked, indicating the potu on her forehead and the way she wore her sari, in the Tamil style with the palu wrapped around her waist.

"No," Annalukshmi said. "I'm from Colombo. Actually, I'm from Malaya."

He looked at her, puzzled, and she explained to him that her father worked in Malaya in the civil service.

"And you, Mr. Jayaweera?" she asked. "You are from Galle?"

"No, miss. I went to school in Galle, but I am from small village called Weeragama."

Annalukshmi shook her head to say she had not heard of it.

"It is in south. A very poor area, very dry. Sometimes we have to walk two miles to get water. Through the jungle. It is very dangerous because there are lots of snakes, some of them very poisonous. Even the not-so poisonous ones, when they bite, the pain is something I have never felt before."

"Are you telling me that you have been bitten by a snake?"

"In poor villages it is very common. Fortunately my brother was with me when it happened. It is not good to be alone because it is hard to tie your leg and make the cut." He smiled at her aghast expression. "First, you have to tie the leg very, very tight above wound. Then you must take a knife and cut V shape with the point of the V on wound and facing towards the heart. That way, the poison will flow out with the blood and not into the rest of your body. Then, you put snake stone on wound."

"A *snake* stone?"

He nodded, amused by her sceptical yet captivated tone. "Yes. It's a healing stone. When it is held against the wound, it sticks on and sucks out the poison. Then you boil stone in milk, which becomes black immediately. After that, you can use stone again."

"But what makes the stone able to cure a person?"

"Nobody knows. The stone we have has been in our family many generations." He smiled. "Some people say that a snake itself vomits it out. But that is just fable."

Annalukshmi raised her eyebrows.

At that moment, Miss Lawton walked in, putting an end to their conversation. Mr. Jayaweera returned to his work, and Annalukshmi went back to the table. As she took her seat, she glanced at Mr. Jayaweera, even more intrigued by him than she had been before.

6

What is stronger than fate which foils
Every ploy to counter it?
— The Tirukkural, *verse 380*

The gold rush, as F. C. Wijewardena predicted, was in full swing. Two weeks had passed since the Mudaliyar's birthday. The Donoughmore commissioners had arrived in Ceylon and were happily ensconced at Queen's House.

Richard Howland, in Colombo two days, had already received a briefing from the colonial secretary that left him confused and bewildered by the numerous claims and counter-claims of the various groups in Ceylon. He sat at a desk in his room at the Galle Face Hotel, hand on forehead as he went through the notes he had quickly made while talking to the colonial secretary. Though not a large room, it was extremely pleasant, with burma teak flooring and Persian carpets. At one end stood a big four-poster bed with a lace canopy and mosquito netting on all sides. Next to it was an intricately carved antique almirah of tamarind wood against the wall. At the other end of the room was a desk and chair, also of tamarind wood, and, adjacent to it, two wing-back chairs. Despite the fact that his desk was advantageously placed with a wonderful view of the sea, Richard was not cognizant of his surroundings. His mind was on the notes in front of him.

"What a mess, what a mess," he murmured.

He turned to his companion, James Alliston, who stood by the window, looking down at the hotel gardens.

"This is a nightmare, Alli," he said. "I didn't realize just how bloody labyrinthine the whole thing was."

"Have you noticed," Alli replied, "that when the waiters stand in a certain light all is visible through their white sarongs."

"For heaven's sake, Alli," Richard said. "Don't you ever listen when I talk?"

Alli smiled and glanced at his watch. "The love of your life has probably arrived. In fact, he must be down in the foyer as we speak."

"Don't be silly. You know he's not the love of my life," Richard tried to sound casually dismissive. Yet, at the thought of Balendran already in the foyer, a feeling of panic took hold of him. He had not seen Balendran for more than twenty years. Not since that day their relationship suddenly ended.

He tried to speak to himself sensibly. He knew from the moment he decided to travel to Ceylon that he might meet Balendran. He had been prepared for the possibility, that chance meeting on the street or at one of those receptions that were bound to be thrown for the commission. He had imagined such a meeting in his mind. In the best of possible scenarios it was he who spotted Balendran, which would have prepared him, ready with a smile when his friend finally did see him. In the worst scenario, someone would tap his shoulder from behind, taking him by surprise, and there he would be, Balendran. What he had never expected was, that on his arrival at the hotel, hot and tired from the hassles of disembarking, from the formalities of customs, and the haggling with the taxi driver, to find a note waiting for him. "Richard, I heard you were arriving in Colombo. I would very much like to see you. If you were willing. Bala." Then the phone number.

He thought of the call he was finally able to make after much agonizing.

"Bala."

"Richard! I'm glad you phoned."

There was an uncomfortable silence.

"I was told you were travelling with the commission," Balendran said.

"No, I'm not with the commission. I'm here to study the commission. For a paper."

Another silence. "Well, we should meet."

"Very well. Come tomorrow at four. My friend Mr. Alliston will join us."

"I'd like you to meet my wife, Sonia. I'll bring her along."

So, Balendran had married. But, after all, wasn't that inevitable? Richard found himself thinking about this "wife" with a certain disdain, remembering the Ceylonese women on board the ship. There had been modern women, but he thought of the traditional ones — the way they drew their saris or shawls over their head when they passed him, as if he might carry an infectious disease. He felt sure she was a cloistered, traditional woman, naïve to the ways of the world and certainly to the ways of her husband. Probably some cousin from Jaffna, judging from what Bala had told him about Tamil marriage customs.

Richard looked at Alli. Yes, he thought to himself, you might have a wife, but I am not solitary either. Balendran would have to admit Alli was handsome in a voluptuous way. Tall with nice shoulders, a mop of curly, black hair, ivory skin, and full lips that always looked like they had been touched with red salve. Yet Alli was twenty-seven, fourteen years younger than himself, and Richard could not help remembering the way Balendran and he used to make fun of those middle-aged men with their pretty young things. He wondered now if Balendran would look at Alli and think he was Richard's old folly. He felt disheartened by the thought.

Alli had turned to Richard, aware he was under scrutiny.

"I've told you it was all over, a long time ago," Richard said. "I'm a big boy now."

"Well, big boy, you could have picked Jamaica or Mauritius to study."

"I've explained to you numerous times the importance of this commission, the precedent it might set for self-government in other colonies." Richard looked at Alli closely. He could not tell if Alli was simply amused or if he was jealous about this meeting.

At that moment, there was a knock on their door and Alli went to answer it. It was a bellhop. "Mr. Balendran is waiting for you in the foyer, sir." he said.

Richard rose from his table hurriedly, almost knocking the chair backwards. "We'll be down right away."

The bellhop bowed and shut the door.

Richard hastened to the almirah to get his coat. In taking it out, he fumbled and the coat slipped off the hanger and fell to the ground. Alli quickly retrieved it and held it out to him. "Not nervous are we, dearest," he said with a smug smile.

"Stop it, Alli," Richard replied irritably.

Balendran and Sonia sat in the lounge. Even though it was only mid-November, the hotel had already put out its Christmas decorations. As Sonia chatted away about how incongruous and silly the fake holly and mistletoe looked in the tropics, Balendran found himself gazing out over Galle Face Green, where a horse rider was cantering across the field. He thought of that walk he had taken across the green two weeks ago, just after his father had told him of Richard's arrival. All the rationalizations he had used to convince himself that this meeting would be painless, even banal, seemed senseless now in the face of this impending encounter.

From where Balendran was sitting, he could see into the foyer of the hotel, where a great wooden staircase rose up to the second floor. To the left of the staircase was the lift. The door to the lift now swung open and Richard stepped out. Balendran rose to his feet and stared at Richard. How much older he looked, how changed. His friend had seen him and he started to come across the foyer. Richard, so slim in his youth, had become heavyset, especially around the jaws. His hair was thinning out and had receded halfway up his head. It was the face of a middle-aged man. Balendran felt a sudden pang of sadness, for there in Richard's face, like the physical distance between them across the foyer, were the missing years of their lives.

Richard was now in front of him. "Bala," he said gruffly and extended his hand.

Balendran took it, but could not speak for a moment because of the sadness in him. "Richard."

Their gaze met and, in that instant, Richard saw that Balendran's eyes were unguarded. His own defensiveness fell away. As they held each other's hands, there passed between them the understanding of their history together, of the life that had been theirs. It settled on them like fine dust.

Sonia had risen from her seat now and Balendran let go of

Richard's hand. "This is my wife, Sonia," Balendran said, turning to her.

Richard saw with surprise that she was of mixed blood, that the cut of her sari blouse, with its short sleeves, was modern. She was holding out her hand and he took it. "Pleased to meet you," they both said at the same time, and then smiled at their synchronization.

"And this my friend, Mr. Alliston," Richard said and turned towards Alli, who was standing a little away from them.

He came forward and offered his hand to Sonia first since she was the woman in their party.

This gave Balendran a moment to look him over. How young he is, he thought immediately and then was careful not to let the surprise show in his face. Mr. Alliston had turned to him now. Balendran shook his hand and said warmly. "Welcome to Ceylon. I hope you have a very pleasant stay here."

They all stood for a moment, not knowing what to say next.

"Well, shall we?" Richard said and pointed in the direction of the garden.

The Galle Face Hotel garden opened directly onto the beach. The upper part of the lawn was a terrace with wrought-iron tables and wicker chairs for tea. The terrace was bordered by a balustrade, and a set of steps led down to the lower garden that was shaded by coconut trees. Beyond it was the sea. As they came into the garden, they could hear music wafting down from the ballroom gallery upstairs. The band was playing a jaunty Charleston.

When they were all seated on the terrace and had ordered tea, there was an awkward pause, then Richard and Balendran spoke at the same time.

"I must say it was a surprise —"

"It's impossible to believe you are —"

Richard indicated for Balendran to speak first.

"It's impossible to believe you are actually in Ceylon. When we heard you were travelling here as Dr. Shiels' so-called assistant, we were surprised."

"I couldn't think of a worse position to be in. The political situation here is more complex than I could ever have imagined. This Donoughmore Commission is rushing in where angels fear to tread."

"Yes," Balendran said, relieved that they had found something to discuss. Something that would alleviate the awkwardness. "It is a complex society with numerous horizontal and vertical divisions. It's going to be very hard to find a constitution that works. Still, one must hope."

"I thought I could assess the situation in one month," Richard said, leaning forward. "It needs many months of work. I don't know how this commission dares to think they can make a reasoned recommendation in such a short period of time."

"That's the British for you," Alli said. "Think they can barge in and tell everyone what to do. Then act put out when their brilliant solutions don't work."

"Hear, hear," Sonia said, "I'm with Mr. Alliston on that."

"I think both of you are a bit harsh on the British," Richard said. It was just like Alli to come out with some naïve statement like that. "They are, after all, trying their best to remedy past wrongs."

"Rubbish," Alli replied. "They're trying to have their cake and eat it. Making it look like they're being fair and treating the colonies well while they rob them blind. Mark my words, this commission's recommendations will make sure the British continue to have their way."

Richard, not wanting to get into an argument with Alli, abruptly changed the subject. "Do you think this country is ready for universal franchise?" Richard asked Balendran.

"No. But I think it should be given anyway. The country is a whitened sepulchre." He waved his hand at his surroundings. "Don't be fooled by all this. You only have to step out into the countryside to find the crippling poverty, the illiteracy, people dying from malaria and lack of proper medical facilities. Already so much has been remedied through limited franchise."

"Such as?" Richard said, searching his pockets for a pencil and notebook.

"Such as the repealing of a bill the British and some of the local élite were using to appropriate land that traditionally belonged to the village communities. Of course, there was a huge hue and cry from the European community in particular."

"The Europeans?" Richard asked, somewhat puzzled by whom the term might cover.

"Forgive me," Balendran said. "By Europeans, we Ceylonese often mean anyone of European descent, including British, Americans, Australians."

Richard gestured for him to continue.

"They said they were an endangered minority whose rights needed to be protected. This, despite their controlling eighty-five per cent of the tea and sixty per cent of the rubber of this country."

Before he could go any further, Alli stood up, bored with the conversation.

"Where are you going?" Richard asked quickly.

"Down to the bottom of the garden to look at the sea."

"I'll come with you, Mr. Alliston," Sonia said and stood up. "I always love the view from there."

Balendran was alarmed that she was going, leaving them alone. But Mr. Alliston had already held out his arm to Sonia gallantly. She took it and they began to walk down the steps chatting to each other. Balendran caught Richard's glance and he saw that his friend was feeling as uneasy as he was.

"Your wife, she's charming," Richard said after a moment. "Where did you meet her?"

"We met in London at —" Balendran paused. "We met at her aunt's house."

Richard stared at him in surprise. He looked down the garden at Sonia, a disturbing thought forming in his mind. "While you were a student there?" he asked.

Balendran moved in his chair uncomfortably. "Richard, let's not dwell on the past."

An uncomfortable silence fell between them, punctured by Richard tapping his pencil on his notebook and the sound of the band upstairs playing a soulful ballad.

On the way home, Sonia turned to Balendran in the car and said, "I like Mr. Alliston very much. At first his indolent manner was off-putting. But I think he has a lot of sense. Sees things with remarkable clarity. He's good for your friend, Mr. Howland. Keeps him from hoisting the British flag too high."

She leant back in her seat and folded her arms. "And so good-looking too. It's funny how those sorts always are. Even Mr. Howland, you can tell he was —"

A quick movement from Balendran made her break off and look at him. He was staring at her in astonishment.

"Bala, darling," she said and took his hand, smiling. "Surely you could tell, couldn't you?"

"Tell what?" Balendran said, trying to conceal his fear.

"They're, you know . . . inverts. 'Friends of Oscar,' as Aunty Ethel used to say."

Balendran withdrew his hand from hers. "Don't be crass, Sonia. What a terrible thing to say about someone you claim to like."

Sonia looked at him, hurt that he had chastised her.

"Besides, how could you tell?" Balendran said gruffly. "There was nothing to indicate that."

"Perhaps some of us are more astute than others," Sonia replied stiffly. Then she added, "It was the difference in their ages. Besides, Mr. Alliston is a little 'outre,' as Aunty Ethel would say."

Balendran looked out of the window and, after a few moments, he realized that his heart was beating furiously.

❧

That evening, Balendran retired to his study under the auspices of working on some estate affairs, but he sat at his desk, thinking of the meeting with Richard. It shocked him that Sonia had discerned what he had never expected she would, that Sonia actually knew what inversion was. "Friends of Oscar," Lady Boxton had called them. A thing he would have thought beyond the pale of refined society, beyond the understanding of decent women. Yet they were both decent women, ladies, and their knowing such a thing took him aback.

Balendran sighed as he thought of Richard's question about Sonia. Everything had gone fairly well until that moment. Now he regretted having cut him off so abruptly. He could have easily said something like, "No, I met her after you left." Alluding indirectly to their relationship and separation and not leaving

Richard with the false impression that he had been unfaithful. He shook his head at his own stupidity.

Balendran found himself thinking of the first time he had seen Richard, coming across the lawn of Lincoln's Inn, his gown flapping out behind him. It had been a fine autumn day and he, Balendran, had been leaning on the balustrade, too lazy to go into the library and study. He had watched Richard come up the step and Richard, looking up, had seen him too. "Hello," Richard said, as if they had met before.

"Hello," Balendran had replied shyly.

"Care for a tea or coffee?"

Balendran had nodded.

Balendran wondered, even to this day, how Richard had simply glanced at him and seen his desire. He, who was so very careful not to be detected watching men. He thought of the shock of blond hair that fell over Richard's forehead in those days, the charming way he had of tossing his head to get it off his face, pulling it back tightly when contemplating a dilemma, blowing it away from his eyes when he was tired or exasperated. He wondered if Richard had got used to not having that shock of hair, if he still tossed his head or ran his hand up his forehead forgetfully.

***

The meeting with Balendran had left Richard in a state of agitation and, as he always did, he sought exercise as a solace.

The swimming bath at the Galle Face Hotel was deserted, since the sun had long set, and he had the pleasure of having it to himself. Alli, who disdained the very idea of exercise, sat in the shadow of the garden keeping him company.

As he swam from one end to the other, Richard pondered over the fact that Balendran had met Sonia while studying in England. Reason told him that, since Sonia was Balendran's cousin (she had told Alli this), he must have called on her often during his years in England. Yet Balendran had never spoken of her. The very fact that he had not made Richard feel strongly that, even while they had been together, Balendran had already started to move away. This truly disturbed Richard. Their relationship, before it had been so brutally severed, had been the only one that had met his criterion of fidelity. They had refused, unlike other couples, to seek gratification outside their alliance. Now, to think that, all the while, Balendran had been unfaithful, and with a *woman* at that.

Richard glanced at Alli and felt, as always, a sense of failure at Alli's constant need to seek gratification outside their relationship. Alli sought young, rough, well-built working men. All that Richard was not. Richard preferred what Alli and their set called "tootsie trade." Men like himself and Alli, not overly masculine. Unfortunately, those men most often sought their opposite. "Bala and I were compatible in that respect," he thought. Then he remembered Sonia. Not compatible enough, obviously.

Richard paused at one end of the pool. Had he, as Alli said, unconsciously chosen Ceylon because of some unsettled feelings for Balendran? He shook his head. He did not believe in the unconscious and Freudian slips and all that fashionable nonsense. He knew precisely why he had come. The Donoughmore Commission. Besides, there was Alli. Things were not perfect, but, still, after these seven years here they were together.

7

As Gods in heaven are fed through fire,
So men on earth are fed through their ears.
— The Tirukkural, *verse 413*

The colonial administrators of Ceylon often said that the common man — the farmer in his fields, the labourer, the fisher-folk — had no aspirations for freedom from colonial patronage. The British government agents in the provinces of Ceylon under-stood the problems of the common man and what solutions needed to be implemented. The Ceylonese élite who sought self-government had scanty knowledge of how the common man lived, had very little real contact with him. They could thus hardly assert the right to represent him.

These claims were made with disregard for the crippling poverty and illiteracy, the terrible health and sanitary conditions that colonial rule had brought to the "common man." There was, however, an element of truth to it. For the common man knew that self-government would not shatter any of the shack-les that held him in his position of feudal subservience. He would simply exchange one set of masters for another.

Annalukshmi, in a curious way, shared the views of the

"common man." The bid for self-rule did not promise to provide her with any greater freedom, any amelioration of her position as a woman, that had not already been achieved under colonial rule.

The conversation Annalukshmi had overheard about the Women's Franchise Union had, however, sparked her interest for the first time in the Donoughmore Commission and the possibility it presented for the female vote. Her Aunt Sonia held good to her promise and invited her to attend the union's first meeting, which took place a few days after the Donoughmore Commission arrived in Ceylon.

When it came time to tell her mother about Sonia's invitation to take her to the Women's Franchise Union meeting, Annalukshmi was concerned what her mother's reaction would be. Still, it was her Aunt Sonia who had invited her, and she knew this would be an advantage in securing her mother's consent. When she was a little girl and they had visited Ceylon from Malaya, she had been very enamoured of her aunt and spent as much time as she could with her, listening to her stories of life in England.

Though Louisa had some reservations, she was indeed delighted that Annalukshmi would be spending an evening with her aunt.

The meeting was held at the Girls' Friendly Society building on Green Path, which had, at one time, been the home of the society's benefactress. The living and dining rooms and the bedrooms on either side had been amalgamated into one large hall, and it was here that the meeting took place. At one end of the hall was a narrow wooden stage, on which there was a table with chairs. The rest of the room was taken up with rows of wooden chairs with cane seats. The space was relatively small, and by the time Annalukshmi and Sonia arrived they were only able to find seats at the back. The hall was noisy with the whirring of the fans, chatter, the rustle of saris. After a few moments, a group of women who had been sitting in the front row got up and solemnly filed onto the stage. A lot of them were well-known Cinnamon Gardens ladies. As they took their seats, a hush descended. The first speaker now rose to address the audience. She was a diminutive woman, a Canadian doctor named Mary Rutnam who had married a Tamil man and now lived in Colombo. Though she was well respected for her charitable work in the slums of Colombo, she, as a proponent of contraception, was a slightly controversial figure. Her speech, however, was not unorthodox in the least. She merely explained what the Women's Franchise Union was going to ask the commission. It was going to recommend limited franchise, whereby only women of property and education would be eligible for the vote.

As Annalukshmi listened to this, she understood that, by virtue of her teacher's certificate, she would qualify. Despite her aunt's frown of reservation, Annalukshmi could not help feeling pleased.

The next speaker was more exciting. She was Mrs. George E. De Silva, a woman who, though from a good family, had married a man from a low caste. Her husband was a lawyer and a prominent member of the Labour Union, and Mrs. George E. De Silva, in the tradition of Labour, did not mince her words as she castigated the narrow-mindedness and selfishness of the men who opposed giving women the vote.

Following the speeches, there was an election of the office bearers for the union and then the meeting was called to a close. A small reception followed, after which Sonia and Annalukshmi left.

When Annalukshmi got back to Lotus Cottage, Manohari and Kumudini were seated on the verandah. She saw them and hurried up the front path ahead of Sonia.

"It was magnificent," she cried as she came up the steps. "You should have come." She struck a pose and, extemporizing on the speeches she had heard, said in a loud, declamatory voice, "Women of Ceylon, of all nationalities, have now organized and united for the purpose of gaining franchise. Men regard us as their household goods and chattels. But we are not so ignorant of the political life of this country as people think. We could teach men a thing or two. We could —"

"Annalukshmi!"

She turned to find Louisa standing in the doorway.

"Are you mad or something? Shouting and screaming like that."

"It's your fault, cousin," a voice said from inside. "Who attends political meetings but hooligans."

Philomena Barnett appeared in the doorway, a cup of tea in one hand, a thick slice of cake in the other. She bit into the cake with gusto, then continued, "Only manly women get involved in men's affairs. Normal women think of their husbands and of their homes and nothing else."

"It's precisely because women think of their homes that they are getting involved," Sonia said as she joined them on the verandah. "Many laws relate to women and children, and it is only right that they should have some say in those laws."

"I, for one, am quite happy to depend on the chivalry of men," Philomena retorted. "Once women start getting involved in politics, then their children are sure to be neglected. Instead, if women spend more time being better mothers, all the ills of society will be cured."

"Ah, but how can women be better mothers when they don't have the education to be able to provide the best care. To know what's best for their children," Sonia said gently.

"Then ask men to provide that. I am all for educating girls up to a *certain* point." Here Philomena glanced at Annalukshmi.

"And that is precisely why women are demanding the vote," Sonia said with a smile. "So they can use the vote to ask – to get – men to provide better education, better health for them and their children."

"Yes," Annalukshmi cried. "With the vote we can make a big difference."

Philomena had been argued into a corner. So she sought support in the words of others. "Sir Ponnambalam Ramanathan, who is after all a knight and a politician for *many* years – a shining example to all us Tamils – is completely opposed to it. He feels it is against our great Tamil tradition. The purity, the nobility, the modesty of women would be ruined if they are given the vote. Besides, we women are far too ignorant about matters like that. He is quite right when he says it would be like throwing pearls before swine."

"Mrs. George E. De Silva, who was one of the speakers, said that men like Sir Ponnambalam are narrow-minded and selfish," Annalukshmi said, drawing strength from Sonia. "She said that such men were swine and that women were the pearls and that good pearls cannot be crushed that easily. Even by men."

Philomena put her hand to her cheek and stared at her niece to convey her shock at such rudeness. Then she shook her head to say she wasn't a bit surprised. "Agnes Nell is this Mrs. George E. De Silva," she said to Louisa. "You know, *the* Nells. A good Burgher family. And that girl went and married a low-caste Sinhalese." She lowered her voice as if she were telling a dirty secret. "A Labour Union man.

"See how low she has fallen," Philomena continued. "Talking just like a real Mattakkuliya fishwife."

Philomena nodded her head sagaciously at the girls to show them the depths to which they, too, could sink if they were not careful.

Once Sonia had gone and they were all seated down to tea again, Annalukshmi found out that, unbeknownst to her, her mother had passed on a photograph of herself to Philomena, who had sent it to the Macintoshes. Annalukshmi was furious. "How could you do that without asking me?" she cried.

"But, kunju, you agreed to see the boy," Louisa said placatingly.

"I did not agree that a photograph be sent. What am I . . . a piece of furniture? It is outrageous that a complete stranger should be looking at my photograph, passing it around to his friends and relatives as if I were some souvenir. I don't even know the name of this Macintosh boy."

"Chandran," Philomena said.

"What?" Annalukshmi was momentarily distracted from her tirade.

"His name is Chandran Macintosh."

Annalukshmi had a sudden image of her Uncle Balendran's study. "Chandran Macintosh?" she repeated. The name was familiar. Had she met this Macintosh boy before at her uncle's? She repeated the name over to herself to see if a face would arise in her mind, but none did. Yet Annalukshmi knew how bad her memory was. She could have very well met him, might have actually spoken with him.

"In any case," Annalukshmi concluded, "do not go to any extra bother on my behalf. I have pretty much concluded I will not marry this Macintosh boy . . . or anyone else for that matter."

She began to eat her piece of cake, pretending to ignore the silent exchange – the rolling of eyes and shaking of heads – that passed between the others at the table.

❧

Annalukshmi had arranged with Sonia that she would visit them at Sevena the following Saturday and spend the afternoon. There were some books of her uncle's that she had finished reading, and she wished to return them. Now the visit would allow her the opportunity to find out more about this Chandran Macintosh, even if she had no intention of marrying him.

On Saturday morning, Balendran's car came to pick her up at Lotus Cottage.

Annalukshmi loved her uncle's house for its peaceful surroundings, its view of the sea, the lulling sound of the waves breaking rhythmically on the beach. Of all the houses she knew, this was her favourite. It was big enough, but not too large. Unlike Brighton, it did not have rooms that looked like tombs, the furniture covered in dust sheets that were only removed for special occasions. The ceilings were high, which meant that the sea breeze circulated constantly through the house and kept it cool, even in April. The furniture, though smart, was comfortable. And, of course, her aunt's touch was everywhere, from the araliya and jasmine flowers floating in carved, red clay bowls to the arrangement of furniture, with comfortable chairs in corners for curling up and reading in.

As the car pulled in through the gates, Annalukshmi saw Balendran and Sonia standing on the front verandah. She felt that, if there was one couple whose marriage she might wish to emulate, whose relations were equitable, who existed in a companionable sharing of ideas, it was her uncle and aunt.

When the car stopped in front of the house, Annalukshmi got out, came up the verandah steps, and kissed her aunt and uncle on the cheek.

"I hear you've become a real fighter for women's suffrage," Balendran said, taking her arm.

"Yes, maama," she said, "and you men would do well to watch your step from now on."

Once they went inside, Annalukshmi said to them, "There's something I need to ask you."

"Sounds mysterious," Sonia said.

"Chandran Macintosh. Do you know him?"

They stared at her in surprise. Then Balendran groaned and Sonia rolled her eyes.

"Why? What's wrong with him?"

Sonia smiled and raised her hands as if protecting herself. "I don't want to hear about that story again. Your maama can tell you. I'm going to see about lunch."

When she had gone inside, Balendran said, "I'm very curious to know why you asked about him. But first I'll explain our story." He indicated for her to follow and he led the way to his study.

Once she was seated across the desk from him, he went to a stack of *Punch* magazines on the floor and, from behind them, drew out a piece of white board. He placed it in front of his niece. Now Annalukshmi knew why the name Chandran Macintosh was familiar. Mounted on the board was a pencil sketch of Sonia, with a signature at the bottom. She had seen it standing behind that stack of magazines many times before. "He's an artist," she exclaimed in astonishment.

"Artistic pretensions would be more accurate."

Annalukshmi looked at the drawing again. The artist had captured a likeness of her aunt's features, yet the straining upwards of the muscles of the neck, the smile that contrasted oddly with the look of disquiet in the eyes, was not her aunt at all. There was detailed attention given to the beauty of her aunt's face, to the choker around her neck, to her sari that made it clear the artist had genuinely thought he was capturing her aunt.

"When was this done?" she asked.

Balendran shook his head. "That was the most insulting thing. It was done without us knowing, at the Governor's Ball in Nuwara Eliya. He secretly sketched it."

"So you've never actually met him?"

"Thankfully not. It was sent to us with the compliments of the artist."

He took the sketch away from her. "Now it's my turn," he said and smiled.

Annalukshmi looked at her hands, finding it hard to begin, given his disapproval of the artist. "Aunt Philomena is trying to set up a meeting," she said.

"With this boy?" He sat down across from her. "Merlay, why didn't you say something? I wouldn't have said what I said."

"No, maama," she said. "I'm glad you did."

"Hmmm, I wish I could tell you more." Balendran tapped his letter opener on the desk. "I suppose he must be handsome," he said. "I was in school with the father, and he certainly was." He frowned. "In fact," he said. "In fact . . ." He got up, went to his bookshelf, searched around a bit, and then took down a large, heavy book entitled *Twentieth Century Impressions of Ceylon.*

"It was a book that was done in the early years of this century," he said. "A lot of the Cinnamon Gardens families are in it."

He put the book on his desk and opened it. Annalukshmi went around and looked at the photographs over his shoulder. He had turned to the Colombo section and she already recognized some of the families, even though the book was so old. How strange and ridiculous they looked, the women in particular in their cumbersome Edwardian dresses and hats against the tropical landscape. "This was before the dress reform movement," Balendran said, as if reading her mind. "Ah, here it is," he pointed at a family portrait. "That is Chandran Macintosh's father, Reginald." Annalukshmi bent low and looked at the young man her uncle was pointing to. His dark skin and the monochrome of the picture made his features stand out, almost as if an artist had highlighted in white the smooth expanse of his forehead, his straight nose, the firm curve of his chin. As Annalukshmi looked at him, she was not certain whether it was her wish or her fear that Chandran be as handsome as his father was.

At that moment, the houseboy was at the door announcing that the chief priest from the family temple had arrived for his appointment.

Annalukshmi went to look for her aunt. She found Sonia in her bedroom, writing a letter. When she knocked on the door and came in, Sonia gestured to her to be seated on the bed. She finished the last words to the letter, pressed a blotter to the paper, and turned to her niece.

"Well? Don't keep me in suspense, I'm dying to know."

"It's Aunt Philomena's nonsense. Trying to arrange a marriage for me with this Chandran Macintosh."

Sonia raised her eyebrows. "My goodness, you sound as if you are contemplating a funeral."

Annalukshmi ran her finger over the design on the counterpane.

"You know, my dear, it's very easy to tell if you love someone of not. It's not advanced algebra. You know almost immediately, in fact, so soon that at first you doubt what you're really feeling is love."

Sonia paused and peered at her niece. She saw that her words were not addressing what concerned her.

"Suppose I don't want to give up something I treasure like . . . well, like, teaching?"

Sonia breathed out slowly. "That is a difficult one, isn't it?" She leant back in her chair. "Perhaps the best thing I can say is that you'll just have to wait and see how things unfold."

Annalukshmi gestured impatiently, as if to say that she rejected the idea of waiting passively.

Sonia played with the bangles on her wrist. "You know, Annalukshmi, we can't expect our life to be pat, our future to be a decided and fixed thing. The fact is, life simply does not work like that. Especially when you are young and the world lies before you and truly anything is possible. One must be pliant, one must not be afraid to say one doesn't know where one is going, to simply stand still without moving until the path one must take becomes clear. Otherwise a person is quite liable to grab on to the first thing that comes along and live to regret it all her life."

"Yes, maamee."

"Well, let's go in to lunch. Do let me know how things progress with this proposal." Sonia held out her hand to Annalukshmi and they left the room.

⁂

Mr. Jayaweera had been at the school six days, but, apart from that first conversation, Annalukshmi had not been able to exchange more than a nod and a smile with him. This Saturday, she had once again been invited to have dinner and spend the night at Miss Lawton's. Once she had finished a late tea with her aunt and uncle, Balendran's car took her to the headmistress's bungalow.

When Joseph dropped her at the gate, she walked up the front path and saw Mr. Jayaweera and Nancy together in the garden. The shadows of the evening were beginning to appear on the lawn. Nancy was seated on a stone bench under an araliya tree, listening intently to Mr. Jayaweera, who was standing with his foot on the bench, bent towards her. Annalukshmi, not altogether certain whether she should interrupt, came towards them. When Nancy saw her, she waved and Mr. Jayaweera straightened up, smiling.

"Miss Lawton has gone to see a friend. She'll be back soon," Nancy said as Annalukshmi came up to them. She patted the bench next to her and Annalukshmi sat down. "We were having a fascinating discussion here. Do you believe in evil spirits, that a person can actually be possessed by one?"

Annalukshmi was taken aback by the question. "No. At least, I don't think so."

Nancy gestured to Mr. Jayaweera. "Why don't you tell her your story."

"I'm sure Miss Annalukshmi is not interested in our village superstitions," he protested. "Besides, it is getting late."

"Of course I am interested," Annalukshmi said. "Now that you have baited my curiosity, I will be very upset if you don't tell me, Mr. Jayaweera."

"Very well, then," he said.

"My oldest sister, Dayawathy," he began, leaning against the trunk of the araliya tree, "was calm and gentle girl, fervent Buddhist, always offering flowers at the temple near our village. One day, she went to make offering. When she did not return, my mother went to look for her. She found my sister on the path. She had fainted. When she revived, she had become a different person. For no reason at all, she would scream and run from our hut, trying to tear off her clothes. Sometimes she would disappear in the evenings only to return in the morning exhausted."

While Mr. Jayaweera spoke, the shadows, as they did so swiftly in the evening, had lengthened and his face was half in darkness. "Of course, the people in village said that there was only one thing wrong with her. She was possessed by a devil, and from the state of her condition it had to be most feared demon, Maha Sohona. So my mother decided that a sanni yakuma would be held to exorcise the devil.

"I was studying in Galle at the time and was asked to come home for the ceremony. Now, as young man of sixteen who had lived for many years in the Galle Mission School, who had studied science and mathematics, I was suspicious of the whole thing and told my mother it was superstitious old thinking. Still, she decided to do it. A circle was cleared in front of our home and an altar was made out of coconut leaves. That night the whole village gathered to watch the ceremony. My sister was brought out on her cot and placed in front of circle and then the ceremony began. First there was chanting. Then the exorcist lit a flare, ate the flames, and the ceremony was well under way."

As Mr. Jayaweera spoke, his voice unconsciously dropped and Annalukshmi found herself leaning forward, drawn into the story. "The air was so full of incense I could hardly see in front of me, and I don't know whether it was because of the fumes or not, but I began to feel very strange. Giddy, but also as if my mind was detaching from my body."

Annalukshmi, because they were in shadow, because of his tone, felt a slight shiver go through her. From the far corner of the garden, she could hear the mournful calling of a bird.

"The chanting got louder and louder, drums faster and faster, and I felt as if those drums were in my chest and the chanting was ringing inside my head. Then there was deafening roar and a demon jumped into the centre of the circle. He wore nothing but a garment of burulla leaves and his face was black and hideous. He began to dance, spinning round and round the circle."

Here Mr. Jayaweera broke off to add that the "demon" was another exorcist into whom the spirit of the demon had entered.

"Of course all the villagers said that it was Maha Sohona's," he said, resuming his story. "Now exorcist began to talk to Maha Sohona. First he pleaded with him to leave my sister in peace. When the spirit refused, exorcist threatened him in the name of our Lord Buddha. Then the devil became frightened and promised to do as he was asked. Exorcist commanded him to enter my sister's body. My sister began to have a fit. After a little while she became quiet. She began to speak, but it was not her voice at all. The devil speaking through her said that he would only leave if he was given sacrifice of a rooster." Mr. Jayaweera leant forward towards Annalukshmi and Nancy. "Then the most horrific thing happened. The priest gave my sister the rooster and she, kind and gentle girl that she was and fervent Buddhist, immediately rang its neck and drank the blood."

Annalukshmi and Nancy exchanged glances.

Just then, they heard the front gate open. It was Miss Lawton. She stopped on the front path when she saw them. "Hadn't you better come in, girls?" she called. "The mosquitoes are terrible at this time of the evening. Dinner should be ready soon."

Annalukshmi and Nancy got up.

"If I am ever possessed by a devil, I shall certainly come to you, Mr. Jayaweera," Nancy said teasingly.

He smiled. "I will be at your service, then." He bowed with mock gravity.

Miss Lawton was waiting for them. Nancy and Annalukshmi began to walk across the garden towards her.

Nancy took Annalukshmi's arm and said softly, "Just a word of caution. I wouldn't mention his story to Miss Lawton."

"I think Miss Lawton might find it fascinating."

"I dearly love her, but we all have our limitations. And you know how she is about non-Christian things. I don't want her lecturing him about these matters and then dismissing what he and his family believes. In any event, how are we to know that it didn't happen exactly that way."

Annalukshmi nodded to say she would not speak of it. Much as she esteemed Miss Lawton, she was not blind to this prejudice of hers.

"In fact, she was not even going to hire Mr. Jayaweera because he was Buddhist," Nancy continued. "But Mr. Wesley was very persuasive and once he told her about the plight of Mr. Jayaweera's family, her heart melted."

Since it was nearly December and the school year was drawing to an end, it was time to select the students who would be admitted to the junior school next year. After dinner, when the table was cleared, Miss Lawton asked Nancy and Annalukshmi to help her go through the applications.

They had barely sat down at the dining table, the pile of applications in front of them, when Nancy picked up one and said, "Now I know you don't like to admit non-Christian girls to the school, but here is a girl – this Niloufer Akbarally – I really think we should consider."

Miss Lawton smiled and shook her head. "Unfortunately, this year I have been asked by the missionary board to be stricter than usual. As you very well know, certain members of the Legislative Council have successfully lobbied the Ministry of Education to have some of the money it allots us Christian schools reallocated to non-Christian schools. It is time to look after our own, Nancy dear. First Mission Church girls, then Protestant girls. I might give in on a few Catholics, but that's it."

"But the Akbarallys have been students at Colpetty Mission School for generations. You know they've won numerous prizes and brought much honour to our school."

"But there are so many non-Christian schools now, wouldn't the Akbarallys be far better off sending their daughter to a school where she would be amongst her own?"

"But the teaching standard is so low in those schools. Miss Lawton, you always say that us Christian women have greater freedoms than women of other faiths because of the very nature of Christianity. That its message of tolerance and love has bred the European cultures that in turn have given women these freedoms. Is it not necessary then to share this enlightenment with those who might be less at liberty?"

"Why don't we return to the Akbarally application later," Annalukshmi said.

"I could not agree with you more about liberty, Nancy dear," Miss Lawton said, as if not hearing Annalukshmi's comment, "but look at this pile of applications. I'm sure that more than half of them are from non-Christians, most of them highly eligible. Our school is one of the finest in this country, so everyone wants their daughters to be in it. I cannot put our Christian girls at a disadvantage by admitting others before them."

Annalukshmi could see she would get nowhere trying to stop the disagreement she had heard so many times before, and she excused herself from the room.

She walked out onto the back verandah. Mr. Jayaweera was sitting at the far end in an armchair outside his room, reading a book by the light of a kerosene lamp. He had changed into a sarong and a shirt. When he saw her approaching, he stood up. She gestured for him to be seated.

"What are you reading, Mr. Jayaweera?" she asked.

"It's a book by a writer named W. A. Silva. About life in rural Ceylon."

She stood by the verandah post. "I keep thinking about your story," she said after a moment. "Do you really believe your sister was possessed?"

"I was not prepared to believe it. But if you had seen Dayawathy, you would have believed it too. To think that my sister could ring the neck of a rooster and drink its blood!" He put his book on his knee. "We live in age when science reigns. We are both educated to think so. If it can't be demonstrated with proof and evidence, it does not exist. But perhaps there are many things that cannot be explained in such a way. Perhaps the old ways, our old ways which we have been taught to ignore, have some things to teach us."

Annalukshmi was silent, taking in what he had said. "And your sister, Mr. Jayaweera, since then she has never experienced the same malady?"

He was silent, looking down at his hands. "No," he said after a moment with a sadness in his voice. "She has not experienced anything like that. My sister died few years ago."

Annalukshmi stared at him in the half-light of the kerosene lamp. "I'm sorry."

He nodded. "Malaria. It's quite common in that part of Ceylon. Almost every family has experienced one death because of it."

Annalukshmi nodded her head in sympathy. "Your life has been so hard, Mr. Jayaweera, first your sister, then your brother." She stopped, realizing what she had said.

"You know about that?"

"Yes," Annalukshmi said reluctantly. "Miss Lawton mentioned it to me."

There was a silence between them broken only by the sound of an owl hooting in the garden.

"You know, Mr. Jayaweera, I . . . I don't think badly of your brother."

He looked up at her, taken aback.

"In fact, I think it's admirable what he did. Not many people truly care about the poor. Care enough to put themselves at risk."

"You are too idealistic, Miss Annalukshmi. Because of what happened, I lost my post and my family nearly starved. If not for kindness of Mr. Wesley, if not for this job, we would be beggars now. People with big ideas never think what the cost is to others."

He opened his book and began to read.

Annalukshmi saw that she had offended him, but why or how she did not know. The stern expression on his face did not invite further conversation. After a moment, she turned and made her way back along the verandah.

8

When the foe approaches like a friend
Smile, but don't befriend.
— The Tirukkural, *verse 830*

In the days following his meeting with Richard, Balendran had intended to tell his father that Richard was not, in fact, Dr. Shiels' assistant. Yet every time he thought to do so, he kept deferring it. Speaking to his father about Richard was an unpleasant, embarrassing task, especially when he took into account his lack of composure the last time they had discussed the subject.

It was the Mudaliyar's habit to lunch every Wednesday at the Grand Oriental Hotel in the commercial district of Fort, a popular haunt for affluent Ceylonese. The hotel was next to the landing dock of the Colombo harbour. It had a palm court where a band played and a beautifully appointed dining room with a European chef. For his weekly luncheons, the Mudaliyar engaged a private dining room upstairs. It had a view of the harbour, with its interesting spectacle of stately ships passing in and out. Balendran and Sonia were always his guests on these occasions.

One Wednesday afternoon, the three of them were coming out of the Grand Oriental Hotel when Balendran saw Richard and Mr. Alliston walking towards them along the arcade that ran the length of the hotel.

Sonia had spotted them as well. "Bala, it's your friends."

She waved, then turned to Balendran. The look on his face spoke of an error she did not understand.

The Mudaliyar peered down the arcade. "It's your friend, Mr. Howland, isn't it?" he asked.

Richard and Mr. Alliston had come closer. Richard faltered when he saw the Mudaliyar, a look of dismay on his face.

"Mr. Howland," the Mudaliyar said grandly and held out his hand, "a pleasure indeed, after all these years."

Richard hesitated, then came forward and offered his hand to the Mudaliyar. "Sir," he said and briefly shook his hand. Then he introduced Alli.

"Ah, I see you've got your trusty companion with you," Sonia said, pointing to Cave's *The Book of Ceylon*, which Richard had in his hand.

"Yes," Richard said. "We've been following it faithfully."

"Too faithfully," Alli added. "One doesn't come halfway across the world to walk along streets that look like London."

"Ah, Mr. Alliston," the Mudaliyar said, "you should then visit the sites of our glorious past, Anuradhapura and Polonnaruwa."

"Thank you, sir," Alli said politely, "but that's not the sort of travelling I enjoy. It's the Greeks in their little tavernas that interest me, not the Acropolis."

The Mudaliyar looked at his son.

"What Mr. Alliston is trying to say, Appa, is that he would rather see how the people of Ceylon live than the ancient sites," Balendran explained.

"Ah," the Mudaliyar cried, "that's easily arranged." He drew his watch out and glanced at it. "In fact, if you are free, I would be delighted to invite you both to tea at my residence. You will get to see how a typical Ceylonese family lives." He beamed at everyone's astonished faces.

"I thank you very much, sir —" Richard started to say, but Alli cut him short.

"We'd be delighted to accept," he said.

"Well then, it's settled." The Mudaliyar led the way to where his car was parked.

As they followed, Balendran glanced at his father, dismayed. The Mudaliyar was going to impress his ideas on Richard and, through him, Dr. Shiels. Balendran noted that Richard gave Mr. Alliston a furious look, which he returned with an innocent smile.

"I'm afraid you might be disappointed, Mr. Alliston," Sonia said softly. "It's hardly a typical Ceylonese family."

"It will be wonderfully charming," Alli said.

They had reached the Mudaliyar's car now and the driver held the door open for them. The automobile was a grey-green 1925 Delahaye and, by its very length, ostentatious. Yet there was a stuffiness inside it, as the roof was low and not detachable.

When they entered Brighton, Nalamma came hurrying into the vestibule. She saw the two Europeans with her family and she stopped in surprise.

"They have come for tea," the Mudaliyar said in Tamil.

Nalamma hurried away to instruct the servants to make the necessary preparations, and the Mudaliyar led the way to the drawing room.

Once tea had been served, the Mudaliyar sat back in his chair and clasped his hands in front of him. A coldness crept up

Balendran's neck. His father was about to bring up the topic of the commission.

"The whole experience of this commission must be fascinating to you, Mr. Howland," the Mudaliyar said.

"Indeed, sir."

"I'm sure Dr. Shiels must find it so as well."

Richard's eyes narrowed. "I'm sure he does, sir."

The Mudaliyar leant forward. "I hope that Dr. Shiels, when he makes his recommendations, does so with care, having considered the implications of reform on an Oriental society. You see, Mr. Howland, I have always felt that the problem with modern Europe is that it has forgotten its aristocracy and the obedience to its will. If every man's voice is to count equally, the voice of those who think will be drowned out by those who do not think, because they have no leisure to think. This position leaves all classes alike at the mercy of unscrupulous opportunists."

As the Mudaliyar spoke, Balendran noticed that Richard began to frown, as if he were gradually realizing something. When the Mudaliyar paused for a moment, he said, "Sir, I hope you are not still under the impression that I am Dr. Shiels' assistant."

Balendran felt his mouth go dry.

"You ought to understand that I have no influence over Dr. Shiels whatsoever." Richard's voice had a biting anger to it. "It would be useless to think I could sway Dr. Shiels' decisions."

Sonia and Mr. Alliston were staring at Richard, discomfited by the sharpness of his voice.

The Mudaliyar looked as though he had been slapped.

Richard stood. "We should be going," he said to Alli. He turned to the Mudaliyar. "I thank you, sir, for your hospitality."

The Mudaliyar raised his hand slightly in acknowledgement.

Balendran got up and followed Richard out.

Alli was still bidding everyone goodbye, so they had a few moments alone in the vestibule.

"Richard," Balendran said softly, "I'm so sorry about all this. I was going to tell my father but –"

"So this is why you were so anxious to contact me, Bala. Not out of friendship, not because of the memory of what we had –"

"Sssh."

"– but because you wanted to do your bloody father's business." He gestured towards the drawing room. "Did you actually think you could get me to accept that drivel?"

Balendran did not reply.

"I suppose you thought you could. Dupe foolish old Richard again." Balendran's eyes widened, understanding what he was talking about.

Richard took his comprehension as an admission of culpability. Somewhere in him, he had hoped that his suspicions about Balendran's infidelity would be wrong. "You disappoint me, Bala. For the second time," he said, his voice shaking. "You disappoint me to the very core."

"Richard –"

At that moment, Alli came out, followed by an anxious Sonia.

Richard tipped his hat and left, indicating for Alli to follow him.

Balendran watched them go down the driveway, Richard walking briskly, as if he wished to be as far away from Brighton as possible.

"Did you explain and apologize to Mr. Howland?" Sonia asked.

Before Balendran could reply, his father came out of the drawing room.

"Why didn't you tell me he was not with the commission?" the Mudaliyar shouted at him.

"I was going to, Appa. This very afternoon."

"You let me make a complete fool of myself. To think I wasted my hospitality on those two. To think . . ." Words failed the Mudaliyar. He turned away and stormed up the stairs.

Balendran signalled to Sonia and they went to the car.

"Well, it serves Appa right. Mr. Howland had every reason to be angry," Sonia said once they were in the car going home.

"Do not speak about things you don't understand, do you hear?"

Balendran had never spoken to her like that before and the anger boiled up inside her. She was hardly able to contain herself until they got home.

Once they reached Sevena, Balendran and Sonia got out of the car and hurried up the steps into the house. The moment they were alone, Sonia spoke. "It makes me sick at heart. Why do you allow him to treat you like that?"

"I told you, this is not your business."

"Why this terrible sense of duty? This absolute obedience to him? It makes no sense."

"He is my father. It is our way. Perhaps you can't understand it." He spoke as if contemptuous of the fact that she was half British.

"Bala," she said. "Bala. It has nothing to do with 'your ways' and 'our ways.'" She put her hand on his arm.

He pulled away from her roughly and went into his study, slamming the door after him.

She stood staring at the door for a moment. Then she sat down slowly on the sofa, despairing that once again she and her husband had reached that point on which there could be no resolution.

Once Balendran was in his study, he removed his coat, put on the fan, and stood by the window, feeling the sea breeze and the wind from the fan cool his body down. He could not forget the look on Richard's face when Richard said he was disappointed in him to the very core. The shame he had carried with him all these years over how the relationship had ended came back to him in full force. A melancholy began to take hold of him. It was a gloom he recognized from the times he and Richard had fought in the past. Waking in the morning after a bitter quarrel, he arose with a grimness that would last through the day; a bleakness that would enter his bones, making it difficult even to summon up the will to go from the living room to the kitchen to prepare a pot of tea. It could not be so. After all these years, it was impossible that Richard could have such an effect on him.

However, that night, as Balendran sat in his study attending to the temple accounts, he was aware of a listlessness in him that made it difficult to concentrate on his work. After adding the figures inaccurately for the third time, he shook his head and closed the book. The house was silent. He got up quietly and went out of his study. He would go for a walk along the railway line. Yet, after he had put on his hat and taken his walking-stick out of the stand, he stood staring at himself in the mirror, feeling the lethargy in him like a dull fever. He could not find the strength or the desire to go out. With a sigh, he took off his hat and returned the walking-stick to the stand.

❧

The moment they were back in their hotel room, Richard turned to Alli furiously. "Why did you ignore my wishes? You could tell that the last thing I wanted to do was go to that bloody house."

Alli looked at him, amazed by his anger.

"That vile, filthy man. Trying to bribe me with his stupid hospitality."

"For goodness sake, Richard," Alli said. "You're blowing this whole thing out of proportion. He's a pompous, old fool. He was more humiliated than you were when he found out –"

"You don't know what you're talking about." Richard stormed off to the almirah to look for his bathing suit.

By the time Richard got to the swimming bath, his anger had abated. As he climbed down the steps into the water, his legs were shaking. He crouched down in the shallow end, feeling vulnerable and distraught.

The memory of his earlier encounter with the Mudaliyar was one Richard never dwelt on, the excess of it, the humiliation. Yet seeing the Mudaliyar today had brought it all back.

When he returned to his room, Alli was seated on the bed, his legs out in front of him, reading Leonard Woolf's *The Village in the Jungle*. He looked up when Richard entered, but, seeing the stiff look on Richard's face, he thought he was still in a bad temper and quickly returned to his book.

Once Richard had changed into his dressing gown, he came and sat down on the bed next to him.

"I need to talk to you," he said after a moment. "To tell you something I've never mentioned before." He took Alli's feet onto his lap.

Alli put his book down on his chest and waited.

"I never explained to you how things ended with Balendran."

"No, my dear, you never did."

Richard shook his head and looked away from Alli, ashamed of what he had hidden from him all these years. "The old man, the Mudaliyar, just turned up at our flat one day."

Alli drew in his breath.

"One look at his face and we saw that somehow he knew about us."

"But how would he have found out such a thing?"

"A friend of Bala's, I think. A chap named F. C. Wijewardena. It was horrible. More so for poor Bala than for me, I'm afraid."

Richard was silent, lost in the memory of that time. "The moment the old man started in on us, Bala fled the apartment, without even a coat, in the middle of winter. When we were left alone, his father told me I was vile, that I had ruined his son. At first I tried to assert myself, to order him out of the flat. Then he threatened to have the police charge me with sodomy." Richard paused. "I was terrified. After all, it hadn't been that long since the Wilde trial." He looked at Alli. "Our lives are so fragile. One word to the law can shatter our lives into a thousand pieces. The old man saw his advantage and he broke me down." Richard shook his head. "Soon I was on my knees pleading with him not to go to the police. He even slapped me and I did not defend myself." Richard looked away. "He ordered me to leave the flat. He was going to move in, take charge of his son. I obeyed his command. I left, went back to my parents' home in Bournemouth."

Alli took Richard's hand.

"After all those promises of love and being together always, I never heard from him again."

Alli drew Richard towards him and held him tightly. They were both still, listening to the sound of the waves breaking against the shore. Richard looked up at Alli. "There must have been a good reason for Bala's silence. Don't despise him for what he did."

Alli shook his head to say that he did not do so. After a moment, he took Richard's face in his hand. "Don't take this the wrong way, sweetest," he said, "but I do feel, even more strongly now, that it wasn't the commission that brought you here."

Richard drew away from him in protest.

"I know you don't believe in psychology, but I think we sometimes do things for reasons we're not aware of."

"You're not suggesting I'm still in love with Bala?"

"I don't know," Alli said. "But I do think that one must rush into one's dilemmas and not away from them."

Alli got off of the bed, went to the window and looked out. "This Ceylon is a bore," he said. "There is nothing to see here. Centuries of imperialism have completely obliterated the culture." He turned to Richard. "I was thinking that I might take a trip to India. See the temples of the south."

Richard started to protest, but Alli held up his hand. "I know what you're thinking and that is partly the reason. My time away will give you a chance to settle this thing once and for all."

He smiled slightly. "Of course I could be doing a very foolish thing. You could go and fall in love with this Balendran all over again and then where would I be?"

"Oh no, Alli. Never, never."

"*Qui vivra verra*," Alli said and turned to look out at the sea again.

9

My love saying "No one knows me"
Has budded and blown in the streets.
— The Tirukkural, *verse 1139*

Kumudini's desire to see Annalukshmi married, though coming from a genuine wish for her sister's happiness, was motivated to some degree by self-interest. If all went well with the Macintosh boy, it meant that her own possibilities would open up. With her elder sister married, she would be able to receive offers herself. In the days that followed the sending of the photograph to the Macintoshes, she found herself thinking of one prospect in particular.

The Van Der Hoot School for Ladies that Kumudini attended was run by Mrs. Van Der Hoot, a Dutch Burgher lady. The school operated out of her home. Mrs. Van Der Hoot had a daughter, Sylvia, and a son, Dicky. Dicky was a house officer at the General Hospital and his fellow house officers often visited while the School for Ladies was in progress. It was a situation that Mrs. Van Der Hoot did not discourage because she knew that the popularity of her school had something to do with the presence of these highly eligible bachelors. She would often engineer her ballroom class to coincide with their arrival. Then the bachelors would be persuaded to accompany the young ladies. Mrs. Van Der Hoot, well tuned to the racial and caste sensitivities of Ceylon, was very careful to pair off like with like, Karava Sinhalese with Karava Sinhalese, Goyigamas with Goyigamas, Burghers with Burghers, Tamils with Tamils, and so on. Since Kumudini was the only Tamil at the school, she invariably found herself partnered by a young Tamil doctor named Ronald Nesiah. Through Sylvia, Kumudini heard of Ronald's interest in her (conveyed through Dicky). He had, of course, not dared to speak to her about it. She would never have forgiven him that impropriety. When they danced together, they maintained the strictest formalities, always addressing each other as Dr. Nesiah and Miss Kumudini. Yet it was delicious knowing all the while that he liked her. As they danced, she was very conscious of the warmth of his hand against her back, the feel of his palm in hers. Occasionally, she would steal a look at him and what she saw did not displease her. He had a nice moustache, which was fashionably curved at both ends. He had a rather big nose and a too-prominent forehead, but these were not serious deterrents. His slow, measured way of speaking suggested a man who was calm and thought carefully before he acted. A man who would make a patient and caring husband.

A few days after Kumudini found out about the Macintosh boy, she told Sylvia about the possible proposal for her sister.

"Oh fabulous, Kumudini!" Sylvia enthused, clapping her hands together. "I'm sure your doctor will be delighted."

"You're not to say anything." Kumudini blushed.

"Why not? You know he has been waiting for this opportunity."

"Has he?" Kumudini blinked in confusion, wanting to know more.

"Dicky tells me that your doctor is like a racehorse chomping at the bit. It's all Dicky can do to keep him from falling on his knees in the middle of our drawing room and proposing to you."

"He's not 'my doctor,'" Kumudini said primly.

Sylvia narrowed her eyes. "I say, Kumudini, why don't I whisper your news in Dicky's ear. It won't hurt to get a jump-start on things, no?"

Before Kumudini could reply, Sylvia said, "Leave it to me. I'll be the model of discretion."

❧

Sylvia Van Der Hoot's little whisperings had a greater effect than either she or Kumudini could have predicted.

A few days later, Louisa was in the garden supervising Ramu as he trimmed the roses when she heard a shrill "Cousin!" She turned to see Philomena Barnett making her way up the front path, waving her hand excitedly. Louisa sent Ramu to the kitchen for a glass of thambili. She removed her hat and went up the garden to meet her cousin. As she stepped up onto the verandah, Cousin Philomena, who had reached the verandah by now, cried out, "Such good news, cousin, such good news."

Then she refused to say any more until she had her glass of thambili. "Cousin!" she said once she was done. "Another inquiry has arrived."

"For Annalukshmi? How thrilling!"

"No, cousin. Not for Annalukshmi. For Kumudini."

Louisa sat down in a chair, astounded. "But . . . but who is it?"

"Ronald Nesiah, son of D. S. Nesiah," Philomena said triumphantly. "*Doctor* Ronald Nesiah."

Louisa breathed out. The son of D. S. Nesiah. The man people said would be the first chief justice, if the position were ever opened up to a Ceylonese. "How . . . where did he see Kumudini?"

"It seems he is a good friend of Mrs. Van Der Hoot's son. He has met her there."

"But what do we know about him?"

"Cousin," Philomena said with a smile, "what is there to know with a family like that?"

She leant forward in her chair. "Now, I know Annalukshmi has to be married first. But it won't hurt to look into this proposal. Mrs. Nesiah has asked to see you in person. To discuss the matter further."

Louisa narrowed her eyes doubtfully. "Couldn't we wait until Annalukshmi's proposal is settled?"

"The truth is, Mrs. Nesiah has received another proposal for her son. But he kept putting it off, putting it off, and no one knew why. Then yesterday he came home and mentioned Kumudini. That's why the mother wants to see you, so she can decide what to do about the other proposal."

Louisa was silent.

"Cousin, this is a golden opportunity. Don't let it slip. After all, your options are not many, all things considered."

Louisa understood that Philomena was speaking of Annalukshmi and her "reputation," which might put off suitors for the other girls. After a moment, Louisa nodded and said she agreed to the meeting.

Once Philomena Barnett had left, the reality of the news she had brought sunk in. Louisa felt joy, but at the same time concern as to just how far things had progressed between Kumudini and this Dr. Nesiah. She felt anxious that there had been improprieties in their relations.

Kumudini generally got back before her sisters, but today she was delayed. By the time she arrived, Annalukshmi and Manohari were already seated at the dining table about to begin lunch. Louisa could not bear to wait until lunch was over and she said to Kumudini, "I want to speak to you. In my room."

Kumudini looked at her, alarmed.

Annalukshmi and Manohari glanced at their mother too. Kumudini had done something wrong. This was indeed a novelty.

The moment Louisa and Kumudini had gone into her room, Manohari got up from the table and made her way stealthily towards her mother's door.

"Chutta," Annalukshmi began to protest, but Manohari held up her hand to silence her. Since Annalukshmi, too, was keen to know what this was about, she did not object further.

The moment Louisa had shut the door behind her, she turned to Kumudini. "I have some news. Another proposal has come."

"How wonderful, Amma!" Kumudini said, relieved that her mother's seriousness was not due to some misdemeanour of hers.

"Not for Annalukshmi. For you."

Kumudini stared at Louisa, then her face became red.

"I suppose I don't have to tell you who it is."

Kumudini was silent.

"Merlay, you haven't . . . you know . . . given him any encouragement."

"No, Amma," Kumudini cried.

The insulted look in her daughter's eyes comforted Louisa. "Good," she said. "I didn't think you had."

She proceeded to tell Kumudini everything that Philomena had told her. When she was done, she said to Kumudini, "What do you think of the young man? Are you interested?"

Kumudini looked away from her, but Louisa saw the brightness in her eyes.

"Well, we shall see what happens with Mrs. Nesiah," Louisa said. "Meanwhile, merlay, you must maintain the strictest formalities with this young Nesiah. It would not do for people to say that you flung yourself at him."

Kumudini nodded.

Louisa crossed to the door.

Manohari, hearing her mother's footsteps, ran back to the dining table and sat down. She had just enough time to whisper, "A proposal. For Kumudini, akka," before her mother and sister came out. Manohari began to dish out some rice for herself, an innocent expression on her face.

Annalukshmi's astounded look, however, gave it all away. Louisa frowned and Kumudini blushed again.

"Well, I guess there is nothing to tell *you*," Louisa said.

"But what . . . who is the boy?" Annalukshmi cried.

Louisa explained who he was and how it had come about. While she did so, Annalukshmi continued to stare at her sister.

"Congratulations, Kumu," she cried. She got up from the table, came around to her sister, and gave her a big hug.

Kumudini, completely overwhelmed, burst into tears.

"Now, now," Louisa said mildly, as she poured the rasam out into cups, "let's not count our chickens before they're hatched."

That afternoon, Mrs. Van Der Hoot showed them how to cut sari blouses. As Kumudini stood around with the other girls, following what was being done, she thought of all she had learnt at the School for Ladies and how it might now have a practical use. As she looked at the blouse patterns, she imagined her own wedding, the sari she would pick for herself, the bridesmaids, the flower arrangements. Then there was married life – the new house to be decorated and taken care of. She had always known exactly what she wanted in her home, what fabric for the curtains and serviettes, what design of crockery.

Ronald Nesiah did not come by that afternoon with the other house officers, and Kumudini, though disappointed, admired him for his discretion. As she sat out the dancing class, she felt as if she were already a matron, watching with interest this year's debutantes, judging them from the comfortable position of someone who no longer had to put herself forward for a husband.

❧

Philomena Barnett, not being one to procrastinate, arranged the meeting between Louisa and Mrs. Nesiah a few days later. It was to take place at the Nesiah residence on Rosmead Place, which was just two streets away from Horton Place.

Louisa was surprised that, despite D. S. Nesiah's reputation as a lawyer, the house was modest. It was a one-storey bungalow, well kept, the garden in impeccable condition.

A houseboy ushered them to some chairs on the verandah and went to fetch his mistress. The doors to the drawing room were open and they saw him knock on Mrs. Nesiah's door and tell her she had visitors. To their surprise, Mrs. Nesiah did not come out immediately. Ten minutes passed and she still did not appear. Louisa leant over and whispered, "Cousin, was it eleven o'clock she asked us to come?"

"Yes, yes," Philomena replied.

Another five minutes passed and Louisa was about to ask her cousin if she were sure she had got the day right when Mrs. Nesiah's door opened. She came across the drawing room to the verandah. Rather than acknowledge their presence at once, she directed the houseboy to bring out two glasses of lime juice. Then, with a slight nod and a smile, she sat in the chair across from them. She looked at them expectantly, almost as if she did not know why they had come. Philomena sat forward in her chair. "Louisa, this is Rani Nesiah. Rani, this is my cousin, Louisa."

Louisa and Mrs. Nesiah nodded at each other.

Mrs. Nesiah, Louisa noted, was one of those very dark-skinned women who insisted on wearing talcum powder, which gave her a strange greyish colour, like a corpse.

Mrs. Nesiah waited until the houseboy had served their drinks, then said abruptly, "About this proposal, anyway." They waited for her to continue, but she was silent again. "You know we have had another one, too. A girl from a very good family and we have to consider your daughter in the light of this other proposal."

Louisa watched her carefully, wondering where this was leading.

"Ronald has to complete his studies. He must go to England to get his F.R.C.S. With just Ceylonese qualifications, he will be good for nothing. The thing is, we cannot afford to send him. So we are looking for a girl whose family will educate him in England. That must be part of the dowry."

They stared at her in shock.

Louisa sat back, feeling her heart sink. Educating a husband in England was an expensive venture, more than Kumudini's share of the estate would cover.

Philomena was the first to recover. "How . . . how much would it cost?"

Mrs. Nesiah stated the figure.

Louisa sighed. It was far beyond anything they could afford. Mrs. Nesiah turned to her. "Ronald's education is very important to us. I'm sorry, but you must understand that." She waited for some acknowledgement of this fact and, after a moment, Louisa nodded.

Mrs. Nesiah stood to indicate that the meeting was over. "Thank you for taking the time to come," she said. Then, without waiting for them to even go down the verandah steps, she turned and went into the house.

By the time Louisa reached the road, she was furious. She opened her umbrella with a snap and began to walk briskly towards Albert Crescent. Philomena had to hurry to keep up with her, not even having a chance to open her umbrella. "The cheek," Louisa cried. She stopped and turned to her cousin. "How dare she treat us like that, as if we were beggars?"

She stalked away again. Philomena opened her umbrella and went after her.

"Who do they think they are?" Louisa said. "Just because their son is a doctor they can treat people like dirt!"

"Unfortunately, that is the way it is, cousin," Philomena said placatingly. "If you have a doctor for a son, you can ask for the world and get it."

"I'm glad Kumudini is not marrying into that family. Very glad indeed." Yet, even as she said it, Louisa felt a keen disappointment. She slowed her pace and they walked along in silence.

"Well," Louisa said, trying to cheer herself up, "other offers will come along. And, besides, there is Annalukshmi's proposal to look forward to."

"I'm sure that will go very well, cousin," Philomena said soothingly. "I have given the photograph and so far nothing. But no news is good news."

Louisa could not help being troubled. This meeting had made her realize just how small the girls' dowries were once the rubber estate in Malaya was divided amongst them.

Philomena hailed a rickshaw at the top of Horton Place and they parted company. Louisa walked back to Lotus Cottage, every now and again shaking her head. She would have to face Kumudini and tell her what had happened.

When Louisa got home, Kumudini had already come back from the School for Ladies, anxious to find out the result of the meeting. She was tidying the glass-fronted bookshelf in the drawing room, taking the books out and wiping them with a feather duster. When she saw her mother, she continued to busy herself, not wanting to appear eager.

Louisa had seen her daughter's darting look and a sense of dread took hold of her. She came in and put her umbrella away in the stand by the front door. Then she sat down on the drawing-room sofa. "Come here, Kumudini," she said and indicated to the spot next to her.

A shiver of excitement went through Kumudini. She came and sat down on the sofa, her duster still in her hand.

Louisa felt a throb of sorrow for her daughter. "My dear," she said.

Kumudini held her breath, waiting for her mother to speak.

"I'm afraid it's bad news. They have refused."

"Refused?" Kumudini said incredulously.

"We . . . we just don't have the sort of dowry they want. It seems that Ronald, their son . . . there is the F.R.C.S. he must do in England."

Kumudini got up and went to the bookshelf. She took out a book and began to dust it. She was curiously calm, yet she was aware that calmness was not the appropriate reaction. She tried to think why she was so collected, then realized that she knew this refusal could not be genuine. There had been a mistake. Ronald was enamoured of her. He had told Sylvia's brother that over and over again. He would not be moved by such considerations as the size of her dowry. She was confident that Ronald, once he had heard about the interview, would be furious and would rectify the situation. Her mother had not reckoned on the strength of Ronald's feelings.

Kumudini was distracted from her thoughts by the sound of her sisters coming in through the gate. Not wanting Louisa to tell them the news, thus forcing her to have to explain her own belief, she went out to greet them with a composed expression on her face. They were walking up the path and the moment they saw her, they cried out, "What happened?"

She shrugged and waited for them to reach the verandah steps. "There are some things to be ironed out," she said.

Louisa had come out onto the verandah. She stared at Kumudini incredulously.

Annalukshmi and Manohari glanced from Louisa to Kumudini, not sure what had happened. Kumudini, seeing that she was under scrutiny, turned and went inside. The moment she was out of earshot, Louisa grimaced, "They have refused."

Annalukshmi and Manohari drew in their breath in dismay.

"Why?" Annalukshmi finally asked.

"It had to do with the dowry. It just wasn't enough."

Annalukshmi walked past her and went inside to look for her sister. She found her in their bedroom, sitting on the edge of her bed, still holding the duster. "Kumu?" she said uncertainly.

After a moment, Kumudini looked up at her. "Amma has got it all wrong. Ronald will not care about the size of my dowry. When he hears what happened, he will correct things." Yet, now that she had actually spoken her hopes, a sinking feeling began to take hold of her. "After all," she said, her voice catching, "after all, why is this F.R.C.S. so important? He can be a doctor without it and earn a very good living."

Her sister's expression did not support any of her hopes.

"Akka," she said and now her voice was plaintive, "he loves me. I know he does. He told Sylvia and Dicky. I could see from the way he looked at me."

Annalukshmi put her bag down. She came and sat by her sister. "Kumu," she said, and her tone made Kumudini shudder.

Annalukshmi put her arms around her sister and drew her tightly to her. Louisa and Manohari had come to the bedroom door, but Annalukshmi gestured for them to leave. She gently stroked her sister's hair and Kumudini began to weep.

That evening, as Annalukshmi watched Kumudini sitting in a chair on the verandah, her hands in her lap, uncharacteristically idle, she felt some of her sister's melancholia transfer itself to her. She found herself thinking of Mr. Jayaweera and the distinct coolness that had sprung up between them since their last conversation at Miss Lawton's house a week ago. Annalukshmi had gone over and over that conversation in her mind, wondering what she had said about his brother that had so deeply offended him. After all, she had only tried to speak well of him, tried to place his brother's deeds in a favourable light. What was all the more alienating was that Nancy's friendship with him seemed to have deepened. She had come upon them a few times in conversation, but somehow she had not felt comfortable joining in.

❧

The next day, Annalukshmi had a free period in the morning. When she arrived at the staff room, she saw that Mr. Jayaweera was alone in Miss Lawton's office. She recalled her thoughts of the night before and, on impulse, went and stood in the doorway. He rose from his chair.

They were both silent and then she said, "Mr. Jayaweera, I feel that I have offended you in some way and I would like to apologize for whatever it is."

A darkness descended over Mr. Jayaweera's face.

"When I spoke about your brother," Annalukshmi proceeded anxiously, "it was only in the most respectful way. But of course I can see how his actions have inconvenienced your family, I understand —"

"No, Miss Annalukshmi, you do not. You do not understand at all." He paused for a moment, playing nervously with the pencil on his desk. "That story Miss Lawton told you about my brother at the estate, it is wrong. I am the one who influenced workers to strike."

"I thought —"

"Oh no, it is my brother who is in the Labour Union. But I was the one who encouraged workers to fight for their rights. They work so hard, their lives are so difficult, living one family in one room, no toilet. Like slaves."

"But it was your brother who went to jail."

Mr. Jayaweera was silent again. "Remember I said that people with big ideas never think what the cost is to others? I was talking about myself. I never thought about my mother and my sisters. I am the one who is breadwinner, that is my role in the family. My brother convinced me to allow him to go to jail, so I could continue to support my family."

He saw the appalled look on her face. "Now you must think I am a very bad man. And a very foolish one."

Annalukshmi made an attempt to protest, but he held up his hand. "It is something I am very ashamed of."

They were both silent. In the quadrangle, a physical training class was in progress and they could hear the whistle of the teacher, the thud of the ball. "I know that ladies who are best friends tell each other everything," Mr. Jayaweera said. "But please, do not tell Miss Nancy."

Annalukshmi shook her head to say that she would not do so.

10

The lute is bent, the arrow straight: judge men
Not by their looks but acts.
— The Tirukkural, *verse 279*

On the morning following the unpleasantness between Balendran and Sonia, he apologized for his rudeness of the night before, explaining that tiredness had been the cause. Things went on as usual. Then, two days later, Balendran came home to find that Richard had paid a visit and left his card behind. As he put Richard's card into his wallet, Balendran felt a heady relief, and the gloom that had stayed with him since that fraught moment between them in his father's house partially lifted.

Balendran knew Richard well enough to know that his visit was not a sign of forgiveness, but rather the opening of a door. As Balendran went to wash before lunch, he felt a little ashamed that he had not made the first effort, since the onus of explanation was so clearly on him.

He had, in all honesty, thought of it yesterday when his car had passed the Galle Face Hotel. Yet the understanding that he might have to discuss how their relationship ended made him defer his visit for another day. Now Richard had come to see him, and Balendran knew it was his duty to return the visit, to offer Richard an explanation. As he bent over the sink and splashed his face and neck with water, he decided that he would try, as much as possible, to avoid discussing their relationship and particularly its ending.

Balendran cancelled his afternoon appointments and went to see Richard. When he arrived at the hotel, he was informed that Mr. Howland had left to observe the sittings of the commission. Rather than return in the evening, he decided to go to the Town Hall and see if he could find Richard there.

The Town Hall was on the north side of Victoria Park. It was an imposing, domed white building with a tall colonnade in front.

As his car drew near, Balendran saw that the street in front of the Town Hall was lined with cars. He told Joseph to drop him at the entrance and then go and find a place to park.

As he entered the public gallery, Balendran saw that the Ceylon National Congress was before the commission today. Their deputation consisted of the president, E. W. Perera, the secretaries, S. W. R. D. Bandaranaike and R. S. S. Gunawardena, and a few others. There were a lot of Congress members present in the gallery. Balendran spotted Richard sitting in the front, his head bent over his notepad, but it was too crowded for him to find a place by him. He heard someone call his name quietly and turned to see his friend, F. C. Wijewardena, indicating a spot next to him. Balendran made his way down the row. As he did so, a number of Congress members around him, all old boys of his alma mater, the Colombo Academy, called to him softly and a few shook his hand.

"Well, well, what a surprise," F. C. said ironically when

Balendran was seated. "I thought you avoided the fracas of hands-on politics. Preferred to see things from your ivory tower."

Balendran smiled. "I do make exceptions."

F. C. bent across him to the Congress member on his other side, also an old classmate of theirs. "This bugger is useless," he said. "How many times I have asked him to join our congress."

"Yes, yes, Bala," the man said. "Bad form. This is in the service of your country, no?"

Balendran smiled again but did not reply. He tried to concentrate instead on the session. The Congress position was as he had expected from everything F. C. had told him. They were for restricting the franchise because if the vote was made universal it would allow in a class of men who would not use responsibility in exercising their vote. They were also against communal representation and they wanted self-government.

As Balendran listened to the Congress deputation, his eyes kept wandering to Richard, who was intently writing notes.

Finally the session was over. People began to get up and make their way out of the public gallery. Balendran stood up.

"Why don't you have some tea with us?" F. C. asked.

Balendran shook his head. "I'm . . . actually here to meet a friend." And he looked over at Richard, who was walking in their direction.

"Well," F. C. said. "Here's a vision from the past." Then he glanced at Balendran.

Richard now saw them and his steps faltered. He straightened up and came towards him. "How nice to see you," he said formally to Balendran, then nodded politely at F. C.

"Mr. Howland," F. C. said and held out his hand. "It's been a long time."

Richard regarded him for a moment, puzzled, then he recognized him. A cold look passed over his face. He bowed slightly in reply.

F. C. withdrew his hand. "Well, Bala," he said, "we'll be seeing you and Sonia tonight for dinner." He patted Balendran on the shoulder and left.

The public gallery was clear by now. Balendran and Richard were silent, looking at each other.

"Sonia said you called on me."

Richard nodded.

"So I thought I'd come right away."

They began to walk out of the gallery together. When they got outside, the colonnaded verandah was deserted. Richard looked at him inquiringly. Balendran, seeing that his friend was waiting for him to say something, said, "We . . . we should go somewhere quiet, where we can talk." His voice wavered slightly.

"How about the hotel?"

The hotel garden was crowded, most of the tables taken by people having tea. Balendran and Richard stood looking around, not knowing where to seat themselves. The head waiter came up and pointed out a table, but it was sandwiched between two groups of noisy Europeans. Balendran looked at his friend for guidance.

"It will not do," Richard said to the waiter. "Have some tea sent up to my room."

"Will we not be disturbing Mr. Alliston?"

"Oh, Alli," he said. "Alli has left. Gone to India."

"India?"

Richard smiled. "Evidently, Ceylon does not provide enough stimulation for our Alli."

An uneasy silence fell between Richard and Balendran as they walked down the red-carpeted corridor to Richard's room. Once Richard had opened the door and let them in, Balendran stood awkwardly, looking around him. It was a small room, not one of the hotel's lavish suites, as Balendran had imagined.

"Make yourself at home," Richard said and pointed to a wing-back chair. Then he went to put his coat away. Balendran sat down.

After a moment, Richard came and stood in front of him. "Well, here we are," he said and lifted his hands. He let them fall by his side, then went to sit down in the chair opposite.

They were silent for a while, Balendran with his head turned, gazing out of the window, Richard looking at his hands.

"I think there has been a misunderstanding," Balendran said suddenly. "There is something I need to explain. About Sonia."

"I already know about you and Sonia," Richard said. "I asked Sonia how you'd met when I had tea with her this morning."

Balendran looked at him in astonishment.

Richard got up and went to stand by the window. "There are other things. Things we need to talk about."

Balendran stood up as well. "Richard, I don't want to speak of that time. I only came to clear up what I thought had been a misunderstanding."

"After you left the flat that day in London," Richard continued, as if he had not heard him, "your father threatened —"

"Please, Richard." Balendran began to walk towards the door.

Richard came after him and held his arm. "Did you know that your father threatened to call the police and have me charged?

It was horrible. So I had no choice but to leave. I went to my parents in Bournemouth, where I waited. Waited for some word from you. Something. I thought I knew the person you were. But I was wrong."

Balendran stepped away from Richard, stung by his words. After a moment, he started to walk back towards his chair, then turned to his friend. "Richard, you must understand, things were difficult for me too."

"After twenty years of silence, this is all you have to say."

"I haven't allowed myself to think about that time for so long."

"Well, there is nothing to talk about, then," Richard said.

"After I senselessly ran out of our flat, I was terrified of going back, of facing my father, so I walked the streets, even though it was raining. Eventually, I hailed a taxi to take me home. When I got there, my father was waiting for me. He told me that you had gone. His bags were in your room. I became ill after that. Pneumonia. During the weeks of my illness, even though my father nursed me, he did not say a single word to me. Not a word. I have never felt such despair. By the time I recuperated, I had thought things through, and I realized that my father was right. Our relationship could not continue." He looked at Richard. "Of course I thought many times of writing to you, but, at the time, I thought it best to leave things as they were since the break had already happened." He paused. "Over the years . . . this is something I have felt ashamed for. It is something I will always live with."

"Had you contacted me, it would have made a difference in both our lives." Richard sat down. "But one cannot reverse the past."

He smiled. "Well, here we are after all this time. Finally talking."

Balendran sat down as well. "You know there is one thing I've never been able to find out. How did my father learn of our relationship?"

"F. C. Wijewardena."

Balendran stared at him, speechless.

"Your father said he had received a note. An anonymous note. After I started going to the Salisbury again – you know the pub on St. Martin's Lane – I found out that a Ceylonese chap from Oxford had been making inquiries about you and me."

"F. C.? But are you sure? There must be some mistake."

"No, there isn't. The pub owner remembered that tortoise-shell cigarette case your friend carried. And you had only one friend studying at Oxford."

There was a knock on the door. Richard went to answer it. Balendran leant back in his chair. He felt as if his head were spinning. A waiter wheeled a tea trolley inside and began to pour the tea. This respite gave Balendran a chance to sort through what Richard had told him.

F. C. had come down from Oxford, made inquiries about him, and then actually written to his father. He had deliberately set out to destroy things between him and Richard. F. C. Wijewardena. A man he had considered his closest friend. It was impossible to comprehend. He thought about F. C. this afternoon, the way he had beckoned him to a seat, teased him for staying aloof of the Congress. He was going to dine with him tonight.

The waiter had now left and Richard brought Balendran a cup of tea. "I hope I haven't shocked you too much. I always knew that man was a snake in the grass."

Balendran took the cup and placed it on the table in front of him. "And I always trusted him."

"Snakes in the grass notwithstanding, I'm glad we are here together."

❧

F. C. Wijewardena's house, Swansea, was on Ward Place. It had belonged to his parents, but after they had retired to their estate near Kandy, F. C. and Sriyani had taken it over. It was one of the bigger residences of Ward Place, with fifteen bedrooms and many acres of land around it. The house resembled Brighton, as there was a curved front driveway that wound around an oval garden, a colonnaded verandah, and three storeys. In the very centre of the façade, however, a tower with a red tile roof rose high above the house. This tower served no purpose and had been built purely at the whim of the owners. Behind the house there was a stable for horses. F. C. had a passion for horses and owned quite a few that he ran regularly in the Colombo and Nuwara Eliya race seasons.

As Balendran and Sonia were driven to F. C.'s house, Balendran was unsure how he was going to get through the evening. How could he possibly look his friend in the face again? He had now had time to ponder the fact of F. C.'s betrayal and it had taken on more substance, more dimension. It surprised him that he had never considered that F. C., during his visits to them in London, had guessed Richard and he were not merely flatmates. Not understanding the innate nature of inversion, F. C. probably sent a note to the Mudaliyar, thinking he would be rescuing Balendran, that Balendran had fallen under the bad influences of Richard. Perhaps in other circumstances, at another time, Balendran might have been able to forgive him this interference in his life, but his conversation with Richard had brought back all the agony, the torment that both he and his friend had suffered. He could not bring himself to pardon F. C. for being the perpetrator of that. Now, as he looked out at the darkness, he felt himself burn with anger that F. C. had thought he had the right, the duty, to interfere in his life, his happiness, and thus set his future on the course it had taken from then onwards. Balendran knew that his outrage was impotent. Somehow he would have to make a pretence of cordiality for Sonia's sake this evening. After that, as far as he was concerned, their friendship was over.

When the car came to a stop in front of the house, F. C. and Sriyani were at the steps to greet them.

"So what's this I hear, Bala?" Sriyani said gaily, as Balendran and Sonia got out of the car. "Rumour has it you are actually descending from your ivory tower."

Both she and F. C. laughed.

Balendran forced himself to smile. Sonia was looking at him for clarification, and he said, "I was at the hearings today."

"Oh, you didn't mention you were going."

"Yes, I wanted to see Richard Howland, so I thought I'd drop in at the hearings." As Balendran mentioned Richard's name, he glanced inadvertently at F. C. and was sure he saw a flicker of an expression cross his face.

They went in to the house now, Sriyani and Sonia together, F. C. and Balendran following.

F. C. put his arm around Balendran's shoulders. "I am eager to know what you thought of the hearings today," he said.

Balendran could barely control the urge to shake off F. C.'s arm. "Mm," he said in reply.

"Now didn't you think the Congress deputation did marvellously today?" F. C. said as they entered the drawing room and sat down.

"Actually," Balendran said, "what I thought marvellous was Dr. Drummond Shiels' comment to the Congress, when he asked how they could dare demand self-rule and at the same time not recommend universal franchise. How the Congress could have the gall to ask for more power, without responsibility to all the peoples of Ceylon."

The others looked at him, surprised by the anger in his voice.

"I mean, F. C., how pathetic that a British man is more concerned about the poor of this country than the Congress which purports to be the voice of the people. Listening to the Congress today, I think I would rather us remain as we are, under the thumb of the British."

"Come, Bala, you don't really believe that," Sonia interjected with a warning glance, telling him to keep his tone civil.

"Oh yes, indeed I do. What in God's name is the point of a free Ceylon when that freedom is only to be enjoyed by an oligarchy of the rich and high born? Congress, British, it's all the same."

"Now, Bala, I might take exception to that," F. C. said with an attempt at joviality.

"You can take exception to whatever you like," Balendran retorted. "Your Congress is ultimately no different from the British. You want power to do exactly what the British have done. Come in on your high horse, think you know exactly what needs doing, meddle in other people's lives, make decisions for them, because, after all, aren't you superior to them, don't you know what's best? I have nothing but contempt for people who are like that."

"Bala," Sonia said firmly, "you're clearly overwrought. You might go into the garden for a breath of air. And when you come back, there will be no more talk of politics."

"You couldn't be more right, Sonia." Balendran got up. "If I were you, I'd be ashamed, F. C." He crossed to open French doors that led out onto the verandah. He turned to Sriyani and Sonia and excused himself.

Despite the coolness of the air in the garden, Balendran was sweating from his tirade. Yet he felt a sense of relief. The burden of his anger had momentarily lifted. Through the window, he could hear voices from the drawing room as the others attempted to make conversation, and he was reminded of his brother and the party he would throw every year before the big cricket match between the Colombo Academy and St. Thomas' College. It was for the boys in Arul's class, senior boys. Balendran, still a junior and not interested in cricket anyway, was not included. So he ate his dinner on the verandah in front of the kitchen, listening to the sounds of the boys' voices drifting across to him. Now Balendran felt as if he were that boy again, alienated from the others. He could hear Sriyani talking of their recent trip to Europe, and he thought to himself, They don't know me. None of these people have any idea who I really am. Then Balendran was overcome by the loneliness of an outsider who finds himself at a gathering of close friends or family. And, just like a stranger in such a gathering might think with longing of his own home, his wife and children assembled around the dining table, Balendran now thought of Richard's room and of his friend seated in the chair across from him. He wondered if Richard was in fact the only person who really knew him, truly understood his nature, for he was hidden to the people around whom he'd woven the fabric of his life. And with this thought, Balendran had an overwhelming desire to be with Richard, to speak with him of their shared past. So strong was this need that he knew the only way he could bear to go back into this party, bear to make pleasant conversation at the dinner table, was to offer himself the promise that, after he and Sonia got home, he would tell her there were some articles from the newspaper about the commission that he had promised Richard.

When Balendran arrived at the Galle Face Hotel, the reception was deserted. He went to the lift and asked the attendant to take him to the third floor.

When he knocked on Richard's door, his friend called out, "It's open. You can bring in the coffee."

Balendran pushed the door open and went in. Richard was sitting at his desk going through some of his notes. He stood up when he saw Balendran. "Hello?" he said. "This is a surprise."

Balendran shut the door behind him. He walked towards Richard, squeezed his shoulder as he passed him, and sat down. "Have you ever seen Colombo at night?" he asked.

Richard shook his head.

"Well, get your hat. The car is waiting."

The next morning when Balendran awoke, he lay in bed and thought of the time he had spent with Richard last night, their reminiscences about the past, their shared humane view of the world. He felt a keen gratitude and warmth towards his friend. He had such an overwhelming desire to be in Richard's company again that he knew it would be useless to attempt to resist his wish.

When Balendran arrived at the hotel, Richard had already gone to the hearings. Impetuously, he cancelled his appointments and errands and went to the Town Hall.

Richard was sitting at the rear of the public gallery this time, in the very last row. When Balendran walked in, his friend looked at him, smiled and lifted his eyebrows to say that he had been expected. As Balendran made his way down the row, Richard lifted his hat off the chair he had reserved. Once Balendran was seated, they nodded to each other but, as the session was on, they did not speak. After a while, Richard leant forward to jot down notes in his book. Balendran, looking at his friend, had the simple desire to rest his cheek against Richard's back.

11

Given in time, even a trifling help
Exceeds the earth.
— The Tirukkural, *verse 102*

Sunday was always a relaxing day at Lotus Cottage, a do-nothing day in an otherwise busy week. In the morning, after church, a woman would come to the house and give each girl a massage with gingelly oil. Then they would engage in quiet activities until it was time for their bath in water that had been boiled with ciacca seeds and other herbs. For Manohari and Kumudini, this meant homework and sewing. Annalukshmi would drag a big cane armchair into the garden and sit herself down under the flamboyant tree for a good read. These hours were sacred, and everyone at Lotus Cottage knew better than to disturb her.

This Sunday, Annalukshmi was reading George Eliot's *Silas Marner* and was two-thirds of the way through. The last part of a novel was always her favourite. There was a quality of breathless excitement, a sense of rushing towards a future that was already decided, but which she could only try and guess at as it approached.

She was so engrossed in her book that she did not hear the bicycle bell at the gate. It was only the call "Telegram" that made her look up. Kumudini had already gone down to the gate. Annalukshmi hurried up the garden, a feeling of trepidation beginning to build in her. Telegrams seldom brought good news.

Louisa, having heard the call, came out onto the verandah, wiping her hands with a dishcloth.

Kumudini brought the telegram up the front path and silently proffered it to her mother. Louisa quickly opened it as the girls crowded around to read it with her. PARVATHY AND MUTTIAH ARRIVE WEDNESDAY WEEK ON EMPRESS OF TOKYO. STOP. IN CEYLON ONLY TWO WEEKS. STOP. MARRY ANNALUKSHMI TO MUTTIAH AND SEND HER BACK. STOP. WILL NOT BROOK OPPOSITION. STOP. MUST MEET MY DAUGHTER IN MALAYA A BRIDE. STOP. MURUGASU. STOP.

Louisa cried out and raised her hand to her mouth.

Annalukshmi felt the blood rush to her head. She thought she was going to faint and sat down quickly in a chair. Wednesday week, ten days from now! It took two weeks by ship from Malaya to Ceylon. Parvathy and Muttiah were already halfway across the Indian Ocean, on their way for her.

"Amma, did you know about this?" Kumudini asked, rereading the telegram.

After a moment, Louisa nodded. Then she told them about the arrival of that letter from Murugasu over a month ago and her attempts to avoid his orders by trying to arrange a marriage for Annalukshmi. When she was done, Kumudini said, "The Macintosh boy. He is our only hope. You must tell Aunt Philomena to find out if he is interested in akka and if so to arrange a meeting right away."

"I've told you I am not interested in marrying anyone," Annalukshmi started to say, but they ignored her.

"How can I tell Philomena that?" Louisa said. "She'll want to know why."

"You must tell her that akka is getting difficult," Kumudini said with complete disregard for Annalukshmi's feelings. "Tell her that akka is threatening to abscond."

"Really, Kumudini," Louisa said crossly, then glanced appraisingly at Annalukshmi.

"I've never heard of anything more ridiculous," Annalukshmi protested. "Bad enough there is this proposal from Malaya. Now —"

"Well, then what, Amma?" Kumudini asked, cutting her sister short.

Louisa turned and went into the house. Kumudini followed, elaborating on her idea.

"If this thing with the Macintosh boy fails, you are finished," Manohari said with relish. "Patas! Before you know it, you'll be in Malaya." She held out her hand, as if displaying a name board. "Mrs. A. Muttiah."

"Be quiet," Annalukshmi cried. "Just be quiet."

She stepped off the verandah and made her way back to her chair. She sat, picked up her book, and then slammed it shut.

Muttiah as her husband. How preposterous. Muttal Muttiah. For he was a "muttal" chap, an oaf, an idiot. She pictured him as she had known him seven years ago, before she left Malaya. His heavy eyelids, the frown of effort when he spoke, his sputtering of words, and then, what he had to say so dull, so inconsequential. He was tall with strong arms and legs. Yet his very physique, usually sprawled in a chair, added to his indolence, his witlessness. She felt her skin prickle with repulsion at the thought of his touch, his embrace. Her abhorrence went even deeper than that. In Parvathy's house, she knew, from the times she had visited, that she would be expected to conduct herself in a traditional manner. Avoid the company of male visitors and sit in the back room; only leave the house when accompanied by a male relative; attend to her housewifely duties in a compliant manner; never contradict her husband even if she knew he was wrong. She would be expected to exemplify the True Wife of the *Tirukkural*, whose husband is her only God. And to think she was being ordered by her father to marry a Hindu. It was an affront to her mother. What utter madness, she thought. I don't care if he will brook opposition or not. My father will never meet *me* in Malaya, a bride.

❧

Louisa knew that Kumudini's suggestion was the only solution. So she ordered a rickshaw and went to see Philomena Barnett that evening.

Cousin Philomena lived in a modest house on Flower Road. A house that was plain and practical with none of the charm of Lotus Cottage. As Louisa came up the front path, she could hear Philomena's unmarried (and some said unmarriageable) daughter Dolly hammering out "Leaning on the Everlasting Arms of Jesus" on the piano, her quavering voice never quite reaching the "leaning" in the chorus, making her sound as if she desperately needed to lean on something. Philomena was sitting on the verandah playing solitaire. When she saw Louisa, she tried to hoist herself out of her chair but gave up. "Cousin," she said. "Come, sit, sit."

She turned towards the drawing room and screeched out for Dolly. It took a few tries before Dolly finally heard her. When she appeared at the doorway, Philomena sent her to get a drink, then turned to Louisa.

Louisa now told Philomena about Annalukshmi's supposed threats not to cooperate with any attempts to arrange a marriage.

When she was finished, Philomena cried out "Hah!" in amazement, then shook her head to say she was not a bit surprised.

After that, it did not take Louisa much work to convince her cousin to try to expedite matters with the Macintoshes.

Philomena Barnett acted quickly and, on Tuesday, she arrived at Lotus Cottage with the news. The Macintoshes had agreed to a meeting. It was to take place on Thursday evening at Lotus Cottage.

Annalukshmi felt that there were more important consider-ations at the moment than for her to be bothered with nonsense that would lead nowhere. Yet she had, after all, given her initial permission for things to proceed with this Macintosh boy. The meeting with him would have to be gone through.

❧

The smell of freshly mown grass was something that Annalukshmi always associated with special occasions, usually birthdays. When she came home early on Thursday afternoon, Ramu was cutting the lawn with a long knife, the piles of grass like tiny hills all over the garden. As she stood on the verandah watching him, she felt as if it was indeed someone's birthday, but, instead of joy, she felt the slight biliousness that had been with her the whole day return, strengthened. She went to find her mother and Kumudini, shaking her head at her foolishness for ever agreeing to go along with this. As she came out of the back door and made her way along the verandah to the kitchen, she smelt the odour of pastry frying in coconut oil, yet another thing she associated with birthdays. Usually the smell made her hungry, but now it increased her feeling of queasiness. When she came into the kitchen, Louisa and Kumudini were making patties. "Akka," Kumudini said on seeing her, "I want you to look at something."

She washed her hands and led Annalukshmi to their bedroom. Manohari was at the desk making a garland of jasmine flowers. On the bed was a sari of Kumudini's. A pink Paris chiffon with a pattern of little birds on it. Annalukshmi disliked it immediately. The sari was too girlish for her.

"What do you think?" Kumudini asked.

"You'll look like a delicate, feminine flower of Tamil womanhood in it," Manohari added caustically.

"No thank you," Annalukshmi said to Kumudini. "I think I'll wear my plain white cotton sari."

Kumudini looked at her aghast. "You can't be serious, akka," she said. "That's a daily-wear sari."

"I'm not about to get all dressed up for nothing."

"Very well, akka," Kumudini said. "In that case, you can heat up the coals and iron the sari yourself. I'm not going to do it."

Annalukshmi envisioned the laborious process of ironing the six yards of material that constituted a sari. "Well, I suppose it will do," she said rather ungraciously.

Kumudini saw she had the advantage and decided to press further. She held up the garland of jasmine flowers. "How about this?" she asked.

"Absolutely not. I hate the heaviness of it in my hair."

"Chutta has gone through a lot of trouble to make it."
Annalukshmi shook her head.

"Look, akka. Either you do it my way or yours." Kumudini began to pick up her sari.

"Oh, for God's sake," Annalukshmi said. "I'll wear the wretched garland."

Kumudini not only got Annalukshmi to wear the sari and the hair garland but, with some resistance, was able to apply a little red salve to her sister's lips, some kohl around her eyes, and powder to lighten her darkness.

When Kumudini was done, she stepped aside so that her sister could see the result of her handiwork in the mirror.

Annalukshmi looked at herself and grimaced.

"You look very nice," Kumudini said.

Annalukshmi looked at Manohari, who nodded her approval. She stared at herself in the mirror, still unsure.

At that moment, they heard the gate opening.

"My goodness," Kumudini cried and glanced at the clock on the wall. "They couldn't have arrived already."

Footsteps could be heard coming along the verandah. They got up and went to see who it was.

As they came out of the bedroom, Louisa was hurrying across the drawing room ahead of them.

Philomena Barnett appeared at the front door. One look at her distraught face and they knew there had been a catastrophe.

"Oh cousin," Philomena gasped. "Oh cousin, cousin, a terrible thing has happened. The boy has bolted."

"What!"

"He's run away, cousin," Philomena said. "The dirty, dirty fellow has run away."

Louisa cried out in horror.

"Akka has been abandoned," Manohari exclaimed. "Deserted like Miss Havisham in *Great Expectations*."

This was too much for Louisa. She slapped Manohari, sat down in a chair, and burst into tears.

Louisa and the girls were able gradually to extract the story from the nearly hysterical Philomena. The Macintosh boy, it turned out, had run away to live with a woman who had a house in Pettah. An older woman. A rich woman. A divorced woman. A low-class parvenu, Philomena added. His parents had tried to dissuade him from this woman. They had come up with the proposal of Annalukshmi. Once he had seen Annalukshmi's photograph, he had actually been willing to meet her. Then this morning he had left, taking hardly anything with him. A real filthy, useless cad, Philomena declared. He was now living in sin with this woman.

Once Annalukshmi had heard the whole story, she stood up and began to walk towards the bedroom. Kumudini rose and followed her.

"Akka," she said and touched her arm.

Annalukshmi shrugged off her sister's hand. "Well, that's an end to that, isn't it," she said and went off to her room.

When she got inside, she bolted the door, then sat down at the mirror and stared at her made-up face. What bloody nonsense, what a waste of time all this had been. She was a fool not to have put her foot down before. There were more important concerns in her life right now than that Macintosh boy. Picking up a towel, she began to take her make-up off, scrubbing viciously at her skin. She unwound the jasmine garland from her hair, threw it in the wastepaper basket, and tied her plait into a knot at the back of her head. She quickly removed the sari.

For the rest of the afternoon, Annalukshmi read, not as if she hoped to find a solution to the impending marriage with Muttiah in the book, but because she knew, instinctively, that what she was to do next would come to her only if her mind was otherwise occupied. Pacing the room fretfully would not provide the solution.

In the evening, a package came for Annalukshmi. She was still in the bedroom, despite repeated attempts by Louisa and her sisters to come in as, after all, it was her sisters' room too.

The package for Annalukshmi had been delivered brusquely. A man had knocked on the gate, handed the parcel wordlessly to Letchumi, and left. Louisa and the girls had risen from their chairs when Letchumi had brought the parcel to them, a piece of cardboard wrapped in brown paper and string. "Miss Annalukshmi Kandiah" was written on it. There was no sender's name or address. They eyed the parcel as if they expected it to explode. After some deliberation, they took it in to Annalukshmi.

When Louisa knocked on the bedroom door, they heard a rustle as Annalukshmi got up from the bed and came to the door. "I just want to be left alone, Amma," Annalukshmi said in a pleasant voice.

"The thing is, kunju, a package has come for you."

There was silence from the other side. Then the bolt was drawn and the door opened. They stared at Annalukshmi. There was a certain serenity in her eyes, a certain set to her jaw, that they had never seen before. Annalukshmi held out her hand for the parcel and Louisa reluctantly relinquished it. "Are you all right, kunju?"

She nodded and shut the door.

Annalukshmi took the parcel to her bed, untied the string, and pulled aside the paper. It was a sketch of herself, based on the photograph they had sent the Macintoshes. Yet it was different from the photograph. The Macintosh boy had changed the perspective and she was being looked at from below, her lap disproportionately large. The folds of her sari had been simplified too and that, combined with the perspective, gave her a sense of grandness.

Annalukshmi lifted the sketch out of its covering to get a better look. As she did so, a note fell to the ground. She picked it up. "I wish it could have been otherwise," it said. "But that would have been dishonest."

Holding the note in one hand, the sketch in the other, she sat on the bed. Yes, she thought, it would have been dishonest. In a strange way, he had done right by her. He could have easily married her for the sake of respectability and then continued his affair with this woman. She would not have known about it and, even if she did find out, she would have been powerless to do anything. She thought of how Aunt Philomena had described the woman. Older, divorced, perhaps a parvenu. All qualities that did not fit in a Cinnamon Gardens family. He had chosen the more difficult route, but, she saw with admiration, he had followed his heart. Rather than bow to his family's dictates, he had simply run away. The solution Annalukshmi had been looking for was now before her.

She smiled. It's a pity we didn't meet, she thought. We would have been good friends.

12

What is the raft of "Will" and "Wont"
Against love's raging waters?
— The Tirukkural, *verse 1134*

"Bala, where on earth have you been?" Sonia asked, a hint of accusation in her voice.

Balendran came up the steps to the verandah. It was a rhetorical question, for Sonia knew he had been at the commission sittings with Richard, as he had for the last week.

"Sorry I'm late for lunch," he replied guiltily.

"It's not about lunch," Sonia replied. "The world has been to see you this morning. First it was Appa. He paid an unexpected visit to the temple and found that the tills have not been cleared this week. I told him you had been at the hearings with Mr. Howland and he was not too pleased about that, as you can imagine."

Balendran felt a twinge of nervousness. "I'll go by tomorrow," he mumbled.

"Then there's trouble at the estate. Your kangany is up to his old tricks."

Balendran sighed. He was eternally involved in the tussles

between the foreman and the workers. "Has he been skimming the workers' pay again?"

Sonia shook her head. "He's found a whole new way of getting up to devilment."

She told him what had happened. The kangany's sister had reached a marriageable age and he was looking for a prospective groom for her. He had hit upon a young man named Naathan, who was, however, already promised to a young woman named Uma. In order to divide them, he had convinced Naathan that his betrothed was unfaithful. Now Uma had come to Balendran to seek redress and was waiting in the servants' quarters for him to return.

Balendran remembered Uma well. A pretty, vivacious young woman who was a good worker. While they waited for lunch to be laid out on the table, Balendran sent for her.

Uma wore a calf-length sari. In the style of many low-caste women, she did not wear a blouse, the fall wrapped tightly around her breasts for modesty. The heavy gold mukkuthi in her nose enhanced the darkness of her skin.

When she saw Balendran, she started to weep. She got down on her knees and tried to touch his feet. He was never comfortable with this sign of respect and he hurriedly told her to stand up.

"Aiyo, durai," she said in Tamil. "You are our mother and our father. Please help me."

He had her repeat the story because Sonia's Tamil was poor and he wanted to make sure that he got it right. When Uma was finished, Balendran said, "I will come the following week."

"But we are to be married the following week, durai."

"You must go immediately, Bala," Sonia said. "This weekend, at least."

"But I promised Richard I would take him to Galle on Saturday," Balendran started to protest. Then he looked at Uma's tear-stained face. "All right," he said to her, "I'll come this weekend."

Her face lit up with joy and she attempted to touch his feet again.

The rubber estate, out of all his numerous duties, was Balendran's pet child. It had been badly abused before he took over, the manager, Mr. Nalliah, keeping some of the profits from the sale of rubber, the workers poorly paid and living in miserable conditions. Balendran had set into motion some of his own liberal notions on work and the rights of employees. He had fired the manager, rebuilt the houses of the workers with proper water and sanitary facilities, and introduced the concept of bonuses to keep his workers happy and productive. Most of all, he had broken the stranglehold the kangany had on them. Uma's gratitude would have usually pleased him tremendously. Yet now he felt irritated by her dependency on him. It had interfered with his much looked forward to trip with Richard.

"When will these damn people ever solve their own problems," he muttered to himself as he went to wash up before lunch.

While Balendran splashed his face with water, he thought of Richard and him walking on the ramparts of the Galle fort. He sighed in exasperation at the good time he would be missing. Then an idea struck him. Since the commission did not sit on the weekend, he could ask Richard to come with him to the estate. He dried his hands on his towel and went to the dining room, his humour restored.

Balendran arrived for the Donoughmore hearings late that afternoon. A. E. Goonesinha and the Labour Union were before the commissioners, and, as Balendran walked in, Goonesinha was telling them that the Labour Union was in favour of adult suffrage irrespective of race, caste, or creed because they felt it would raise the status of the poor. They were for female franchise, too, especially for the working woman because, unlike the more fortunate women, she faced the stern realities of life. She had to earn her livelihood.

In other circumstances, Balendran would have paid great attention to Goonesinha's testimony, happy to finally hear his own views expressed by someone to the commissioners. But now he looked around for Richard, his mind solely on their trip to the estate.

Richard was sitting in the back row and, as always, had reserved a seat for him.

Balendran noticed that F. C. Wijewardena was looking at him, and Balendran nodded in greeting but did not make any move towards him. Balendran made his way along the back row to Richard.

"You were late. What happened?" Richard whispered as Balendran sat down next to him.

"Some ruckus at the estate," he whispered back. "I have to go up this weekend to see about it."

"The trip to Galle is off?"

Balendran shook his head. "I was thinking we could visit Galle and then go to the estate."

"But really, Bala," Richard began to protest, "I don't want to inconvenience you."

"Rubbish," Balendran said. "The estate is my pride and joy. I would be disappointed if I couldn't show you around and boast a little at what I've done there."

Richard scrutinized his friend's face to make sure he was genuine, then he smiled to express his consent.

After the session was over and people were leaving, F. C. called out to Balendran to wait for him.

"I'll meet you outside," Richard said.

"Bala," F. C. said as he came up to him, "it's so nice to see you at the sessions." He patted him on the back.

Balendran did not venture any comment.

"By the way," F. C. said, "about that night. Let's just put it behind us, all right?"

"I don't know if that will be possible," Balendran replied. "It seems that our attitudes are fundamentally different. I don't know what we will have to say to each other in the future."

"Now, now, Bala, it's silly to let our opinions get between us."

"Our opinions are part of ourselves, F. C. They are not so easily overlooked. As you well know, when we act according to our opinions we can end up ruining other people's lives."

"My goodness," F. C. said with an attempt at levity. "You sound dreadfully dull and serious, like one of those Labour Union chaps."

Balendran did not reply. He bowed slightly and then left to find Richard.

That evening when Balendran got home, he informed Sonia about his plans to take Richard to the estate. As he told her, he knew that he should ask her if she wanted to come too, that if he did, she would say yes. But he refrained from doing so. He knew he was being selfish in excluding her, yet he felt irritated with her for wanting to come. Still, the sight of his wife's hurt face at the table made him feel he would try in some way to make it up to her.

⁂

Richard and Balendran left Colombo on Friday afternoon. They were both companionably silent as they drove along. Occasionally, Richard would ask a question about a sight they had just passed and Balendran would explain it to him.

When they reached Galle, however, Richard became very animated, excited by the seventeenth-century Dutch fort in front of them. Balendran had Joseph take them in through the old entrance so he could show Richard the Dutch East India Company coat of arms, with its rooster and lion crest and 1669 date above the portal.

The extensive fort enclosed the modern town, whose streets were clean and shaded by suriya trees. As they drove into the fort and down one of its narrow roads, Richard sat up in his seat and began to look around him, asking numerous questions about the old buildings, the dwellings with their deep, shady, pillared verandahs.

Joseph stopped the car by the ramparts. Richard got down and hurried towards the edge to look down at the sea below. Balendran followed. Richard grinned in delight. He opened his arms and held them there, feeling the wind flap against the underside of his coat. "Ah, this is wonderful, Bala." He looked down at the bay below. "Let's go for a swim. I'm dying to get into the water."

Balendran nodded and they went back to the car to leave their coats and get their bathing costumes.

A flight of steps led down to a room in the ramparts that had probably served as a guard room during the time the Dutch occupied the fort. Balendran knew of it, for his family had often come to this very spot for picnics and sea baths. He took Richard to it.

The room was dark except for the light that came down the steps. There was a fair amount of litter on the ground, but not the obligatory smell of urine that one encountered in any abandoned edifice in Ceylon. As Balendran reached the doorway, he remembered that when he had changed here in the past with his brother or his son, they had taken turns holding each other's clothes, there being no clean spot to put them down. He realized he would have to do the same for Richard. "I . . . I'll hold your clothes. There's nowhere to set them down," he said.

Richard nodded, yet he did not look at Balendran.

When they were inside, Richard turned away and started to undress, his hands fumbling with the buttons of his shirt. He handed it to Balendran, then paused, as if unsure what to do next. He turned away and began to unbuckle his trousers. Balendran, despite his uneasiness, found himself looking at Richard's back, the way the muscles around his shoulder blades flexed and relaxed as he moved his arms. Richard pulled his trousers down, revealing the smooth whiteness of his buttocks. He had to turn now to hand his trousers to Balendran and get his bathing costume from him. As he did so, Balendran could not help looking at his nakedness, so familiar even after all these years, the scar below his right hip, the unusual sparseness of hair at his groin, the crinkled tightness of his testicles, the fold of his penis over it. A pocket of warmth formed at the base of Balendran's spine and spread down his thighs. He looked away quickly at the walls of the room to distract himself.

When it was Balendran's turn to change, he undressed quickly, handing Richard his clothes. Once he had put on his bathing costume, he turned to his friend. Richard was looking at him intently. Balendran frowned questioningly. In reply, Richard stepped up to him and kissed him lightly on the lips. He handed Balendran his clothes, turned abruptly, and went out of the room. Balendran was astounded. After a moment he followed.

His friend was at the bottom of the steps, waiting.

"Richard . . ."

"Yes, I know," he smiled. "Let the hearings begin."

Balendran did not smile. He looked at the ground in front of him, trying to think of what he wanted to say. "What happened in the guard room —"

"Yes, I understand."

"What?" Balendran asked in surprise.

"I'm sorry," Richard said. "I jumped the gun. I thought you were going to say it was an abberation that should never happen again."

Balendran was silent. "I was going to say it was a surprise."

Richard looked at the clothes in his hands. Something about his expression made Balendran bend forward and peer at him. "You . . . you were surprised too, weren't you?"

Richard shrugged. "I don't know. Yes, yes, I suppose I was."

Balendran stared at his friend in astonishment.

"What?" Richard snapped. "Why are you staring at me?" He turned and hurriedly went up the steps.

Balendran gazed after his friend, a realization before him. In the last week, he had come to enjoy, even covet, his company, the strain of being reunited having lifted. He realized that, with

Richard, he could truly be himself. He felt now that Richard had sought, and had been gratified by, his attention for different reasons.

"Wait," he called out.

Richard stood at the top of the steps, a sullen expression on his face.

Balendran went up the steps to him.

"I value our friendship too highly to let things pass like this, Richard. Tell me, honestly, what are your feelings."

Richard looked at his feet. "Very well," he said. "In this last week, I have fallen in love with you. All over again."

Balendran, now that he had heard it, could no longer hope it was not so.

"I understand, obviously, that you don't feel the same. Though I was mistaken in thinking you did."

They were both silent. Balendran could think of only one way to respond – to say that he was married, had a son, and a home, that Richard had Mr. Alliston, that they led different lives in different countries – but he knew this would only sound patronizing. The fact was that Richard had fallen in love with him and he did not return that feeling, something he could not bring himself to say. Balendran felt their friendship begin to come apart, like the creaking close of an ancient door.

By the time they left the Galle fort, the sun was setting rapidly and long shadows lay across the ramparts. Some of the narrow streets of the fort were already in darkness because of the shade cast by the buildings on either side. A brisk wind had come in from the sea and it blew pieces of scrap paper and tin cans along in front of the car. As they went out through the fort entrance, Balendran looked back and found it difficult to believe that just an hour ago they had driven in through this very entrance. Days seemed to have passed. As he turned back in his seat, the sight of his friend's face was a reminder of just how much had changed in this brief time. For now their silence was no longer companionable. It sat between them like the growing darkness outside.

Balendran sat back in his seat, staring straight ahead. A deep melancholy began to take hold of him.

When the car pulled up in front of the estate bungalow, Uma was standing by the front steps. She had been waiting for Balendran's arrival, and her expression told him that she expected him to come and settle her problem right away. He nodded towards her, then led Richard inside.

The estate bungalow was a simple building, constructed for inspections. Its architecture was closer to a village hut than a colonial-style bungalow. The roof was of thatched coconut palms and the walls of wattle and daub, whitewashed. A verandah ran around the entire house. It was a cool house, the wattle and daub and the roofing kept it so. There were two bedrooms to the right of the living and dining room. Balendran looked in both and, seeing that one room was better made up than the other, he offered it to Richard and took the remaining one. The houseboy was helping Joseph unload the provisions that had been sent along for their meals. Balendran told him to look after Richard's needs, then he said to Richard, "I have to go and see about this matter," he gestured towards Uma. "The girl has been waiting for me."

Richard looked at him, not sure if he was using it as an excuse to get away, but Uma's anxious face dispelled his suspicion and he nodded.

Balendran took his hat and walking-stick and followed Uma as she went down the front steps holding a kerosene lantern in front of her.

Balendran was usually very careful to placate and humour the kangany while, at the same time, ensuring the welfare of the workers. This time, because of what had happened between him and Richard, he displayed none of his usual diplomacy and was particularly harsh with the kangany. Uma's future husband, quick to see his stupidity, begged Uma's forgiveness. By the time the whole affair was settled, Balendran was exhausted. He glanced at his watch and saw that it was already 9:30. Richard was waiting for dinner.

Uma and her grateful mother accompanied him back, swinging their lanterns in front of him to light his way. Understanding his tiredness, they escorted him in silence. When they were almost at the bungalow, however, Uma's mother said, "Durai, we would be honoured by your presence at my daughter's wedding next week."

"Next week," Balendran said and thought immediately about the Donoughmore hearings. "I'm afraid I will be —" He stopped himself. Next week, the commission began its tour of the country and Richard went with them. The plan had been that he would accompany Richard. Given their current estrangement, however, this would not be so. Then a realization was before Balendran. This was the last time he and Richard would be together. It was unbearable that they should part this way.

He had reached the end of the path and he gestured to the women to leave him. He hurried towards the lights of the bungalow.

When he came in through the front door, Balendran stopped in dismay. Richard was not in the living room and his bedroom door was closed. Only Balendran's share of the dinner was on the table. The houseboy had placed it under a fly cover and left the bungalow for the night. Balendran stared at Richard's bedroom door, unsure only for a moment. Then he crossed over, knocked on the door, and, without waiting for a response, went inside.

Richard had changed into his pyjamas and was in bed.

"I refuse to let our friendship end as it stands," Balendran said to a startled Richard. "In silence."

He came and sat by him on the edge of the bed. "Our friendship means something important to me. In the time you've been here I have come to realize that in some sense you are the only one who truly understands me." He took Richard's hand in his. "You'll be gone in a few weeks and —" Balendran stopped, a swift sadness rising in him. Then, before he quite knew what he was doing, Balendran reached over and kissed Richard on the lips. When he withdrew, Richard, with a quick movement, held Balendran's face between his hands. They were still, looking at each other.

"You *do* love me," Richard said.

And this time, Balendran did not protest.

After a moment, Richard drew him down onto the bed, next to him.

13

Swift as one's hand to slipping clothes
Is a friend in need.
— The Tirukkural, *verse 778*

Time was running out. Paravathy and Muttiah would be here in two days.

At the end of the morning session the next day, Annalukshmi asked Miss Lawton and Nancy if she might have a word with them. Standing in the headmistress's office, Annalukshmi told them of the arrival of Parvathy and Muttiah and the marriage that was being forced upon her.

"This is terrible," Miss Lawton cried. "You cannot allow yourself to be married to a man you dislike, Anna. You simply cannot allow it. And a Hindu at that."

Nancy looked at her friend. "You have some plan up your sleeve, don't you?"

Annalukshmi nodded, then turned to Miss Lawton. "I am thinking," she said, "of your friend Mary Sisler."

She then told them of her notion. Her idea was to run away to Mary Sisler's and stay there for the two weeks that Muttiah and Parvathy were in Ceylon. Mary Sisler was an old school friend of Miss Lawton. The three of them had often spent time together during their school holidays at the tea plantation in Nanu Oya where she lived with her husband. It would not be as if she were staying with a complete stranger. The month-long Christmas holidays began at the end of the week, so Miss Lawton would only have to arrange a relief teacher for a short while.

Miss Lawton placed a telephone call to her friend and explained that Annalukshmi was in a "spot of bother" and needed to stay with her for two weeks. Mary Sisler immediately agreed.

It was decided that Annalukshmi would take the morning train on Wednesday, the day that Parvathy and Muttiah arrived. Now that her escape was more of a reality, Annalukshmi felt a great sense of relief, a lightness within her.

It was further decided that afternoon that Mr. Jayaweera would chaperon her. At first Annalukshmi was reluctant to put him to such trouble, as he would have to take the train there and then immediately return, a seven-hour journey each way. Mr. Jayaweera was, however, insistent, pointing out that it was not safe for a young woman to travel alone.

That evening, as Annalukshmi sat in the window-seat watching her mother busy herself around the drawing room, she felt, for the first time, a sinking feeling in her stomach at the thought of having to deceive her. She had decided that she would send a letter to her mother on Wednesday morning, once she was at Miss Lawton's bungalow. In the letter, she would tell her mother that she had gone away to a safe place and would be back once their relatives had left. The letter would reach Louisa the same evening. Yet there would be those few hours in the afternoon when her mother would have no idea what had happened to her. She tried to tell herself that her mother, once she received that letter, would be secretly relieved she had run away, relieved that this marriage would not go through. Yet she knew her mother would only be troubled about where her daughter was, if she were really in safe hands. Annalukshmi tried to be angry with her mother, silently accusing her of being inept at resisting her husband's order, of being cowardly for not standing up to her father. But she found it difficult to sustain her wrath when she thought of the terrible embarrassment of her mother when Parvathy and Muttiah arrived all the way from Malaya on a wasted journey. She even contemplated, for a moment, telling her mother of her plan but immediately dismissed the notion.

The thought of one parent led inevitably to the other. In all her deliberations, Annalukshmi had forgotten that her father would be irate when he found out about her disobedience. She recalled with a shudder the quarrel with her father, her helplessness to prevent him from striking her, her weakness against his strength. Her wariness of him and his understanding of it made the month he spent in Colombo every year truly unbearable for both of them. She was filled with fear now that all the irritation and anger he harboured towards her would find a new outlet. She would suffer the physical effect of it.

But she would rather face her father's wrath for a short time than acquiesce to a lifetime of misery as Muttiah's wife.

❧

When Annalukshmi arrived at Miss Lawton's bungalow on Wednesday morning, she found the headmistress, Nancy, and Mr. Jayaweera waiting for her. As already planned, Nancy had packed a bag with some of her clothes for Annalukshmi to take with her. It was by Mr. Jayaweera's feet.

"Well, Anna," Miss Lawton said. "Everything's in order. I have called for a taxi and it should be here momentarily." Then, seeing her downcast expression, she added, "Mary is very hospitable, as you well know. You will be in fine hands. And don't forget, we will be up on the weekend to see you. So you won't be alone very long."

Miss Lawton now handed her the train tickets. The nervousness that had been with Annalukshmi from the time she got up this morning now turned to dread. She excused herself and went to the toilet.

Once she had shut the door behind her, she quickly splashed her face with water, hoping that this would calm her down. But it did not help. At that moment, she heard the honk of the taxi outside the gate. Annalukshmi stood unable to move.

There was a knock at the door.

"Hurry up," Nancy said. "The taxi is here."

She was silent.

"Annalukshmi, are you all right?" Nancy turned the doorknob. Annalukshmi had not locked it and her friend came inside. She stood looking at her, concerned.

"You know, you don't have to do this," Nancy said.

"No . . . I'm fine."

When they came out of the house, Miss Lawton and Mr. Jayaweera were waiting. The taxi was at the gate and the driver pressed his horn impatiently.

"Well, come along then," Miss Lawton said.

Annalukshmi, feeling slightly disoriented, began to follow Miss Lawton and Mr. Jayaweera.

The taxi driver was, by now, very angry at being kept waiting, and when he saw them come out of the gate, he started to harangue them about wasting his time.

"Be quiet, you stupid, stupid man," Miss Lawton yelled at him, losing her temper.

At this, the driver got into the taxi and slammed the door.

Miss Lawton quickly ushered Annalukshmi inside. Mr. Jayaweera got in too.

Nancy leant in through the window. "I'll see you in a few days," she said.

She had barely spoken when the driver revved his engine and took off, his tires grinding up the dust.

"Goodbye, goodbye," Miss Lawton and Nancy cried out.

Annalukshmi did not wave back. She rested her head against the seat and closed her eyes.

For a Wednesday afternoon, the train proved to be surprisingly crowded. Once Annalukshmi and Mr. Jayaweera had found their seats in the last car of the train, they sat across from each other by the window. Their compartment was full. There were two older Ceylonese ladies seated next to Mr. Jayaweera. Annalukshmi could tell that one of them was Tamil. Like her, she wore a pottu on her forehead and draped her sari in the Tamil style, the palu wound around the hips and tucked in at the back. Both ladies wore expensive Paris chiffon saris. On Annalukshmi's left was an older Ceylonese man and, next to him, an European lady.

They had not been seated long when the door slid open and another Ceylonese gentleman entered. He was in his late forties and, just from the cut of his suit and his fine walking-stick, it was clear that he was wealthy. He stopped in surprise when he saw that the compartment was full. He glanced at his ticket and then at the seat numbers. "Excuse me, sir," he said to Mr. Jayaweera civilly. "I believe you are in my seat."

Annalukshmi and Mr. Jayaweera looked at each other in surprise. All the other passengers were now staring at them.

They took out their tickets and checked them, wondering if they were in the wrong compartment. But they were not.

"I am sorry, sir, but you are making mistake," Mr. Jayaweera said politely.

The man looked Mr. Jayaweera up and down, noting his threadbare suit. "Sir," he said and his manner was no longer civil, "I am sure you are the one who is mistaken. This is a first-class carriage." He looked around at the other passengers and saw that the Ceylonese were in complicity with him. The European woman had her lips pursed to say that, as far as she was concerned, they were all in the wrong compartment.

Against this united opposition, Mr. Jayaweera seemed unsure of himself. He glanced at his ticket again.

"These are our seats, sir," Annalukshmi said, "You must be mistaken."

The gentleman took in her polished speech and manner, her nice Georgette sari. His face registered his surprise. "Madam," he said politely, "may I see your tickets."

Annalukshmi and Mr. Jayaweera handed him their tickets. He looked at them carefully and then gave them back. "It seems there must have been an overbooking," he said, addressing himself solely to Annalukshmi. "Perhaps, madam, we could reach a compromise. You can stay here and I can ask the railway guard to find your man a seat in another compartment, though it probably will be second class as first class appears to be full."

Annalukshmi bristled at how he had referred to Mr. Jayaweera as "your man," as if he were a gardener or a labourer.

She straightened her back. "I am afraid it is you who will have to find yourself another seat, sir."

The gentleman recoiled from her words as if he had been slapped. The other passengers murmured in disapproval. The European lady stood up and left the compartment.

"Madam, I have tried to be polite but —"

"Please, Miss Annalukshmi, don't concern —"

"Sir, your politeness is neither here nor there. These are our seats. We were here first. If there is an overbooking, since you arrived later, you must pay the consequence of it."

The gentleman's face became red, and the other Ceylonese passengers now began to add their bit.

"Why don't you behave like a lady," the Tamil woman said to Annalukshmi.

"Yes, shouting and screaming like a street vendor," her companion added.

"It is terrible what the younger generation has come to," said the older man.

"And what exactly are your relations to this man?" the gentleman demanded. "Are you married to him?"

Annalukshmi flushed in anger and mortification at what the man was implying.

"I thought so," he said, nodding knowingly.

Mr. Jayaweera now stood up. "Sir," he said, "there is no reason to speak like that." He turned to Annalukshmi. "I will settle this and go to second class." And, with that, he walked out of the compartment.

"No," Annalukshmi said, and she stood up. "Since you have forced this man to give up his seat for you, then I will have to leave with him and you will be guilty of denying a lady her seat."

For the first time, she saw the gentleman become unsure of himself. She pressed her advantage. "You have also insulted my honour by implying that my relations are improper with this man who has been sent along to chaperon me."

"Madam, I did not mean to say that there was anything improper –"

"Sir, you implied it." She allowed a tremulous note to enter her voice. "You have insulted my honour in front of all these people, dragged me down from my position as a lady."

"Yes, sir," the Tamil lady said, now switching sides in that way interested bystanders often did. "It was disgraceful to say that."

"You are not wanted in here, sir," her companion added. "We are ladies and God knows who you will insult next."

The gentleman saw that he had been worsted. He turned and left without a word.

Annalukshmi went to look for Mr. Jayaweera. She saw him at the end of the carriage, standing in the open doorway, smoking a cigarette.

She walked over to him. "I'm sorry about all that. Please come back, that dreadful man has gone."

"Why don't you go back," he replied after a moment. "I'll follow you once I have finished my cigarette."

14

Duty is not for reward:
Does the world recompense the rain-cloud?
— The Tirukkural, *verse 211*

Balendran and Richard had extended their stay at the estate by
a few days. Balendran had sent word to Sonia.

On their return to Colombo, Balendran left Richard at the
hotel. When the car turned down Seaside Place, Balendran was
aware of how much had changed in his life. He found himself
observing Sevena keenly, as if he expected it to have altered.

When he approached the verandah, Sonia did not come out
to greet him. He went up the front steps into the drawing room.
It was empty. He felt a strange foreboding take hold of him.
"Sonia," he called out.

"Here," Sonia replied from his study.

He walked quickly to the door and went inside. She was in
front of the flower bowl making an arrangement. She looked up
at him briefly. "Oh, hello," she said, then returned to her work.

A momentary panic took hold of him. Sonia knew, she had
somehow found out about him and Richard. He shook himself,
aware that he was being foolish. She was just resentful that she

had been left behind. He placed his hat and walking-stick on a chair. Then he turned to her and waited, willing to deal with her disaffection, so much preferable was it to the alternative he had just considered.

She continued to busy herself with the flower arrangement. "Did Richard find the estate interesting?" she finally asked.

"Yes," he replied, "I think he was impressed by my work."

"Good."

There was a silence between them.

"Well," Balendran said, "perhaps I should go and wash up before dinner."

Sonia nodded imperceptibly.

Balendran walked away from her. He was almost at the door when she said, "By the way, there is a note from Appa on the desk for you."

She spoke casually, yet Balendran felt the air was charged with peril. He went quickly to the desk, picked up the note, and opened it.

I have been to the temple again and the tills are still not cleared. I came looking for you today to find you were at the estate. I must travel to Jaffna by the night train and be there when the commission arrives. In my absence, attend to my affairs at Brighton.

Balendran put the piece of paper down. "What . . . what did you tell Appa?" he asked, trying to keep his voice from shaking.

"That you had been to the estate."

"You know how Appa feels about Richard. I hope you didn't mention that he accompanied me."

"Yes, when your father came by and asked where you were, I told him that you had gone to the estate, that Mr. Howland went with you."

Balendran felt a quick anger rise in him. "What on earth possessed you to say that?" he demanded.

"Why should I have to lie?" Sonia replied. She stood back, looked at her arrangement, nodded in satisfaction, then walked towards the door. "Dinner will be in half an hour," she added as she went out.

The moment she had left, Balendran sat down and placed his head in his hands. He stared at the note in front of him and wondered how much his father knew, what he suspected. The very fact that his father had made no mention of Richard going with him was extremely ominous. Despite his efforts to reassure himself about what conclusions his father had drawn, Balendran felt as if he were playing a mental game of blind man's bluff. He was possessed by an overwhelming desire to be in his father's presence, to read for himself, in his father's eyes and manner, what his thoughts were. Balendran quickly stood and picked up his hat and walking-stick from the chair. His father would not have left yet.

Sonia was in the drawing room and she looked up at him in surprise as he walked towards the front door. "I am going to see Appa," he said.

She raised her eyebrows questioningly, but he felt he owed her no explanation.

When Balendran arrived at Brighton, there was a flurry of activity going on around his father's car. As he came through the front door, his mother was walking up the stairs, Pillai's wife,

Rajini, following her with a pile of laundered sheets. She saw her son and came quickly downstairs again. She took his face between her hands, kissed him on both cheeks, and said, "We are preparing your old room. Just the way it used to be."

He looked at her, not comprehending, and she frowned, puzzled. "Don't you know?" she asked. "Appa has asked you to come and keep me company during his absence."

Balendran stared at her in shock.

"I told him it was unnecessary. But, you know, I have been a little sick recently and he was concerned about leaving me alone."

Even before he saw his father, Balendran had the answer he sought. He felt light-headed.

The study door opened. His father came out, followed by Miss Adamson.

When the Mudaliyar saw Balendran, he stopped in surprise. Balendran glanced quickly at his father and then away, afraid to meet his gaze.

"What is this?" Nalamma demanded of the Mudaliyar. "Thambi-boy doesn't know he is to stay with me?"

"Come," the Mudaliyar said to Balendran and went back into his study.

Balendran followed. As soon as he was in front of his father's desk, he sat down in a chair, afraid his legs would give way under him. He put his walking-stick and hat on the chair next to him.

"I'm glad I was able to see you," the Mudaliyar said. Then he busied himself at his table, searching through his documents.

The Mudaliyar took a long time, and Balendran, after a moment, glanced up at his father, perplexed. Then he saw that his father was finding it difficult to look at him.

"I made up this list of things I need you to do." The Mudaliyar held out a sheet of paper to Balendran.

Balendran took it, his hand trembling.

"Also, I would like you and Sonia to come and stay with your mother. She has not been too well of late and I am worried about leaving her alone at night. How does this suit you?"

Balendran looked up and their eyes met for the first time. Then an expression flickered across the Mudaliyar's face, an anxious, almost pleading look. His father was begging for confirmation that his fears were unfounded.

"Yes, Appa," Balendran said, trying to keep his voice steady. "You don't have to worry. All will be fine in your absence."

The relief flooded his father's face.

"I knew I could count on you," the Mudaliyar said.

At that moment, Miss Adamson came in to announce that everything was ready. As the Mudaliyar came around the side of his desk, he placed his hand on Balendran's shoulder and squeezed it, then he went out. This gesture of affection, so rare from the Mudaliyar, filled Balendran with love for his father. Yet, simultaneous with this love, he felt a burning shame. There was a photograph of his son, Lukshman, prominently displayed on his father's desk. Balendran picked it up. The photograph had been taken in Nuwara Eliya during the racing season. Lukshman stood with the Mudaliyar's favourite horse, Nellie. It was a lovely photograph, Lukshman leaning his head against the horse's neck, a contented smile on his face, the sun in his hair. As Balendran stared at the photograph, he had a sudden vision of that smile leaving his son's face replaced by horror and revulsion at his father's crime. He thought of his wife. Sonia was so dependent for her happiness, her existence, on the life they had created together. Their house, Sevena, was all the world she had. How such a revelation would shatter her he could not even allow himself to imagine. Just then he heard his father's car starting up.

He went to the window and stood watching as it began to inch forward, past the study window and along the driveway. As he gazed at its disappearing lights, he felt his illusions leaving him. Balendran picked up his hat and walking-stick and went to find his own car.

At the Galle Face Hotel, the receptionist was busy with visitors. Rather than waiting for a message to be sent, Balendran went quickly to the lift and had the attendant take him to Richard's floor.

As the lift started to rise, Balendran felt fear in the pit of his stomach. Yet he reminded himself of his son, his father, his wife, his life here in Ceylon, and this steadied him for the encounter with Richard.

He knocked on the door, and, after a moment, Richard opened it. He was in his dressing gown and was drying his hair with a towel. "Well, what a pleasant surprise." He opened his arms and Balendran started to move past him. Richard held his wrist and looked at his friend's face searchingly. "What have we here?"

Balendran did not reply. Then he said, "My father knows . . . at least suspects what's happened between us."

Richard swallowed hard and sat down on the bed. "How?" he asked softly.

Balendran waved his hand to say that it was not important. "Anyway, I allayed his suspicions." He crossed to the window.

Richard waited, watching him.

"At a price, however." Balendran paused. "My father is going to Jaffna for the hearings. I am to stay at Brighton with my mother. Attend to my father's business."

"Well, that's not too bad, is it?" Richard said with relief. "I'll just stay behind. Being together is more important than the wretched hearings."

The relief on Richard's face pained Balendran. He found it difficult to go on. He knew when he next spoke he would shatter his friend. Yet he had to get this done with for the sake of his son, his family. Then, gazing out the window, he took a deep breath and said, "I think you should go."

He heard Richard exhale and he turned to him. Richard was staring at him in astonishment. Then Balendran saw the apprehension enter his friend's eyes. "What . . . what are you saying to me, Bala?" Richard asked, his voice shaking.

Balendran felt an aching sorrow, an overwhelming urge to take Richard in his arms. Instead, he looked away at the sea, gripping the windowsill until this urge passed and he recovered his resolve.

Richard got up and came to him. He took him by the shoulders and forced him to turn around. Balendran kept his head down, but Richard grabbed his face in his hands. "Do you love me?" he demanded.

Balendran did not reply.

"Well?"

"No . . . I don't know."

"You don't know," Richard shouted. "That's not good enough. Not good enough at all."

Balendran moved his head, trying to break away from Richard's hands, but his friend tightened his grip. Richard then bent over and kissed him roughly, biting down hard on his lower lip. Balendran cried out in pain and broke from his hold. He touched his lip and saw that it was bleeding. He took his handkerchief out and dabbed at his wound. Then he glared at Richard. "What did you expect?" he cried. "Where did you think all this would go? Did you actually expect me to leave my life here for . . . for what?"

"I would willingly leave my life with Alli for you."

"I am married with a child. How can you compare what I have with what you have."

Richard drew himself together. "Get out," he said. "Just get out of my room."

Balendran started towards the door, but, as he passed him, Richard grabbed his arm and tried to twist it behind his back. Balendran broke away from him. "Stop it, Richard," he said, "just stop it."

Richard hit out, but Balendran grabbed his hand and pulled Richard to him. "Just stop it," he said softly as he held him. "It's over, don't you see? It's all over."

After a moment, he pushed Richard away gently and hurried to the door.

"Bala," Richard called out. "Please wait."

Balendran opened the door and went out into the corridor. He began to walk quickly towards the lift, finally breaking into a run when he heard Richard call out to him again. Rather than wait for the lift, he went down the stairs. On the first landing, he leant against the wall and breathed in deeply, trying to gain control of himself. Then he walked down the last few steps to the Galle Face Hotel foyer.

As Balendran's car began to pull away, he looked back at the hotel and felt a terrible emptiness. He wanted to put his head in his hands and rub at his face in an attempt to erase that last image of Richard, the entreaty in his eyes as he had begged him to wait. He wanted to weep. Yet he was the Mudaliyar Navaratnam's son and such things were not permitted in the presence of the driver. Decorum compelled him to sit up straight like a gentleman, his hands clasped uselessly in his lap.

℈

That very night, Balendran and Sonia went to stay with his mother at Brighton. As the car took them through the darkened streets of Colombo, they were both silent, lost in their own worlds, looking out at the looming, great trees on either side of the road, the occasional streetlamp that cast a pool of light on the deserted pavements. After a while, Balendran became aware that his wife was looking at him, and he turned to her.

"I've been thinking about something," Sonia said. "It's been a shamefully long time since I've seen Aunt Ethel and she is getting old. I'd like to go to England for a little while. Spend some time with her and Lukshman."

Balendran felt a foreboding in the pit of his stomach. He tried to see the expression on Sonia's face, but she was half hidden in the darkness of the car. "When . . . when you say a little while, what do you mean?"

"Oh, I was thinking that perhaps I would go right after Christmas and return by April."

"Well," he said, "of course. If that's what you want."

"I had even thought of going for Christmas," Sonia said. "To spend it with Lukshman, but I would not feel good about leaving you alone."

They were silent again.

When the car turned into Brighton, Balendran felt along the

seat for his wife's hand, took it, and squeezed it. Sonia did not return his pressure.

In the days that followed, Balendran silently thanked his father for having asked him to stay at Brighton. In his childhood home, in the very room in which he had grown up, with its pictures on the walls, the creaking of the old fan that lulled him to sleep at night, Balendran found a constant reminder of the life he had in Ceylon, the life that, he told himself, ultimately mattered. His mother, so happy to have her child back in her home, re-created the food of his childhood: uppuma in the morning, ravva ladu spiced with cardamom in the way he liked them. He took comfort in these foods, as if he were an invalid slowly recovering from a long illness.

Yet Balendran was far from free of the pain of Richard. During the day, his father's duties kept him from thinking too much of his friend. In the evenings, however, when he would sit on the front verandah of Brighton and read in the newspapers about the hearings of the commission in various cities, a searing ache would build in his chest. Still, even as he felt the pain of Richard, Balendran would look out at Sonia cutting flowers in the garden alongside his mother, their heads companionably side by side. The look of contentment and serenity on her face made more horrible the thought of discovery.

His revulsion was comforting to him. It questioned the depth of his love for Richard and made him aware that he did love his wife, that she was, in many ways, his dear friend. This understanding made him hopeful that somewhere in the future his love for Richard would diminish or become simply a famil-iar impediment.

When the shadows grew long across the lawns of Brighton, Balendran would put down his paper and go out to join his wife. Taking Sonia's hand in his, they walked around the grounds, reviewing the happenings of the day and examining any changes that had come to the garden.

15

Learn well what should be learnt, and then
Live your learning.
— The Tirukkural, *verse 391*

The Sisler estate bungalow in Nanu Oya was perched along a ridge. There was a semicircular terrace at the back of the bungalow and, from here, the estate sloped sharply down to the valley below, the green of the tea bushes spotted with the brightly clad tea pluckers at work. There was a bench at the edge of the terrace, shaded by a cypress tree. It was here that Annalukshmi spent most of her days, gazing out at the hills, lost in thought. The book she had brought with her lay face down on the bench next to her. Every time she tried to read, she felt vaguely nauseated, in the same way she would if she tried reading with a fever. Her thoughts constantly drifted to what her mother must have felt when she received her letter. She wondered if Louisa had suspected Miss Lawton was involved, if she had confronted the headmistress and demanded the truth from her. Would she, Annalukshmi, look up from her deliberations one day to find her mother standing at the back door of the bungalow, her arms folded in anger? That image made her apprehensive, but it was the thought of her father that truly made her feel terror. Every time she thought of his wrath, she shivered, pacing the terrace to try to dismiss him from her mind. The constant worry soured her stomach, making it difficult for her to eat.

Her unhappiness had been observed by both Mary Sisler and her cook. They tried in their different ways to remedy it. The cook would approach her each morning and, under the guise of narrating his life history, describe all the delicious meals he had prepared for the various masters and mistresses he had worked for. Annalukshmi, finally taking pity on him, would ask a question about a particular meal, knowing that she would be sure to find it waiting for her at the table. Mary Sisler, a kind but rather shy woman, had her own remedy. Every evening, she would insist that Annalukshmi sit in the drawing room with her husband and her and listen to their Gilbert and Sullivan records. "Nothing like a jolly old tune in the evening," she would say at the end of every record, and Annalukshmi would nod in agreement.

Annalukshmi eagerly awaited Miss Lawton and Nancy's arrival. From Friday afternoon, she went to the top of the driveway every hour or so and scanned the road to see if a taxi was approaching, hoping that, somehow, they had left Colombo earlier.

As it happened, Annalukshmi missed them when they finally came, having gone into the house briefly. But when she heard a car door slam, she hurried through the drawing room and out to the front. Miss Lawton and Nancy were at the centre of a flurry of activity as the various houseservants handled their luggage, supervised by Mary Sisler. When Miss Lawton and Nancy saw Annalukshmi, they both cried out. Miss Lawton hurried to her and grasped her hands. "Anna, dear Anna, there has been a very, very strange development in Colombo."

Miss Lawton put her arm around Annalukshmi's shoulders. She led her inside to the drawing room and made her sit down in a chair. Then she silently handed her a letter. "I hope you don't mind," she said. "I took the liberty of reading it in case there was an emergency that required your return."

Annalukshmi opened the letter and recognized Kumudini's writing.

Akka,

I feel that Miss Lawton knows where you are. Hence, I have sent this to her.

Certain things have happened since you left and, as I am at the centre of them, Manohari and I feel that I should be the one to inform you.

You can well imagine our panic and horror when you didn't turn up after school. Parvathy Maamee and Muttiah had already arrived by then. Amma was frantic and was all set to go to the police station when your letter arrived. From all her worry, Amma fainted on the spot. Manohari and I both feel that you should know this. Just to understand the difficulty you have caused her and all of us. It was very selfish and hard of you to subject us to this. Poor Amma, she had to face the terrible, terrible embarrassment of explaining your absence to Parvathy Maamee.

Now, here is the surprising thing. You know how we have always hated Parvathy Maamee, called her Snotty Mukkuthi and blamed her for Appa becoming a Hindu again. So, naturally, we expected that she would be very angry. Instead, she clapped her hands together, laughing in delight. "Like father, like daughter," she said. Then she told us how Appa had fled their house in Jaffna in the same way, leaving a note behind. Her kindness and good humour in the face of your inconsideration (don't forget they travelled for two weeks <u>on deck</u> to get here) completely changed how we felt about her. Since then, we have come to see her for what she might truly be. A kind aunt with a gentle temperament.

Akka, it is about Muttiah that I now wish to speak. Two days after they arrived, Parvathy Maamee approached Amma with a curious request. Would Amma consent to Muttiah marrying me? Of course Amma was not at all happy about this, as you can imagine, since Muttiah is a Hindu. She graciously but firmly refused, without even consulting me. When I heard about her rejection of their offer, I was not pleased. To tell you the truth, I had noticed, since they arrived, that Muttiah looked at me often. I must confess that, right from the start, I found him very pleasant and handsome too. So I had a long talk with Amma and convinced her to see things differently, that as long as we had a Christian wedding, as long as I remained a Christian and my children too, no harm was done by my marrying Muttiah. Poor Parvathy Maamee. I felt sorry for her that I had to make these conditions. At the same time, I cannot and will not agree to the marriage without these conditions. She finally consented.

There rests only one further issue and that is your permission. Please think of this carefully before you agree. Promise me you will put yourself first in this matter knowing that, if the marriage goes through, it will place you on the shelf with very little prospect of getting married. Later, it will seem that you were passed over because of some defect – you can only imagine the fabrications that will ensue about your mental state, morals, etc.

Manohari wishes me to add that you must not be afraid to come home and face Amma. Parvathy Maamee's good humour in the face of all these difficulties has helped to calm Amma down. However, expect some ranting and raving on Amma's part.

I feel confident that this letter will reach you, and I await your reply. Kumu.

When Annalukshmi finished the letter, questions crowded her mind. One thought, however, dominated. She had to return home. She turned to Miss Lawton. "I must go back," she said.

Miss Lawton nodded to say that she had expected she would. "A train leaves from Nanu Oya early tomorrow morning," she said. "I have already asked Mr. Jayaweera to meet you at the Fort station with a taxi."

❧

Nancy offered to accompany Annalukshmi; Miss Lawton, at Mary Sisler's insistence, would stay the balance of the weekend.

On the train back to Colombo, Annalukshmi still felt stunned by the contents of Kumudini's letter, and by her sister's astonishing decision.

"I don't understand it at all," she said at one point. "I fear that Kumudini's desire to marry Muttiah comes out of desperation." She told Nancy now about the failure of the Nesiah proposal.

"I'm not disagreeing that she might feel desperate," Nancy said, "but on the other hand you can't ignore the possibility that she might actually like him."

Annalukshmi looked out at the green hills of the tea plantations. "I hope she knows what she's getting into," she said. "My mother has had such misery in her marriage because of religious differences." She turned to Nancy. "It was because of those differences and the trouble it caused that we finally came to Ceylon."

Nancy nodded for her to go on.

"My father and I . . . at one time, were devoted to each other. People used to say they were sorry for him because he didn't have a son. But my father said he did not care at all about it, that I was better than a son. He took me with him to the rubber estate, instructed me how to do the accounts, showed me how rubber was made. He even taught me to swim in the river that ran through our estate. He told me that, because there was no son in the family, he was training me to do the job, so that, when he was gone, I would be in charge. Then my Aunt Parvathy arrived in Malaya."

Annalukshmi was silent, thinking back to that time. "She brought with her the news that my grandfather had died. This changed my father. He became filled with remorse that he and his father had never reconciled, that he had not been there to do the most important task a son does for his father – light his funeral pyre. I think he began to regret his conversion to Christianity, his marriage to a Christian. My parents had a stormy marriage, always yelling at each other, but it was clear that underneath they loved each other. Now he began to treat my mother with the politeness one uses on strangers. I felt so sad for him because I could tell he was miserable, so I tried to be more affectionate, to do the little things he loved like massage his head with coconut oil. But he slowly began to change towards me too.

"A few weeks after my aunt arrived, he took us to visit her for the first time. We were sent to the back room where the other women were. Of course, in our house we sat wherever we wanted, so, after some time, without even thinking, I went into the front room to ask him a question. When I walked in, all the men became silent. My father looked away from me as if I had shamed him. On the way home that day he rebuked me. He told me I was uncouth, that he wanted me to learn from my aunt how to behave like a proper Jaffna Tamil woman. When he went to the estate the next time, he took my cousin Muttiah instead. I came back from school to find out that he had gone, without telling me.

"A few weeks later, my mother sent me to the shop to buy some rice for her. On my way back I took a shortcut that led past the local Hindu temple. I couldn't believe what I saw. Among the devotees leaving the temple, there was my father. He was furtively wiping the holy ash from his forehead so we wouldn't see it when he came home. It was at that moment that he looked up and saw me. He turned quickly and walked in the other direction, as if he hadn't seen me. It was then that I truly knew that the foundation of my parents' marriage was breaking. From then onwards, my father and I were locked together in this deception. An uneasy silence had fallen between us. Whenever he would try to approach me, to talk to me, ask me to do some chore, I held myself stiffly back. One day, he began to scold me because it was my turn to sweep the drawing room and I had forgotten. I let him go on for a while and then I said very quietly, 'Don't try to pretend we didn't see each other. At least have the decency to respect my intelligence.' Then he went mad. He grabbed me by the hair and began to hit me on my face and hands and shoulders. If my mother had not come in and stopped it, he might have seriously hurt me. When he finally let me go, my mother said to him, 'This is enough. I will not let our unhappiness affect the girls.' A few months later, we came to Ceylon."

By now the train had pulled into a station. Both of them watched the activity on the platform, Annalukshmi thinking about that difficult time in Malaya, Nancy considering what her friend had told her.

Once the train was moving again, Annalukshmi turned to Nancy. "I've never talked about this to anyone before."

"I, too, have things in my life that I keep hidden from others," Nancy said. "I have never told you the real story about my own family.

"My parents did not die of cholera. In fact, they didn't die of anything." She looked down at her hands. "They were murdered."

Annalukshmi drew in her breath, aghast.

"During the 1915 riots between the Muslims and Sinhalese."

"I . . . I don't know much about it. We were in Malaya then."

"I was a girl at the time, thirteen years old. A rumour came to our village that Muslims had murdered a Buddhist monk and hanged him from a tree. Of course this was not so at all, as I was to learn later. There had simply been some disagreement between Muslims and Sinhala Buddhists about parades and playing music in front of each other's places of worship. There was only one Muslim family in our village and they owned the village shop. A group of thugs attacked the shop that night, they looted the goods, then burned it down once they had locked the family inside. It was so terrible. It still comes back to me from time to time, the faces of that family in the window, their cries begging us villagers to unbar the door. But nobody did. The thugs were employed by the village headman who wanted to start up a shop of his own.

"Our village had just one Muslim family. In others there were many and in the towns whole sections were Muslim. So you can only imagine the carnage. The British, however, misinterpreted the whole thing as being an anti-colonial protest. So they armed British planters with guns and told them to go into the villages and shoot on sight. One night they came to our village.

"We were awakened by the sound of shouting and then there were shots. My mother immediately pushed me into a large wooden chest that was in our hut and shut the lid. From there I heard it all," Nancy's voice shook. "The harsh command of the planter, his servants dragging my parents from the house. Then there was silence and that was followed by gunfire. I don't know how long I stayed there. I think I fainted at one point, for when the villagers who had survived came to get me, the dawn was already breaking."

Annalukshmi placed her hand on her friend's shoulder. "I'm so sorry, Nancy. You should have told me before. Does Miss Lawton even know?"

"Oh, yes," Nancy said after a moment. "The planter who killed my parents was someone she knew. He felt remorseful, I suppose, and asked her to adopt me. I was always told by Miss Lawton that when people asked me about my parents, in order not to upset myself, or them, it was best to say that they had died of cholera. Why stir up a hornet's nest, etc. As a young girl, I accepted that Miss Lawton was right. Over the years, I admit I have felt resentful about the lie she asked me to tell."

Annalukshmi shook her head, amazed by what her friend was telling her.

Nancy smiled ruefully. "It's the British way. I suppose when you think you have the right to rule half the world for its own good, it's hard to admit that you are capable of making mistakes, that you are sorry and in need of forgiveness." She turned to Annalukshmi. "Whatever the circumstances, it was an act of benevolence on Miss Lawton's part. I don't want you thinking horribly of her, turning on her or something like that. She has loved me almost as she would a daughter. She has never made me feel like an object of charity or a burden. And just think of how my life would have been otherwise. Some poor girl in an orphanage, or sent off to work as a servant in some house."

Nancy was silent. "Miss Lawton's life has had its difficult moments," she said. "Here she might be a respected and influential figure, but in England, in the little town from which she comes, she is merely the daughter of a poor pastor. And one around whom there was some kind of scandal. It seems there was something to do with improper use of church funds. Though Miss Lawton has never said so directly, I gather he may have been relieved of his clerical duties. Can you imagine the shame for poor Miss Lawton? A young woman in a small town constantly living with the burden of her father's mistake. Perhaps this contributed to the reason why she decided to come out here and work in the colonies. Yet the fact is that one day Miss Lawton will have to retire, and if she were to leave Ceylon and return to her town, she would go back to simply being Amelia Lawton, the daughter of Reverend Lawton."

Nancy took her friend's hand. "So you see, Annalukshmi, it's not often easy to say that a person, be it your father or Miss Lawton or your aunt or your cousin, is simply this or that, bad or good."

The train now rounded a sharp bend, making their carriage

rock slightly from side to side. They could see the tail end of the train, the passengers in the crowded third class hanging out of the doorways, some even on the roof. The train let out a long, mournful whistle that echoed against the sides of the hills. Annalukshmi glanced at her friend. She realized she would never see Miss Lawton and Nancy the same way again.

ॐ

When Annalukshmi alighted from the taxi at Lotus Cottage, she saw Parvathy sitting on the front verandah and she felt her hands go cold. She pushed open the gate and went inside. At the creak of the gate, Parvathy turned to squint down the driveway. Then she rose from her chair in astonishment. "Kadavale!" she cried.

The sound of her voice brought Louisa and the girls out onto the verandah.

"Annalukshmi?" Louisa said as if she could not believe it was her daughter standing there at the bottom of the steps.

Annalukshmi waited, not sure what to expect.

Louisa recovered. "Do you think this house is a hotel, miss?" she cried. "You think you can come and go as you like?" She shook your finger at her. "You're lucky that I even let you in through the gate. And that Miss Lawton, I am disappointed that —"

"Miss Lawton had nothing to do with this, Amma. I've acted entirely of my own volition."

"Don't you try and talk back to me, miss."

Parvathy touched Louisa's arm. "Let her be, thangachi," she said. "She must be very tired after her long journey."

Louisa glared at Annalukshmi, then turned and walked back into the house.

The moment she was gone, Kumudini and Manohari rushed down to greet their sister. Manohari took her bag solicitously and Kumudini put her arm around her sister's shoulders. "Poor akka," she said. "You must be exhausted."

They led her up the verandah steps. Annalukshmi was before her aunt and she bent down quickly and touched her aunt's feet, as was the Hindu custom. Parvathy raised her to a standing position. She looked at her carefully and then patted her on the arm. "You need to have a bath after your trip."

They started towards the front door, when someone cleared his throat. Annalukshmi turned and saw Muttiah. He had come around the side of the house and was standing at the other end of the verandah. He looked the same as when she'd last seen him seven years before. The only difference was his luxuriant moustache stylishly curled at both ends.

Muttiah now spoke. "You . . . you are back."

He talked just as she remembered, the frown of concentration, the stumbling over his words, and, finally, the inanity of what he said. Muttal Muttiah. She glanced at Kumudini quickly. There was a demure smile on her face. She looked at Muttiah, again perplexed by what her sister might see in him.

"Do you remember that you planted an . . . an oleander shoot in your Malaya house garden many years ago?"

Annalukshmi looked at him, bewildered.

"And it died," he continued. "You were so upset. Do you remember how . . . how we teased you?" He smiled. "Annalukshmi is a silly bee, can't even plant a tree." He threw back his head and laughed, well pleased with himself.

Now she studied her cousin, noting the fastidiousness of his cream China silk suit, the carefully manicured nails, the absolutely straight part in his hair worn à la Valentino. He thinks he's the cat's meow, she thought to herself, partly amazed that he could actually think so. Such conceit would surely make him a selfish husband.

"Come, akka," Kumudini said gently and took her by the arm. "Come inside the house and have your bath."

"I don't think you know what you are doing, Kumu," Annalukshmi said as she sat down at the toilette table to dry her hair with a towel.

Kumudini, who was seated on the edge of her bed, drew herself together with injured dignity. "Oh and why is that, akka?"

"You know how Parvathy Maamee runs her house, Kumu. Could you be happy living like that?"

"Akka, I am not like you. I don't feel the need to go out all the time and have a say in every conversation."

"Well, do you love him?"

"I have some intelligence, akka. He has only been here a few days. I'm not foolish enough to think that love is like fireworks, puta-puta-puta the moment you meet someone. He is kind and very charming. Why shouldn't I grow to love him?"

Annalukshmi looked at Manohari, who was standing by the chest of drawers. "And what do you think?"

"To each his own, the old lady said, kissing her cow," Manohari replied tartly, adding, "I suppose he is handsome in his own way. He does dress very stylishly."

As Manohari spoke, Annalukshmi watched Kumudini in the toilette-table mirror and saw what she had never seen in her sister's face before — the flicker of desire in her eyes. She pictured Muttiah again, trying to see him as her sister did, but failed to do so. Still, there was another issue at stake. To marry Muttiah would slight their mother. And hadn't her mother's marriage suffered as a result of these very differences?

"The real question, akka, is whether you will consent or not," Manohari said.

"What about the fact that he is a Hindu?" Annalukshmi said, ignoring Manohari. "You know this would be a blow to Amma."

"She is not overly happy about it, but in time I hope she comes to accept it," Kumudini said.

"Don't forget, akka," Manohari added, "if Kumudini returns to Malaya as Muttiah's wife, Appa will let you off the hook for running away."

Annalukshmi had finished drying her hair, and she tossed her towel on the bed rather peevishly. "Well I don't see why my permission is needed. You have all pretty much decided what is to be done. Anyway, you seem to know what you are doing, so I suppose I must give my consent."

Kumudini's face flushed. "I know I will be happy. And I won't forget, akka, that you've put me before yourself." She came and hugged her sister. "Thank you," she said softly. Then she and Manohari went out of the bedroom to tell their mother.

Annalukshmi, left alone, picked up her brush and began to run it through her hair, a pensive expression on her face.

Book Two

16

Do I dwell in his thoughts always
As he in mine?
— The Tirukkural, *verse 1204*

In the four months that followed Richard's departure, Balendran set himself with great purposefulness to put aside the memory of his friend. Sonia had left in early January for England to visit her son and Lady Boxton. She would be away for three months.

The realization of what he had nearly lost helped Balendran in his endeavour. He tried hard to draw pleasure from the things around him. The estate gave him new delight. The reforms he had put into place over the years were now truly bearing fruit, the productivity of the estate soaring. It had become a showpiece and he was often solicited both by Europeans and Ceylonese for a tour so they could study his reforms. These excursion never amounted to anything, however, as the cornerstone of his success, labour reform, was unpalatable to his guests. Still, he felt vindicated that liberal measures could actually result in higher gains. Further, the price of rubber was at a peak, and the debit column of his ledger filled him with satisfaction.

Balendran had also taken up a long-time dream of his, to write a book on Jaffna culture. He was soon absorbed in this task, and came to love the time he spent with the villagers of Jaffna, discussing their rituals, understanding, with surprise, the variance of custom and language from village to village; the radically different culture of the barren little islands that surrounded the Jaffna peninsula, the language of the inhabitants almost a medieval Tamil.

All in all, it might be said that Balendran's attempt to forget his friend was an overwhelming success.

∾

One evening, towards the end of April, Balendran stopped by at Brighton on his return from a research trip. He had promised to inform his father about a sale he had conducted on a piece of family property in Jaffna. Learning from a servant that his father was not in, he was walking along the verandah to his car when he heard Pillai calling to him. He turned to see his father's servant hurrying down the front verandah towards him.

"Sin-Aiyah," Pillai said urgently, "Peri-Amma wants to see you upstairs."

Balendran looked at him closely, wondering what was wrong. Pillai took out his bunch of keys and let Balendran into the vestibule.

When Balendran reached the top of the stairs, he saw his mother pacing her drawing room. She came forward without a word and took his hands. "A terrible thing has happened. We got word today your brother is very ill."

Balendran stared at her in astonishment. "What did Arul say is wrong?"

"Not Arul. The servants told me. It's fatal."

Balendran glanced towards the stairs, but Pillai had left.

"Wouldn't Arul have contacted us directly if there was a problem like this?"

"Pillai's wife, Rajini, told me."

"Nonsense, Amma," Balendran said. "Rajini can't read or write. How would she have been in contact with them?"

Nalamma waved her hand impatiently. "What matters is not how we heard, but what we're going to do about it."

"Let us wait a few days and see," he said soothingly. "Perhaps some news will come to us."

"A few days might be too late."

When Balendran came out of the house, he noticed Pillai supervising the gardeners as they gathered up the leaves on the lawn. It struck him now that Pillai, unlike the other servants, was literate. Could Rajini have got the news from him? He recalled the way Pakkiam, his brother's wife, would sit between Rajini's legs every evening as Rajini combed out her hair. Pakkiam had been a surrogate daughter to the childless couple. He thought of the urgency with which Pillai had approached him to go and see his mother. Had Pillai been in contact with his brother? Even as he thought this, Balendran dismissed the notion. Pillai's favoured position as head servant was due to his absolute loyalty to his father, his absolute dedication to the welfare of the family, his absolute honesty. His father had made them all, Pillai included, swear in the household shrine not to have any contact with Arul. Pillai would never have defied his father in this manner. Even as he said this to himself, however, he remembered that his mother, so dutiful and obedient, had maintained some connection with his brother's family, enmeshing him in her duplicity.

As Balendran's car left Brighton, he leant back against his seat, exhausted from his long journey but also from the terrible

April heat. He thought of his brother's marriage to Pakkiam, who had worked as a servant for them. Twenty-eight years had passed since Arul had gone with her to India, and Balendran pondered, as he sometimes did, if there were problems between them, given their differences.

His brother was the son of a rich landowner, educated in English and European culture. He had spent his life in luxury. She was a Koviar, a low caste. As such, Pakkiam belonged to a different world. Before she came to Brighton, she had never seen electricity or running water, never sat on a chair, never had more than a single change of clothing. She could not read or write. Had it been a struggle to find a common base on which to build a life?

When Balendran got home, Sonia, now back from England a few weeks, was on the verandah, a troubled look on her face. He remembered immediately the news of his brother.

"Something has happened," he said as he came up the verandah steps.

She held out a telegram to him. "It's your brother."

He took it from her. FATHER VERY ILL. STOP. WON'T LAST A MONTH. STOP. WISHES TO SEE YOU. STOP. AT BOMBAY. STOP. YOUR NEPHEW, SEELAN.

Balendran felt the blood rush to his head. He sat down in a chair, afraid that his legs would give way under him.

"Are you going to go?" Sonia asked.

"I don't know," Balendran said after a moment. "I have to talk to Appa about it."

"And what if he says no?"

Balendran was silent, not having an answer. His mind was

too confounded by the shocking news. He stood up and straightened his coat. "I'm going back to Brighton," he said.

He picked up the telegram and went down the steps.

Sonia watched Balendran leave. She hoped he would have the strength to do as his heart wished in this matter and not obey his father's orders out of a sense of duty. She knew well the sadness of being at a distance when the death of a loved one was impending. Although she had basked in the happiness of her son's company once again during her time in London, her visit there had been coloured by some regret. Sonia had not been in London for twenty years, and, despite her regular correspondence with her aunt, Lady Boxton, Sonia felt that they had become strangers to each other. Her aunt's letters, chatty with news of social events in London, had not conveyed her growing frailty. Sonia, understanding that she might never see her aunt alive again, had endeavoured to bridge the missing years. During their afternoon teas, their mornings together while Lukshman was at his classes, Sonia would try to engage her aunt with stories of her life in Ceylon, but Lady Boxton, though she seemed to take in what Sonia said, appeared to be in the world of her own thoughts. Now Sonia wanted Balendran to have the opportunity to speak with his brother, at least make some attempt to re-establish the bonds that had been broken, before it was too late.

As the car left his house, Balendran looked at the telegram and felt a sense of disbelief that his brother was dying. He had got used to his absence, but, at the same time, he had also got used to the fact of his alternate life in Bombay. This other existence his mother kept alive and, in order to do so, she had involved him in her conspiracy. It was he who had to accompany her to the temple on his brother's birthday so she could offer a pooja; he who, after she had an inauspicious dream about Arul, had to instruct the priest to make an offering to Ganesh or go, himself, to St. Anthony's in Kochchikade. Then there was the son, Seelan. They had been sent a notice of his birth by Arul. A terse, typewritten, unsigned note. Every year, his mother sent a gold sovereign for Seelan's birthday. She directed it to the bank manager, Mr. Govind, who was responsible for paying the monthly stipend his father allotted Arul. Balendran had been aware of his brother's life and, in a strange way, had participated in it. Now he found it difficult to imagine that life ending, their connection being completely severed.

He looked at the telegram again, thinking of whether he would go or not. He knew that it depended on his father, but he had to admit that he did not wish to go.

Seven years separated the two brothers and, while that gap would be insignificant now, when Balendran was twelve, his brother had been nineteen and left Brighton with Pakkiam. They had never known each other as adults. His brother was, in many ways, a stranger to him. Compounding this alienation was the antagonism between them. Arul, until his relationship with Pakkiam was discovered, had enjoyed his father's favour. While Balendran spent his leisure time reading or looking after his stamp collection, Arul and his father shared a love of the outdoors. They would go on a shooting trip to Vavuniya or pearl fishing in Mannar and not think to invite Balendran. He had stood little chance against his brother's forceful personality. Arul's voice, gestures, actions were all passionate. He could take over a room, a conversation, a holiday. Further, Arul had viewed Balendran with contempt. He had considered Balendran's love of reading and quiet activities effeminate. He had tormented

Balendran over his inadequacies in sports, mocked his distaste for hunting.

Balendran's dislike for Arul extended to his wife as well. Pakkiam had come to work for them when she was fifteen. She was beautiful, with almond-shaped eyes, long, glossy black hair, skin the colour of milk tea, and a shapely figure. For the first two years of her time at Brighton, he had hardly noticed her. She had been a pleasant, happy girl, constantly breaking into song while she worked, adorning herself with flowers from their garden. Then, in her last year at Brighton, before she went off to India with Arul, her temperament had changed. She had become rude and aggressive, likely to burst into tears at the slightest reprimand from his mother. Her belligerence had turned against him for reasons he had never understood. She had begun to call out greetings every time she saw him. The words themselves were innocuous, things like "Ah here comes, thambi," "Good health to you, thambi," "thambi is looking well today." Yet her tone had been mocking and cruel, and she would glance at his thin, awkward body and smirk. Though he was the master's son, he had felt helpless against her aggression. It was never overt enough for him to complain to his mother. Also it would have been a loss of face for him to do so, would have showed that he did not have the manliness to deal with a female servant.

Balendran dated the change in Pakkiam from the time she had begun her relations with Arul. He felt that her familiarity with him was an attempt to lift herself to his level, to be considered his equal now that she was having an affair with his brother.

Though he believed firmly in the rights of the poor, and was concerned about their misery, Balendran did not think that the downtrodden, were they given power, would handle it any more magnanimously than the rich did. Someone like Pakkiam would not know how to exercise power except in the way she had seen it used against her.

Despite his feelings of dislike for his brother, Balendran was moved to concern for his reduced circumstances. Arul, he knew, worked in a lowly clerical position at the Post Office. Even with the allowance from his father, their circumstances would be difficult. A meagre house with a pocket handkerchief of a garden. They had raised a son. Arul's inability to provide for him, in a way that befitted what he knew his son could have had in Ceylon, must have eaten away at him.

Balendran folded the telegram and put it away. "It's too late to mend all that," Balendran said to himself. "It's best that I don't go." Yet, even as he thought this, he was filled with the discomfort of unfinished business. It was as if he had been called to dinner while in the middle of an irksome accounts problem. A sense of relief to be away from it but, at the same time, an understanding that it was still there to be attended to.

Balendran's car had turned into Brighton and he glanced ahead of him. His speculations, his desires were unimportant. Ultimately, his father would decide on the matter.

The Mudaliyar hated the unnecessary use of electricity, so Brighton was in darkness except for the lights in his father's study and his mother's drawing room. Balendran could hear the faint sound of the piano coming from Lotus Cottage and one of the Kandiah sisters singing along to it. Joseph took him to the back entrance. He went up the steps to the verandah that joined the kitchen to the main part of the house. As he made his way towards the back door, he noticed that a fire had been lit by the servants' quarters. Their dwellings were screened from the house by trees and, through them, he could make out figures dancing while others sang. He was reminded of the night of his father's birthday, twenty-eight years ago, when he had followed his brother out there. It made him shiver now to think of that moment when he had heard his father cry out. He had run towards the quarters, but, as he reached the trees, Pillai had been there. He had struggled, but Pillai, with the help of the two gardeners, had held him tightly, forcing him back across the lawn in the direction of the house. Yet he had seen it, his father with the red stain on his arm and his brother holding the knife. Balendran turned away, not wanting to dwell on that memory, and went into the house.

When Balendran came into the vestibule, he noticed the light spilling onto the stairs from his mother's drawing room. As he looked up, he felt he should go to her first, and a chill passed through him. He was going up there to tell his mother that her son was dying. He gripped the banister tightly and began to go slowly upstairs.

Nalamma looked up from her sewing and caught her breath as she saw Balendran come up the last few steps. He seemed to rise out of the darkness and she felt a foreboding.

"What is it, mahan?" she asked in fear.

He came forward, took her hands between his and kissed them. Then he knelt in front of her.

She watched him, wanting him to speak and yet afraid that, after he spoke, the world would fall around her.

"Its Arulanandan," he said, using his brother's full name.

A sound escaped from her lips. Then she reached out and drew Balendran tightly to her, arms circling him as if afraid that this son, too, might slip away.

"How long?" Nalamma asked. "How long do we have?"

"About a month, perhaps less."

She released him. Her face was tear-stained. She stood up. "Come. We must speak to your appa."

Wiping her face with the edge of her sari palu, she tucked it back into her waist. He followed her as she led the way towards the stairs.

When she got to the vestibule, her courage gave way and she indicated for him to knock on the door.

He did so and, after a moment, his father called out for them to enter. He went first and she followed.

The Mudaliyar was at the window, looking out over the lawn of Brighton. He turned to them.

"Appa," Balendran said timidly, "I . . . I received this telegram today."

He handed it to his father and then watched as he read it, wondering if the pain of his son dying would be too much for him.

The Mudaliyar kept his face inscrutable so that neither his son nor his wife could tell that he was already aware of the telegram's contents. Even though he had made them swear to have no communication with Arul, he had been unable to cut his son off completely. Along with the monthly allowance he sent Arul, he had arranged for the bank manager, Mr. Govind, to make inquiries about his son and convey the news to him. Mr. Govind had telegraphed him the same information a few hours ago. The Mudaliyar had been pacing his study agitatedly contemplating this terrible news when his son and wife had knocked on the door.

He put down the telegram.

"Appa," Balendran said, aware of his mother's eyes on him. "Should I go to him?"

The Mudaliyar had already anticipated this question and had decided that, of course, Balendran should go. Arul was his son and despite the fact that he had disobeyed him and caused him much pain, the Mudaliyar still loved him as he did Balendran. In fact, hardly a week went by when the sight of Balendran or the photograph of Lukshman on his desk did not make him sigh at the loss of that other son and grandson. For they were irrevocably lost to him, his son by his marriage, his grandson by the blood he carried in him. Now that Arul was close to death, the Mudaliyar felt it was absolutely essential Balendran go and convince Arul's family to send the body back to Ceylon so that his son could be buried in a way that befitted his heritage. In India, there would be no Koviars to bathe the body and accompany it to the cremation grounds, no Parayars to beat their drums, no Pallars to cut the firewood and make the funeral pyre. His son, his oldest son, would be buried like a nameless pauper. It would be a shame on him, an insult to the family name. Silk, as his father used to say, remained silk even if it was torn. His son was still of their blood and should be given a funeral that was worthy of his lineage.

Yet the Mudaliyar was confronted by a dilemma. While he wished to send Balendran, he did not want it to seem that he lightly dismissed the vow he had made his household take at the family shrine. "You know my wishes on this subject and I expect them to be obeyed," he said and waited for his son's appeal.

Balendran nodded in acquiescence, relieved that he was not to be sent.

"Is there a reason I should alter my mind?"

Before Balendran could answer, Nalamma burst out, "What reason do you want? Are you a man or a piece of stone?"

She had never spoken like this to her husband. The Mudaliyar straightened up. "Are you forgetting who you are talking to?" he said, his voice awful.

Much to his surprise, Nalamma stared back at him. The Mudaliyar grew furious at her refusal to be penitent, his outrage exacerbated by the tumult over his son's impending death. "Get out!" he shouted. Nalamma's gaze wavered. "Get out of my study, you disrespectful woman!"

"Take her away," the Mudaliyar said to Balendran. "There is nothing more to be said."

Once his wife and son had gone, and the door was closed, the Mudaliyar hit the table with his palm. He began to pace the room, cursing his wife for interrupting and thus preventing his son from begging his permission to go to Bombay.

When Balendran and his mother reached the top of the stairs, she let go of his arm.

"I can go by myself."

"Are you sure?"

She nodded. "There is something you must do. Go to the vellakari."

He stared at her in astonishment. "Miss Adamson?"

She looked away from him, but not before he saw the expression on her face — a mixture of uneasiness and cunning.

"She exerts great influence over him," she said. "You know how he is about Europeans. Anything they say, he will believe." She pushed at him gently. "Go now."

"But, Amma, this is a family matter. We can't drag a stranger into it."

"What is wrong with you?" Nalamma cried. "I am your mother. Do as I say."

Balendran sighed. There was no point arguing with either of his parents when they were in this state. He turned and went down the stairs.

Miss Adamson's bedroom was along the passage behind the stairs. He stood for a moment outside the door, listening to her moving around inside, then he knocked.

"Who is it?" she called out softly.

He cleared his throat. "It's Balendran."

She came to the door, opened it a crack, and peered out at him.

"I wonder if I could speak with you," he said, feeling as if he were intruding on her privacy.

She bowed her head in acquiescence. "If you could give me a moment." She shut the door.

He waited in the passage, feeling irritable. Why had he agreed to this damn-fool mission? His father had expressed his wish and that was that. There was no point approaching this woman who was a stranger, who knew nothing about their family.

Miss Adamson finally emerged from her room and Balendran signalled for them to walk down the passage to the dining room. She was wearing a long silk housecoat and kept her hand at her throat to prevent the neckline from opening up. Her hair was in a plait down her back and she kept her head bent demurely. Balendran thought this was the first time he had seen her look what she was — a Western woman. Seeing her in these clothes that belonged to her earlier life, he thought how incongruent the sari really was on her.

When they reached the dining room, he stood aside so she could enter, then followed her in. He reached to turn on the light, but she said softly, "The master will not like it."

He paused awkwardly, then lowered his hand to his side.

"I have asked to speak with you alone about a private matter . . . a family matter," he began, wanting to get this over with as soon as possible.

She waited, her head bent.

"I don't know if you are aware that I have an older brother. Who lives in India."

She nodded.

"Do you know the circumstances surrounding his going to India?"

"A marriage that the master didn't approve of."

Balendran nodded. "Now my brother is dying and it is important that someone from the family goes to him. Unfortunately, my father has forbidden it."

He paused again, finding it very difficult to continue. "My mother feels that you exert an influence over him . . . some good influence."

He stopped, as Miss Adamson had moved slightly.

"Do you think this is so?" he asked. "Do you think you could get him to change his mind?"

Miss Adamson released the neckline of her gown. She crossed her arms. He thought she looked strangely troubled.

"Do you think this would be possible?" he asked again.

"I don't know," she said. "Your mother exaggerates my influence over the master. But I will try. I will talk to him."

He bowed slightly and left the room.

As Balendran's car left Brighton, he glanced back at his father's study window. The memory of that terrible night Arul had used a knife on his father came back to him. How much havoc and shame Arul had caused their family.

Balendran knew that, to his father, caste differences were as real as the earth being flat and inhabited by spirits had been to his forebears. One's birth, one's caste were tangible, as if these differences were manifest in the blood in one's veins, one's ligaments, the very smell of one's sweat. His father had a story that he often told of how, unknowingly, he had drunk from the cup of an untouchable and had spontaneously vomited. His body, aware of the very poison, had rejected it. Balendran did not agree with his father at all, but he would have taken his father's feelings into consideration if he had been in Arul's position. His brother, in his characteristically single-minded fashion, had not only refused to see things from his father's perspective but had been enraged with him. But what had been his father's crime? After all, his father had reacted to the affair in the same way any parent of their peers might. He had ordered Pakkiam to return to her village. And for that his brother had stabbed him. Balendran remembered shuddering when he thought about what would have happened if his brother had killed his father – not just the loss of his father but also the scandal, the shame, that would have haunted them the rest of their lives. As it was, it had been very hard.

Their family doctor had been discreet and kept the stabbing to himself. After Arul left for India, however, his marriage to Pakkiam became public knowledge. Balendran had suffered at school because of it. His schoolmates had taunted him, never allowing a woman labourer to pass without calling Balendran's attention to his future wife. Once, he had seen a schoolmate surreptitiously wipe something he had handled, as if Pakkiam's untouchability had affected him too. His father's blood pressure had soared, and he had been compelled to take to bed for a month. His mother had been forced to endure visits from relatives and other "well wishers" who had come to find out what they could and spread it around. The first time they had gone into public as a family, at an at-home given by F. C. Wijewardena's parents, a hush had fallen on the room as they entered. They had spent most of the evening shunned by the other people.

Still, his father had arranged for Arul to have a monthly allowance. For that, Balendran admired him.

The next morning, Balendran received a summons from his father. He arrived at the appointed time and found his father pacing up and down his study. When the Mudaliyar saw him, he stopped and waited for him to approach.

"I have decided that you must go," the Mudaliyar said. "We don't know how long your brother has. Therefore, you must leave tomorrow evening."

Balendran stared at him in astonishment.

The Mudaliyar held out the ticket for his passage to Bombay. "I want you to speak to his family and arrange for the body to be brought back here," the Mudaliyar continued. "He must be buried with full honours in Jaffna. If they refuse, threaten to cut off their allowance."

As his father spoke, Balendran half listened. He was looking at Miss Adamson, who sat at her table attending to the correspondence, seemingly oblivious to what was going on. He felt not so much respect or gratitude, but rather confirmation of her significance in this, his father's house.

In a few days, Balendran would be seeing Arul, and now, as his car took him home, the reality of his brother's death was before him. He felt for the first time sorrow, like a hardness in his chest. How devastating it was, how terrible for Arul to have his life cut down like this when it had only half run its course. He could only imagine how Arul must agonize over his wife and son, wonder how they would survive without him. Balendran thought of this sad reunion with Arul, after all these years of absence. To meet now, in the face of death, was almost unbearable. What would he say to Arul after all this time? The long absence had made them strangers to each other. Seelan. He would be twenty-seven years old now. What would he have to say to him? Would his nephew resent the fact that he had been deprived of his heritage? Would he hate Balendran? All the time he had known Pakkiam she had been a servant in his house. Now she was his sister-in-law. Though he had every intention of treating her with the due respect of a sister-in-law, it would sit awkwardly on both of them.

Then there was his father's order to bring Arul's body back so that it could be cremated in Ceylon. Balendran sat up in his seat. While his father had spoken, this had not sunk in. Now the full significance of his father's command was before him. He was going to meet his brother and his family and ask for the return of his brother's body. Arul had a temper to match their father's, even exceed it. His anger had, after all, made him stab his own father. He imagined telling Arul of their father's request and he felt himself wither at the tirade that would be unleashed against him. Pakkiam and Seelan would support Arul too. He would not have a hope against them. Pakkiam would never let Arul be buried away from them. Seelan would never allow anyone else to light the funeral pyre. It was the most important duty a son ever performed for his father! But the Mudaliyar was determined to see his beloved son, even if only in his death, determined to give him the honours he deserved as a member of their family.

Balendran wiped the sweat off his face with his handkerchief and sighed at the task before him.

17

Friendship curbs wrong, guides right,
And shares distress.
— The Tirukkural, *verse 787*

April was the hottest month of the year. Despite the proximity to the sea and the presence of Beira Lake, an inert sultriness hung over Colombo. On the tree-shaded streets, a shimmering heat seemed to have become trapped between the canopy of dusty leaves overhead and the tarred road. Even the nights were sweltering, and one went to sleep on a warm mattress, tossing and turning through uneasy dreams only to wake in a sweat. It was a time when tempers, both public and private, were frayed. The year of 1928 was no exception, for April had brought with it the murmuring of Labour Union unrest. Taxi drivers of the Minerva Hiring Company had taken a vote to join the Labour Union, but the company had refused to recognize unionism by its employees. The owner had dismissed the driver who was the union representative, telling him to get out as he did not want his "damned union." Discontent was brewing amongst the other drivers.

A deserted air hung over Cinnamon Gardens as most of its residents had fled to the cooler climate of the hill country, to the town of Nuwara Eliya, a hill station once the exclusive domain of the British but now increasingly populated by wealthy Ceylonese, many of whom owned cottages there. In April, Cinnamon Gardens resembled nothing so much as a ghost town. This impression was enhanced by the fact that the scores of servants, who were so present everywhere, had also departed. They had gone to their villages for the Sinhala and Tamil New Year. Those occupants of Cinnamon Gardens who remained could not help but be possessed by a feeling of melancholy, a sense of being abandoned.

Since schools were closed for the April holidays, Annalukshmi had gone back to the Sisler estate with Miss Lawton and Nancy. But deprived of Letchumi and Ramu, and with Kumudini married and in Malaya, Louisa asked Annalukshmi to come home after only a week, to help with the numerous domestic chores that had fallen on her shoulders.

As one unbearably hot day gave way to another, Annalukshmi found herself restless and pensive as she ground the spices for the curry, stood over steaming pots in the stifling kitchen, swept the verandah, or watered the garden.

After her sister's marriage, she had thrown herself with increased vigour into her teaching. Besides paying more attention to her classes, she had taken time after school hours to tutor the weaker students. She had also volunteered her services to direct the school's drama society for the forthcoming inter-school Shakespeare competition in June, in which they would be performing an act from *As You Like It*. She had tried to schedule some rehearsals for the April holidays, but the girls had all rebelled against the idea, most of them having plans to spend the month in Nuwara Eliya.

Annalukshmi found herself longing for the end of the April holidays or at least the return of her friends from Nanu Oya.

To add to Annalukshmi's irritations, her Aunt Philomena, who was also deprived of domestic help, had taken to dropping in too often. Her visits were conveniently engineered to coincide with meals and, over lunch or dinner, the residents of Lotus Cottage had to put up with a litany of their faults, particularly the new thorn they had pierced in Philomena's side, this marriage of Kumudini to a Hindu (even though wild dogs could not have kept Philomena away from the wedding).

One morning, Philomena Barnett arrived at the gates of Lotus Cottage. She walked up the front path with a bustle and energy that was unusual for her at this time of year. She came up the verandah steps, an expression of sly pleasure on her face.

Louisa was dusting the verandah furniture and Annalukshmi and Manohari were sweeping the verandah and breaking cobwebs. They paused in their work, sighing inwardly at the prospect of another tedious visit.

"Well, cousin," Philomena declared, "I am flabbergasted. How many days I have been coming here and you never thought to mention this news about Kumudini."

"News?" Louisa said, not knowing what she was talking about.

"You mean, you don't know? Kumudini is pregnant."

"Haaah?" Louisa cried in surprise.

Annalukshmi and Manohari looked at each other, astonished.

Louisa recovered herself. "What are you talking about, cousin? You must be misinformed."

Philomena shook her head. "No. My friend Viola Emannuel is back from Malaya. Her husband is one of the few Tamil gynaecologists in Kuala Lumpur, and she knows for a fact that Kumudini is pregnant. Has been for the last four months. Soon after they were married."

"No, cousin, that can't be." Louisa looked to her daughters for support.

"Why wouldn't we have heard if she was?" Annalukshmi demanded. She was sure that her aunt had got things wrong. "Why wouldn't Kumudini have written and told us?"

"Why indeed," Philomena said. She sank into a chair. "It's certain that Parvathy and your father are keeping her from informing you. They want her to have the child there so they can prevent its baptism."

Louisa sat down as well. Philomena had, unwittingly, touched on one of her own misgivings. Though she had given her grudging permission to this marriage, she was haunted by doubts and concerns. She had begun to speculate whether her husband would honour the pact she had made with Parvathy about the religion of Kumudini's future children. "No," she said firmly. "Parvathy would never do that. She is a woman of her word."

"Don't say I didn't warn you, cousin," Philomena said.

Once Louisa and the girls had retired to the kitchen to put the finishing touches to the lunch, Manohari said, "Imagine if akka got pregnant right after they were married. Out on the first ball."

Louisa frowned at her and told her not to be crude.

"She isn't pregnant," Annalukshmi said impatiently, and she wiped the sweat from her forehead with her sleeve. "It's just Aunt Philomena's rubbish. I don't know why she keeps coming here with her wretched nonsense. I have a good mind to put Epsom salts in her food one of these days."

"I agree it's probably nothing," Louisa said. "But I am going to send a letter to Kumudini today. By express post. Let's clear this up once and for all."

That afternoon, as she lay in bed trying to sleep despite the sluggish heat that the overhead fan merely shifted around, Annalukshmi pondered what her Aunt Philomena had said and felt even more sure that she was wrong. Besides it being custom-ary for girls to return to their mother's house for the later part of their confinement, Ceylonese women in Malaya always came back at the beginning of their pregnancy. Medical facilities in Malaya were backward when compared to Ceylon, and during those early dangerous months it was very important to be near a good hospital and good doctors. She doubted that her aunt or her father, whatever intentions they might have about the child's religion, would take such a risk with her sister or their future grandchild.

Annalukshmi looked over at Kumudini's empty bed and sighed, thinking back to the wedding four months earlier. Since Muttiah and Parvathy had been in Ceylon for only two weeks, there had been a flurry of activity to organize the reception. Her Aunt Philomena, despite her cries of horror when she found out and her threats to disown their family, had been unable to resist a wedding and had arrived with *Mrs. Beeton's Cookery Book* tucked under her arm to supervise preparation of the wedding break-fast. It had been a small affair, just the immediate relatives. The Mudaliyar and Nalamma had made the ballroom at Brighton available for the breakfast. Their Uncle Balendran had given away the bride since their father had not been able to come in time from Malaya. He had, however, sent a long letter castigating Annalukshmi and praising Kumudini for her good sense. At the wedding itself, Annalukshmi had found it difficult to ignore the strange, often pitying looks she got, the whispered conversations behind open fans.

The wedding preparations had been so frantic that it was only once they were at the jetty bidding goodbye to her sister that Annalukshmi had realized what she was losing. When they had returned that day to their now quiet house, she had been filled with despondency. Her gloom had not been helped by the arrival of Christmas. She had missed her sister during the making of the cake, the annual trip to Colombo Cold Stores to buy the suckling pig for Christmas dinner, the shopping for presents. When the holidays were over, she was glad to return to school and the sense of purpose her teaching career offered.

Annalukshmi picked up her book. She glanced at it and then flung it down again. In this heat, even reading was too much of an effort. Besides, she had read this novel before. She thought of going next door, to Brighton, and finding out if her grand-uncle, the Mudaliyar, was going into town on business. She might be able to get a ride with him to Cargills' bookshop. Annalukshmi noticed that Manohari was lying on her side, her head propped up by her arm, looking at her. "I thought you told me Nancy and Miss Lawton were in Nanu Oya," Manohari said.

"They are."

"That's how much you know then. Yesterday when Amma and I were shopping at the market in Pettah, I saw Nancy with that Mr. Jayaweera."

"How can that be? Miss Lawton and Nancy would have told me that they had returned to Colombo."

"Well, I know what I saw."

Annalukshmi lay back in bed, puzzled. Surely if Nancy and Miss Lawton had returned, they would have sent word that they had arrived. Mr. Jayaweera had recently moved to a rooming house in Pettah. Annalukshmi wondered if Miss Lawton and Nancy had been to visit him without her. She felt put out that this might be so, given they had said they would go together to see his new lodgings. However, she would not let this spoil the pleasure she felt at their return, which would no doubt provide some relief from the drudgery of her domestic chores.

She decided to get a rickshaw this evening, once it was less warm, and go to visit them.

Annalukshmi pushed open the gate to Miss Lawton's bungalow. As she entered, she noticed that the grass had not been cut in the last two weeks as the gardener had gone back to his village. The front path, usually well swept, was covered in dry leaves. She saw that the front door was still locked and none of the verandah furniture had been put out. She felt sure now that they had not come back, that Manohari had made a mistake.

Annalukshmi knew that Miss Lawton's servant, Rosa, had not gone to her village this year, and she went around the side of the house to look for her.

As she walked along, she was startled to suddenly hear Nancy's and Mr. Jayaweera's voices on the side verandah behind a thick screen of foliage. Annalukshmi stopped, pleased. Nancy and Miss Lawton had indeed come back from Nanu Oya. She walked up to where the foliage began and she was about to part the leaves when she heard Nancy say, with a deep sigh, "You can't understand how hard this is for me. I am not by nature a deceitful person. I am miserable about this."

"Yes, I know, I know," Mr. Jayaweera said soothingly in Sinhalese. "But it will only be for a few weeks more."

Annalukshmi carefully pushed aside the foliage to try to understand what was happening. What she saw startled her.

Mr. Jayaweera and Nancy were seated on a wooden bench. He had his arm around her and he was stroking her head, which was resting on his shoulder.

Annalukshmi started to move away, but it was too late, they had seen her. Everyone was still, then Mr. Jayaweera and Nancy quickly broke apart. He stood up and she turned her face in the other direction.

After a moment, Mr. Jayaweera silently extended his hand to help Annalukshmi climb up on the verandah. They stood again, looking at each other. Then Nancy began to cry. "Forgive me, Annalukshmi," she said. "I am so very, very sorry. I did not want you to find out in this way." She got up and went quickly into the house.

"Please, Miss Annalukshmi," Mr. Jayaweera said, "go and talk with her." He inclined his head slightly towards her and left.

Annalukshmi went inside to go after her friend.

As she crossed the gloomy drawing room, she felt a hundred questions crowd into her mind. But, more than that, she felt curiously betrayed by what had been revealed. Had she mistaken her and Nancy's closeness. They had shared their pasts with each other, yet, her friend, all along, had kept this important secret from her.

She found Nancy seated on the bed. She was no longer crying. She glanced up at Annalukshmi. "Are you very hurt?" Nancy asked after a moment.

Annalukshmi did not reply immediately. "I . . . I can't deny that I am," she said. "A little. After all we've told each other."

"Yes," Nancy said. "But I wanted to protect our friendship."

"What do you mean?"

"I have not yet told Miss Lawton. I simply did not feel it was fair to involve you in my problems, causing you discomfort with her."

Annalukshmi saw the distress in her friend's face. She came and sat down next to Nancy on the bed. "You will have to tell Miss Lawton eventually. It is not as if she would throw you out like some Ceylonese parent would."

"No. But this will upset her deeply, my involvement with a man who is poor with a family to support, who has no real prospects. And a non-Christian at that." Nancy stood up and crossed the room, then turned back to her friend. "Miss Lawton has often expressed worry about my future, you know, realizing that my position is neither here nor there, that I don't quite fit in. But I believe, though we haven't always seen eye to eye, or agreed on everything . . . I suppose I want to believe that if I were to find something I really wanted and was happy, she would come to accept it"

"Yes, Nancy, I'm certain of it."

"I will have to be careful though. Choose my time carefully. Vijith — Mr. Jayaweera — is vulnerable. I don't want her blaming him, asking him to leave the school."

"But the longer you wait, the worse it gets, Nancy. It's better to tell her now and take the consequences."

"Vijith and I want to wait a few weeks. The lady who owns his boarding house has promised to find him employment in a bank. Once the school finds out about us, it is going to look very bad for Miss Lawton. The parents will think that she committed an impropriety by encouraging the affair while he was living in our house. Or they will think she was not clever enough to see what was going on under her very nose, so how can she be trusted with their daughters. Vijith and I both feel that the honourable thing is for him to find another job."

That evening, as the sun set over the lawn, they walked about the garden and Nancy told her of how her alliance with Mr. Jayaweera had begun very shortly after he had come to the school. She had felt almost immediately a sense of ease with him, liked the fact that, when they were alone together, he spoke to her in Sinhalese, a language she used so infrequently now and one that brought her back to the life she had lived before she came to Miss Lawton. It had soon been clear to her that Mr. Jayaweera returned her admiration. He was barely at the school a month before he told her that his feelings for her went beyond friendship. As she spoke, moments in the past began to reveal themselves to Annalukshmi in a different light. And though she was pleased for her friend, she could not help but feel concern.

❧

In January, Nancy and Annalukshmi had decided to join the Ceylon Lawn Tennis Association Club, which was in Victoria Park. Over the past few months they met often for a game. One evening, a few days after Nancy had told Annalukshmi about Mr. Jayaweera, they came together for a round of tennis. When they finished their game, Nancy began to hurriedly put her things away. "I hope you don't mind," she said, "but I won't have a drink today. I've arranged to meet Vijith for a little while in the park."

"Of course," Annalukshmi said, trying to keep the disappointment from her voice.

Nancy patted her on the shoulder in thanks. Then she got on her bicycle and set off across Victoria Park.

Annalukshmi watched her go, feeling abandoned. She had asked her rickshaw man to come fifteen minutes late, so she and Nancy would have time for their drink. Now she would have to wait for him alone. She made her way to the lawn in front of the clubhouse and sat down at one of the wrought-iron tables. Other players sat at the tables around her, chatting. Their camaraderie increased her isolation. The sky above was beginning to darken now, a precursor to one of those evening thundershowers that briefly relieved the heat of April. After a few moments of sitting thus, she could not bear it any longer. She would leave some money with a ball boy to pay the rickshaw man for his wasted effort.

Once she had done this, Annalukshmi began to walk across Victoria Park.

She had no sooner left the club when she saw Nancy and Mr. Jayaweera ahead of her. He was wheeling Nancy's bicycle and she walked beside him. Annalukshmi quickly stepped off the path so they would not see her, and she watched them. Mr. Jayaweera was holding Nancy's hand tucked tightly under his arm and he was looking down at her with great fondness. Nancy's face was suffused with a glow of happiness.

Miss Lawton returned from Nanu Oya a few days later and suggested that Annalukshmi come for a visit. The headmistress's face lit up with pleasure when she saw her, yet Annalukshmi was barely able to look her in the eye as Miss Lawton pressed her hand warmly. She stayed for dinner that night, but, rather than it being a pleasure, she found it a strain. She had always valued Miss Lawton's company for the freedom she had to discuss any dilemma with her, the assurance that she would find a sympathetic and discerning ear. In Miss Lawton's presence, she was now conscious of the things she could not speak of, and found it difficult to talk about anything else.

∽

A week after Philomena Barnett had told them about Kumudini, the family at Lotus Cottage received a letter. It was from Parvathy and was addressed to Louisa.

> My dear thangachi,
> Rejoice for Kumudini is pregnant! By the time you receive this letter, she will be on her way to Ceylon for her confinement.
> You should know, however, that she is actually four months' pregnant. Murugasu thambi and I have been urging her to return to Colombo these last months but, displaying a will she has no doubt inherited from her father, she has refused to leave, insisting that her place is with her husband, that scores of women give birth every year in the hospitals of Kuala Lumpur without harm either to themselves or the child. She did not even want you to know of her condition, saying you would worry unnecessarily. Finally, Murugasu thambi and I put our foot down and so now she is on her way to you. She will

arrive in two weeks. I remain pledged to our agreement
about the child's religion.

Parvathy.

The letter Louisa had sent her daughter could not have
arrived in Malaya yet, so this was not a response to it. Parvathy's
last sentence, her commitment to the baptism of the child,
removed any suspicions they could have had on this point. In
fact, it seemed deliberately mentioned to allay any doubts they
might have. As they reread the letter and discussed it, they could
not help but feel that the culprit in this delay was Kumudini
herself. They wondered how she, so well known for her good
sense, could have held up her return in this way.

"It's love," Manohari finally declared with mock sentimen-
tality. "She cannot bear to be parted from the one who brings
rays of sunshine into her life."

It quickly came to dominate Louisa's mind that she was going
to be a grandmother. That very morning, despite the blistering
heat, which made their leather slippers stick to the tar of the
roads, Louisa went into Pettah to shop for cotton cloth that
she would use to make shirts for the baby. She expected that
Annalukshmi accompany her.

Pettah, being one of the oldest districts of Colombo, didn't
have any of the wide, tree-lined streets the rest of the city boasted.
Instead, its narrow jumble of lanes were open mercilessly to the
sun, and the mixed smells of bloody meat and putrefying fruit
and vegetables were heightened by the heat. Annalukshmi, grimly
carrying the parcels, watched her mother jostling with the
crowds, hurrying from shop to shop, buying lace and ribbons

and buttons and cotton cloth, bargaining with enthusiasm and fierceness. It was clear to Annalukshmi that for the next five months, her mother would have one thing alone on her mind: the birth of her grandchild.

That afternoon, after they came home, Louisa told Annalukshmi that she wanted her to give up her tennis game with Nancy that evening and, indeed, for the rest of the week. She was to devote herself to smocking little shirts for Kumudini's child.

"I'm not giving up anything," Annalukshmi cried, now truly infuriated. "You're acting as if the child is going to be born next week."

"Don't be selfish," Louisa said. "You have enough time in the world to go and play tennis with Nancy."

"So will Kumudini have time when she gets here. She'll have nothing to do the whole day but sit and smock shirts for her child."

"A fine aunt you'll make," Manohari said. "Just like that evil Mrs. Reed in *Jane Eyre*."

"Kadavale," Annalukshmi cried. "You'd think this was the second coming."

Louisa looked at her as if she had committed a sacrilege.

❧

The new school term was to begin in a few days and Annalukshmi volunteered to help Miss Lawton and Nancy tidy up the staff room. They met one morning to do so.

Annalukshmi was in the process of cleaning out the teachers' cubicles when she said to the headmistress and Nancy, "We've had some good news this week. My sister, Kumudini, is pregnant."

Miss Lawton was at the table going through old correspondence, sorting out what needed to be thrown away. Nancy was up on a chair taking down the curtains so they could be washed. They both stopped what they were doing. "Congratulations," Miss Lawton exclaimed.

"You must be delighted at the prospect of being an aunt," Nancy added.

Annalukshmi shrugged.

"But it is a wonderful thing, isn't it? A grandchild for your mother, a niece or nephew for you."

"Yes, indeed. But does it have to consume every conversation a person has, take up every waking moment of my life? After all, village women give birth in the fields and then continue their work, none of this fussing and running around."

Annalukshmi went back to her cleaning, and thus did not see the headmistress looking at her intently. Nancy, however, observed her doing so.

"Well, do convey my congratulations to your family," Miss Lawton said. She glanced at a few more letters and discarded them on the floor. "You know, I've been thinking, Anna," she said. "The Ministry of Education has sent around a prospectus asking if there are any teachers who would be interested in taking an enhancement course. It would lead to further qualifications, allow you ultimately to become a senior teacher and instruct upper classes. Would you be interested?"

Annalukshmi turned around. "Yes, indeed I would be very interested."

"Good," Miss Lawton said. "I thought you would be. Remind me to get you a form from my office before you leave today."

Later that day, when Nancy and Annalukshmi were walking across the quadrangle towards the headmistress's bungalow, she said to her friend, "I'm pleased about this. It will give me something to really look forward to in the coming term. This may be a good opportunity to move up. Perhaps even to the top."

Nancy looked at her, worried.

"What do you suppose my chances might be of becoming a headmistress some day?" She looked at her friend for support and now saw the reservation on her face.

They had reached a clump of araliya trees and Nancy stopped in the shade. She was silent, looking down at her hands. "I do applaud your ambition, Annalukshmi, and I think that you would make an excellent headmistress. But I think you are forgetting how things are. Being Ceylonese, neither you nor I will get a chance to be headmistress."

"But surely the world is changing."

"Is it? Look at the Buddhist and Hindu schools that were started up as a protest against the missionary schools. Even they have hired European headmasters and headmistresses, despite the nationalistic talk of their founders. Ceylonese parents want the prestige of sending their children to schools run by Europeans."

Annalukshmi felt something beginning to come unravelled in her mind, like a spool of thread that had slipped off a table and was tumbling across the floor. "But things are bound to change," she said. "And I am sure that Miss Lawton, for example, would support me. I'm sure she would take on the missionary board and Ceylonese parents if she needed to."

Nancy placed her hand on Annalukshmi's arm. "Are you so sure, knowing Miss Lawton's attitudes? Last year, when Miss Blake left the school, she was unable to secure a replacement from England. She could have promoted one of the teachers then. Instead, she hired Vijith as a clerk."

Annalukshmi looked at her friend. The spool of thread was unravelling faster and faster. Now that Nancy mentioned it, when Miss Lawton had asked her to help with Miss Blake's duties, there had been no intimation that she, Annalukshmi, might assume the role of assistant headmistress then or ever. She suddenly remembered Miss Lawton's reply when she had said that she did not know very much about the assistant headmistress's job. Miss Lawton had replied, "Well, of course I wouldn't expect you to do all of it. That would be beyond you."

"I've forgotten something in my classroom. Excuse me." Annalukshmi began to walk away.

Nancy looked after her, troubled, then continued on in the direction of the headmistress's bungalow.

Annalukshmi walked quickly towards the senior classroom block. Instead of going to her classroom, she found herself in the music room. She shut the door behind her, then walked to the open window from where she had an uninterrupted view of the sea. The rhythmic movement of the waves, crashing against the beach, then receding, the breeze that blew on her face, all had a calming effect on her.

Annalukshmi turned to look around the music room. She remembered an evening when the three of them had come here and played the pianos together, singing along. Her mind drifted to many other moments of pleasure with Miss Lawton and Nancy, the sea baths, the holidays in Nanu Oya, the nights at the headmistress's bungalow. She could not deny that she had been happy here at the school, that Miss Lawton had been extremely kind to her. Still, she was aware now that those happy times had been lined with the hidden bars of her limitations.

18

The mark of wisdom is to see the reality
Behind each appearance.
— The Tirukkural, *verse 355*

On the five-day-long voyage from Colombo to Bombay, Balendran paced up and down the steamer deck or leant against the rails going over and over in his mind the appalling situation towards which he was heading, the terrible task he was to perform. He considered not conveying his father's message. He would simply avoid mentioning the issue at all and tell his father that the family had refused. He pictured his father's fury and, while he feared it, he felt it would be more tolerable than asking for his brother's body. Then he recalled his father's threat to cut off his brother's allowance. Arul's death was sure to make his family even more dependent on that allowance. Through no fault of their own, not understanding the reason, they would find themselves destitute. He could not extricate himself from the task. He would have to convey his father's request, he would have to let them decide what they wished to do.

By the time the shoreline of Bombay was visible, Balendran was exhausted from his ruminations, his nerves on edge.

Bombay. Balendran could already smell it from the railings, a mixture of sewers and sea breeze. The gangway was being lowered. He looked down at the crowd on the jetty and it dawned on him that in all likelihood someone from his brother's family waited for him. The thought made his hands go cold.

The gangway had been secured and passengers began to disembark. Balendran gathered his things together. Even though the last days on the ship had been difficult, the thought of leaving it was now unpalatable.

When he got down to the jetty, he looked around him.

"Sir, are you Mr. Balendran?"

Balendran turned quickly to find a young man before him. "Seelan?"

They stood for a moment, staring at each other.

His nephew was fashionably dressed in a double-breasted coat, white trousers, a Trilby hat in one hand, a good walking-stick in the other. Recollecting himself, Balendran quickly extended his hand.

They shook hands.

"It is an honour and pleasure to have you here, sir," Seelan said.

Balendran was taken aback by his formal, almost oratorical, tone, the British intonation to his voice. "Thank you," he replied.

Seelan pointed to his bags. "Are these yours?"

He nodded.

Seelan signalled to a couple of porters. He said something to them in what Balendran presumed was Hindi, then he led the way towards their buggy. Balendran followed. He was free to examine his nephew again and he noted that Seelan, at twenty-seven, resembled Arul and had only inherited from his mother her eyes. Yet it had taken him a second look to recognize the similarity, and, after studying his nephew keenly for a moment, he realized why. Though Seelan had his father's features, their arrangement was completely different. The unruly hair he had inherited from his father had been flattened down with brilliantine. His nephew's full lips were primly tightened, banishing from his face the expressive energy that had been so much a part of Arul. Balendran inspected his nephew's clothes again. He knew how to spot a suit made in Europe from one that had been sewn in the East, and Seelan's was definitely the former. He frowned, puzzled. How could he afford it? He knew that the circumstances they lived in were strained. Seelan's clothes spoke of an affluence that equalled his own or that of any Cinnamon Gardens family. Like the son of a Cinnamon Gardens family, Seelan carried himself with a sense of importance. In fact, Balendran thought, as he looked at the rakish angle of Seelan's hat, his nephew was quite a dandy and, judging from his British intonation, an anglophile as well. How strange this was, how unexpected.

They had reached the buggy. Balendran got in and waited as Seelan instructed the driver and the porters to tie the bags to the back. Balendran noticed a book lying on the seat next to him and he picked it up. It was Thomas Hardy's *The Mayor of Casterbridge*. He was surprised. He had not expected a love of reading to go hand in hand with his nephew's foppish ways. Such young men usually preferred cars and racehorses and gramophones.

Seelan got into the buggy. When he saw the book in Balendran's hands, he looked at him eagerly, as if he expected some comment.

"I see that you like Thomas Hardy."

"Indeed, sir," Seelan replied promptly. "Reading is one of my greatest pleasures."

The buggy had set off and an uneasy silence fell between them.
"How is your appa?" Balendran asked.

A brief sadness crossed his nephew's face. "I'm afraid in the very last stages, sir. A week or two, at best."

"But what is the cause?"

"Cancer of the lung, sir."

"Is he . . . is he suffering with a lot of pain?"

"Unfortunately, it has spread to the bones. But he's kept highly sedated. With morphine."

"Will he recognize me?"

"Oh, indeed, sir."

This line of conversation had run its course. Balendran stared out at the city around him, feigning interest in it while he tried to think of what to say next. Gradually, he became aware that he was under scrutiny. He turned his head quickly to find his nephew studying him, a curious, almost hungry expression in his eyes. Seelan looked hastily away from him. Balendran, too, averted his eyes, wondering why his nephew had looked at him like that. It was not desire, for that he knew, but something akin to it that he could not quite name. Covetousness was the word that came to mind, but what it had to do with his nephew's expression he could not discern. Balendran did not want to look at his nephew's face again, yet he could not stop himself from glancing at Seelan's hands, which were clasped together tightly, too tightly. Balendran saw that, beneath his formal and confident manner, his nephew was not sure of himself.

They travelled through endless overcrowded and dirty streets. After a while, they turned into an alleyway and the horses slowed to a halt. Balendran looked around in dismay at the filth on the street. A stench rose from an open drain. He had thought they were merely passing through and would ultimately emerge into a better residential area. He turned to Seelan. "Have we arrived?"

The young man blushed. "Yes we have," he mumbled and hastily got out of the buggy and began to help the driver unload the bags.

Balendran stepped out after him, silently cursing himself for unintentionally embarrassing his nephew. Yet he could hardly stop himself from staring around with shock.

The alleyway ended in a courtyard surrounded on three sides by a two-storey building containing numerous flats. A balcony ran along the second floor, the washing hanging over it obliterating the doors to the flats. The building had, at one time, been whitewashed, but now the dirt and damp had spread black stains over the walls. Refuse was piled in one corner, and a few emaciated stray dogs were nosing their way through it. From the various flats, he could hear a wireless, someone banging something, two women having a fierce argument, a child crying. Balendran shook his head. This was not what he had expected at all. With the allowance and Arul's salary, he had thought they would live in a small house, not in this terrible squalor.

A woman dressed in a blue sari was walking across the courtyard. He watched her, not sure if it was Pakkiam. Yet she was coming in his direction. It had to be her. Balendran felt his heart beat rapidly. He had never known her as this, his sister-in-law. What was he expected to say? Should he call her anney or akka? What if he slipped up and used the diminutive "you" with her? The insult of that would be unforgivable, especially in the presence of his nephew.

Pakkiam was before him and they stood a moment looking at each other.

The Pakkiam he had known was a girl of seventeen. The woman who stood before him was in her forties. Her features, despite aging, were recognizable. It was her expression that made him feel he was before a stranger. Her eyes, which had always been lively, were now hooded, and when she lifted them to him, he saw that she had been crying. Her mouth that had always been busy with song and later defiance and sarcasm was now firmly held together, as if to keep in her grief.

She bowed slightly and said softly, in Tamil, "Welcome, thambi."

He bowed back, trying to think of what to say, what words of comfort he could use, but he hardly knew her at all and whatever he said would sound inappropriate and distanced.

Seelan had picked up the bags and he came up to them. "How is Appa?" he asked anxiously.

"He's having a bad day," she replied. "He wants another injection but will wait until he has seen his brother."

Seelan nodded and started to lead the way up the stairs to the second floor of the building, then he remembered himself and stood aside for Balendran to go first. He and Pakkiam followed behind.

As Balendran walked up the stairs, he felt a heaviness build in him that, with each step, he was drawing closer to that moment when he would see his brother.

The flat, in contrast to the outside, was clean. The drawing room also served as the dining room. Balendran noted immediately the signs of poverty in the worn upholstery of the settee, the scarred dining table with a vase of cheap cloth flowers on it, the old dresser with a few plates, the faded curtains that hung in the doorways of the bedrooms. The walls were bare and badly needed a coat of paint.

"Seelan, is that you?" a querulous, tired voice called out from one of the rooms. "Have you all arrived?"

Balendran turned to Pakkiam inquiringly. She nodded to say that it was, indeed, Arul.

"Yes, Appa. I'll be with you in a minute."

Seelan took the bags towards the bedroom in which Balendran would be staying. He had been given Seelan's room. Balendran began to follow him, but Pakkiam placed her hand on his arm. "He's awake now, thambi. It's best to speak with him before he has another injection."

Balendran felt a coldness pass down his neck. Pakkiam was waiting. He had no choice but to do as she requested. He crossed the drawing room, drew back the curtain, and went inside.

It took a moment for Balendran's eyes to adjust to the dim room. Then he saw his brother lying on the bed. Arul had not noticed him enter and his face was turned to one side on the pillow. As Balendran stood in the shadows of the doorway staring at his brother, he realized that he had not prepared himself for this moment, that, even though he knew his brother was dying, he had imagined him with the force of character he had possessed in youth. He remembered that Arul had always been a terrible patient and he had expected to find him bitter, frightened by his death, raging at the slipping away of his life when he was only forty-seven. Instead, the man on the bed looked older than his father, his mouth open as he struggled to breathe, his face so gaunt the outline of his skull was visible, his hair thin and limp. Arul made a noise in his throat, a rasping, rattling sound. Balendran wondered if he should go and fetch Pakkiam. Then he realized that his brother, with the greatest difficulty, was clearing his throat. Balendran's nervousness fell away, replaced by a terrible sorrow.

Arul had seen him. They were both still a moment, staring at each other. Then Balendran began to walk towards the bed and Arul said softly, "Thambi-boy" and struggled to smile.

Balendran was by the bed now and Arul gestured for him to lean closer, then took his brother's face in his hands and looked at him for a long time. This close to him, Balendran could smell, beneath the eau de cologne and powder, the odour of decay in his brother, like stagnant water. Arul put his hands down on the bed and made a satisfied grunt. He went through the rattling, rasping effort of clearing his throat. Then he spoke. "You look well," he said, barely audible. "I am glad."

"You are looking quite fine –"

Arul waved his hand impatiently to say such niceties were not necessary. "Sit, sit," he said.

There was a chair in a corner of the room and Balendran brought it over and sat down. They stared at each other again, neither one knowing how to start. Then they both spoke at the same moment.

"Amma sends her –"

"How was your –"

They were silent, each waiting for the other to speak.

"Amma sends her love," Balendran repeated.

Arul nodded and they were silent again.

From another flat, Balendran could hear a child shrieking, a mother scolding.

Arul was no longer looking at him. His head was turned to the side, as if something else had caught his attention. Balendran could see from the expression on his brother's face that he was in intense pain.

Balendran noticed a walking-stick leaning up in a corner. It was Arul's, one he had carved for himself when he was boy. He had a sudden memory of Arul striding ahead of him as they went for a walk, beating at the vegetation with the walking-stick in order to frighten away snakes, singing loudly to himself.

Pakkiam and Seelan came into the room.

"Now you're happy. Your thambi is here," Pakkiam said, and propped Arul up with her body as she patted his pillows and turned them over. She smiled as she did so, but Balendran could see she was aware of the distress she was causing her husband. Arul's face seemed to collapse under the pain, his mouth hanging open. Yet, when she was done, he touched her hand in gratitude.

Seelan, Balendran noticed, was standing by the window, heating a teaspoon over a burner. He deftly picked up a syringe with his other hand and drew up the liquid on the teaspoon. Balendran noticed a white coat and a stethoscope hanging over the chair by the desk. "You're a doctor!" he said in astonishment.

Seelan blushed with pleasure.

Balendran turned to his brother in wonder. Arul and Pakkiam smiled, delighted with his surprise.

"You're looking at a University Scholarship student, thambi. London-trained," Arul said. "Just came back last month."

The University Scholarship was a rare honour, only given to the very brightest students in the colonies. Balendran looked at his nephew with doubled admiration.

Seelan came forward with the syringe, a shy but gratified smile on his face.

Arul extended his arm. Seelan took it and, with a quick movement, inserted the needle. Arul hissed and then sighed. Seelan withdrew the needle.

Both Pakkiam and Arul turned to Balendran, seeking his endorsement for the marvellous manoeuvre their son had performed. He shook his head to show his admiration, glad that they had taken his surprise as a compliment, that they had not understood it came from his very scant expectations of his brother's existence in Bombay.

Balendran watched his nephew walk back to the table by the window, followed by his parents' proud gaze. Nothing was as he had anticipated. His brother and his wife were at peace with each other. The enormous gap that existed between them had not destroyed their affections.

Balendran remembered the purpose of his visit and his father's threat to cancel Arul's allowance. Seelan had finished his work at the table and he came back and sat on the edge of his father's bed. It occurred to Balendran, as he looked at his nephew, that with him being a doctor and now practising, Pakkiam would not be dependent on his father's allowance any more. Seelan could easily provide for her on a doctor's salary. Balendran realized that his father's threat had become empty, all its power diffused.

❧

On his first morning in Bombay, Balendran went for a walk to look at the neighbourhood. He found it as dismal as his brother's residence, but then saw, amidst the squalor, a well-kept little park. He sat there for a while watching the traffic. Even the busiest streets in Ceylon were slow and uncluttered in comparison, and he found something exciting about the rush of traffic, the hooting of horns, the pedestrians who crossed willy-nilly, the cows that simply stood in the middle of the road.

When Balendran returned to his brother's flat, he heard the sound of raised voices inside and he knew that something had happened.

Upon entering, the conversation in Arul's room ceased. Pakkiam pushed open the curtain and looked out. She signalled to him. She was distraught and he dreaded that Arul's illness had taken a turn for the worse. When he went in, he was surprised to find his brother sitting up in bed, stronger than he had been yesterday. There was an enraged expression on Arul's face as he glared at his brother. A crumpled letter was lying on the bed.

"How dare you, Bala, how dare you come here with such a request," Arul cried at him. "You bastard, you bloody vulture, picking at my dead bones."

Balendran drew in his breath in dismay. His brother had found out about his father's decree.

Arul's shouting had brought on a coughing fit.

Pakkiam put her arm around him. "Don't get excited, Appa."

She nodded for Balendran to sit down in the chair by the bed. He did so. Arul had called him a "bloody vulture." His brother believed that he had remained silent with the devious intention of fighting for his body after he had died. Balendran cursed himself for not telling his brother last night.

Arul's coughing caused the letter to slip from his lap and fall to the ground. Balendran picked it up. It was in Tamil. He quickly turned it over and saw the name at the bottom. Pillai. He stared at his brother in astonishment. Even though Arul was coughing, he was watching for his brother's reaction and he managed through his coughing to nod his head as if to say, "Yes, you are surprised, aren't you? It serves you right."

Pakkiam, seeing that the coughing was not going to cease, went to get Arul some medicine from the side table.

Balendran gazed at the letter again and remembered how his mother had known of Arul's impending death through Pillai.

Pakkiam gave Arul some medicine and his coughing stopped. He lay there exhausted, breathing raspingly. After a moment, he muttered something. Pakkiam bent close to him, but he waved her away and stretched his hand out towards Balendran, who came around the side of the bed and knelt close to him. Arul muttered something in Tamil and Balendran recognized it as a verse from the *Tirukkural*. "'Knowledge is a weapon of defense, an inner fortress no foe can raze.'" Arul, seeing the puzzled look on Balendran's face, gestured to the letter. Then Balendran understood what he meant. He was talking about the knowledge of servants, their awareness of what went on in a house. Pillai was a servant *par excellence*, never supervised, his household accounts never checked, so implicit was his father's trust in him. Yet that very same Pillai had acted on his own conscience and had, all these years, maintained contact with Arul. He had flagrantly defied his master's dictates, ignored the vow he took in front of the family Gods.

Arul was looking at him, his eyes bright with the understanding that his brother knew what he meant. He beckoned Balendran close to him. "You are a fool, Bala, a damn fool." Then he quoted the *Tirukkural* again. "'Only the learned have eyes — others two sores on their face.'"

Balendran nodded, thinking his brother was talking about his ignorance of Pillai's insubordination.

Arul shook his head to say that Balendran had not understood. He gripped his arm tightly and drew him forward again. "You have been blind to the reality of life, Bala. You have spent your whole life living by codes everyone lays down but nobody follows." It was the longest sentence Arul had uttered since his coughing began and he lay back on his pillow, drained.

Pakkiam took over now. She gestured to Balendran that it was best to leave Arul to rest. Balendran nodded and got up. Arul started to protest, but Pakkiam put her hand on his shoulder and said firmly, "Enough, Appa. Your thambi and you can talk later."

Arul pushed her hand away in annoyance, but he acquiesced.

Balendran went to his bedroom, his brother's words echoing in his head. He ran the sentence over and over again in his mind, pondering what these codes were his brother was talking about. The word "everyone" lingered for a moment and he wondered if his brother was not really speaking of "everyone" but of their father. Yet what codes could he be following that his father was not?

Balendran's contemplations were disturbed by Pakkiam calling "Thambi" from the other side of the curtain in his doorway. He told her to enter. She was dressed to go out. "I need to visit the pharmacy, thambi, to get more morphine. I'll be a few minutes."

He nodded to say that he would take care of Arul in her absence. She looked at him for a moment, as if she wished to say something. Then she changed her mind and left. He heard the front door closing behind her.

The moment she was gone, he got up and went out of his room. He paused outside Arul's doorway, uncertain if he should go in or not, then he drew back the curtain and entered. Arul was propped up in bed, staring at him. He had seen him beyond the curtain. Balendran came up to the bed. He could tell his brother was not comfortable, as his head kept lolling to one side from time to time, as if keeping it straight was too great an effort. Balendran sat down on the bed. "I need to ask you something."

Arul nodded.

Balendran paused. "This . . . this code you talk about. What does it mean?"

Arul cleared his throat. "A set of rules. We are told we must follow them. Some of us obey in spite of our natures. Others only make a pretence."

Balendran looked at his brother carefully. "I always live by what I believe."

"Do you, Bala?"

"I don't understand."

Arul studied him for a moment. "Your stay in England."

Balendran was astonished. He found it difficult to believe that Arul knew anything about Richard, yet his heart was beating rapidly.

"What about England?"

Arul rolled his eyes upwards trying to think of how to express himself.

Balendran clenched his hands, waiting.

"A friend of yours there."

Balendran felt the blood rush to his face. He got up and went to the table by the window and poured a glass of water, no longer able to look at his brother.

Arul clapped his hands to get Balendran's attention. Balendran turned to him. His brother beckoned him to come and sit on the bed again. When he had done so, Arul took his hand and held it tightly in his. He cleared his throat slowly and painfully and then said, very softly, "I do not judge you."

"But how? How did you find out?"

"Pillai," Arul said. "An anonymous note. Sent to Appa."

"So Pillai reads English," Balendran said. He was silent for a moment. "Then you know."

Arul patted his hand. "Pillai wrote to me, concerned about the consequences of Appa's anger."

Balendran was silent again. His brother did not judge him. Something which might have been catastrophic had actually passed with great ease. And Pillai. He had known about all of it, but never changed his demeanour towards him.

"I'm sorry. I'm sorry things turned out the way they did," Arul said. "I blame Appa. Most of all for his own hypocrisy."

Arul was silent then, gazing ahead of him. After a moment, he made the effort to clear his throat and Balendran leant close to him. "Pakkiam's mother," Arul finally whispered.

Balendran drew back and looked at him, not understanding.

Arul sighed. "Appa only made a pretence of living by those rules he laid down so firmly. He and Pakkiam's mother . . ."

Balendran stared at his brother in disbelief. His father and Pakkiam's mother. "But . . . but it's impossible. Where would they have met?"

"In Jaffna," Arul said. "When he would go to make his inspections."

At that moment, Pakkiam entered the flat. Balendran got up from the bed hastily.

She drew the curtain aside and came into the bedroom. When she saw them both staring at her, she stopped in the doorway and looked from one to the other. Then she went to the side table and began to put out the vials of morphine she had bought.

Balendran left the room.

He felt that he had to get away from the flat in order to think clearly, so he made his way to the little park he had discovered that morning. It was deserted. He found a bench under a banyan tree and sat down, staring ahead of him. In the short course of this morning, much had changed. He was content for the moment to put aside the fact that Arul and Pillai knew of his inversion. He concentrated his mind, instead, on what he had learnt about his father. Numerous questions swarmed into his mind like buzzing flies.

With his scant knowledge, it was impossible for his father's indiscretion to become an actuality to him. He needed to know more, he needed to feel the facts, like rounded stones in his palm, rub them over and over until they became real to him. Balendran got up. It was useless for him to sit here.

When Balendran returned to the flat, he found Pakkiam sitting at the head of the dining table. She gestured for him to keep his voice low, that Arul was sleeping. He removed his hat and stood running his hand through his hair, wanting to speak with her but understanding that he had to consider her feelings, had to consider what she might wish or not wish to discuss. Pakkiam had seen his hesitancy and she beckoned for him to come and sit down at the chair on her left.

Once he was seated, they were both silent, not looking at each other.

"Ask what you will, thambi," Pakkiam finally said. She opened her palms as a gesture of her willingness, but he saw that she was tired and indifferent to his quest. Her husband, the love of her life, was slipping away from her and, in the light of that enormity, his quest, or even her past, seemed trifling and irrelevant.

Balendran was silent, ashamed to be imposing his needs on her at a time like this. "The relationship between your mother and my father . . ."

"For my mother, it wasn't love. I'm not sure what it was for him. Once my father had died, she was a widow, a desperately poor widow with a daughter to raise."

"And did you know from the beginning?"

"No. A man would come to say that my mother was wanted at the big house. I thought she had work there. I only understood, once my mother had died and I was brought to Brighton from Jaffna."

"How did you find out?"

"I was told by that very man who came to fetch my mother."

"Pillai?"

She nodded.

"But what a difficult thing for you to have been told about your own mother."

She was silent. "I was told for my own safety," she finally said, then looked away from him.

Balendran stared at her in shock.

She shook her head slowly to say that nothing had happened between his father and her.

In the silence, they could hear the hissing of the fire as water boiled out of a pot onto the stove. Pakkiam got up to attend to it. Before she left, however, she said, "Our son does not know any of this."

Now that the facts were in his hand like hard, rounded stones, Balendran, as he sat on his bed, began to feel his emotions push to the surface. He thought again of the fifteen-year-old Pakkiam and he felt a deep abhorrence for his father. His father had brought her from Jaffna to Brighton like the sacrificial Dipavali goat, fed her, clothed her, all with the intention of seducing her once she had reached a more mature age. He thought of Pakkiam's mother and wondered what had gone through her mind when she had been called to their house in Jaffna, the revulsion she must have had to control in order to keep her daughter fed. What had his father thought as he forced himself on Pakkiam's mother, as he prepared Pakkiam to take her place? A quote from the *Tirukkural* that his father often declaimed rose in his mind. "Integrity and shame are natural, only to the well born." His father must have told himself that they, being of a low caste, could not possibly have the same sentiments as those of his own wife or niece, could not possibly feel shame or the loss of self. Balendran felt an anger begin to stir within him. What terrible, offensive hypocrisy. His father felt no more revulsion for a person because of their caste than he did. Yet Arul had committed the crime. He had fallen in love with Pakkiam, he had wanted to make her his wife. He had loved where he should have simply lusted.

Balendran's anger, however, was impotent. The damage had long been done. His anger, lacking a release, turned inward. Balendran berated himself that he had justified what his father had done to Arul, that he had been understanding of his father's views.

"I, too, am a hypocrite," Balendran said, disgusted with himself. He got up and began to pace around the room. Arul was right. He had been blind, blind to the realities of life.

But Arul had said something else. About those who lived by the rules despite their nature.

Balendran looked around him at the shabby furniture of Seelan's bedroom, the bare walls, the faded, threadbare coverlet, the almirah propped up by bricks where the legs had fallen off. Arul had foregone his wealth, his status. He had worked in a lowly job. Yet he had a happiness that eluded Balendran with his fine house and high position. He thought of his own study, its expensive furniture, shelves of books, the ebony stand with the bowl of flowers on it, the sea breeze that gently moved the lace curtains back and forth. He recalled the day, six months earlier, when he had heard about Richard's imminent arrival in Ceylon, how he had stood in his study, Edward Carpenter's book in his hands, and said that he truly believed what his father had done had been for the best, saving him from an unhappy fate.

Balendran saw that what had changed now was that the thing which had comforted him in his exile from himself had been taken away. His love and admiration for his father, his understanding that his father had, ultimately, done what was right for him, were gone. The prop of his existence had been dislodged. He could no longer count on it for succour. All that was left was the heaviness of regret for a time, for a moment, that was irredeemably past.

⁂

In the days that followed, Balendran mourned the loss of his father, the one he had imagined was his, though he was not conscious that he was mourning. In fact, he would have been hardpressed to give a name to the variety of emotions that passed through him in a day.

Mirroring Balendran's volatile emotional state, Arul's disease ebbed and flowed, changing direction sometimes from hour to hour. None of them was quite certain what to expect, save that the end would come soon. There were mornings when Arul was not conscious of the world around him and they were sure he would be gone by the evening. Then by mid-afternoon he would stir to life, able to talk without coughing much. Balendran and Arul spent most of their time in companionable silence, because of his brother's increasing breathlessness. When they did talk, they chose not to discuss their father. Instead, they talked about their holidays, their escapades as boys, the old neighbours, the Kandiah girls at Lotus Cottage. A bond grew between the brothers that had not existed before. Or perhaps it had. For as they talked of their childhood, even of their quarrels, they found in those shared memories a life lived together.

Balendran began to call Pakkiam "akka" to show his respect for the person she had become despite her past, to show his desire to be accepted as family by her. Pakkiam tried to return his affection and respect, though understandably her attention was absorbed by the impending catastrophe of her husband's death.

With Seelan, Balendran saw, one evening, the person beneath his nephew's formal manner. Pakkiam had retired early to bed from exhaustion, leaving them alone to watch over Arul. They sat in silence, Seelan reading and Balendran lost in his thoughts. After a while, Balendran glanced up to find his nephew staring at him. Seelan quickly looked away. Yet, after a moment, he returned his gaze to his uncle. Balendran could tell that his nephew was struggling with something and he waited.

"What is it like . . . Brighton?"

Balendran was surprised. "It . . . it's quite nice. A three-storey house. A large front garden."

"Do you live there?"

"No. I . . . my wife and I live alone."

"I've often thought that I should like to pay a visit to Ceylon."

Seelan had spoken casually, yet he was watching Balendran intently all the while to gauge his reaction.

"Well, I don't see why not," Balendran said, because he could not think of what else to say without sounding rude. "You should come and visit us."

Seelan's face lit up, making him suddenly handsome. "Do you really mean it?" he asked.

"Yes, of course."

Seelan looked down at his hands, then glanced up shyly. "I would like that," he said, a depth of feeling in his voice. Then he was silent, playing with the pages of his book. He spoke again, his voice low. "I'm finding it so hard to get used to life here after London. I was so happy there. I . . . I really felt as if I belonged. I hated to come back."

At that moment, Arul stirred in his bed and moaned. Seelan got up and went to see if he needed anything.

Balendran looked at his nephew and he felt a welling up of tenderness towards him, the same tenderness he would have felt for a lame cat or a broken-winged bird.

When Balendran had been in London, he had been well provided for. Yet there had been other students from the colonies, scholarship holders or those from less-affluent families. They had lived in unheated garrets, sometimes three or four to a room; hollow-cheeked, constantly coughing or sniffling. They were despised by their landlords and shunned by the more prosperous students from the colonies. This was probably how Seelan had lived. It must have plagued him to see students like his son, Lukshman, carefree and rich, and know that, if not for his parents' banishment, he would have been of their rank. Then to come back from even that poor existence to this flat, surrounded by people who did not understand his aspirations or tastes. It must be truly unbearable. His nephew's self-important, dandyish manner, his anglophilia was an attempt to bridge, in some way, the space between who he was and who he felt he should be.

When Balendran retired for the night, he noticed that the doors to Seelan's almirah had been left open. He was aware of the sparsity of clothes and their shabbiness. The suit Seelan had worn to meet him was his only fine one. It was carefully sheathed in a cloth covering. Balendran thought of his son's almirah, with its abundance of clothes, the bottom lined with shoes, and he felt the unfairness, that the only thing that stood between Seelan and his desires was his grandfather. Then an idea struck him. Once Pakkiam was settled and provided for, if his nephew wanted to come to Colombo to visit, why shouldn't he do so?

❧

The next morning, Balendran was returning from an errand when he noticed a lot of activity on the balcony of the second floor. As he got closer, he saw that people were congregated outside his brother's doorway.

When he entered the flat, the curtain to Arul's room had been pulled back. Some neighbours had gathered in the flat, while others hovered outside. Seelan was by the side of the bed, feeling Arul's pulse. He was still in his white doctor's coat so he must have rushed back from the hospital. Pakkiam was at the foot of the bed, watching anxiously. They looked up as Balendran entered.

Seelan straightened up. "His pulse is barely there." He repeated the same thing in Tamil to Pakkiam. She kneaded her arm with her hand, her face distraught.

Seelan started to leave the room. As he passed Balendran he said, "It's Amma's wish that she is alone with Appa when he dies."

Balendran did not hear him. He was staring at his brother, stunned by this rapid turn of events, despite everything unprepared for his brother's death.

Seelan repeated himself. Balendran nodded and followed him out. As he left, he saw Pakkiam sit down on the side of the bed and take Arul's hand. Just before Seelan drew the curtain across, he turned to see her lying her head on Arul's chest.

The neighbours had left, giving them their privacy. Balendran and Seelan sat in the drawing room for what seemed to them an interminable amount of time. Balendran glanced at his nephew, at the frightened look on his face, and wondered how he could have ever seriously thought he would ask for the return of his brother's body to Ceylon. He vowed to not even request a little ash to release into the sea at Keerimalai.

His thoughts were interrupted by a movement from the bedroom. They stood up quickly.

"Mahan," Pakkiam called out, "mahan."

Seelan hurried into the room and Balendran followed. Pakkiam was standing by the bed, her eyes wide with fear. She stared intently at her son, her entire body an entreaty that what she suspected was not so. He went to the bed and took Arul's hand in his.

After a moment, Seelan laid his father's hand down and looked up at his mother. The room became still. Then Pakkiam sank to her knees by the side of the bed. She buried her face in

Arul's arm. After a moment, her hand fell open, palm upwards. "Mahan," she said in a muffled tone. "Please give me something. This pain is unbearable."

⨓

The funeral was the next day and, contrary to the Mudaliyar's wishes, it was a simple affair. Arul had laid down very clear instructions for his funeral and, when Balendran saw them, he felt admiration for his brother. They were exactly what his father would have feared. It was a burial that befitted a simple man whose family name was not important. Balendran tried to offset whatever expenses there were, but Arul had put away enough to pay for his funeral. Balendran was surprised by the number of friends Arul had made in his time in India. Every neighbour from the building dropped in to pay their respects, as did his fellow workers.

Balendran and Seelan accompanied the bier to the crematorium. There, Balendran watched as Seelan began to walk around the pyre, setting it alight with a torch at each corner.

Seelan had come to the last corner now and he turned on impulse and offered the torch to his uncle. Balendran looked at him, surprised. The kurukkal who was conducting the funeral came towards them to try and stop the irregularity of the proceedings, but Balendran quickly took the torch from Seelan and set fire to the last corner. Then he handed the torch to the kurukkal and stepped back. He looked at his brother's corpse as the flames began to surround it.

19

A peacock's feather can break the axle-tree
Of an overloaded cart.
   — The Tirukkural, *verse 475*

Hσω marriage changes a person, Annalukshmi thought. She looked at Kumudini propped up on their mother's bed, the bulge in her stomach beginning to show through her sari. Kumudini had been back only a day, and Annalukshmi saw that there was a strange new confidence to her sister that had not been there before. A slightly superior, bossy manner, a way of ordering everyone around. Kumudini said she was happy, yet Annalukshmi could not help feeling that there was something amiss. She had come upon her sister once or twice crying, and when she questioned her, Kumudini had put it down simply to the emotional vagaries of a pregnant woman.

Kumudini noted her sister looking at her and smiled, patting the bed for Annalukshmi to come and sit beside her. "How are things going with you at the school, akka?" she asked.

"Fine," Annalukshmi replied as she sat down.

"Chutta tells me that you don't visit Miss Lawton as much as you used to."

"What rubbish," Annalukshmi said. "Of course I do. It's just that with this play, I don't have much time."

At that moment, they heard the sound of a bicycle bell at the gate.

"Akka, it's the mail, run along like a dear and see if there is anything for me."

As Annalukshmi went towards the front door, she thought, as she had done so often over the last two weeks, about Miss Lawton. It was not as if she had been unaware of the head-mistress's attitudes. She had chosen not to reflect on them too deeply. Something that had been there all along had now moved into the foreground. It was like walking into one's bedroom with its familiar bric-à-brac and, because of the passing away of a loved one, being sharply conscious of their photograph that had been for years in the same place on the dresser.

Miss Lawton had often spoken with such fervour of the ameliorated position of women in England since the beginning of this century, how her work here in Ceylon was committed to helping women better themselves. Yet it was clear that for Miss Lawton the right of women to be free to pursue whatever they chose did not truly encompass women of the colonies. Annalukshmi felt saddened. It seemed that something irrevocable now stood between them.

When she came out onto the verandah, Letchumi, who had returned from her holidays last week, was already bringing the post to the front door. Annalukshmi took the letters from her, glanced at the addresses, and saw that there was one from Muttiah. She asked Letchumi to take it to her sister directly. Then she heard the gate open. She looked out and saw Philomena Barnett coming up the front path. "Amma, Aunt Philomena is here," she called out.

After a moment, Louisa came in, shaking her head. She knew Philomena could not wait to find out what had kept Kumudini in Malaya.

After Louisa had met Kumudini's ship at the harbour and they were driving home, Kumudini had seemed distant and quiet. When Louisa asked her why she had waited so long to come home, Kumudini had at first seemed annoyed, but then explained that medical standards in Malaya were quite advanced enough and that she felt this habit of women coming home for their confinement was out of date and unnecessary. Louisa knew, however, that Philomena would try to create an intrigue around this.

"Cousin," Philomena said in an urgent whisper when Louisa came out of the front door to greet her. "So, so, what happened? What took her so long?"

Louisa told her what Kumudini had said, but Philomena immediately dismissed this explanation with a wave of her hand. "You don't know these Hindus. Very crafty. I am sure that her in-laws have influenced her, no matter what she says."

"I assure you, cousin, that was not the case."

"Then why did she not come before?"

"I've told you why," Louisa snapped at her.

"Well, well, let me talk to her."

Philomena nodded a greeting to Annalukshmi, then went in to look for Kumudini.

Annalukshmi hurried after her aunt. "Let me make sure Kumudini is not asleep."

Annalukshmi went quietly into the bedroom. Kumudini was propped up in bed. The opened letter was on her lap and there was a pensive expression on her face. Then, when she noticed Annalukshmi, she quickly folded the letter.

Philomena now barged into the room.

"Well, hmmm, it's very nice to see you, Kumudini," Philomena said.

Kumudini's eyes narrowed and she said with hostility, "I hope you haven't come to tire me out, Aunt Philomena."

Philomena, not used to being spoken to in this way, looked at her, open-mouthed.

∾

A few days after school had begun, Annalukshmi walked into the staff room one morning to find herself witness to a conversation between Nancy and Mr. Jayaweera. They were in Miss Lawton's office and did not hear her enter. Mr. Jayaweera's brother, she overheard, had finally returned from exile in India. He had visited Mr. Jayaweera the previous night at his lodgings in Pettah. Nancy was pleading with Mr. Jayaweera to be careful about seeing his brother openly or too often, as it could lead to trouble again.

Finally, Nancy pushed her chair back. "Well, I can only advise you," she said. "But you must think of your mother and sisters and the plight they will be in if anything happens to you." With that, she came out of the office.

Annalukshmi, who was seated at the table by now, hurriedly bent over a student's exercise book.

Nancy stopped in surprise when she saw her friend, then came up to her. "Oh . . . I didn't realize you were here," she said.

"Yes, the bell rang a little while ago," Annalukshmi replied without looking up.

In the days that followed, Nancy made no mention of her unhappiness, or of the fact that Mr. Jayaweera's brother had returned. Yet Annalukshmi could not help but feel concern for her friend and wonder what the consequences would be for Mr. Jayaweera.

༅

One afternoon, a week later, Annalukshmi was tidying up her classroom after the last bell when Nancy came and stood in the doorway, surveying her with the smile of someone who knew a delicious secret. "Hello," she said.

"Hello," Annalukshmi replied. She beckoned for her to enter the classroom, then picked up the duster and began to clean the blackboard.

Nancy walked into the class and sat on the edge of a desk. "You'll never guess who one of the other boarders is at the house where Vijith is staying. Grace Macintosh's brother."

Annalukshmi dropped her duster. It fell to the floor with a clatter. She turned quickly to her friend.

Nancy smiled. "Yes," she said. "Your Macintosh boy."

Annalukshmi picked up the duster. "How . . . how do you know this?" she asked, as she could think of nothing else to say.

"Vijith told me yesterday, when we met in Victoria Park. He happened to mention your name, and Mackie, as they call him, asked if it was you. He even showed Vijith a photograph your family sent him of you."

The photograph, as yet unreturned, gave a sudden concreteness to what Nancy was saying. Annalukshmi recalled now that Mr. Jayaweera had mentioned that a woman owned the boarding house. It was the Macintosh boy's lover! She turned to Nancy.

"Her name is Srimani," Nancy said. "You better sit down and prepare yourself for this." Annalukshmi leant against her desk. "He didn't run away to be with her," Nancy said.

"But we were told that —"

"Your Macintosh boy ran away not for a woman but for a box of paints."

"Nancy, what are you talking about?"

"He left his parents' house because he wanted to devote his life to his art. Srimani provided him with a haven to work in. According to Vijith, she's always offering a hand to various waifs and strays."

"Isn't that extraordinary."

"He wants to see you."

Annalukshmi stared at her, stunned.

Nancy took out a note from her book and put it on the desk. "Let me know what you want to do," she said and left the classroom.

Once Nancy had gone, Annalukshmi continued to clean the board. She worked deliberately and meticulously, concentrating on carefully erasing even the chalk marks on the very edges. The task gave her the necessary calmness she needed. When she was finished, she wiped her hands with her handkerchief, then sat down to read the note.

"It seems that we must be destined to meet," the note began without any salutation. "Could you accompany your friend next Saturday? I would like very much to meet you and show you my paintings."

She put it down and rubbed her temples with her fingers. In her mind, the Macintosh boy had run away to be with the love of his life. This she had accepted as a fact. She had even imagined the woman, given her the beauty and the intelligence of a younger version of her Aunt Sonia. Now to discover that the Macintosh boy had run away for a "box of paints." There arose in her mind the image she had formed of the Macintosh boy – handsome like his father and, because he had stood by his convictions, a man of courage and honesty. A sliver of light opened in her, as if someone had separated the louvres of a blind. "This is foolish," she said aloud.

She began to busy herself straightening the desks in the classroom, hoping to rid herself of this ludicrous feeling. Yet it danced before her mind, like the streamers of a kite blowing gaily in the breeze. "It seems we are destined to meet," the note had said. Perhaps he regretted his earlier hastiness, perhaps he realized the irrationality of his fears. For they were irrational. She would never think to interfere with his art. She was not the kind of woman who would cling to her husband. She liked to be alone. Her Sunday reading under the flamboyant tree, she guarded fiercely. Was it possible that the Macintosh boy wanted to open up a chapter that was closed?

∞

Once she agreed to go with Nancy the following Saturday, Annalukshmi passed the week in a state of some nervousness. She decided that she would not dress too well, as this might make it appear that she had certain expectations. Yet she chose one of her favourite saris. A minutely checked red-and-cream Japanese Georgette. With it, she wore a simple cream cotton blouse with a V neckline and elbow-length sleeves.

When Saturday came, Annalukshmi and Nancy took the train to Pettah. It was a short journey from Colpetty, a mere ten-minute ride. When they got off at the Pettah station, Mr. Jayaweera was waiting for them. Once they had left the station, he led them along a busy street. Halfway down, they stopped in front of a very old house, built in the early nineteenth century. The house was elevated high above the street to prevent flooding during monsoon season. Two flights of stairs rose up from either side to a common landing. From there, a few steps led to a pillared verandah. What was unique and whimsical about the house was that the doors, the lattice-work windows, the fretwork mal lallis were all painted a sky blue, which contrasted sharply with the whitewashed walls.

Mr. Jayaweera went up the steps and they followed him. He took a key out of his pocket, opened the door, and they entered.

Like most of the houses of the period, its exterior was deceptively small. A corridor led to a meda midula, open to the sky, and beyond it there was another corridor that stretched far into the distance. A woman came out of a room and peered inquiringly at them.

"Oh, it's you," she said to Mr. Jayaweera. She came towards them.

Annalukshmi stared at her. She wore a man's sarong and a man's shirt that was open at the neck. On her feet were a pair of men's slippers. Her top knot and simple pearl necklace emphasized the long elegance of her neck. She had a cigarette between her fingers.

She had reached them now and she held out her hand. "I'm Srimani," she said. "You are both most welcome here." She waved her hand to her surroundings. "We are a relaxed household, so please make yourself at home and do as you like."

Then she turned away as if she had forgotten them and drifted back towards the room.

Mr. Jayaweera took them down the corridor. He stopped in front of an open door and looked at Annalukshmi meaningfully. She felt a quick coldness travel down her spine.

Mr. Jayaweera knocked.

"Come in," a voice called out.

They entered. It was a studio filled with canvases and half-finished paintings. At first they could not see anyone, then he stepped out from behind an easel. The Macintosh boy.

When she had thought of him at all, Annalukshmi had imagined him as someone whose appearance was somehow noteworthy. What she had not expected was that he would look like a person she could easily pass on the street and never remember. He was of average height and build and wore a painter's smock. The most defining feature of his face was his moustache, which drooped down on either side, giving him a sad look that was promptly dispelled when he smiled, his eyes merry. He came up to her. "At last, we meet," he said and held his hand out. His voice had a pleasant, resonant timber.

She shook his hand, tongue-tied. She had not expected him to be so much at ease, to refer so casually to their failed meeting and, at the same time, lightly smooth over it.

He now shook hands with Nancy. "Make yourself at home," he said, pointing to some chairs. Then he went behind a curtain and they heard him fiddling around with plates and cups.

"Annalukshmi," Nancy whispered.

She turned to her.

"We are going," Nancy mouthed at her.

Annalukshmi raised her eyebrows in alarm, but before she could protest, Nancy took Mr. Jayaweera by the hand and they went out of the room.

Annalukshmi looked after them in panic. She had not envisioned being left unaccompanied with the Macintosh boy.

Chandran Macintosh came out from behind the curtain with a tray. He stopped when he saw that they were alone. A look of discomfort passed over his face. Annalukshmi felt her own uneasiness increase. He gestured towards a chair and she went and sat down. He put the tea tray on the table between them and settled down in the other armchair across from her.

"What do you take in your tea?" he asked.

She told him and he prepared it for her. She noted that the cups and saucers did not match.

He offered her the tea and then sat back in his chair, his cup in his hand. The preparation of the tea had provided a rest in their awkwardness. Now an uncomfortable silence fell between them.

Annalukshmi, to avoid meeting his eyes, looked around the studio.

"Oh yes, I forgot," Chandran Macintosh said with relief. "I am supposed to give you a tour."

He put down his cup and stood up. She did the same, equally glad that they had found something to fill in the silence. He led her to the picture he was painting. It was nearly finished.

The first thing Annalukshmi noticed was that the three women in the picture were bare-breasted. She felt a momentary embarrassment but, knowing that art was art, she quelled this feeling and tried to look at the painting objectively. On the left side of the canvas, a woman was lying in the arms of a blue-skinned man. The other two women were on the right.

"I call it *Mrs. X At-Home,*" he said.

She looked at him, not understanding.

"You know," he said, somewhat impatiently. "At-homes, those tea parties Cinnamon Gardens ladies have."

Annalukshmi nodded quickly and gazed at the painting. He was a little put out that she did not understand, but honestly she could not comprehend what the painting had to do with an at-home.

"It was inspired by a conversation I heard at one of my mother's at-homes. The ladies were discussing a servant girl who had been caught . . . you know . . . with the gardener. Their righteous indignation made me want to portray them as crows picking at the servant girl's entrails, but that would have been too obvious. Instead, it struck me that they might, deep in themselves, envy the servant girl. So I painted it like that."

Annalukshmi looked at the painting again, recognizing the servant girl with the gardener and the imperious-looking woman at the extreme right of the picture as Mrs. X. Then, with a start, she realized that the desolate-looking third woman was Mrs X's image in a mirror. "It's jolly good," Annalukshmi cried, forgetting herself. She pointed to the two white lines, at right angles, that denoted the mirror. Chandran Macintosh smiled in pleasure. "Come, let me show you some others," he said.

She gestured to him that she was not finished and stood back, surveying the painting. Annalukshmi's knowledge of art was what she had been taught in school, mostly Renaissance painters. As she gazed at this painting, she felt as if she were learning a new grammar, a new language. For a change of space was indicated not by doors or walls or gates, but by a change of colour in the background; objects like the mirror were merely suggested and not fully represented.

When she was ready to move on, she turned to him and smiled. Their eyes met and held. In that instant, Annalukshmi felt her wonder and delight at the painting transfer itself onto him. A warmth broke open inside her.

Chandran Macintosh led the way to another painting and she followed.

Annalukshmi had been unsure what she thought of the Macintosh boy's appearance, but now she knew that she found him handsome. She liked his thick, curly hair that made him look like he had just got out of bed, his rather large nose. He was not wearing a shirt under his smock and, through the white cotton, she could make out the hair on his chest, the darkness of his nipples.

They had come to another painting. One of a horse being tamed by two men. As he began to explain this to her, Annalukshmi found herself thinking about the moment when their eyes had met. She was sure that something had passed through his face that had not been there before.

The last painting he showed her was one of herself developed from the sketch he had done. When he swung it around for her to see, she drew in her breath in surprise. He stood back and looked at it critically. "Hmm," he said. "I should have made you darker."

He picked up a brush, dipped it in a colour on his palette, and touched up her hand until it was closer to her own colour.

"I am planning to include it in an exhibition I am having in July." He went to a large wooden desk by the window to get something. "I'd like it very much if you would come," he said, handing her a printed card that announced the exhibition and gave the time and place.

"Thank you," she said. "I've never been to an exhibition before." And she tucked the invitation away.

"Tell me, do you like what I've done with your portrait?" he asked.

She nodded. "Very much."

"Then I shall give it to you, after the exhibition."

She began to protest, but he held up his hand. "Please. It's my way of saying I am sorry for the whole débâcle . . . you know."

Chandran Macintosh had spoken with good intentions, yet his words were like cold water thrown at Annalukshmi. He was talking about what happened as if it were something far past, something long over.

The buoyancy Annalukshmi felt since that moment their eyes had met began to drain out of her.

Chandran Macintosh had become awkward as well. He gestured to her to come and have her tea.

When they were seated, cups in hand, he said, "So I am forgiven, I hope . . . for that."

"Yes," she said, not looking at him.

"It was not you," he said. "The fact is I don't ever intend to get married." He waved his hand to his canvases. "I am married to this and no woman would agree to take second place to it. I hope you understand."

Annalukshmi looked up at him quickly, then away.

"Marriage would mean family," he said, leaning forward. "And family would mean I'd have to give up what I love and get a proper job. Some boring appointment in the civil service."

The slightly beseeching tone in his voice made her glance at him again. She saw, much to her dismay, that he must have assumed that she had come to see him with an expectation that his ideas about marriage had changed. A terrible embarrassment took hold of her. She put her cup on the table, afraid it might rattle in her hand. She knew that she had to look up at him, had to say something to save herself from shame.

"I don't intend to get married either," she said. "Marriage would mean giving up my career as a teacher."

"Good. That makes me feel better about the whole thing."

She felt that he did not believe her, that he thought she had made it up on the spur of the moment.

He put down his cup, pushed his chair back, and stood up. She stood up too. "Thank you very much for coming."

She bowed slightly. "Thank you for the tour of your studio. It was very informative."

Then she turned and left.

When Annalukshmi came out into the corridor, she did not know which way to go. She could feel the tears welling up deep inside her, like the beginnings of an infection. She knew she had to leave this house before she lost control of herself. Fortunately, at that moment, Nancy and Mr. Jayaweera came down the corridor. Nancy hurried up to her with a look of concern. "What happened?" she asked.

"Nothing," Annalukshmi replied, keeping careful command over her voice and face. "He had to get back to his work."

"Well, never mind, come and have some lunch with us and we'll go back together after tea."

Annalukshmi gave a tight smile. "I think I'll go home."

"But Srimani is expecting us to stay for lunch."

"No thank you." What did Nancy want her to do? Follow them around like an unwanted guest? Sit by herself in a room for the whole afternoon? She turned to Mr. Jayaweera. "Can you get me a rickshaw to take me back to the station?"

He nodded and went to attend to it.

Nancy walked her to the door. "Are you sure, Annalukshmi? Are you sure you don't want to stay?" she asked.

Annalukshmi glared at her. "Why?" she snapped. "Do you want me to stay?"

Nancy raised her eyebrows to say that Annalukshmi was being unnecessarily cross.

They went out of the door in silence, and Mr. Jayaweera soon appeared with a rickshaw.

Once the rickshaw had set off, Annalukshmi leant back in the seat and allowed her tears to flow. She berated her own naïveté. How foolish she must have looked to him. How foolish she had been to imagine that because he had not run away for another woman he might be interested in her. He had asked her to visit him not because he wished to consider her as a potential wife, but so that he could apologize for disappearing as he had. She thought of the portrait of herself he had offered. She knew he was sincere, but, in her current mood, she could not stop herself from thinking, What audacity, what gall to think I needed to be appeased in that way? Who does he think he is to imagine that I would need his apologies, his gift? She tried to come up with disparaging thoughts about his paintings, but her admiration was genuine. The best she could do was comment to herself on the preponderance of nude women and wonder cattily if he had not noticed that most women did keep their clothes on.

When Annalukshmi came in through the gates of Lotus Cottage, she saw Kumudini seated on the verandah alone, her hands resting on her stomach, a smile on her face, and she felt strongly the fetters of her own narrow life. Her soul stretched tightly against the edges of her existence, longing to burst out, but it was frustratingly confined.

20

Many spotted minds bathe in holy streams
And lead a double life.
  — The Tirukkural, *verse 278*

When Balendran's steamer reached Colombo, it was evening. Instead of going home, he decided to proceed to Brighton by taxi and face his father. Balendran felt his heart begin to beat rapidly as he saw the familiar whitewashed façade of the house.

He instructed the taxi to take him to the back. He got out of the car, told the driver to wait, and walked along the open corridor that connected the main house and the kitchen.

The door that led from the study into the vestibule was open, and Balendran went in without knocking. The Mudaliyar was sitting at his table, reading. Balendran stared at his father. Somewhere in his mind, he had expected to find the changes he felt towards his father reflected in his face, but he looked the same.

The Mudaliyar glanced up and saw Balendran. He stood quickly. They were still, looking at each other.

"We didn't know you were coming back so soon," the Mudaliyar said almost as an accusation.

"Yes, Appa. Death came and I saw no reason to remain."

For a moment, the Mudaliyar's stern expression slipped. Then he regained composure. "You should have telegraphed. What have you arranged for the coffin?"

Balendran did not meet his gaze.

"Is it still at the docks?"

Again Balendran did not answer.

The Mudaliyar came around the table. He stood in front of him. "Did the coffin not come with you? Has there been some delay?"

After a moment, Balendran shook his head.

"*When* does it come?"

Balendran's hands had been clasped together tightly, and he now relaxed his grip. "The truth is, it does not," he said. "The funeral took place in Bombay."

The Mudaliyar stepped back, a stricken look on his face.

"Yes," Balendran said, his voice gaining confidence. "The funeral has taken place according to Arul's instructions."

The Mudaliyar sat down in his chair. "But didn't you try to stop it?" he asked, his voice quavering.

"It would have made no difference if I had," Balendran said. "Arul had left instructions and they were to be carried out. Besides, they are not in need of your assistance."

The Mudaliyar leant forward. "Am I to understand that you did not broach the subject at all?" he said, his voice awful with anger.

"What would you have me do? Did you really think I could ask my nephew to let his father be cremated by people he doesn't know, people who have rejected him because of his birth? How could you have even expected that?"

The Mudaliyar stared at him, astounded.

Before either one of them could continue, the study door

opened and Nalamma entered. She stood still when she saw her son.

"Amma," Balendran said gently. "It's over."

"Aiyo," she said. "Aiyo, aiyo."

She swayed slightly.

Balendran, afraid she was going to faint, went and put his arm around her.

She looked from the Mudaliyar to Balendran. "When can I see him?"

The Mudaliyar glared at Balendran, as if to say that, since he had failed to bring Arul back, he could be the one to tell his mother.

"Come," Balendran said, "let's go upstairs. We can talk there."

With his arm around his mother, he guided her out. As he left his father's study, he glanced back and saw the Mudaliyar staring at him with a look of anger and hatred on his face he had never seen before.

When Balendran entered Sevena, Sonia was sitting in a corner of the drawing room, looking over some paperwork that related to the Girls' Friendly Society. "Bala," she cried and stood up quickly.

She looked at him for a long moment. "I'm sorry."

He came to her and kissed her on the cheek, then sat down in a chair, suddenly very tired. Now that the strain of meeting his father was over, Balendran felt the sadness of his brother's death take hold of him once again.

Sonia came and stood behind him. "Poor Bala," she said and put her arms around his shoulders. He held her hands and kissed them. "Would you like some tea? A drink?" she asked.

He shook his head.

"When is the funeral to be?"

"It already happened."

Sonia came around the side of the chair. "What do you mean?"

"All according to his instructions. A simple funeral for a simple man. No pomp and ceremony. He died as he had lived."

"Have you told your father?"

He nodded. "Appa didn't take it very well."

"Well, that's fine," Sonia said with spirit. "I am proud of you, Bala. You did what was right."

Balendran squeezed her hand in gratitude, comforted by her approval.

"And your mother?" Sonia said. "Should I go to her tonight?"

He shook his head. "She has retired to bed. Perhaps in the morning."

"Very well then, let me go and tell the cook to prepare something for you to eat."

Once Sonia had left, Balendran thought of his mother's terrible grief. When he had explained why he could not ask that his brother's body be returned to Colombo, he had been taken aback by her understanding and her support of his decision.

He found himself wondering, for the first time, how much she might have known about Pakkiam and his father. He tried to recall her treatment of Pakkiam, if there had been harshness, but he could not remember that being so. In all the interactions he recalled between them, his mother had handled her just like she would another servant.

The sorrow that Balendran felt made it difficult for him to sleep, despite his exhaustion. As he paced his bedroom, he found himself thinking about those yearly holidays his family took in Jaffna at their ancestral home. During the holiday he would be bored, alienated in this strange place, away from his friends, his familiar books and hobbies, forced to play with his Jaffna cousins who, in the ensuing year, had become strangers. Yet, when it was all over and he came back to Colombo, he would remember the holiday with nostalgia, suddenly missing the company of his cousins, the sea baths, the huge prawns from the Jaffna lagoon, the barren landscape with its palmyra trees, even the saline water of Jaffna. In the same way, Balendran felt a longing now for Bombay and his time there. Forgotten was the squalor outside his brother's flat, the meagre meals, the stifling room in which he had slept. Instead, he remembered the conversations with his brother; Pakkiam, Seelan, and he sitting down to a meal in companionable silence.

The next morning, Balendran resumed his normal duties.

He went first to their temple in Pettah. It was on a road that at one time had been one of the most exclusive residential streets in Ceylon. From the turn of this century, it had become increasingly a commercial street. The temple was a simple structure and would have had very little business were it not for the statue of the dancing Siva that was supposed to have miraculous powers. The Mudaliyar's grandfather had owned a fleet of boats for pearl fishing. The legend was that, in a dream, Siva appeared to him, instructing him to cast his net at a certain place. He had obeyed, but, instead of a fine catch of oysters, his workers had drawn up the statue entangled in the nets.

The man outside the temple who took care of people's shoes for a small fee bowed low when Balendran got out of the car. He pushed at his assistant, and the boy ran inside to alert the chief priest of Balendran's arrival. Balendran removed his shoes, stepped into the temple, and stood looking around him. This was his favourite time to visit, when no devotees were present. An air of repose permeated the interior. In one part of the temple was a shrine to the goddess Durga, where supplicants lit lamps made of halves of limes. Balendran noted the area was cluttered and untidy. He looked towards the office, wondering why the chief priest had not come out yet. Impatient with waiting, Balendran went to the office. There was no one there and he walked around the back to the chief priest's quarters. He stood outside his house and called to him. After a few moments, the chief priest emerged, chewing beetal.

"I have been waiting," Balendran said angrily.

"Oh, durai, I'm sorry," the chief priest said. "The boy came and told me you were here, but I thought, Why would durai come?"

Balendran frowned. "Why not?"

The chief priest opened his eyes wide. "Durai doesn't know? Your father's worker, Pillai, was here early this morning to empty the tills."

Balendran looked at him in astonishment. The chief priest turned away to spit beetal juice into an old can, but Balendran saw the sly look on his face. The priest knew that Balendran was not aware Pillai had been.

"Is there anything else the durai needs?"

"Let's inspect the temple," Balendran said brusquely.

"But your father's worker already —"

"Never mind. I wish to do it."

The chief priest reluctantly led the way and Balendran followed. The meaning of this was clear. His father, because of his failure to comply with his orders, was punishing him by withdrawing responsibilities. In order to win back a sense of honour, to demonstrate that he was still in charge, Balendran was more than normally critical, pointing out the slight tarnishing on the brass lamps, the old offerings that needed to be cleaned out, the fact that some of the statues had been lackadaisically dressed that morning. The chief priest nodded at all his comments and promised to fix everything he pointed out. Yet there was an indulgence to his tone, as if he were humouring him.

When Balendran got into his car again, his hands were shaking with anger. "Home, Sin-Aiyah?" Joseph asked.

"No," Balendran said. "Take me to Brighton."

Even though Brighton's verandah was crowded with petitioners, Balendran instructed Joseph to drive around to the front of the house. Rather than ringing the bell, he went along the verandah to the door that led into his father's study. "Is anyone in there with my father?" he asked the next petitioner in line, a poor man.

"Yes, aiyah," he replied.

Balendran stood outside the door, waiting. Everyone on the verandah was looking at him curiously, aware that he was the Mudaliyar Navaratnam's son, but he did not care what they thought or how they felt about him standing outside his father's door like a petitioner.

Finally, a widow in a white sari emerged. Miss Adamson led her out. Balendran quickly stepped up to the door and said to a surprised Miss Adamson, "I want to see my father."

Balendran brushed past her and went inside.

The Mudaliyar was pretending to attend to business at his desk, a thing he always did with the poorer petitioners. He would keep them standing by his desk for quite a while before he put down his work and turned to them with a weary air, as if they had disturbed him in the middle of some very important deliberation. Thus he did not glance up as Balendran approached the desk and stood in front of it.

"Appa."

The Mudaliyar looked at him, startled.

"I want to talk to you, alone." He looked pointedly at Miss Adamson.

After a moment, the Mudaliyar waved his hand at Miss Adamson and she left the room, going out into the vestibule.

"I went to the temple today, but Pillai had already been."

The Mudaliyar indicated for Balendran to sit, but he shook his head, preferring to stand.

"Yes," the Mudaliyar said. "I thought it best. You have taken on more than you can handle. So I am relieving you of some of your duties. That way you can concentrate better on the others. Do them right."

Balendran's face grew hot at this insult. "What?" he cried. "Which one of my duties have I not done right?"

"I will not have my son raise his voice to me. Sit down. How dare you stand over me like this."

Balendran folded his arms to his chest. "That's not the real reason."

"I don't understand what you are talking about."

Balendran stared at him, disconcerted. His father had backed him into a corner by feigning ignorance. If he pointed out the actual cause, his father would dismiss it as fanciful imaginings. He felt a frustration boil up in him, so strong that he wanted to smash something.

"Pillai has become lazy," the Mudaliyar continued. "All he does the whole day is eat and sleep. This new responsibility will —"

Balendran turned away and walked towards the door.

"I haven't finished speaking."

Balendran ignored him and left the study.

As he stepped out, he noticed that all eyes were upon him and he wondered if the petitioners had overheard the conversation. He did not care. He walked quickly down the verandah. As he approached his car, he saw Pillai and Joseph deep in conversation. Seeing him, Pillai straightened up respectfully.

"Sin-Aiyah," Pillai said and opened the car door.

Balendran ignored him and got in.

"There is something for Sin-Aiyah on the back seat."

Balendran nodded curtly. He glanced at the parcel wrapped in newspaper. Pillai closed the door and bowed.

As the car began to pull away from the house, Balendran looked at the parcel. After a few moments, he pulled aside the newspaper. It was some jumbu fruit. Pillai had picked them from the trees at the back, knowing how much Balendran loved them. He sighed deeply. It was a peace offering from Pillai, a way of making amends for taking over his duties. He folded the newspaper over the fruit and felt sorry he had been so rude to Pillai for something that was not his fault.

When Balendran got home, he went into his study and slammed the door.

After a few moments, Sonia knocked on the door and came in. "Is everything all right?" she asked.

Balendran was sitting at his desk, his arms folded on his chest. "It seems I have been relieved of my temple duties. This has to do, no doubt, with my father's anger."

Sonia walked over to him. "And what reason did he give you?"

"It seems as if I have too many duties," Balendran said sarcastically. "I need to concentrate on a few and get them right, rather than do all of them badly."

"Badly?" Sonia said, incredulous.

Balendran felt comforted by the incredulous look on her face.

"You perform your duties much more thoroughly than he ever did. Why, that chief priest was robbing the temple blind. I remember the first time I visited the temple with you. It was a pigsty. There were even pariah dogs in there. Ever since then, it's been spotless."

She leant forward, her hands on the desk. "I've often thought you feel grateful that your father gave you these responsibilities. But really, Bala, it wasn't simply some act of goodwill. He had to do so. His affairs were in chaos. Without you, without your effort, none of us would be able to live the way we do. You are the true breadwinner in this family."

After Sonia had gone to see about lunch, Balendran stared ahead of him, thinking of the condition of the rubber estate when he took it over twenty years ago, the trees dying, the manager selling off part of the rubber and keeping the profits, the labourers living in squalor. He had sacked the manager, improved the houses of the labourers, and introduced the notion of bonuses to keep his workers happy and productive.

Balendran had known these facts before, but they came to him as a sort of revelation. He thought of the day his father had called him into his study to announce the transfer of responsibilities. He had wanted to cry in gratitude and kiss his father's hand. For the granting of these duties had been more than an acknowledgement of his status as a married man and father to a son. It had been his father's way of telling him that he was pardoned for what had happened in England. Now Balendran thought of his gratitude with irony.

A notion suggested itself to Balendran. He would turn his punishment back on his father. He knew perfectly well his father would not be able to get along without him, that the family fortunes depended on his continued management of the rubber estate.

Balendran opened a desk drawer and brought out some writing paper. The time to act was now, before his anger abated and he lost courage. He dipped his pen in the inkwell and began to write.

> Dear Appa,
>
> I see now that you were right. My mind has not been on my duties of late. This book I am writing obsesses me. I fear, therefore, that not only have I been remiss in my duties towards the temple, but, further, I have not attended to the estate and other family affairs as I should. I think, in the best interests of all concerned, I should be relieved of all my duties until such time as I have finished my book.
>
> Your son, Balendran.

Balendran had Joseph take the note to his father right away.

That evening, Miss Adamson telephoned Balendran to say that his father wanted to see him. Balendran felt nervous at the impending confrontation, but his trepidation was easily surpassed by his exhilaration and excitement over seeing his father routed, over having his father at his mercy.

When his car entered Brighton, Balendran instructed Joseph to take him around to the back. As if in anticipation of what was to come, there were no servants around.

The door to his father's study was slightly ajar. He knocked and went in. His father was dressed in a verti, with a shawl around his upper body. He was writing and he waved his hand at Balendran to come in and sit down, then he continued with his work. Balendran saw that the Mudaliyar was trying to gain an advantage over him by keeping him waiting. The very transparency of what he was doing made Balendran relax. The seriousness of his expression, his father's frown, reminded Balendran of a child who had not learnt his letters but applied himself with great assiduity to his scribblings.

The Mudaliyar finally finished, pressed a blotter to the paper, and put it away. He picked up the note Balendran had written to him and glanced at it again. Then he took off his spectacles. "Yes," he said. "I have received your letter and thought about it carefully."

He clasped his hands in front of him on the desk. "You are freed of your duties."

Balendran breathed out, astounded.

"You should devote yourself to your book and finish it. I, myself, am a scholar and am aware of just how much effort goes into a work such as yours. This afternoon I have hired back Mr. Nalliah, our old manager."

"What?" Balendran cried. "But he was robbing us blind, Appa."

"I think Mr. Nalliah has learnt his lesson. People are capable of bettering themselves, you know."

Balendran stared at his father, unable to believe what he was hearing.

"He must be paid a salary," the Mudaliyar continued. "This, of course, means that there must be economizing in other areas. We are old people, your mother and I. At our stage of life, we cannot live without the few things we allow ourselves. You must, therefore, bear Mr. Nalliah's salary. Whatever money you have drawn from the running of the estate must be reduced to meet the salary."

"Appa —" Balendran began to protest.

"There is also the matter of your car. I have told Mr. Nalliah it will be at his disposal every morning and when he has to go to the estate."

Balendran started to protest again, but the Mudaliyar interrupted to say that the meeting was over. "Once you have finished your book and are ready to resume your activities, I will have Mr. Nalliah relieved of his." With that, the Mudaliyar rose to his feet, waiting for his son to leave.

"Good night, Appa," Balendran said softly.

The Mudaliyar nodded in reply.

As Balendran came out of his father's study, he heard someone coming down the passageway. Wanting to avoid having to make pleasantries with anyone, he stepped back and waited. After a few moments, Miss Adamson appeared. She was wearing a housecoat. Without knocking, she went inside the Mudaliyar's study, shutting the door softly after her. In the silence, Balendran could faintly hear the sound of the clapping and singing that often emanated from the servants' quarters at night.

The study door opened. Balendran stood back in the shadow of the stairs. Miss Adamson went down the passageway and, after a few moments, his father followed. Balendran stepped forward just in time to see his father enter Miss Adamson's room.

A sound in his mother's drawing room made Balendran glance upstairs. A memory came back to him of that time his mother had asked him to go to Miss Adamson for help, the half-sly, half-discomforted look on her face. Balendran felt giddy. He gripped the banister to steady himself. After a moment, he went shakily down the stairs.

When he was outside, his legs felt as if they would give way under him. He sat down on the edge of the verandah and leant back against a pillar, breathing deeply. He thought of his mother. Behind her docile, naïve façade was a woman who was wise to the ways of the world. He felt a deep anguish for what she must suffer every day, what effort it must take for her to go about her daily routine, knowing all the while of this encroachment into her very home about which she could do nothing, like being constantly assailed by a pestilence of termites or rats. Not only had she grieved over the banishment of Arul all these years, but now she had this humiliating liaison to contend with. Even as Balendran was agonized by his mother's terrible situation, he also felt a certain respect for her strength. While such a thing could have made someone unbearable to live with, his mother had remained kind and magnanimous to everyone.

The singing from the servants' quarters intruded on his thoughts. He glanced in that direction and he felt a terrible anger well up in him against the unfairness of a world in which people like his father managed to do as they pleased with no consequence. He would not let his father triumph over all of them.

From tomorrow Mr. Nalliah would take over his duties, take over the use of his car. His car? It was not his car at all. It belonged to his father and he had only assumed the use of it. Balendran thought of his brother's flat in Bombay. The furniture was broken and used, but it was his. He, Balendran, had worked hard at the family affairs, had considered whatever money he drew from the estate and temple to be rightfully his. Now he saw that he had been a fool to think so. The only thing that was his was Sevena; that and an inheritance he had from his grandmother.

When Balendran got home, he found Sonia reading in the drawing room. She was so engrossed in her book that she did not hear him enter. He stood watching her for a moment, then called out her name. She looked up quickly and rose to her feet.

"What did your father want, Bala?"

"I need to talk with you," Balendran replied.

She was frightened by the seriousness of his tone.

He came and sat down next to her, took her hand in his and pressed it. Then he got up and went to stand by the bookcase. "The thing I want to tell you is very hard for me to speak of . . . it has to do with my father. Something I learnt about him in India."

Then, not looking up, he told her about his father's relations with Pakkiam's mother, the reason he had brought Pakkiam to Brighton. He did not describe what he had seen this evening. It was too new for him to be able to speak about yet.

When he was done, he glanced at Sonia. She was looking at him, appalled. He went and sat down beside her and took her hands in his again. Then he told her of the letter he had written to his father and the consequences of it.

"You did what was right, Bala," Sonia cried out. "I don't care if we have to take rickshaws. It doesn't matter."

The fierceness with which she spoke filled his heart with gratitude.

"We'll show him that we can manage very well without him."

"It's not a question of our managing or not, Sonia. Certain wrongs must be righted. Others have suffered and they must be recompensed."

Sonia said she understood.

"Before I left, Seelan and I found a small house for the two of them in a more pleasant part of Bombay. Yet that is not enough. When I was there, Seelan expressed a desire to see Ceylon. I will write and suggest a short holiday here, telling him that once he is ready to come, I will arrange his passage. If he finds that he likes it in Colombo, as a place to live, then I will help him establish himself here."

"What about your father? He will never want to set eyes on this grandson. How can you subject the boy to this?"

"I will explain that his grandfather may not accept him at first, but will ultimately have to come to terms with his presence here. That he must not let his grandfather stand in the way of his happiness."

At the same time, Balendran knew the role a grandchild fulfilled in the Mudaliyar's life. A grandson was a continuance of his lineage, the aristocratic blood of his family. According to his father, Seelan would never fulfil this function as his blood was tainted. An image of his son with the Mudaliyar's favourite horse, Nellie, came into his mind. Whenever Nellie won at the Colombo or Nuwara Eliya races, it was Lukshman whom the Mudaliyar invited to lead Nellie past the grandstand and receive the applause of the spectators. Balendran had seen the absolute pride in his father's eyes as he had looked at Lukshman, so hand-some as he bowed charmingly to the grandstand.

"And his mother?" Sonia said, interrupting his thoughts. "I doubt she will be happy to let him come, given the way her husband was treated by his own family."

Balendran nodded. "Her reaction to the suggestion of her son coming here was, of course, cautious. But, being wise, I feel she would do nothing to dissuade him from pursuing what he wants."

Balendran turned to his wife. "And I will ensure to the best of my ability that, for the sake of my brother, my nephew has all the advantages Lukshman would enjoy. I will help Seelan in his endeavours wherever he may see that they lie."

That evening, Balendran and Sonia sat, hands clasped, discussing their plans for their nephew, closer to each other than they had been in a long time.

21

Seas may whelm, but men of character
Will stand like the shore.
— The Tirukkural, *verse 989*

The escalating tensions between the Minerva Hiring Company and its taxi drivers had taken a new direction. Faced with an intractable management, the taxi drivers, under the advice of the Labour Union, had gone on strike. For the first time in Ceylon, a boycott had also been organized. It was directed at any business that supported the taxi company and, as a result, a chain of petrol sheds found themselves blacklisted.

One morning, Annalukshmi was alone in the staff room, correcting students' exercise books, when the groundskeeper put his head in through the door and said, "Where is Principal Nona, missie?"

"She's teaching."

"Aiyo, missie, there's two police mahattayas at the gate."

"Policemen?" Annalukshmi stood up. "What do they want?"

"To see the Principal Nona."

Mr. Jayaweera had gone on an errand to the bank, so Annalukshmi felt that she should go and invite the policemen to come inside. She put the cap back on her pen. "Go to the senior classroom block and tell the Nona. I will let them in."

As Annalukshmi left the staff room, she wondered what trouble had brought the police to the school. When she reached the gate, she grew a little alarmed. For there, on the other side, was the Inspector General of Police, an Englishman notorious for his cruelty. She recognized him from pictures she had seen of him in the newspapers. Another policeman was with him, of low rank, Annalukshmi could tell, from the way he stood at attention looking straight ahead of him.

The inspector was obviously irritated with having been kept waiting, as he snapped at her, "I ask for Miss Lawton and I get every other person in the school."

Annalukshmi opened the gate and said, her voice catching slightly, "I have sent the groundskeeper for her."

She noticed that the inspector smiled slightly, pleased that she was nervous.

They had nearly reached the building that housed the office when she saw Miss Lawton hurrying across the quadrangle, followed by the groundskeeper. When Miss Lawton reached them, the inspector's demeanour changed and he became courteous. "I am terribly sorry to take you away from your class, madam, but this is a matter of some urgency."

"Indeed," Miss Lawton said, still breathless. She indicated for them to go inside.

Annalukshmi followed and seated herself in the staff room. She picked up an exercise book, but her ears were attuned to the murmur of voices behind the closed door of the headmistress's office. After a few moments, Miss Lawton gave a little cry and Annalukshmi heard her say, "Oh no, inspector, that can't be so. I'm sure Mr. Jayaweera is not involved."

She did not hear the inspector's reply.

Annalukshmi felt a fear come over her. She thought of the ongoing taxi strike. Was Mr. Jayaweera involved in labour unrest again? She contemplated going to the gate and waiting for him there to warn him of the presence of the police. Yet, even as she deliberated this, the school bell rang announcing the end of the period. She had a class of girls waiting for her and she had no choice but to gather her books and leave the staff room.

For the rest of the morning, Annalukshmi found it difficult to conduct her lessons with much attention. What did the police want with him? The more she thought about it, the more she wondered if Mr. Jayaweera had involved himself in this taxi strike. She felt a sense of dread.

By lunchtime, the entire school knew of the inspector's visit. Annalukshmi returned to the staff room to find all the teachers in an excited state, discussing what had happened in lowered voices as they gathered their belongings to go home for lunch. Annalukshmi was dismayed to learn that, upon his return, the police had taken Mr. Jayaweera away for questioning. None of the teachers seemed to know why, or what it was that he had done. Nancy was in the staff room and she indicated, with a slight nod, for Annalukshmi to follow her outside.

The moment they were walking across the quadrangle, Nancy said, "Miss Lawton has told me everything. It seems that the taxi strike turned violent last evening. A stone was thrown into a taxi and it blinded a woman in one eye."

Annalukshmi drew in her breath in dismay.

"The wife of an Australian mayor."

They both looked at each other, understanding the significance of this. If it had been a Ceylonese woman, the implications would not have been so grave. But with a European woman, something else was at stake. The honour of European men. No wonder the Inspector General of Police himself had come by the school.

"The police say Vijith's brother threw the stone. They went to his house last night to arrest him. There was a scuffle and he managed to escape. The police think Vijith knows where his brother is. I'm scared that he's got himself involved again."

Annalukshmi took her friend's hand. "I don't blame you for being worried, but let's not get upset until we know for certain what's going on."

That afternoon, as Annalukshmi was conducting a rehearsal of *As You Like It* under the trees at the edge of the quadrangle, she saw Mr. Jayaweera come in through the school gate. She put one of her students in charge and went quickly towards him. He had seen her and he waited for her at the steps that led into the staff room. As she came up to him, she saw, from the grim expression on his face, that his time at the police station had been extremely unpleasant.

"Rosa has saved some lunch for you," she said. "Perhaps you should go and have something to eat."

"Thank you, but I am not hungry."

"Then you must at least have a cup of tea. I'll send one of my girls to get you one."

She started to go away and he said softly, "Miss Annalukshmi."

She turned back to him.

"I would like to protect Nancy from this. The situation is not good. After police station, I went to my brother's house to talk with the people there. Last night, police did not even knock on the door. Just broke it down and came inside. My brother jumped from the window and was running away, but they shot him in arm. The people in the house found blood on the road this morning."

Annalukshmi looked at him, horrified. "My God, this is terrible."

Mr. Jayaweera looked at his hands. "I think I know where my brother is. He told me if ever he was in trouble he would go to hide in a certain house in Pettah."

"Do you think your brother is guilty?"

"No, but that is not the question. Knowing my brother was in prison once for labour problems, police have chosen easy victim. But I cannot stand by again and let my brother go to prison for something he did not do. I have found out he was seen at Labour Union meeting last night when incident occurred. If I go to him I risk leading police to his door."

"You shouldn't take that chance, Mr. Jayaweera."

"But he is hurt. I don't know if he has had wound attended. It's better that the police find him alive than dead."

"When we were in Malaya," Annalukshmi said, "there were sometimes bandits on the road from Kuala Lumpur to our rubber estate. Once, my father, who always travelled with a pistol in his car, shot one of them in the leg. Days later, my sisters and I found the man dead in the forest near the estate. It was the terrible foul smell that led us to his hiding place. His leg had turned black and festered from gangrene. If your brother has not had treatment for his wound, he will indeed need it soon."

❧

The next morning, when Annalukshmi arrived at the school, she found a student at the gate with a message from Nancy. She was to go immediately to the chapel and meet her there. She hurried up the path that led to the chapel. When she entered, she found Nancy sitting in one of the pews, her arms folded to her chest, rocking back and forth. Nancy heard Annalukshmi enter and she turned and beckoned to her urgently. Annalukshmi went and sat down by her side.

"What has happened?" Annalukshmi asked.

"It's Vijith. He hasn't come to school today."

A feeling of foreboding began to creep through Annalukshmi. "Perhaps he's just late," she said lamely.

"He's never late. In fact, he's always the first to arrive."

Annalukshmi pressed her friend's hand. "It's nothing," she said, trying to convince herself and Nancy. "With the taxi strike, the trams and buses are also delayed."

"Miss Lawton sent the groundskeeper to his house in Pettah to find out what is wrong. I promised him some money to come and tell me first. I've been waiting in here for more than an hour."

At that moment, they heard someone enter the chapel. The groundskeeper was walking quickly towards them. The expression on his face told them that something unfortunate had happened.

Nancy stood up and went to meet him in the aisle. Annalukshmi followed, her hands cold.

"Aiyo, missie," he said. "What a thing. Jayaweera mahattaya went out last night and never came back."

Nancy froze.

"Did anyone say where he might have gone?" Annalukshmi asked, even though she feared that she knew.

The groundskeeper shook his head. "He left late at night when everyone was asleep."

Annalukshmi tried to hide her dismay from her friend.

Nancy had, however, seen something in Annalukshmi's eyes. She pressed a coin into the groundskeeper's hand and he bowed and left the chapel. She now turned to Annalukshmi and grasped her tightly by the arm. "You know something, don't you?"

"I don't know anything for certain, Nancy, but yesterday he told me he thought he knew where his brother was."

"You should have told me," Nancy cried. "I would have pleaded with him not to go. I would have tried to make him see sense."

"He told me his brother had been shot by the police. He had to stop him from going to prison again for something he did not —" Annalukshmi, seeing Nancy's surprised expression, stopped short.

"I have always known that it was something like that," Nancy said after a moment.

"I'm sorry. I didn't realize he hadn't told you."

Nancy shook her head. "When you love someone, when you know them intimately, you read their silences. You see how, again and again, they avoid certain subjects. I always wondered why he wasn't more bitter when speaking of his brother. Now I clearly see that Vijith owes him something important."

The school bell now rang announcing the beginning of prayers. As the students and teachers began to file in,

Annalukshmi and Nancy walked slowly to the front of the chapel where they would join the other teachers.

In the period before lunch, a prefect came to Annalukshmi's class to tell her that Miss Lawton wanted to see her at once. She put the class monitor in charge and left. She was almost at the office when she noticed Nancy also hurrying across the quadrangle. She waited for her friend to catch up. They both stood for a moment, looking at each other, apprehensive.

The door to the headmistress's office was open. Miss Lawton was waiting for them. "Come in, girls," she called out.

The sober expression on Miss Lawton's face boded no good. She gestured for them to be seated in the chairs across from the desk and then, rather than sitting down herself, she came and stood in front of them, leaning against the desk. "I'm afraid it's not good news," she said. "I wanted to tell you right away."

Annalukshmi glanced at her friend, whose knuckles were white from gripping the arms of the chair.

"The police have been watching Mr. Jayaweera. Last night he left his house in Pettah and they followed him to where his brother was hiding. They've taken both of them to the police station, where they're being held in custody."

Nancy and Annalukshmi looked at each other.

"I've had a long talk with the Inspector General of Police," Miss Lawton continued. "I don't think they are going to be able to indict the brother for the blinding of that poor, innocent woman, more's the pity. It seems he has gone and got himself a very strong alibi. The entire Labour Union is willing to swear themselves blue that he was at a meeting. It is likely that Mr. Jayaweera will therefore soon be released."

Nancy slowly breathed out and relaxed back in her chair.

"This is such a relief to hear," Annalukshmi said.

Miss Lawton was twisting a pencil between her fingers. After a moment, she looked up at them. "This will, of course, end Mr. Jayaweera's career here."

They stared at her in shock "But why should that be?" Annalukshmi cried. "He hasn't committed a crime."

"There is no crime, surely, in helping your brother," Nancy said, her voice shaking.

"You have to understand my situation. You know what a small place Colombo is. No sooner was Mr. Jayaweera taken away for questioning yesterday than I had a telephone call from someone on the missionary board who had heard about it from someone with whom he plays golf. I was advised to seriously consider the reputation of the school. It's been only a matter of hours since Mr. Jayaweera has been taken into custody, and I have already received a call from an important benefactor to this school. It is impossible to keep him on here. By tomorrow, his name and the place where he works will probably be in all the newspapers."

"But what about his family! How are they to manage?" Annalukshmi said.

"Mr. Jayaweera should have thought of them before he got involved with his brother again."

"But his brother was wounded. What would you –"

"My hands are tied, Anna. Even if I wanted to give Mr. Jayaweera a chance, I couldn't. I blame myself for this in a way. I should never have hired someone who –"

"Stop!" Nancy cried and stood up.

Annalukshmi and Miss Lawton looked at Nancy. Her eyes were filled with tears.

"Nancy?" Miss Lawton touched her shoulder.

At this, Nancy turned her head and brushed her cheek with her hand.

Miss Lawton stared at her, puzzled as to why the usually unperturbed Nancy was in such a state. She glanced at Annalukshmi questioningly, but Annalukshmi looked away from her.

"What is all this about?" Miss Lawton said, holding Nancy's hands. "Nancy, answer me."

"There is something you should know . . . Vijith — Mr. Jayaweera — is in trouble so I must be free to help him."

"What are you saying?"

Nancy was silent. "That Vijith and I have deep feelings for each other."

Miss Lawton went to the other side of the desk and sat down.

"Oh? And how long have you both known this?"

"For a while."

Miss Lawton suddenly pushed her chair back from the desk and stood up. "Have you taken complete leave of your senses? This man has nothing to offer you. A poor clerk, with a family to support. I didn't bring you up a good Christian to have you give yourself to this."

"I have thought about all this," Nancy said, looking Miss Lawton straight in the eye.

"Your Mr. Jayaweera is now an unemployed clerk who has had a tangle with the law. Have you thought about that as well?"

Nancy sat down. "I understand how you must feel. But please promise you will try to understand my feelings."

"Do not ask me to condone an alliance that will ultimately make you unhappy. I cannot do that." Miss Lawton straightened the collar of her dress. "I beg you to stop seeing him."

A silence fell among them. The school choir could be heard practising, their voices drifting across from the senior classroom block. Feeling uncomfortable, Annalukshmi quickly excused herself and left the room.

She came out into the quadrangle. A wind had picked up and was blowing leaves and scraps of paper around her. The sky had darkened in patches. This was, as the newspapers had been predicting, the precursor to the monsoon. In the distance, she could hear the sea, now stormy, waves thundering against the rocks. She slowly began to make her way across the deserted quadrangle towards her classroom. As she walked along, a tin can blown by the wind rattled along in front of her, as if leading the way.

22

A thoughtless foray only dresses
The enemy's field for him.
— The Tirukkural, *verse 465*

The monsoon, which had been greeted with such relief when it arrived in early June to dispel the heat, had quite outstayed its welcome by July. The residents of Colombo found it vexatious to have their days governed by the great gusts of rain that materialized with little forewarning. For, when they arrived, everything had to stop until their tumult had subsided. Pedestrians and rickshaw riders would find themselves rushing for inadequate cover under the nearest tree or in a building. There they would find themselves stranded, shivering in their damp clothes for five minutes or an hour, it being useless to try to brave the rain with umbrellas, which would quickly sail away in the wind broken and twisted. Even those with the privilege of cars were not much better off. In a few minutes, a road could flood, forcing them to abandon their automobiles and also run for protection.

The insides of houses were not inviolate either. The monsoon's dampness, like a thief, had slyly crept through Lotus Cottage. The residents of the house constantly came upon evidence of it in their personal belongings. Louisa would open her spice chest to find that the curry powder had clumped into useless, earth-smelling lumps. Annalukshmi, much as she tried to protect her small collection of books by wrapping them in cloth and storing them in her almirah, would inevitably discover that the ends of pages had curled up, the books developed a hump in the middle. The verandahs on which they conducted so much of their life were now mostly out of bounds. They were forced to spend their time inside the house, the constantly grey sky making the drawing room gloomy, the electric lights permanently on. It was inevitable that, in this confined situation, the habits of one would come to annoy the other. *As You Like It* had won second place at the inter-school Shakespeare competition. With her afternoons and evenings free again, Annalukshmi found that time and her family sat heavily on her. There were moments when she felt close to snapping at Kumudini, whose stomach by this time was very large, and who constantly moaned about the rain or asked her in a helpless tone to fetch things for her. Manohari had colonized the dining-room table, where she left her homework long after it should have been put away. To provoke her sister, Manohari from time to time would look up from her work and, in a tremulous, high-pitched voice, declaim a line from *As You Like It*.

Nancy was busy with her own affairs and Annalukshmi saw her infrequently. Mr. Jayaweera, with some degree of difficulty, had been able to find himself a low-paying job as a clerk in a small mercantile firm. While on the surface, Nancy and Miss Lawton seemed to carry on as usual, Annalukshmi thought the headmistress looked strained. Nancy had confided that visiting Mr. Jayaweera in Pettah was a continuing source of dissent between her and Miss Lawton. Because of this unfortunate state of affairs, Annalukshmi's contact with Miss Lawton took on a distanced quality.

Annalukshmi felt an unsettled yearning for something, some sense that her life was not confined to a repetition of the same things. It was in this spirit that she sent Ramu, their gardener, to the top of the road for a rickshaw one Saturday morning. She would go and see her Aunt Sonia, who was always a source of new ideas and intelligent conversation.

When Annalukshmi arrived at Sevena, the houseboy let her in, explaining that her aunt and uncle were not home, but that her uncle would be returning soon. She went into the study and began to browse through the bookshelves while she waited for Balendran.

Annalukshmi had gone up the ladder to look at the books on the top shelf when the front door opened and she heard someone enter. A man with an unfamiliar voice was talking to the houseboy. After a moment, a young gentleman appeared in the doorway of the study. Because she was at the top of the ladder, Annalukshmi hastily drew her sari in around her legs.

He inclined his head formally. "Good morning," he said, without any sense of surprise at seeing her there.

She nodded in reply and came hastily down the ladder, wondering who this stranger was that had walked so casually into her uncle's study. When she got to the bottom, she stood uncertain.

"I am Dr. Govind," he said. "A friend of Mr. Balendran visiting from India."

Annalukshmi stared at him, intimidated by his formal manner, the British intonation to his voice. He was wearing a neatly pressed white cotton suit. Everything, from his carefully parted and brilliantined hair to his polished shoes, was impeccable. Though he looked as if he were in his twenties, she felt as if she was in the presence of a much older man, someone like her grand-uncle, the Mudaliyar.

A silence had fallen between them. It was her turn to say something. "I'm Annalukshmi. . . . Mr. Balendran's cousin's daughter."

"It is a pleasure to meet you."

He extended his hand and she hesitantly shook it.

He gestured to the book in her hand. "Ah, I see you like to read. I, too, am very fond of books. One of my greatest pleasures." He tried to glimpse the title. "May I ask what you are reading?"

She held the book out to him. It was a book discussing the philosophy of Hinduism. Something she had never read anything about before.

"Is this your interest?" he asked, surprised.

"I . . . I've read most of the novels in here and was looking for something new."

"Ah. Then may I interest you in a novel I have just finished? It's called *A Passage to India*."

Annalukshmi nodded to say that she had, of course, heard of the book.

"Have you read it?"

She shook her head.

"Then you must let me lend it to you." Without waiting for her response, he quickly turned and left the room.

Annalukshmi was a bit taken aback.

Just then, the front door opened again and she was relieved to hear her uncle talking to the houseboy. Annalukshmi went into the vestibule to meet him; at the same moment the young man came out of the guest room, holding a book.

Balendran, who was handing a package to the houseboy, stared at them in surprise.

"Bala Maama, I came to see Sonia Maamee," Annalukshmi said.

At the same instant, Seelan, for it was indeed Seelan, said, "I was just getting Miss Annalukshmi a book."

Balendran looked from one to the other, trying to discern what interaction had passed between them, if his niece knew that this was his nephew. Yet the calm expression on her face told him that Seelan had not revealed his identity to her and that he best go along with this for the time being.

Seelan now proffered the book to Annalukshmi and she glanced at Balendran. "Dr. Govind wants to lend me a novel he recommends," she said, unsure whether to take something from someone she hardly knew.

Balendran had turned away to hang up his hat and he dropped it in surprise. He glanced at his nephew as he bent down to retrieve it.

"May I, Bala Maama?"

"Yes, I don't see why not."

Annalukshmi smiled at Dr. Govind to express her thanks for the book and she took it from him. He bowed in return and she could not help thinking what an odd, overly formal person he was.

When Annalukshmi said she would be leaving, Balendran did not insist that she stay for lunch as he usually would have.

Once he had seen her off at the gate, he walked slowly up the front path, lost in thought. Govind. The name was strangely familiar. Then he remembered that it was the name of the bank manager who had allotted Arul his monthly allowance. He understood why Seelan had been reticent about his identity. Annalukshmi's arrival had probably taken him by surprise and, in order to spare himself the embarrassment of her astonishment at who he was, he had told a lie. Balendran felt he was to blame for this. Seelan had only been in Colombo two days, and Balendran had not yet made a point of announcing his nephew's presence. He was waiting for the right moment to do so. For his mother, he knew, seeing Arul's son for the first time would be a moment of tremendous import.

Seelan was in the drawing room, an uneasy look on his face.

"Seelan," Balendran started to say, but Seelan raised his hand.

"I know what you are thinking, Bala Maama," he said, "but I couldn't tell her who I was. So I gave her the first name that came to mind."

"I understand. I will tell her myself, if that makes it easier."

"I would rather stay Dr. Govind for the time being, if you don't mind."

Balendran stared at him, astonished. Then he felt a rush of sympathy for his nephew. He put his hand on Seelan's shoulder. "Seelan, there's no need to keep up this fiction. I would be proud to introduce you as my nephew."

"And then nobody would want anything to do with me."

"No, Seelan. What's in the past is past."

Seelan looked down at his hands, a stubborn expression on his face. "You overestimate people."

Balendran gazed at his nephew, not sure what he could do or say, but hoping it would be only a matter of time until Seelan saw things differently. Meanwhile, he would respect his wishes and delay introducing him to his family.

Yet Seelan's words had left Balendran feeling saddened.

❧

The next evening, Annalukshmi accompanied Kumudini on the walk the doctor recommended she take every day now that she was entering the more advanced stages of her pregnancy. In the two months since Kumudini had arrived home, Annalukshmi had noticed that her sister's moodiness seemed to have passed.

They were returning to Lotus Cottage along Horton Place when they saw a young man standing at the gates of Brighton, looking in. Annalukshmi drew in her breath, for she immediately recognized Dr. Govind.

"Who is it, akka?" Kumudini asked.

Before Annalukshmi could reply, Dr. Govind saw them. A flustered look crossed his face. He hastily removed his hat.

"Miss Annalukshmi," he said and bowed.

"Dr. Govind," she replied and inclined her head.

Kumudini was staring at her questioningly, and she introduced him as their uncle's friend.

They nodded to each other in greeting.

"How is the book, then?" he asked eagerly. "Are you enjoying it?"

"Yes I am," Annalukshmi said, even though she had not begun it, preferring to read the book about Hinduism she had taken from her uncle's study.

"I don't usually enjoy books set in India. But since it was by such as well-known British author, I thought it was worth a try." While he spoke, he extended his gaze to include Kumudini.

He saw the puzzled look on her face and added, "I had the good fortune to meet your sister at Mr. Balendran's and recommend a book of mine."

Kumudini looked at Annalukshmi in unconcealed surprise. In the midst of her own concerns, Annalukshmi had forgotten to mention this meeting at her uncle's. Yet now, under Kumudini's gaze, she felt ill at ease, as if she had been hiding something. She glanced at her sister. Kumudini was regarding her with an appraising look.

Seelan took out his handkerchief and mopped his forehead. "It's such a hot evening, isn't it?"

"We live just over there," Kumudini said, pointing towards the lane to Lotus Cottage. "Would you like to come inside and have a drink?"

"I'd be delighted," he said.

Kumudini began to lead the way with him and Annalukshmi followed, stunned by the way her sister had taken command.

Kumudini was, meanwhile, quizzing Dr. Govind about himself.

"Are you from Britain?" she asked innocently, having noted his British intonation.

"No, madam," he replied, "though I spent a good many years there."

"Qualifying as a doctor," he added and glanced quickly at Kumudini. He was suitably gratified by the awed look on her face.

"I've always wanted to visit Britain," Kumudini said.

"You should, madam. The mother country is a must."

He began to tell her about the sights of London, and Kumudini listened with a feigned eagerness.

They had reached the gate now and he gallantly held it open for them. As Annalukshmi passed him, he smiled at her.

Louisa had gone to a ladies' auxiliary meeting at the church and Manohari was alone on the verandah doing her homework. She put her pencil down in astonishment when she saw the young man with her sisters.

"Chutta," Kumudini said as they came up the steps, "this is Dr. Govind, a friend of Bala Maama."

She nodded to him and glanced curiously at her sisters.

"Please do sit down," Kumudini said. "What would you like to drink?"

"A glass of water would be fine."

Kumudini went to ask Letchumi to bring it, and returned. An awkward silence fell among them. Annalukshmi stood by a verandah pillar and Manohari pretended to busy herself with her homework. Not having brothers, the girls were unaccustomed to the presence of a young man in their house, unsure what to say to him, how he should be treated.

"Tell us more about London," Kumudini said in desperation.

"Ah yes, London, madam," he began, only too happy to oblige.

In the midst of his description of the great dome of St. Paul's Cathedral, Letchumi brought out the glass of water. He took it from her with a nod and drank it. A silence fell again. After a moment, he stood up. "I've presumed too much on your time already."

"Oh no, not at all," Kumudini said, though she was relieved.

He tipped his hat to all of them and left.

The moment the gate had closed behind him, Kumudini turned to Manohari. "Well, chutta, isn't he perfect for akka? A doctor. London-qualified and everything."

"For God's sake, Kumu," Annalukshmi said, now understanding what was behind her hospitality.

"Oh, akka, don't be so blind. What do you think he was doing outside Brighton? He mentioned it was such a hot evening, hoping we would invite him in and he could visit with you."

"Madness. He hardly knows me. We only exchanged a few words yesterday."

"What does one need but a few words."

Annalukshmi shook her head. She was beginning to be truly irritated with her sister.

"Chutta, what do you think?" Kumudini asked, appealing to her younger sister.

"I've presumed too much on your time already," Manohari said in a perfect imitation of Seelan's overly formal manner, his British intonation.

Kumudini was not amused. "Nonsense," she said. "He is a very polite, refined man. He speaks beautifully too."

"Ah yes, London," Manohari said, imitating his "beautiful" speech. "Did I tell you I had tea with the king? Simply marvellous. Scones and Devonshire cream."

Kumudini wagged her finger at her older sister. "You mark my words, akka. He is interested in you."

With that, Kumudini went inside.

Annalukshmi shook her head. Her experience with the Macintosh boy had shown her the wisdom of not interpreting simple events or coincidences in the wrong way. There could be any number of reasons why Dr. Govind was outside Brighton. Since he was a friend of her uncle, he probably knew the

Mudaliyar as well and had come to pay him a visit. It was ridiculous to imagine that he had been standing outside the gates of Brighton in the hope that she would pass by.

∾

Two young women, whether married or not, engaged in a conversation with an unknown man on Horton Place was not something that could escape attention or comment.

Pillai, who was supervising the cleaning up of the driveway, had observed the meeting. He conveyed this unusual sight to his wife, Rajini, who brought it to the attention of Nalamma. That evening, Nalamma sent Rajini, under the pretext of borrowing some cloves, to find out from Letchumi more details about this young man. Letchumi, though by no means fluent in English, was able to tell Rajini that he was a doctor from India by the name of Govind.

At dinner that night, Nalamma looked at her husband until she got his attention. Then she said, "What is the name of the bank manager in India. The one who used to arrange the payments for our son?"

The Mudaliyar stared at her in surprise. "Mr. Govind," he said after a moment.

She nodded and continued to eat her dinner.

"Why?"

She shrugged. "I was thinking about it, for some reason."

23

What good are outward features if they lack
Love, the inward sense?
— The Tirukkural, *verse 79*

The next morning, Balendran was in his study when the bell
rang. He heard Sonia go towards the front door and, after a
moment, the sound of his mother's voice. Quick footsteps
approached his study. Nalamma entered without knocking,
Sonia behind her. He stood up.

"I have always thought you incapable of deceit," Nalamma
said.

She sank into the chair across from him, took out a handkerchief, and wiped her face. "Aiyoo, what a thing."

Balendran stared at her, nonplussed.

"I'm talking about your Dr. Govind," she said, irritated that
he was playing innocent.

He sat down slowly in his chair.

"Bala, what is happening?" Sonia demanded.

He waved his hand at his wife to be silent. "You know," he
said to his mother.

Nalamma told him that Seelan, posing as Dr. Govind, was
seen yesterday on Horton Place outside Brighton. He had been

talking to Annalukshmi and Kumudini and was invited to Lotus Cottage.

When she was finished speaking, Sonia asked Balendran what Nalamma had said, for she had been unable to follow her rapid Tamil. Balendran repeated the story in English. Sonia breathed out in astonishment.

"Where is he now? Where is he staying?" Nalamma asked.

He glanced at his mother. She was twisting her handkerchief between her fingers. "Here."

Nalamma stood up quickly. "In this house? He is here now?"

"No, Amma, he has gone to the Fort. To look around Colombo a bit."

Nalamma was silent, playing with the clasp of her handbag. "How could you not have told me?"

Balendran came to her side. "Forgive me. It was not supposed to happen in this way," he said. "I was trying to give Seelan time to get his bearings first. If you would like to wait and see him, he should be here soon."

For a moment, Nalamma did not reply, then she spoke. "I will go into the garden with Sonia. You can let me know when my grandson arrives."

Nalamma started to walk towards the door and then turned back to Balendran. "You understand, we need to keep this just between us for the present. We must carefully consider how best to tell your father that his grandson is in Colombo."

When he was alone, Balendran walked to the window, lost in thought. So, the power of his father had managed to draw his nephew to him, even before they had met.

Seelan arrived later than he was expected. Nalamma and Sonia had come in from the garden, and they were all seated in the drawing room in anxious silence when they heard the gate open. Balendran stood up and went out to his nephew so that he could prepare him for this meeting with his grandmother.

He was walking up the front path and Balendran signalled to him to stop.

Seelan took his hat off, a look of disquiet on his face as he saw his uncle's serious expression.

"Seelan," Balendran said as he reached him, "there is something you need to know." Then he told him of Nalamma's presence in the drawing room and how she had found out about him.

At first Seelan looked shocked, but Balendran quickly assured him that his grandmother was very keen to meet him and had waited a long time to do so. Yet this did little to assuage Seelan's nervousness. As they walked up the front path, he ran his hand over his hair and straightened his tie.

When they entered the drawing room, both Nalamma and Sonia stood up. For a moment, they were all still.

Then Balendran turned to his nephew. "Seelan," he said in Tamil. "This is your parti." He turned back to his mother. "Amma, this is Arul's son."

Seelan stepped forward and held out his hand. "How do you do?" he said formally in English.

Nalamma took his hand in hers and gazed at him for a moment. "You have your father's face," she said, her voice hushed. "I was unable to come to him before he . . . but I am glad to see him living in you." She pressed something into his hand. It was twenty rupees.

"Oh no," Seelan said to her in Tamil. "It's too much, I can't take it."

She shook her head. "You must obey. You cannot imagine what joy this gives me. You have fulfilled one of the few wishes I had left in this world. I thank you for that."

He nodded, understanding what she meant, but unable to speak because of the mixture of emotions he felt.

That evening at dinner, after dessert was served, Balendran sat back and looked at his nephew. "I'm sure you will understand, Seelan, things are complicated. It is important to your grandmother that we choose the moment carefully when we tell your grandfather about you. In the meantime, take care where you are seen. I'm sure you understand."

"Yes, maama."

"So tell me about your visit to Lotus Cottage."

"It was very pleasant. The sister who is married seemed interested in London and I was happy to oblige her with my experiences of the city."

"That's nice," Balendran said.

"It was particularly nice to see Miss Annalukshmi again. I was very impressed by her during our first meeting."

Balendran stared at his nephew, surprised. The brief conversation between Annalukshmi and his nephew in his study had obviously sparked a strong admiration. He recalled that Seelan had offered his book to Annalukshmi and he saw the gesture in a different light now. He tried to remember his niece's reaction, but, except for her discomfort, her need for his permission that she might borrow the book, he did not recall any particular interest. She had seemed perfectly normal.

Sonia leant forward in her chair. "Seelan, you are quite taken with our niece, then?"

After a moment, he nodded.

"But if so, you must tell her who you really are."

"Yes," Balendran said. "Consider what I told you before. Do you really think she would shun you?"

"Why shouldn't she? If I had a daughter, I wouldn't want her associating with a low-caste man."

Sonia and Balendran stared at their nephew, aghast.

"Seelan," Sonia said after a moment, "I'm sure I speak for your uncle when I say that we would find it difficult to condone such a deceit."

He looked away from them. "Once she has got to know me, once she has come to like me for who I am, I will tell her."

Sonia sat back in her chair. She glanced at Balendran and shook her head imperceptibly.

Seelan retired to bed early. Sonia and Balendran sat in the drawing room in silence. After a while, she turned to her husband. "Your nephew," she said, "what do we really know about him?"

"He is decent man, Sonia," Balendran answered. "During my time in India, it was clear he was a devoted son. It cannot be easy for him to be completely responsible for his mother's welfare now. Yet he bears his load without a murmur of complaint."

"Still, I worry. I'm concerned about Annalukshmi. I do hope his intentions are honourable."

❧

From his wanderings yesterday, Seelan knew that Cargills had a good bookshop and, the next day, he made his way back to it.

The bookshop was in a corner of the department store, enclosed on three sides by bookcases, a gap between two of them providing an entrance.

As Seelan made his way to the literature section, he stopped in surprise. Annalukshmi was standing by one of the shelves, reading. He straightened his tie and walked towards her.

At the sound of his approaching footsteps, Annalukshmi looked up. "Dr. Govind," she said in surprise. She had spoken too loudly and other people turned to look at her.

Seelan smiled. "Good morning, Miss Annalukshmi. How are you?"

"Very well, Dr. Govind."

They were both silent, not knowing what to say next. She held up a copy of Jane Austen's *Mansfield Park*. "Are you familiar with this book?"

"Ah, dear Jane Austen. One of my very favourite writers." He took another copy of the book from the shelf and began to look through it.

At that moment, Manohari walked in with her parcel. When she saw Dr. Govind, she stopped in surprise. "Good morning," he said and bowed.

Manohari nodded back.

"Have you decided yet, akka?"

"I'm not sure."

"The car is probably waiting. You know how impatient he gets if we're not there when he arrives."

Seelan cleared his throat. "If you will allow me, I would like to buy it for you, Miss Annalukshmi."

Annalukshmi and Manohari were taken aback.

"Oh no, Dr. Govind, that's quite all right." Annalukshmi quickly put the copy of *Mansfield Park* back on the shelf.

She indicated to Manohari. They nodded goodbye and started to walk away.

Seelan placed his hand on Annalukshmi's arm. "Please," he said.

She drew in her breath and moved her arm away, as if his touch had scorched her. She and Manohari stared at him, not knowing what to make of his indiscretion, too shocked to be even outraged.

Seelan flushed deeply, losing his composure. He had been unseemly. He looked down and then, after a moment, lifted his gaze to them. His eyes were bright, almost tearful, with appeal. "Please," he said softly.

They did not say anything, and he, taking this as their acquiescence, hurried away to the counter.

Manohari raised her eyebrows at Annalukshmi, as if to say that her sister had brought it on herself.

Annalukshmi narrowed her eyes and turned away.

After a moment, Seelan returned with the book, wrapped in brown paper.

He gave it to Annalukshmi and she reluctantly accepted it with a mumbled thank you. Then she and Manohari hurriedly left the bookshop.

The shaded portico outside Cargills was crowded with shoppers. Street vendors had laid out their wares on mats along the sidewalk and were calling out loudly to the passersby. There was a smell of camphor and incense.

"You're a fine one," Manohari said as they jostled their way through the crowd.

"Madness. I didn't do a thing." Annalukshmi looked at the parcel in her hand. The discomfort of having accepted his gift was beginning to wear off, replaced by a flutter of excitement at his gesture.

"There it is," Manohari said.

Annalukshmi looked in the direction she was pointing and saw the Mudaliyar Navaratnam's car.

"You see, Peri-Appa's already there. He'll never let us ride with him again."

They began to walk quickly towards the grey-green Delahaye.

"You have to sit in the back with him," Manohari said. "I'm not taking the scolding for your offence."

She hurried ahead of Annalukshmi and got into the front seat. Annalukshmi had no choice but to sit in the back with the Mudaliyar. She glanced at him as she got in. He was clearly displeased. "I'm sorry, Peri-Appa," she said. "I was delayed choosing a book."

The Mudaliyar did not reply. He waved his hand for his driver to proceed. They sat in uncomfortable silence. The Mudaliyar glanced at the parcel that Annalukshmi had placed between them, almost as a barricade. "One mustn't waste one's money on frivolities, thangachi," he said.

Annalukshmi looked down at her feet. The Mudaliyar disapproved of her reading habit because he said, "It puts too many ideas into a young girl's head."

He inclined his head towards the parcel. "Well, open it, open it. Let's see what frippery you've bought this time."

She tore open the brown paper and handed the book to him. When he saw the binding, she noticed his eyes widen at her extravagance. He opened the book and looked at the first page, frowning, then snapped the book shut and handed it back to her. She glanced at him anxiously, but he was staring out of the window.

Kumudini was, of course, informed of the meeting with Dr. Govind the moment they got home. Her eyes widened with excitement when Manohari, now relishing the drama, described the way he had held Annalukshmi's arm, an almost tearful look in his eyes.

"Show the book, akka," Kumudini cried. "Open it, open it."

Annalukshmi took the book out of its wrapping, and Kumudini exclaimed over the expensive binding as if it were further proof of Dr. Govind's admiration for her sister. Annalukshmi opened the book and drew in her breath when she saw that he had written an inscription. "May our joy of reading strengthen our regard for each other. Dr. Govind."

Her sisters had crowded behind her and they read it too.

"Our regard!" Kumudini cried in delight.

"What he means is 'strengthen our love,'" Manohari declared.

"Oh, akka, I am so happy for you." Kumudini hugged Annalukshmi, as if Dr. Govind had proposed to her.

Annalukshmi continued to stare at the dedication, which she now realized the Mudaliyar had seen. Kumudini was right after all. When they met Dr. Govind outside Brighton, he was waiting in the hope of meeting her. Annalukshmi felt a quick rush of pleasure go through her. There was no mistaking the look in his eyes when he had touched her arm. In that moment, his formal manner had fallen away and she had glimpsed the person he might really be. With his face flushed, his eyes bright, he had been handsome.

❧

The Mudaliyar felt as if his mind would shatter from the real-ization he had made. His grandson was in Colombo! The moment he had seen that name on the book, he had remembered his wife's question at dinner two nights ago. Then there was her absence at lunch yesterday, an event which, in itself, should have made him realize that something was afoot. Yet he had been engrossed in the family affairs, which were not going well under the current manager, and he had not thought very much about it. He had asked Pillai where his wife was and had been told that she had gone to visit his son. Everything fell into place. His son had brought his grandson to Ceylon! What did he hope to achieve by this? Balendran could not possibly imagine that he would receive the boy in his house? Balendran could not possibly think he would acknowledge that grandchild and thus open himself up to scandal again.

The Mudaliyar thought of the shame and embarrassment when Arul had gone away with Pakkiam to India. He recalled the first time he had got up to speak in the Legislative Council, after the scandal became public. There had been a collective titter from his opponents. He was used to opposition, even welcomed the challenge of a good debate, the exchange of repartee. But this had been different. He had felt completely defenceless, as if he himself had committed a crime.

An anger began to grow in him now. What was his son thinking? Did he want to bring scandal on his head in his old age, when he no longer had the strength to withstand it? A knot of hurt began to build in the Mudaliyar's chest. He leant his head back against the car seat and breathed in deeply.

When the car came to a stop at Brighton, Pillai hurried down the steps and opened the door. The Mudaliyar got out and Pillai bowed respectfully.

When the Mudaliyar came into the vestibule, he found his wife waiting for him.

Pillai had come in with his parcels. As the Mudaliyar looked at him, he felt certain that he, too, knew about his grandson.

"Shall I have lunch served?" Nalamma asked.

He stared at his wife as if he had not heard her.

"If you would rather eat later, that would be fine."

"In an hour," he said and went towards the stairs. "I wish to lie down for a little."

Usually he walked up unaided, yet today he felt tired and he held on to the banister as he went up. When he reached the landing, he turned to see his wife and Pillai looking up at him. The two people he trusted the most, the two he felt he could count on for absolute obedience and loyalty had betrayed him.

From where he lay on his bed, the Mudaliyar could see over the trees into the front garden of Lotus Cottage. He remembered the dedication in that book. "May our joy of reading strengthen our regard for each other."

The Mudaliyar sat up in bed. This boy was making love to his grand-niece and she reciprocated his feelings, for she had accepted the book from him. The reason the girls had been delayed this morning was because of a tryst with that young man. A secret one, obviously, otherwise he would have come to Lotus Cottage as any other decent suitor would have. It was clear that the mother, Louisa, knew nothing.

The Mudaliyar began to form an image in his mind of his grandson. It was not a pleasant one — deceit and wilfulness. Slyness, boastfulness, sloth. The desire to rise up by any means, at the expense of anyone. The young man had arranged to meet his niece secretly. He was a seducer of the worst kind.

The Mudaliyar rang his bell and waited for Pillai to come up to him. His first task was to subjugate his retainer, make him realize his precarious position in this house, that if he, the Mudaliyar, chose, he could reduce him to penury. The threat would ensure that Pillai would be his faithful eyes and ears in the days to come.

24

Wrath is a fire which kills near and far
Burning both kinsmen and life's boat.
   — The Tirukkural, *verse 306*

Louisa had a ladies' auxiliary meeting at the church on Tuesday. Kumudini, determined to facilitate the progress of her sister's friendship with Dr. Govind, and knowing her sister's likely reluctance, took matters into her own hands and decided to invite Dr. Govind to tea in her mother's absence. Her mother, who had never learnt of his first visit, would likely not approve of her matchmaking, or of them entertaining a man when she was not at home. Kumudini also knew she could count on the servants' silence. She worded the invitation carefully, for she judged Dr. Govind to be shy, like an untrained colt, capable of bolting if one moved too swiftly on him. She sent Ramu with a note to her uncle's house. Ramu returned an hour later with the reply that the "Aiyah from India would be very happy to oblige." Kumudini and Letchumi then set about planning the tea.

When Kumudini told Annalukshmi that Dr. Govind was coming for tea, Annalukshmi scolded her sister for not consulting her first, but instantly she felt a mixture of panic and delight. Since the encounter with Dr. Govind at Cargills' bookshop, he had been constantly on her mind. Even though she knew so little about him, her imagination had not been deterred. Her realization of his handsomeness filled his mouth with words of ardour; the warmth of his hand against her arm transformed in her mind into the urgent tenderness with which he would give her pleasure. With the exception of her Uncle Balendran, she did not know another man who read anything more than a newspaper. She held those who truly appreciated literature to be thoughtful, refined, sensitive souls like herself. They were people who looked at life and saw the poetry within it. The understanding that Dr. Govind was such a person raised him high in her esteem.

A few evenings later, Annalukshmi accompanied Kumudini on her evening walk along Horton Place. They took their umbrellas with them as the sky was darkening overhead and there was a faint rumble of thunder. For a while, they walked in silence, both of them lost in thought, then Annalukshmi turned to her sister and said, "Tell me, Kumu, are you truly happy?"

"Well, there is no such thing as a perfect husband, akka."

"But Muttiah is kind to you, isn't he?"

Kumudini was silent for a moment. "Can I trust you with something, as one sister to another?"

"Of course, Kumu."

"There are . . . difficulties. I have come to learn that there is a problem with my husband."

Annalukshmi's eyes widened and she turned to look at her sister.

"He has a terrible weakness. For gambling. Please, akka, you must not tell anyone."

Annalukshmi said that her secret was guarded.

"After we were married, Appa put Muttiah in charge of the rubber estate, as he is getting rather old to look after it himself. We have since learnt that Muttiah has been drawing money for gambling from the estate. Appa had to take back control, especially when Muttiah tried to sell a portion of the estate. Certain problems fell on my shoulders too. It was not possible to leave until they were resolved. I couldn't tell Amma, but that is what kept me from coming sooner."

"Oh, Kumu, I am so sorry. Is there anything we should do?"

"No. Things have a way of resolving themselves. Anyway, what is to be done?" She smiled. "One must go on."

It had now begun to drizzle. They opened their umbrellas and turned back towards Lotus Cottage. As they reached the gate, Kumudini said to her sister, "Look at Dr. Govind. If the two of you grow fond of each other, you must not have unrealistic expectations. He is human like the rest of us, and therefore not perfect."

"Really, Kumu. I'm not about to have expectations of a man I hardly know."

Once they got home and she was alone, Annalukshmi thought of the image of Dr. Govind she had constructed and she saw that she had indeed made him into a perfect lover. She had given him a passion she did not know he had; she had attributed to his formality a shyness and sensitivity that might not be there at all. Her sister was right. She had to be realistic.

❧

On Tuesday, when Annalukshmi returned from school, the nervousness that had ebbed and flowed through her the entire day like a low fever suddenly peaked in a moment of panic. Her mother was still at home. There she was, seated on the verandah checking and correcting the minutes from the last ladies' auxiliary meeting. Kumudini and Manohari were watching her intently, hardly able to suppress their agitation that she had not left yet. Annalukshmi glanced at her wristwatch, dismayed. Dr. Govind would be here in fifteen minutes.

Finally, Louisa closed her minute book and began to gather her things.

The moment their mother's rickshaw disappeared down the lane, Kumudini hurriedly led the way to their bedroom. "Thank God, I thought she would never leave."

On Annalukshmi's bed, Kumudini had laid out one of Louisa's favourite saris, a French chiffon with a cream background and a design of magenta flowers and bright-green leaves. With it was a cream blouse with a lace ruffle along the U-shaped neckline. Annalukshmi took one look at the sari and knew it was all wrong for her. Such flower-filled affairs seldom suited her. Still, they were running out of time and there was no chance to pick another sari, heat up the coals, and have it ironed. It would have to do.

As her rickshaw turned onto Horton Place, Louisa was so engrossed in keeping her handbag, notebook, and umbrella from slipping off her lap that it was only when her rickshaw came to a jarring halt by the gates of Brighton that she looked up and saw the Mudaliyar Navaratnam standing in front of her.

"Thangachi," the Mudaliyar said solemnly, "your daughter is in terrible trouble."

"What!" Louisa cried in astonishment.

"Come with me." The Mudaliyar signalled for her to alight from the rickshaw and follow him inside. She did so, for the serious expression on his face told her that, irrespective of what she thought she knew, trouble was brewing.

The Mudaliyar did not say a word until they were both seated in his study. Then he began.

"I have some distressing news for you, thangachi. Your oldest daughter is having a liaison."

"I don't understand what you mean."

"With a so-called Dr. Govind."

"Dr. Govind?"

The Mudaliyar paused for effect. "My grandson, the son of Arulanandan."

Louisa shook her head, confused, unable to make sense of what he was saying.

The Mudaliyar saw that he had not spoken clearly. He started again, telling her how Balendran had brought Seelan to Colombo. How Seelan had befriended Annalukshmi.

Louisa's eyes widened in amazement as he spoke. "But . . . how does he know Annalukshmi? When would they have met?"

The Mudaliyar told her about Seelan's earlier visit to Lotus Cottage and Louisa gasped. "He was a visitor at our house?"

The Mudaliyar nodded gravely. Then he told her about the dedication in the book, how the girls had arranged a tryst with this young man at Cargills' bookshop. As he spoke, he saw the horror dawning on Louisa's face. To stoke the fire, he said, "I am afraid to say the young man's character is not good. He has all the cunning and deceit one expects of that class." The Mudaliyar paused. Then he played his trump card. "Even as we speak, thangachi, your daughters are preparing to receive him for tea."

Louisa stood up quickly.

The Mudaliyar held up his hand to stay her, as he had not finished. Too agitated to sit down, she remained standing.

The Mudaliyar now told Louisa that he had learnt about this from a very good source. Louisa's horror gave way to outrage. From Annalukshmi she would have expected rash action, but to think that Kumudini and Letchumi, her greatest supports, had gone behind her back and planned such a heinous thing was too much to bear. Louisa hurried to the door, determined to put an end to this disgraceful state of affairs, to save the reputation of her family, to give each of her errant daughters, married or unmarried, thundering slaps. It was with the greatest difficulty that the Mudaliyar was able to stop her, to make her understand that, if she went now, the young man would not have arrived yet and the girls might be able to warn him, making her efforts useless. How Louisa was able to contain herself would remain a marvel to her for the rest of her days.

Dr. Govind arrived promptly. Kumudini had barely finished draping the sari when Manohari, who had been keeping sentry, came running inside to tell them. Annalukshmi immediately felt a weakness take hold of her. She ran her hand over her face, praying that her body would not choose this very moment to give way.

Kumudini left to greet Dr. Govind, and Annalukshmi heard her welcoming him to a seat. She felt light-headed and she quickly sat on the edge of the bed. She stayed there until her weakness passed. Then she stood up, looked in the mirror to ensure that her hair and sari were in place, took a deep breath, and went to meet Dr. Govind.

When she walked out onto the verandah and saw Dr. Govind, she felt disappointed. There he sat stiffly, his hands formally resting in his lap, his legs crossed, his shoulders held back, as if he were posing for a photograph. The expression on his face was pinched and restrained, his smile, as he talked to Kumudini, never quite reaching his eyes. Annalukshmi felt no movement of desire within her.

Dr. Govind had noticed her now and he stood up. For a moment, his expression became uncertain. Then he composed himself. "Miss Annalukshmi, good afternoon." He bowed.

She nodded and looked around for a chair.

Kumudini had carefully rearranged the verandah so that the only seat open to her was directly across from him.

The moment she was seated, Kumudini said, "I must go and see about tea." With a glance at Manohari indicating that she should accompany her, Kumudini went inside.

Annalukshmi looked after her sisters in dismay. Yet she knew they had done what was necessary. This was her chance to get to know Dr. Govind.

There was a moment of silence between them, then he spoke. "How are you enjoying *A Passage to India?*"

"I'm afraid I haven't really read it yet."

He shifted in his chair. "It looks like the rain might hold off this evening."

"Yes." Annalukshmi searched quickly for something to talk about. "Have you read about what is happening now with the Labour Union?" she asked. "It seems that the employees at the Galle Face Hotel and the Grand Oriental might go on strike."

"I have glanced at items in the newspaper," he replied, "but I find such things of very little interest. To be frank, I don't believe that these protests achieve much good. In my opinion, most people who appoint themselves champions of the down-trodden are simply self-aggrandizing."

Annalukshmi looked at him in surprise.

"Take our Mr. Gandhi in India, for example," he continued. "It is all very well for him to issue this or that directive, but in the ensuing commotion so many lives are lost and so many people hurt. We who work in hospitals often have to deal with the results."

"I agree that the loss of lives is a terrible thing, Dr. Govind. But what do you think *should* be done? After all, things can't continue as they do."

"Why shouldn't they, Miss Annalukshmi? Has British imperialism been such a terrible thing for us? It has brought so many advantages, railways, rule of law, postal services, electricity. I, unlike so many others, would be very unhappy to see the British go."

"Yet do you not feel that our — your very own — horizons are limited by their presence, their biases."

He smiled. "I think that their renowned bias is often the fancy of those who are too indolent for the stern realities of life. I am sure that, in the absence of the British, someone else would be found to blame."

Annalukshmi could not think what to say.

"Well, enough of politics," he said. "Tell me, what *are* you reading these days?"

"A wonderful book on Hinduism. You remember, the one I borrowed from my uncle."

"Oh," he said, waiting for her to go on.

"I find it very fascinating," Annalukshmi said. "It's unlocked a whole new world for me. I have just finished a chapter on the dancing Shiva. I don't know how many times I have seen one of those statues without ever understanding it, without comprehending that the entire cycle of creation is depicted in it."

"Yes," he said, "I can see that it must be fascinating. I myself, however, am a great admirer of the marvels of Europe. The Eiffel Tower, St. Paul's Cathedral, the Louvre, the Sistine Chapel." He paused. "One of my favourite writers is George Eliot. Have you ever read her?"

"Of course, I've read every single one of her books," she said, sitting back in her chair.

"*Mill on the Floss* is quite the finest novel I have ever read," he said. He began to describe what he found so compelling about the book, the generous nature of the heroine, her terrible suffering.

As he spoke, his face lost its usual constraint and his eyes shone with passion. A strand of carefully combed hair fell over his forehead, but he hardly seemed to notice it. As she looked at him, Annalukshmi thought what a beautiful colour his skin was, brown with a saffron undertone, like seasoned jak wood, how strong but at the same time vulnerable was the curve of his neck.

Seelan caught himself short. "I am sorry," he said. "I should not go on so."

"No," she said. "Please do. I'm enjoying your analysis."

Their eyes met and a smile passed between them. Then they both looked away to the garden.

"I read *Silas Marner* last year and —"

"When I was in London I visited Eliot's —"

They smiled again. He indicated for her to speak first. Before she could do so, however, she heard an exclamation from the back of the house.

A cup crashed to the floor. Annalukshmi tried to peer in, but she was too far from the front door.

She turned back to Dr. Govind and was about to pick up the conversation when she heard the sound of rapid footsteps coming through the house. There was an all too familiar rhythm to them. Annalukshmi was hardly able to draw in her breath in astonishment before her mother appeared in the doorway, behind her a very frightened Kumudini and Manohari.

Seelan stood up. There was a moment of stunned silence, as everyone surveyed each other. Then Louisa moved into action, spurred on by the sight of Annalukshmi wearing *her* favourite French chiffon sari.

"You devil," she cried.

She rushed at Annalukshmi, who stood up in alarm, knocking the table over.

"This is disgraceful," Louisa cried. "Have you girls no shame at all?"

The Mudaliyar had been waiting inside and he decided that this was the moment to make his entrance. He stepped into the doorway but stopped, for there before him was a living embodiment of his son Arul. This was what the Mudaliyar had not counted on. In that instant, he felt his resolve begin to slip from him with the quickness of falling garments. He clutched desperately at it. "Thangachi," he cried to Annalukshmi and the other girls. "Do you realize this man is an imposter? This . . . this man is no Dr. Govind. He is Seelan, the son of my son Arulanandan."

Seelan stepped back, appalled. Annalukshmi gasped audibly. Kumudini sat down in a chair.

"Sir," Louisa said, "I must ask you to leave my house. Have you no decency coming to visit my daughters in my absence!"

"Madam, please understand that I meant no disrespect."

Seelan then turned beseechingly to Annalukshmi. "You must believe me. This is not as it seems. I —"

"You would do well to be quiet, young man," the Mudaliyar said. "You have violated the kindness and hospitality of these ladies."

"There is no need for this, sir," Seelan said. "I am going."

He looked around at all of them, anguished, then his gaze came to rest on Annalukshmi. "Goodbye," he said to her. "If I never see you again, please believe that I meant no harm." He looked at the Mudaliyar bitterly. "My intentions were honourable, despite what you think, sir."

Annalukshmi, her eyes filling with tears, ran from the room. Seelan picked up his hat and went down the steps of the verandah.

25

The backward step of a battering ram
Is vigour restrained.
— The Tirukkural, *verse 486*

Seelan did not know how he found his way to his uncle's house,
but he finally arrived there.

Balendran and Sonia were seated in the drawing room,
listening to the gramophone when he walked in.

"Where have you been?" Balendran called out.

Seelan did not reply. He came into the drawing room and sat
down in a chair. He looked up at his aunt and uncle and they saw
immediately that something was wrong. Sonia got up quickly
and turned off the gramophone.

After a moment, Seelan began to tell them all that had happened. As he spoke of his humiliation, his voice shook. By the
time he had finished, he had to press his lips together to prevent
himself from crying.

While his nephew spoke, Balendran had a recollection of
himself twenty years ago, when he had fled his apartment in the
face of his father's wrath. He vowed now that he would not let
his father dictate Seelan's destiny. At least one of them would
escape from his clutches.

"I cannot bear the thought that Miss Annalukshmi might feel I meant her harm," Seelan continued, once he had regained his composure. "I want her to know that I had intended to tell her who I was." He looked down at his hands. "The time I spent with her this afternoon has made me all the more sure of my feelings towards her. I would like a chance to explain myself. Then, if she can find it in her heart to forgive me this awful deception, I would like to pursue the possibility of an attachment growing between us . . . of her ultimately becoming my wife."

Balendran and Sonia glanced at each other.

Sonia was the first to speak. "Seelan, don't you think it is a bit soon to be thinking of future possibilities between you and Annalukshmi? After all —"

"I understand that many difficulties exist. Yet I am willing to wait, to be patient." He looked from one to the other beseechingly.

"I think it's best if I speak to my niece on your behalf," Balendran said finally.

Seelan's face brightened a little. "Yes, I would like that very much."

"But you must understand, Seelan, that things are very heated at the moment." Balendran paused. "If you really want something to grow between you and my niece, my sincere advice is that you go back home for a while. Let everyone regain their senses. Then return at a later date, if that is what you want to do."

After a moment, Seelan said, "Yes. I will see if I can change the date of my return passage to Bombay, leave Ceylon as soon as possible. To try to see her again at this time would be awkward for everyone. I will have a letter sent to her tomorrow."

Balendran telephoned for a taxi. He wished to speak with his father about what had happened that afternoon.

As Balendran walked down the hallway that led to his father's dining room, he could hear the clink of cutlery and the low murmur of voices. He paused outside, straightened his coat, and went in.

His father, mother, and Miss Adamson were at the table, Pillai waiting on them. When they saw him, they stopped eating. His mother and Miss Adamson looked surprised, but he saw that his father had been expecting him.

Balendran had envisioned that his father would be triumphant with righteous indignation. Instead, he saw a look of uncertainty in his father's face, present only fleetingly before his countenance regained its usual sternness.

"I want to talk to you," Balendran said.

"As you can see, I am at dinner," the Mudaliyar replied. "You will have to wait until I have finished."

The imperiousness of his tone enraged Balendran. "Your dinner can wait," he snapped back. Pillai was about to offer his father some fish in a white sauce and Balendran signalled him to refrain from doing so.

Pillai looked from father to son, not sure what to do.

The Mudaliyar glared at his retainer and pointed insistently at his plate.

As Pillai bent down to serve the Mudaliyar, Balendran stepped forward on impulse and pushed the plate. It fell out of Pillai's hands and onto the floor with a clatter. Nalamma and Miss Adamson gasped, and the Mudaliyar's face became red. "Get out," he shouted, his voice cracking. "Get out of my house."

Balendran, though shaken by his own action, stood his ground. He walked over to where his mother sat and placed his arm around her, leaning over. "Amma, I am sorry for this, but please allow me to speak to my father alone." She looked as if she were about to say something, but then got up and went towards the door. "And you as well," Balendran said to Miss Adamson. "This is a family matter."

She, too, rose hurriedly and left, with Pillai behind her.

Balendran crossed to the door and shut it.

The Mudaliyar sat where he was, his hands trembling beneath the table.

Since the moment he walked away from Lotus Cottage that afternoon, he had been unable to dispel the image of his grandson's face, the anger and contempt with which he had looked at him before he left. Now, confronted by his son, he felt disturbingly vulnerable.

Balendran turned to his father. "The boy came to me and told me what happened this afternoon. The way you spoke to him. How could I tell him that when you look at him you see your own crimes reflected in his face."

The Mudaliyar started.

"You are reminded of what you did to Arul, to Pakkiam and her mother. And for those things, you hate your grandson."

"I don't know what you are talking about."

Balendran smiled disdainfully. "Arul told me, and his wife confirmed it."

The Mudaliyar tried to conceal his distress.

"How could you have brought Pakkiam here? She was just a girl when you brought her to Brighton to take her mother's place."

Smashing his fist down on the table, the Mudaliyar cried, "You deceived me by bringing that boy here. You had no right."

Balendran waved his hand to dismiss his father's ploy to steer the conversation away from Seelan's mother.

"Why do you try to destroy everything you touch?" he asked

bitterly. "Look what you've done to Seelan. To Arul. Even in his death you tried to master him, demanding that his body be returned to you."

"I did it out of love for my son, out of —"

"The same love that drove you to London to destroy my life?" Balendran had spoken without thinking and he glanced quickly at his father. To his astonishment, the Mudaliyar recoiled from his words.

Balendran was silent, taking this in. When he next spoke, he felt as if he were testing something unknown, prodding at it. "Why didn't you leave me alone in London? I was content then."

"I saved you from that . . . degradation. Look at what you have now. What would you have been in London? Nothing."

"Yes, Appa," Balendran said with gathering strength, "but I might have been truly happy." He took a deep breath. "I loved Richard. That would have been enough."

"Stop," the Mudaliyar cried, raising his hand as if to shield off his son's words. "I forbid you to speak such filth in my house. Apologize immediately."

"No, Appa. I cannot, for this is how things are with me. And there isn't a day that goes by that I don't live with the pain of knowing this and not being able to do anything about it."

The Mudaliyar stared at him, his mouth agape. He ran his hand over his forehead. Balendran could see he was trembling.

His father tried to rise from his seat, then sank back into it, making a pained sound through his gritted teeth. "How dare you," he said, his voice breaking. "How dare you speak like this in my presence. It is not true. I will not accept it."

Balendran did not respond; he simply watched his father. He saw that by confronting his father with his true nature, una-shamed, assured, he had taken something away from him. How strange, how unexpected this was. It was like a tale of enchantment where the quester, by accidently pronouncing the magic words, causes the spell that binds him to fall away. He had come looking for his nephew's freedom and, unwittingly, he had achieved his own.

As Balendran walked towards his waiting taxi, he glanced towards the lights of Lotus Cottage and he knew that there was something else he must do. He sent a gardener to tell Annalukshmi that he wanted to speak to her alone, to meet him just outside the gates of Brighton. In his current frame of mind, Balendran could not bear to deal with Louisa, with her recriminations, her questions, her outrage.

❦

Earlier that afternoon when Annalukshmi had run into the house in tears, she had locked herself in her bedroom and wept at her humiliation and embarrassment, her shock at the terrible cruelty of what had been said and done. When she calmed down, she had lain on her bed, staring up at the ceiling, ignoring her mother's insistent demands that she open the door. She had pondered with some wonder that Dr. Govind was Seelan. The son of Arulanandan. How strange it was to have met someone who, in her mind all these years, she had pictured as a mysterious and doomed figure.

For the rest of the afternoon, she had been turning over and over in her mind her meetings with Seelan. His attention towards her had seemed so sincere. Were his feelings as well not to be trusted? How could she have allowed herself to be taken in like this? The man she thought she knew, however vaguely, she found now that she did not know at all. Was he even a doctor?

Was that story about his studying in London a lie? What were his real thoughts, hopes, and aspirations?

When the gardener came to tell her that her uncle wished to speak with her at Brighton, Annalukshmi felt relieved. Here was someone who would answer some of the numerous questions that had come to dominate her mind.

Annalukshmi emerged from the clump of trees that separated the grounds of Brighton from the garden of Lotus Cottage. She saw her uncle standing by the taxi near the gate and she made her way quickly towards him.

They stood for a moment, regarding each other.

"Are you all right, thangachi?"

She nodded.

He opened the door of the taxi for her. "Come," he said. "I want to talk to you. Let's go for a drive around Victoria Park, then I will bring you back home."

At first, as the taxi left Brighton, they were silent. Then Balendran said, "It's unfortunate that such vicious and unnecessary things were said this afternoon."

"For people who claim to be refined and respectable, their behaviour this afternoon was ill-bred and vulgar," Annalukshmi said.

"Yes, it was indeed."

The taxi began to circle Victoria Park. Except for intermittent streetlamps besides the railings, the park was in darkness. The air was fragrant with the sweet smell of Queen of the Night.

"You know you must not judge my nephew too harshly," Balendran said. "He would have told you but . . . well, it is not easy to speak of certain things. I have good reason to believe that he was afraid. I think he was convinced that if you knew who he really was, you would want nothing at all to do with him. He wanted you to come to like him first."

"I wonder if it was something like that," she said.

"It is very important to him that you understand that he meant you no harm."

"I think I do, now."

"In light of what has happened, Seelan feels that it would be best to leave for Bombay as soon as possible. Give things a chance to settle down. He told me that he will have a letter delivered to you tomorrow."

"I look forward to reading it."

"There is something else . . . something that I feel you should know," Balendran continued after a moment. "Seelan has told us that his feelings for you go beyond mere friendship. He has even talked of marriage."

Annalukshmi turned to him, stunned. Then she remembered the appeal in Seelan's eyes as he had told her that he meant no harm. So, his feelings had not been a lie after all. "I don't know what to say. I hardly know him," she said to her uncle.

Balendran looked out of the window at the swaying trees. A wind had picked up. "Seelan is a very accomplished young man. He won the University Scholarship to London, where he trained as a doctor. He has been practising in Bombay and some day might wish to set up a practice here. I am going to give him a piece of the land connected to Sevena, on which he could build a house. He was brought up in a home where, despite terrible difficulties and poverty, there seems to have been love. Seelan was dutiful and loving towards his mother during Arul's illness and after his death. Much as he desired to come to Ceylon to visit, he held back until he was sure his mother would be well taken care of in his absence. He is a man who, in many senses, is honourable."

"I'm glad you've told me all this about him, Bala Maama. It increases my regard for him."

"Merlay, you know how these things are. One must be very careful. Please do not enter into anything lightly. You must be very, very sure."

✺

The next day was uncharacteristically sunny for July. Yet the mood inside Lotus Cottage was dark and gloomy. The tensions of the previous afternoon had not altogether abated. Nothing at all was said about the incident.

The letter from Seelan had not arrived with the morning post. After lunch, Annalukshmi, wanting to be alone, took a chair from the verandah to the shade of the flamboyant tree, where she sat moodily turning the pages of the newspaper. Something on the last page caught her eye. It was a small item announcing the exhibition of paintings by Chandran Macintosh. It was to take place this evening. Though Nancy had reminded her about it last week, she had forgotten all about it.

Annalukshmi looked up from the newspaper to see her mother making her way down the garden to her.

"We had planned to go and do a little shopping this afternoon," Louisa said when she came up to her. "Are you going to get ready?"

"I don't think I'll go."

After a moment, Louisa put her hand on her shoulder. "It would be good for you to get out of the house. We thought we might have tea at the Cave's Tearoom."

• 371 •

"Thank you, Amma, but I would rather remain."

"Well, merlay, you must do what's best for you."

After her mother and sisters had left, Annalukshmi went into the house to get her book and she found inside it the invitation that Chandran Macintosh had given her that day in his studio, almost two months ago. The location of the exhibition was at a house on Gregory's Road, ten minutes from where she lived.

As she walked down the steps into the garden, she caught sight of a messenger handing Letchumi a letter. Letchumi brought it to her, and she opened it as she sat down again.

> My dear Miss Annalukshmi,
>
> As my uncle has no doubt told you, I am leaving shortly for Bombay. I would have preferred to meet with you face to face, but I thought it would be better in the circumstances to write you. Though one cannot entirely undo an injury caused, one can try to understand the reasons behind it. And this is something I will have to examine within myself. What I can say again is that I never meant to cause you any harm. I pray that you will come to understand, and can forgive me.
>
> From the very first time we met in my uncle's study, you have been constantly in my thoughts. At our meetings since, however brief, my respect for you has only increased. I have always known, and now firmly believe, that the special regard one feels for a certain person is almost instantly known. It is my hope that you return my esteem. If you do, when I am back in Bombay, we might,

through our letters, strengthen the bond between us and give me reason to return to Colombo — so that we may see where our affections lead us.

I remain yours sincerely,

Seelan.

The letter lay open in Annalukshmi's lap as she gazed out over the garden. She was moved by Seelan's words. They were addressed from his heart and brought back the feeling of anticipation she had felt so keenly the day before, as she had awaited his arrival. She remembered the conversation she had with her uncle yesterday. He was right, she thought. Seelan was an honourable man. The devotion with which he had looked after his mother showed that he was a man of kindness and sensitivity, someone who shouldered his burdens with a sense of responsibility that was admirable. He had apologized to her for his deception and asked for her forgiveness. She could imagine that he would make a very caring husband. She found herself picturing the life she would have with Seelan. She saw them living in a house like Sevena, the sea breeze that blew continuously through it, the comfortable armchairs in the corner for curling up and reading in, the bowls of flowers. In a house like this she could be happy. She pictured them walking arm in arm through the garden, watching the steamers going towards the harbour. She imagined him working at his desk late into the evening, his face half lit by the lamp. As she went about some task, he would, without his eyes leaving his book, reach out his hand to touch her as she passed, a smile on his face.

But the possibility of marriage to Seelan seemed so fraught. There would be the obstacle of her family. Her mother and grand-uncle would do everything in their power to stop the marriage. Could she really love him enough to overcome all that?

It was true that they did share some interests. And yet . . . did they really share so much? Were they really suited for each other? She remembered some of the things he said yesterday, opinions they most definitely did not share, the way he seemed to turn away from his own traditions. A person's opinions, as she well knew, were not simply to be dismissed, for they did mark the way someone conducted their life.

Annalukshmi picked up the letter and read it again, remembering the way his eyes had looked into hers when they had spoken on the verandah, the fine features of his face. She sighed at the thought of what she must give up. Seelan had implied that they were to maintain an exchange of letters only if she returned his affection. She would write to him, nevertheless. But how she would express what she felt, she did not know.

❧

Once Annalukshmi had set off along Horton Place, her umbrella open against the sun, she wondered if meeting Chandran Macintosh again would be uncomfortable and embarrassing for the both of them. She almost thought to turn back home, but she had never been to an art exhibition before. Besides, Nancy would be there.

The house where the paintings were being shown was not very different from any of those of Cinnamon Gardens, with its deep verandahs, whitewashed walls, and red roofs. Yet the garden was rather more elaborate than any she had seen before, with a miniature water garden in one corner. There was a gazebo in the middle of the garden and she noticed that a pair of lovers was involved in a passionate embrace on the bench inside. She shifted the position of her umbrella so that they would not notice that she had seen them. From the house she heard a man singing in Sinhalese, accompanied by a sarpina and tablas. The verandah was deserted, but the front doors were wide open. As she came up to them, she could see into a large room. A small stage had been set up at the far end. It was decorated with coconut leaves that had been twisted into the shape of flowers. The singer she had heard from the garden was on the stage, accompanying himself on the sarpina. He and the tabla player were sitting on cushions. Behind them jasmine and araliya garlands hung down from the ceiling, forming a curtain at the back. Chandran Macintosh's paintings were on the wall. As she looked around the people present, she could not see him or Nancy anywhere.

Annalukshmi noticed that the room was empty of furniture. Instead, most of the floor was taken up with a red Persian carpet and there were large, mirror-worked cushions and bolsters scattered around the room. The guests disported themselves amongst the cushions, picking at the rich array of food that was artfully arranged on large platters in front of them. There were beef cutlets, pinwheel sandwiches swirled with orange, green, and dark-red filling, fish patties, crisp kokis in the shape of birds of paradise, slices of moist love cake filled with cashew and pumpkin preserve, devilled prawns with a yoghurt dipping sauce, bibikan fragrant with the smell of cardamom and cloves, kadalay fried with coconut, mustard seeds, and chilli, fruit of various kinds.

A lot of the women present were smoking, and Annalukshmi quickly noted that two of them were not wearing blouses under their saris. One of these women lay with her head in the lap of a woman she recognized as Srimani, Mr. Jayaweera's landlady.

She was wearing a sarong and a shirt. The men were unusually dressed. Instead of suits and ties, most of the men wore sarongs or vertis, clothes that were usually worn at home. One of them had an elaborate shawl draped about his body. From the way he signalled the bearers, he was probably the host. The scene before her was not what Annalukshmi had expected at all.

The performance came to an end and the audience applauded. They began to rise from the cushions. It was now that Annalukshmi noticed Chandran Macintosh stand up from behind a bolster. He was wearing a sarong and a white cotton kurtha shirt open at the neck. He saw her and his face broke into a smile. He came quickly towards her. "I'm so glad you remembered," he said and held out his hand to her.

The friendliness of his greeting, his frank pleasure at seeing her, put Annalukshmi immediately at ease. She shook his hand warmly and said, "How could I forget, after having enjoyed your paintings so much the last time."

"There are people here who would be very keen to meet you, having seen your portrait. Shall I impose them on you?"

"I think I'll sustain myself on your paintings first, Mr. Macintosh."

He bowed slightly and waved his hand to tell her to proceed.

Annalukshmi, ignoring the looks of interest she was getting from people who had obviously recognized her from her portrait, began to examine the paintings. She started to walk around the room, only glancing at the portrait of herself but a little embarrassed to linger in front of it. On the wall next to it was a series of watercolours depicting village life.

She was halfway through the exhibition when she came upon *Mrs. X At-Home*. The painting had not changed. Still the servant woman in the arms of the gardener. Still Mrs. X regarding herself in the mirror. Perhaps it was the angle of the light, perhaps he had altered the picture, but Mrs. X looked different. There was no longer a haughty expression on her face. Instead, she had a smile that Annalukshmi found oddly familiar. She bent closer, but then the face became a blur of paint. She stepped back and studied Mrs. X. Then, with a start, she realized who it reminded her of. That smile on Kumudini's face when she had said, "One must go on." Annalukshmi's eyes now travelled to the mirror image of Mrs. X, her truer, sadder self, and it was there that her gaze rested a long time. Somehow, the painting affirmed for her the importance of being faithful to one's spirit. She knew she must wait, even if it might take a long time, to find whatever it was that she desired.

Annalukshmi folded her arms to her chest and prayed, not to God but to her better self, for the strength to wait, to hold fast to her ideals, even when there was nothing to pin her dreams on.

She heard her name being called. She turned to see Nancy, who had just arrived, coming towards her. Chandran Macintosh, thinking that Annalukshmi had finished her tour of the exhibition, was also making his way in her direction.

26

The Finale

A man's conduct is the touchstone
Of his greatness and littleness.
— The Tirukkural, *verse 505*

It was November and the days were once again cool and pleasant. The recommendations of the Donoughmore Commission had been published in the newspapers. Balendran, as he read them, saw that they would bring satisfaction to hardly anyone.

The members of the Congress Party would be furious and disappointed, for the commissioners had not recommended self-government. The Congress's suggestion of a Whitehall-type cabinet government had also been rejected. Instead, the legislature was to be divided into seven executive councils, each with a minister. The system, modelled on the League of Nations and the London County Council, was the commission's recognition of the multi-faceted nature of Ceylonese society. The councils would give minorities a chance to participate in government. While this would be the first time any executive power had been granted to the Ceylonese, the most important departments — the Treasury, External Affairs, and the Public Service —

remained in the hands of British officers. Since no minister could act without the aid of the Treasury and the Public Service, his ability to make real changes was doubtful. In addition, the authority of the governor to veto any measure was increased. In other words, power had been given with one hand and taken with the other.

The various minority groups, too, would be disappointed, Balendran saw, for all members of the legislature would be territorially elected. There were to be no more seats allocated on the basis of communal representation, thus drastically reducing the number of minority seats in the council. Balendran wondered how Richard would interpret these measures in his report, begun now almost a full year ago.

The commission recommended that the governor no longer had the prerogative to nominate members, who would henceforth be elected by popular vote. This would mean that his father, who would never deign to canvas for votes, would lose his seat on the council. The verandah at Brighton, always crowded with petitioners, would soon be empty of people coming to seek his father's favour. Balendran knew, however, that the men who would replace his father – F. C. Wijewardena and other younger members of the Cinnamon Gardens élite – while they would make the necessary gestures to the lower classes, would continue to maintain, even increase their own advantage. The first families of Ceylon, irrespective of race, would ensure that.

The commission's recommendations, in one aspect, pleased Balendran. The commissioners, displaying a reformative attitude that put the Ceylonese to shame, had recommended universal franchise, making Ceylon the first Asian country to receive it. This, Balendran knew, was perhaps the greatest reform the Donoughmore constitution would bring. With universal franchise, the semi-feudal structures of Ceylon would begin to loosen.

Balendran put down his paper and went to stand at his study window.

In the days that followed his encounter with his father, Balendran had expected to feel a sense of freedom. He had spoken aloud to his father, and in some sense to himself, of his struggle, the difficulty of living with who he really was. But instead of release, a feeling of dejection took hold of him, as if he had reached a goal, an end, and found it curiously hollow.

A few days after the incident at Lotus Cottage, Balendran had told his father about Seelan's return to Bombay. He had tried to convince him to consider passing on to Seelan the share of the family wealth that had belonged to Arul, saying that it was important to make his peace before he died with this restitution in Arul's name. His father had remained obdurate.

One afternoon, not too long after Seelan had departed from Colombo, Nalamma surprised Balendran with a visit. She explained that her husband had let her know what had happened at Lotus Cottage. Balendran told her of his failed attempt to convince his father to allow his grandson an inheritance. Nalamma had said, "You must understand that a man like your father, irrespective of how he appears, always lives with the consequences of his actions."

In the proceeding months, Balendran had visited his father's house rarely. On those occasions that he did, he found his mother distracted and tired. Though from time to time his father expounded loudly about the scoundrels in the Labour Union and their causes, which he said would prove to be the ruination of Ceylon, he seemed otherwise withdrawn and to have aged.

❧

The torches were lit along Brighton's driveway, giving it a festive air. Once again, it was the Mudaliyar's birthday. As Balendran and Sonia's taxi turned into the gate, he saw that his mother had added a new touch to the celebrations. Along both sides of the driveway, stretching from the gate to the porch, was a row of little clay lamps, their lights like fireflies flickering in the darkness.

When the taxi stopped under the porch, Pillai came down the steps to open the car door. He bowed respectfully. "You are wanted upstairs, Sin-Aiyah."

Although Pillai spoke in a neutral tone, Balendran knew immediately that something was wrong. Sonia and he exchanged looks. They went in quickly.

Before they even reached the top of the stairs, Balendran could hear the raised voices. He entered in time to hear Louisa say, "I am at a loss to understand my daughter. An absolute loss."

Balendran quickly surveyed the family present. Louisa shaking her head, distraught. Kumudini holding her arm in comfort, Philomena Barnett by the dining table, a vindicated look on her face. Manohari enjoying the whole proceedings and Nalamma trying not to notice what was going on. He now realized Louisa had been referring to Annalukshmi.

Louisa had seen him and she came towards him. "Thambi, the most dreadful thing has happened. You must talk some sense into Annalukshmi."

"We found a letter," Kumudini said. "It seems that akka has applied to a school in Jaffna."

Balendran raised his eyebrows.

"A Hindu school," Louisa cried.

"Mark my word, it's that Miss Lawton's girl who is encouraging her in this nonsense," Philomena said. She turned to Balendran. "That girl is now living with some man in Pettah. They say she is married, but I have my doubts. He's a Labour Union man, so I would not be in the least surprised if they are living in sin." She began to go around the table, checking the place settings. "Poor Miss Lawton. Her blood pressure went up so high, she had to stay in bed for a week. Still, what can you expect? These foreigners and their notions on raising up low castes. If you rear a snake even from the time it is born, will it not ultimately turn around and sting you? It is in its very nature to do so."

Philomena continued about her business, oblivious to the change in the room. She did not see Nalamma turn away with an expression of sorrow on her face or Balendran and Sonia glance at each other or Louisa fiddle with the palu of her sari. A year ago, Philomena's comment would have hardly been heeded by them. Now, on all their minds, was the thought of Seelan back in India with his mother.

"Where is Annalukshmi?" Balendran said to break the silence.

"Who knows," Manohari said. "She flounced off downstairs a few minutes ago."

Balendran went to look for Annalukshmi, and was told by one of the servants that she was in the study.

He knocked on the door and went inside to find his niece seated in a chair by the desk. There was a stubborn, irritated look on her face.

Balendran came and perched on the desk in front of her.

"I have been sent to rescue you from running off to Jaffna and becoming a Hindu."

He spoke with good-natured irony, and Annalukshmi could not help but smile. "Don't worry, I am quite safe from that," she said satirically. "One faith is enough of a burden."

Balendran looked at her keenly. There was a quiet determination in her face that he had never seen before.

"Do you *really* want to go to Jaffna?" he queried.

"It's a possibility."

He waited for her to go on.

She shrugged. "I am considering many possibilities. I might go to Jaffna, I might go somewhere else, perhaps even Malaya with Kumudini, as she will need some help with her baby girl." She gestured to her surroundings. "Or I might just stay right here. After all, it's not such a bad life, is it? And I am beginning to meet new people . . . interesting people."

She leant forward, her face shining with enthusiasm. "Everything is changing, Bala Maama, I don't really know what I'm going to do." Her face became stern. "But when I do decide, I will do it."

They were both silent for a moment, listening to the voices of servants on the verandah.

"Seelan has finally replied to a letter I sent him," Annalukshmi said.

"Oh?"

"I thought about it for a long time, maama. I don't think Seelan and I would have been well matched. I don't think we would have seen eye to eye on things that are important."

"It is good to know these things before one makes an irrevocable choice."

"I wrote to him and said that I do indeed return his respect, and I hoped we would be able to correspond as cousins."

"I'm so happy to hear it, merlay. It is my wish that some day Seelan will be fully accepted in this, our family, and be able to claim what is rightfully his."

After Annalukshmi had left to go upstairs, Balendran continued to sit where he was, thinking of youth, his youth, and his mind filled with a memory. Richard and he walking from Sheffield to Edward Carpenter's house, the deserted road, the rolling green fields on either side. Richard, as they walked along, had turned to him, held his gaze and, with an ever so slight movement, touched the brim of his hat. It was a gesture of friendship, a confirmation of the amity between them. Matching that memory came a more recent one, the time at the Galle Face Hotel when they had sat together speaking of their shared past.

Balendran now understood clearly the cause of his discontent, his sadness in the last months. He was lonely, not for friendship exactly but for the desire to be able to truly share himself with someone.

He was still for a moment, lost in thought. Then he glanced at his watch and sat down at his father's desk. From his coat pocket he took out his wallet and from it pulled the visiting card Richard had left at his house the one time he had visited. He opened a drawer and took out a sheet of paper. He undid the cap to the inkwell and dipped his father's pen in it.

Dear Richard,
        There is no excuse for not having written this

before. I will not attempt to make justifications, only ask that you let me tell you what's in my thoughts. I feel the need to express my regret over what happened during your visit to Ceylon. I behaved badly, my conduct was inexcusable. What prompted it was not any lack in you. Rather, it was a sadly clear vision of my life as it is, the numerous claims upon me. For, you see, it would be wrong to hold my own desires paramount above those of my wife, my son. Such an act would be grossly selfish. Yet there are times I feel such alienation from the world I live in.

Richard, might I ask for your friendship? This may be very difficult for you, but ask I must. I am trying, by this request, to learn to content myself with what cannot be changed, to draw sustenance from the small comforts. But perhaps that is not such a <u>small</u> comfort after all. Perhaps it is enough to have one person to whom nothing is a secret, to whom one can lay open the inner workings of one's heart. Possibly, at the end of a life, to have said that would be enough.

I have lived so much of my existence not asking for what I wanted, lived so much with half courage, half attempts, half feelings. To ask for your friendship is, then, for me, an immense gesture of bravery. I make it now. And will stop writing before my so long idle courage gives up on me. I would so very much like to hear from you.
Bala.

Balendran sealed the envelope, addressed it, and put a stamp on it. He put it in his coat pocket. He would post it tomorrow.

In the vestibule, Balendran could hear Sonia talking to his father, preparing for the arrival of the guests. He turned the light off by the desk and left the study.

His wife and his father were now by the door. His mother led the way down the stairs with Philomena Barnett. Behind them were Louisa, Kumudini, Manohari, and last, lagging behind, Annalukshmi.

As Balendran looked around at his family, he was filled with a sudden tenderness for them that had not existed before, an affection that sat strangely light on him. In the past, they were the things he had drawn around himself, entangled his soul in, weighed his desires down with. Now they stood apart from him and they had, as a result of this detachment, become strangely sweeter.

The first cars could now be heard coming up the driveway. Balendran straightened his tie and went to take his place amongst his family.

ACKNOWLEDGEMENTS

Kumari Jayawardena greatly influenced the direction this book followed. It is thus fitting that the acknowledgements begin with her. Her unpublished research on the Women's Franchise Union and early feminism in Sri Lanka – which she so generously shared with me – inspired the character of Annalukshmi. Her books, *The Rise of the Labour Movement in Ceylon* and *The White Woman's Other Burden*, were also invaluable. Her stories about various Cinnamon Gardens families helped me get a sense of what went on beneath the polished veneer.

My gratitude to my partner, Andrew Champion, for his enormous patience with my daily doubts; his help with various knots in the plot; coming up with the title; martinis at six o'clock; good sense, plants, cats.

My thanks to my family, as always, for their support and love.

The following people read the early drafts of this novel and I am indebted to them for their valuable input: Rishika Williams and Fernando Sa-Pereira, who helped me with interesting insights into Annalukshmi's and Balendran's characters; also

Sunila Abeysekera, Manel Fonseka, Kumari Jayawardena, Jeff Round, Tony Stephenson.

I would like to give special thanks to my editor Ellen Seligman at McClelland & Stewart for her meticulous and creative editing of this book, for forcing me to go that extra mile (and for her strong faith that I could, indeed, do it); my editor Will Schwalbe at Hyperion in New York, for pointing out that a historical novel can be a metaphor for the present, for his encouraging calls and e-mails while I was in Sri Lanka, for his conviction that I could do it again; John Saddler at Anchor; my agents Bruce Westwood and Jennifer Barclay for, among other things, the box of books they sent me while I was in Sri Lanka – further proof that their regard for me goes beyond their excellent representation of my work internationally; Heather Sangster, formerly of McClelland & Stewart, who stuck with the copyediting even after she had left; Anne Valeri, my publicist at McClelland & Stewart.

This book was heavily reliant on research, so I wish to thank the following people for their time and effort: *In Sri Lanka*: Manel Fonseka, who put me into contact with numerous interesting people; Mr. C. I. Edwards, Sr., who, despite difficulties of speech because of illness, brought the 1920s alive for me; Reverend Lionel Peiries, for interesting reflections on the Cinnamon Gardens crowd; Mrs. Sathasivam of Cambridge Place, for details of Hindu culture and for arranging for me to visit a temple and its trustee; Chloe De Soysa, whose memories of the saris and food at her parents' parties provided helpful detail; Siro Gopallawa, who so patiently photocopied the Donoughmore Commission Report for me, five pages a day; Anjalendran, for help with architectural details; Jan Bruinsma, whose house was a haven for us during the year in Sri Lanka. *In Singapore and Malaysia:*

For the oral histories they shared with me – Dr. S. R. Sayampanathan, Mrs. Jayalukshmi Sivarajah of Klang, Dulcie Abraham, Mrs. Ampalapillai of Scotts Road. Mrs. Shellatay Rao of the Arkrib Negara and Dr. Kathirithamby-Wells pointed me in the right direction in terms of my research. Kurt Crocker and Andreas Wan for their hospitality. Ian Gomez for his friendship and good times, so essential when one is in a foreign country.

Other books were extremely helpful: K. M. De Silva's *A History of Sri Lanka*; S. W. R. D. Bandaranaike's *The Handbook of the Ceylon National Congress 1919-1928*; H. W. Cave's *The Book of Ceylon*; M. D. Raghavan's *Tamil Culture in Ceylon*; S. Namasivayam's *The Legislatures of Ceylon*; Rajakrishnan's *The Tamils of Sri Lankan Origin in the History of West Malaysia*, and Jeffrey Weeks' *Coming Out: Homosexual Politics in Britain from the Nineteenth Century to the Present*. The *Daily News* from 1927 and 1928 was an excellent source for period details, accounts of labour strikes and the Donoughmore hearings.

The photograph of a street in Cinnamon Gardens, which appears on the jacket of this book, is from H. W. Cave's *The Book of Ceylon* and was kindly re-photographed for me by Dominic Sansoni. The two people on the `jacket are, of course, real, and I am very grateful to their families for letting me use these photographs. The lives of these two people, however, in no way bear any resemblance to the lives of the characters in this book.